Reviews for Blood Surge

"Blood Surge is an intriguing mix of Urban Fantasy and Vampiric lore. The characters are complex, flawed, and completely intriguing." — *Book Reviews by Lynn*

"The story Dianna has told just sucked me right in. It definitely had some vampire traits and lore as others have used but she made her vampires also unique in their own glorious way. At least to me as I've not read nor watched anything featuring the main lore here. Let me say I was here for it. I think she's written some of the best ideas for a vampire story I have come across." — *Rhonda McGuire*

"Dianna's characters always have layers, and often complex relationships, which means you're always kept on your toes because you're not quite sure how anything is going to play out."
— *Elizabeth Morgan (author)*

"I was fascinated by the different kinds of vampire in particular - there's just so much attention to detail ... I honestly can't wait to read about what happens next to Sophia, her vampires and her frankly awful family." — *Clare's Little Book Obsession*

"Blood Surge is about vampires and more than one kind. The way it explores the complexities of vampire society and the moral dilemmas faced by its characters kept me on the edge of my seat. Each twist and turn added depth to the story, making it impossible to put down until I reached the last page."
— *Nancy at The Avid Reader*

A VAMPIRIC URBAN FANTASY NOVEL

Blood Surge

DIANNA HARDY

Published by Satin Smoke Press, October 2025
First Edition | ISBN 978-1916840-11-9

Written in British English.

This book is set in 11 pt EB Garamond © The EB Garamond Project Authors, and licensed under the SIL Open Font License, Version 1.1
All fonts used in this publication are done so under open source licenses that allow for commercial use.

Satin Smoke Press
(an imprint of Bitten Fruit Books)
Hampshire, UK

www.satinsmoke.com

Author's Note

Blood Surge is set in a fictional town in the real county of Hampshire, England – fictionalised to capture the authentic quaint feel of the area without reality intruding into the imagination. Most of the small towns and villages in this novel are fictionalised with this in mind, but the larger towns, cities, motorways, and 'A' roads, are named as they really exist.

Huge thanks to my regular readers for always wanting more; thanks to Ninfa and Elizabeth for their support of fifteen years, and thanks to Amanda Pederick, my editor, for her sharp eye.

I hope you all enjoy this new, slow(ish) burn story.

Dianna xx

Blood Surge

PART I

Remembering

Chapter One

"Everything's down!" Abigail's stressed tone was a notch above her usual one.

Sophia wasn't sure she'd actually heard her stressed before, but there wasn't much to get stressed about in the sleepy town of Emerson. Emerson encapsulated everything that was 'Hampshire' – a quaint, English town with fields and humble woodlands surrounding it, just a ten-minute drive from the city of Winchester. "Everything?"

"Yep. The lights, the computers, the printers, and now the Wi-Fi's cut out, too." She thrust a wooden object into Sophia's hand.

"A stamp?"

"*The* stamp." She nodded towards the growing queue by the library's front desk. Even in sleepy Emerson, the library heaved with people almost every Saturday. "Bought in 1995. Hopefully the ink pad's not totally dry. Let's get these books checked out."

"Great. Yay to the old-fashioned ways." And part of her meant that. Old was good, even exciting sometimes. An excitement that was safe to immerse herself in because it was long gone and dead.

Emerson was a historic town. Nothing ever happened in Emerson – that's why Sophia Jameson liked it here. It was nondescript compared to London, and that was exactly what she'd wanted. But it had its gems. The library was one of the oldest in the entire country, so old it had its own stone vaults. Well, okay, they weren't vaults – more like a large basement or cellar – but she called them vaults because it made her imagination happy. The entire building smelled of secrets and knowledge, stirring the inner nerd in her who had gone to university to study archaeology and ancient history.

As Abigail saw to the events desk and telephone, Sophia made the front desk her own with an apology every now and then to the customers waiting. No one was really used to waiting nowadays, technology allowing so many things to happen in an instant. Only two of them ever managed the library on any one day.

It didn't take her long getting into her stride, logging the titles and Dewey numbers being checked out with a good old, reliable pencil and paper. Every thump of the stamp against the front of every book was surprisingly satisfying, a bit like branding it with her heartbeat – every thud a marking claim.

A tad possessive about literature, Sophia?

She smiled to herself. Yes, she was. Ever since she was very, very little.

"Penny for your thoughts?"

The question came with a large, square hardback thrust towards her, both the hand holding it, and the voice, igniting an odd feeling in the pit of her stomach she couldn't place until she looked up and met familiar brown eyes with her own. Familiar in *not* a good way. "Jesus Christ..."

His lips widened to a cheeky smirk at being recognised as he half-raised his left eyebrow at her. "I still just go by Pierce."

Fuck you. She grabbed his book, trying not to snatch it, wishing she couldn't hear her heart walloping in her ears. "This is the last place I expected to see you."

"I could say the same."

"You still live in London?" *Please say yes and hurry back there.*

"I do. I'm passing through on business. I'll be here for a couple of weeks."

Great. Not. She said nothing as she scribbled the title of the book down – something about architecture in the industrial period. Made sense – he worked in engineering. Her eyes were blurry with her rising anxiety. She blinked fast.

"Maybe we could—"

"Not a chance in hell." And she was really proud of the harsh finality in her voice. *Too bloody right.*

Pierce held her gaze for a second longer than necessary, then looked down and cleared his throat. "You never gave me a chance to—"

"How's your wife, Pierce?" Yeah, she'd said that loudly and somewhat angrily.

He stared at her, no regret evident even though it should definitely be there. A smidgen of a warning lit his gaze.

"And your two beautiful kids? I hope they're well?" She brought the stamp down – hard – on his book. The desk shook. No one in the queue bothered to pretend they weren't riveted in the now heated conversation and she could feel Abigail's stare boring into her side. She refused to hide her own glare, daring Pierce to *go there*, because she was not averse to airing his dirty laundry in public; not when he was the one who'd spoiled it all in the first place.

He took his book. "They're well. Thank you."

"Glad to hear it. When you return your book, there's a deposit box out front – there's no need to come in. Since I know how busy you always are."

"I'll be sure to remember that."

"Do. Goodbye."

Without another word, he turned and left, and Abigail was at her side in no time, prising the stamp from her hand. "I've got this, hun. It's your afternoon break anyway, and I left some of my flapjack for you in the cupboard. Take your time."

Grateful at her colleague's interjection and annoyed that she was trembling at that unexpected old wound being prodded, she mumbled a thanks and made her way to the staff room out the back.

She opened both the windows, letting the cool summer breeze float in and clear her head.

Over five minutes had passed before Abi waltzed in. Her face was flushed with how rushed she was, but her gaze was one of curiosity and concern. "I've cleared the queue for now – can't stay back here long, though. Are you okay?"

"I'm so sorry, Abi. That guy's a dickhead."

"Has he been in before?"

"No – he doesn't live here. Never thought I'd see him again – not here."

"Who is he?"

She sighed. "An old boyfriend – one I should never have gone out with, but I was young and an idiot."

"Okay, I get the picture now, I think. Listen, I have a free couple of hours after work – come get a coffee with me. Dark Roast across the road is open until ten tonight because they're hosting movie night. We don't have to watch it, but we can grab a bite to eat and talk."

Talking was the *last* thing she wanted to do – especially if it was about Pierce – but she felt she at the very least owed Abi an explanation for the way she'd handled that. She also never really did the 'socials' with any of the staff here, preferring to keep herself to herself. But she needed to get back onto even ground. "That would be great. Thanks."

"Fab. We'll head over after closing up." Abi smiled, and it was genuine. "Can you tidy up the shelves after your break? I'll take the front desk."

"Sure."

"Thanks. See you out there." She turned and left.

Sophia looked out one of the open windows.

Yuck – that's how she felt. Yucky and like the daft twenty-one-year-old she'd been, and all because of *him*. It had been *his* fault – not hers.

Yeah, you tell yourself that. You're the one who said yes to dating a guy almost twice your age.

You did more than date, Sophia.

Yes, she'd been a stone's throw from falling in love, her past, ironically, being the one thing that had kept her from falling completely. The past no one knew about. The one that always had her looking over her shoulder.

Used to, Soph. Used to have you looking over your shoulder. That's all over now. It's ancient history.

Except a small part of the past had just walked in, waking up a bigger part of an even older past. One that had taken *years* of police visits, lawyers, and therapy to put behind her.

It's done. One small, unrelated flashback doesn't make any of that real again.

Feeling queasy, she stood and made her way to the cupboard and that promised flapjack.

Abigail Carey was cute as a button. At around five foot and two inches, she carried herself with both a homeliness and surety. Whatever she was about, she was comfortable with it. A generally round figure and face did not hide her natural curves but accentuated them, her soft and smiley features framed by light blonde hair, a magnet for strangers wanting to start conversations with her, whether young or old. The large, round glasses on her face made her look like a sweet and very approachable owl who was wise beyond her years. If there was a stereotype of a librarian, then Abi was probably it.

And Sophia probably wasn't, with her ripped blue jeans, short leather jacket, dark chestnut hair (almost always worn in a long ponytail) and a defensiveness she'd definitely *tried* to overcome. But some things were easier said than done. Nevertheless, she tried again now as she took her coffee mug from Abi, placing it on the table at the very back of the café they'd decided to visit.

The film hadn't started yet, but Abi knew the owner, and they had been guaranteed this table for as long as they wanted to stay tonight, at the quietest part of the seating area. They could barely see the screen from here.

"I'm sorry again about earlier with Pierce."

Abi sat down, shrugging her cardigan off. "Is that the old flame's name?"

"Yeah. The whole thing just took me off-guard."

Abi stared at her, waiting. It actually *was* a bit like being stared at by an owl.

If you really want the past to be the past, might as well let it out – get it off your chest and put *it in the past.* "I was twenty-one, at university, and I met Pierce in a library, funnily enough. This was in London. We got talking and had loads in common, and yeah – it was obvious he was an older man, but he was just ... I dunno."

"Sophisticated?"

"I guess. He had that charm about him that older guys have sometimes – that wisdom, you know? He was intelligent and ... yeah. We started dating and ... I had no idea he was married."

"Yikes."

"I didn't find out until pretty much a whole year later. We were having dinner at a restaurant and this kid runs at him, all smiles, and it took me a good few seconds to realise she was calling him Daddy."

"Oh, my God."

"Then, her little brother's there doing the same, and then up comes—"

"The wife?"

"Yeah. With a look of murder on her face. Especially when she saw *my* horrified face. I'm guessing she put two and two together on the spot."

"Did *he* have the decency to look horrified?"

"Hmmn, his face was all stony, giving nothing away."

"Bastard."

"Yeah. I'm ashamed to say he broke my heart."

"Hey, not your fault."

"With hindsight, there were red flags. I ignored them all."

"You were inexperienced. You're *not* the first woman that's happened to and you won't be the last."

"I suppose. But the one good thing is I learned from the experience and I will *never* put myself in that position again. That night I found out was six years ago now, and I honestly hadn't thought about him in ages until he was right in front of me this afternoon. And I handled it badly. I'm sorry."

"Don't you dare say sorry again. I can't say I'd have handled it any better. And I'm glad I know so I can make sure to get rid of him quickly if he comes in again."

"I doubt he will. He seemed just as surprised to see me."

"Well, he's not going anywhere near you as long as I'm around."

Sophia smiled. "Thanks."

"Do you want anything stronger? They have an alcohol license here – I can get you wine."

She laughed. "Maybe after the coffee."

"They also do a gorgeous pasta and salad dish if you want dinner."

She'd been planning on sticking her one-person meal in the microwave later tonight, but hell, it was actually nice to be out, and not as bad as she'd thought it would be getting this shit off her chest. "You know, maybe I will – pasta and wine sounds good."

"I'll go order it now before they get busy with the film."

Sophia reached for her bag. "I'll give you my card."

"Nuh-uh, this is on me."

"No."

"Yes – I promise you I can afford it and I haven't been out in ages, so I want to."

"Are you sure?"

"More than." She went up to the till to order both of them food and wine.

Sophia sighed, feeling oddly calm. Odd for her, anyway. Gingerly, she looked around at all the people seated. *Remember there was a time you'd freak out wondering if they were here because of you? If they were out to get you? Finish the job they started?*

She gulped at the memory, but refused to go there. She'd come a long way. And maybe – just maybe – it would be okay to talk about it. To share it. Talking about Pierce had actually felt good.

"Done!" Abi returned, a huge smile on her face.

"Thank you so much."

"My pleasure. I don't think we've ever been out together, and you've been working at the library for what, a year now?"

"Pretty much. I, um – I don't go out much."

"'Cause of Pierce?"

"No! God no – no way. I just – it's complicated."

"I know that feeling. My parents want me to attend a party next week because it's my birthday, and I'm going to know almost no one there."

"You'll know no one at your own birthday party?"

"Nuh-uh, you see, the party isn't actually for me. It's this huge event for ... something else – they're doing a summer solstice thing – and they always want me to be at these events, which I hate and always try to avoid, but because it's my birthday, they know I'll feel pushed into a corner and say yes. Parents – family history – complicated."

Sophia laughed.

"You know that's *your* cue to tell me more about you, right?"

She narrowed her eyes. "I sort of guessed."

"Only if you want to, that is."

"I ... um..." Yeah, she did want to. "I was adopted when I was seven. My parents – and a couple of aunts, and my grandparents, actually – were all murdered in a house fire."

There. *Right there* – that pin dropping was the most horrible sound.

Abi's expression froze in place and Sophia's mouth went dry.

Take it back!

You can't. "I ... shouldn't have said anything, I'm so sorry."

"No, it's—"

"No one ever expects it and it just sounds so—"

"Sophia, it's fine, and of *course* you can say it; I just—"

The food arrived, bringing a pause to the conversation which Sophia used to try and get her head together and calm her nervousness.

The waiter poured the wine.

Her first gulp of it was a large and welcome one.

Abi wasted no time carrying on as soon as they were alone again. "You're right, I didn't expect it, but I am *totally* here for this and if you want to talk about it you can and should." She poked her fork into fusilli and Sophia did the same, stuffing the largest amount possible into her mouth.

After a few seconds, she swallowed hard, following the food down with more wine. "I *couldn't* talk about it for such a long time – legally, I mean – that it became difficult to after."

"Legally?"

"I was six when the fire happened. I was put into witness protection. It took years for the case to be closed."

"Christ, what happened?"

Maybe this hadn't been such a good idea after all. Her chest was tight as hell. Still, she couldn't exactly erase the last few minutes. Wine made mistakes more bearable, so she drank some more. And she was twenty-eight with no life.

After another swig, she put her glass down and hoped whatever she said made sense because she'd never once told anyone about this before, outside the professionals who had engineered the many years that followed. "I don't remember much about that night, I was so young. We had a lot of family staying over. We had a big house, I think, although I don't even know the address." She frowned. "It's probably in my files, but I've never really looked at them because everyone – all the adults – just took care of everything. I remember waking up that night, and it was screaming that woke me. My mum was there quick, picking me up, carrying me out of bed. I was mostly still asleep, I think, but I heard screaming. And then, there was this horrible smell: hot; burning; wood burning; and worse – maybe skin burning.

"I woke up a bit more then, and my mum was shouting to my dad that she couldn't get out. We were in my bedroom and I don't know where he was. Outside the bedroom, maybe. I remember seeing orange flickering across the walls, and that's when I also felt the heat. Really, really hot like being in front of a bonfire, and I realised everything was on fire.

"Dad yelled to my mum to go out the window, and she carried me to the window. She told me to piggyback her and hold onto her neck. I think I did. But ... I can't remember. I think she was trying to climb down out the window with me on her back or something, but I remember seeing flames on the sill, eating up the wood, and my mum's skin was hot and wet, and she was crying. I think everything was too hot for her to touch. I heard someone shout her name, *Deborah*.

"I don't know if it was Dad who said that or someone else. I don't really remember what happened next. My mum said to me, 'I love you so much. I always will.' And then, I think I was falling. Maybe I was screaming too. Or maybe that was my mum. The only thing I remember next is waking up in a hospital a day later with strangers. No one else in the house made it out."

Abi's fusilli had been forgotten. Her eyes were the size of saucers behind her already huge glasses.

Sophia cleared her throat. "Nurses spoke to me first – they were nice, and then the police, and then social services. They tried to explain things to me in a way I could understand. They believed it was arson. They explained I could be in danger until they could find who did it, so I was hidden during the investigation, but it took years. Years.

"It turned out I had no other living relatives who could take me, so I was given to a new family who adopted me. They are the most wonderful parents I could ask for. I grew up. I had to go to court every now and then and say what I remembered. I remember lawyers arguing about whether my testimony was reliable. I remember someone else stating they didn't have enough evidence for arson and then more arguments about it all. For a long time, I had nightmares, and for a long time I wondered if whoever set the fire would come back if they knew I was alive and ... kill me too.

"My father was a barrister – I think they thought the arson might be connected to a case. My adopted parents were schooled on what to do if they suspected I was in danger. But ... nothing happened. No one came after me. Eventually, with still no leads to go on, no other witnesses, and not enough evidence, the case was effectively closed – that was about ten years ago now. I'd like to say it made me feel better, but – it just felt like nothing got resolved. I still don't know if it was arson or not. I had to teach myself not to look over my shoulder all the time." Sophia shrugged, all words finally leaving her.

Abi took a deep breath in, downed the wine in her glass, and reached for the bottle to pour herself more. "I have no idea what to say except I'm so sorry that happened to you. I can't even begin to imagine..." Her words trailed off.

"I've done okay. I've pulled myself out of it, but ... when Pierce showed up... This is so stupid, but because I felt vulnerable remembering everything about the way he left me, it also took me back to feeling jumpy and scared about all the other stuff."

"That's not stupid – it makes total sense."

"I moved here three years ago because I didn't want to be in London anymore. I've literally dated no one since Pierce and I wanted to start anew in a place that was—"

"Boring?"

She laughed. "I was going for peaceful, quiet, and calm."

"So, boring."

"Wonderfully so, until Pierce walked in."

A comfortable pause followed.

"Hey, look!" Abi gestured to their plates. "We finished our dinners. How the hell did that happen? Do you remember eating?"

Sophia laughed harder. "No."

"Me neither!"

"The wine's gone, too."

"That's easily fixed." She gestured to the waiter and reached for her bag.

"No, no, I shouldn't drink more."

"*Shouldn't* is not a word for tonight, okay? Not after that story." She held up the empty bottle at the waiter and mouthed for one more, then went back to rummaging in her bag.

"What are you doing?"

"Making sure I've got cash for a cab home. It's okay, I don't live far and my car can stay in the car park until tomorrow. You're not driving, are you?"

"No, I'm just a fifteen-minute walk from here."

"Okay, good." She pulled an array of things out of her bag to get to her wallet: a small teddy bear, a lipstick, a book, a keyring with a ridiculous number of keys on, and...

It was Sophia's turn to look surprised. "Abi?" Concern stole over her at the miniature bottles of alcohol lying on the table. Four of them. How did you politely ask someone if they had a drinking problem?

"Hmmn? Oh, yes – I *do* have cash."

"Do you ... er ... drink these during the day?"

Abi looked up from her wallet in confusion, then followed her gaze to the four small bottles. "Ooooh! No – read the labels. Those aren't my secret stash of spirits." She snickered.

Sophia did as instructed, leaning forward to inspect them better. It turned out, little bottles of whiskey and vodka would've made more sense than— "*Why* do you have four bottles of holy water in your bag?"

Abi went beetroot, then smiled possibly the most devilish smile Sophia had ever seen on the woman, before putting everything else back in her bag. The four bottles stayed out.

"Right – spill. I just told you my darkest secret."

"Okay, okay." Except the waiter came over with wine bottle number two and Abi wobbled in her seat with what looked like excitement at what she was bursting to say.

When they were once more alone, with new mouthfuls of wine, Abi shoved two of the small bottles of holy water towards her. "Here, have these two. He keeps giving them to me."

"He— What? Who?"

Abi giggled, going even redder, but looking positively delighted. "I'm dating someone. We started seeing each other about three months ago."

"That's ... great, but..." She looked quizzically at the holy water.

"He's training to be a priest!" squealed Abi, possibly on the wrong side of drunk now as she descended into a fit of further giggles.

"You're dating a *priest*?"

"Training – he's *training* to be a priest."

"*What*? Isn't there, like, a vow of celibacy or something?"

"Yes!" she squealed again, her smile as wide as it could be. Yeah – a little devil disguised as a sweet owl. "Well, for him there is – he's old school Roman Catholic or something."

"You *minx*!"

She snorted, but nothing was wiping away that happiness – it made her glow. "I like him a lot, Soph. He's clever and philosophical and he loves books. He's even poetic."

"And the holy water?"

She laughed. "He keeps giving me a bottle every time we meet. I think it's to assuage his guilt over our illicit affair." She waggled her eyebrows meaningfully over the rim of her glasses.

"Is he trying to cleanse your sins or something?"

Another snort. "More like he's trying to cleanse his own. I don't feel guilty in the slightest."

"Have you slept with him?"

"Not yet. We've only got to second base. I dunno *how* many bottles he's going to give me when we reach third, so here"—she shoved them even closer to Sophia—"you take these."

Sophia picked up one of them, inspecting it from a new angle. According to the tiny writing on the label, the water came from Lourdes in France. "What do you *do* with these?"

"Nothing. I keep them in my bag. I have a couple stashed in my cupboard at home."

"What does *he* think you do with them?"

"He's never asked me and I've never told him, but if it gets me to third base, I'll take more bottles."

"You can't be serious. This guy is *wedded* to God. Did you not hear my doomed story about the guy married to his *wife*.

They don't ever leave."

"He *might*. He's not wedded to God yet – he's in *training*."

"And clearly not a good student."

"Well, I'm having fun feeling sexy trying to woo him away from the Almighty. Do you know how many times I've felt sexy with a guy before? None. I'm not what guys look for. And then I meet Anthony and he's..." She shrugged. "You know."

An awkward silence settled between them.

"Hey, I'm in no way judging – I've just told you all my own mess. Just don't sell yourself short. You are most definitely what any decent guy would go for."

She smiled and nodded to the little glass vessels. "Please take those bottles? Water your plants with them or something."

With a sigh, Sophia picked them both up and put them in her bag.

"Thank you."

Another silence.

"Listen," started Abi, "remember I mentioned this party at my parents' house and how I'm not going to know anyone there? It's on Friday. Do you want to come?"

"Oh ... um..."

"It's out near Arundel – Bannerman House?"

She hadn't heard of it.

"I've got a ride there and back you can share."

Sophia shook her head. "You've already paid for so much."

"Oh, no – my parents are paying for the ride. It's um – it's a chauffeur." She sounded embarrassed saying that. "I so don't want a one-hour ride in the back of a car by myself. *Two* hours if you count coming back. And then there's the five hours at the party when it's supposed to be my twenty-fifth birthday and—"

"Okay, okay ... I would love to come."

"Yay!" She smiled and held her glass up in a toast.

Sophia returned the gesture and they clinked their glasses.

"Here's to boring towns."

Sophia laughed, feeling better than she had in a long time. "To boring towns."

Chapter Two

She *wasn't* drunk – just ... maybe a little too tipsy. And when had the sun set?

They'd left the café a little over ten minutes ago. Sophia had waited with Abi until her cab showed up, refusing a lift herself because she needed the fresh air to clear her fuzzy head. Fifteen minutes was not a long walk home and she liked the walks around here – even in the dark. There were so many pretty tree-lined streets, parks, and little cut-throughs. And most importantly, it was safe. *Way* safer than London, anyway. There was no 'bad side of town' in Emerson. All the residential areas were lovely and its crime statistics were one of the lowest in the country. If she hadn't inherited everything from her family upon their death, there was no way she could afford to live here – certainly not from earnings made from working in a library. It was one of the things she felt grateful for; the money allowed her the time she needed to live life at her own pace without too many material worries following all the legal issues and therapy from her childhood.

She turned into a familiar, small bridleway and looked at her backlit wristwatch. It was just after ten o'clock. In five minutes, she'd be under a hot shower and in bed soon after. She'd had a good night – she really had. Although, recalling her past like that

... it had left her with a strange compulsion to dig into her history. She didn't remember much, if anything, about the first six years of her life. Multiple therapists had told her it was a protective mental reaction to block those years out after such a traumatic experience – all memories before the fire itself were mostly gone. For the first time, a part of her *wanted* to remember despite the pain. She wasn't sure where to start, though.

Glancing at the stars above her on this fabulously clear night, she muttered, "Care to help me with that?"

A few twinkled in response.

Smiling, she picked up pace and hugged her jacket around her a bit tighter, the night breeze turning cooler.

An out-of-place 'shuffling' sounded from somewhere behind her. She was very used to the sounds around here – that one had seemed odd. She stopped in her tracks, waiting with her ears pricked, but nothing further sounded. *Probably just a blackbird or something. Or a pigeon. A badger or fox?*

Shaking away the oddness, she carried on, reminding herself of the usual mental exercises she did to stave off unfounded fear. *Paranoia more like, with everything you've been through.*

Nevertheless, her skin prickled. While this was only a short bridle path – barely a thicket – the leaves, branches, and hedges played merrily with the shadows that made up the dark. She couldn't make out a thing. The next street light was on the first corner beyond the bridle path. Sophia shrugged away the urge to reach for her phone and turn on its torch. It would ruin her night vision and if there was someone behind her who meant her harm, it would give them an advantage.

There it was again.

She froze.

Rustling.

Just an animal, right?

A twig snapped and she caught her breath. Small animals didn't fucking snap twigs – people did that.

Torn, she glanced towards the exit to the bridle path which she could clearly see, but it was at least another forty seconds or so of walking to get there – fifteen to run it, maybe.

Running always excites the hunter.

That wasn't a welcome thought – was she prey?

Fuck this.

Her other option? Turn around and face the problem. Call the person out. She'd taken *some* self-defence classes although it had been quite a few years since her last. She'd never needed to use those moves. And she was pretty sure there was an old atomiser of homemade pepper spray somewhere at the bottom of her bag.

If there's really a person there, they could be a drunk, or homeless. Likely not violent.

Tamping down her fear and steeling herself, she decided on being upfront. "Hello? Are you okay? I can hear you – do you need help?"

Yep – there was a definite rustle in response.

She begged her heart rate to slow down. She *had* this. She was in control. As cautiously and slowly as she could, she reached up with her right arm and undid the snap to her handbag. She'd feel better if that pepper spray was in her hand.

She didn't get time to dive into her bag before a figure stepped out of the shadows. "Hi." A woman's voice. "Sorry. I didn't know you were ahead, and then I heard you, and I got scared, so I hid."

Exhaling in relief, Sophia could feel herself relax. Two women, just walking. "Hey, that's cool. Walk with me if you like. I'm just making my way home." She wished she hadn't said that as soon as she'd said it. She might feel suddenly safer, but it was no one's business where she was heading.

The woman didn't move straight away, then began to edge forwards. Her movements were weird. Was she limping? She seemed in pain or something.

"Are you okay? Are you hurt?" Until now, she hadn't considered the person following her might have been a victim of some kind – maybe that was why she'd been scared of her and hid. "I can get you help if you need."

Half of her face came into view. Her expression looked odd, too. Almost manic and kinda ... wild. Her dark hair was just as untamed, covering the other half of her face. But if she'd been attacked that would explain the dishevelled appearance.

The woman clutched her stomach as if she'd been stabbed or something – maybe hit? – but Sophia saw no blood or obvious bruises; the look on her face didn't quite match her actions, and something *really* didn't feel right about this. The woman's eyes seemed to glint in the dark, the way a cat's would. Sophia looked for a light source – there was only half a moon and a few stars.

"I'm hungry," the woman all but whispered, her voice gravelly.

So ... she was homeless? *And probably on drugs if she looks this crazed.*

"I need to eat."

"Um ... I'm so sorry, I have no food."

"Yes, you do."

And she'd been an idiot for divulging she was making her way home – the woman was going to ask to crash at hers now. "I'm sorry – I've just had dinner out and my fridge is bare until I can go shopping tomorrow. Um ... I can give you a bit of cash?" She pulled her bag off her shoulder, intending to reach for her wallet. "It might not help too much tonight, but in the morning, you can get a full English at a café or something."

A *growl* erupted, and Sophia halted all movement, looking for whatever the hell was making that sound until she realised it came from the woman. Animalistic was an understatement. Did *drugs* do that?

"I want my full English *now*."

What happened next was not anything she could fathom because it happened *so* damn quick no thoughts could form. The woman was on her – *on* her – and Sophia's only saving grace was that her instinct had clocked onto whatever the hell was happening despite her lack of mental capacity.

As she went down hard on her back, she managed to shove her handbag outwards in front of her face, forming a barrier between herself and the *insane* woman, even if for just a second. But a second was all her body needed. Raising her knees, she planted her feet against what she hoped was the woman's abdomen and in some vague recollection of her self-defence classes, used the woman's weight and strength against her when she straightened her knees as fast and hard as she could, kicking her off with a yell.

She went flying with an inhuman yowl as Sophia scrambled to her feet and dove into her bag. *Pepper spray!* But the atomiser was too damn small. *Where the fuck—*

Hand still in her bag, she was knocked sideways and screamed as she landed on her left shoulder. Her hand closed around whatever it made contact with – *anything* would do – and without wasting time, she brought it out and half-punched, half-slammed her fist into the woman's face.

Something cracked and – shit. This lady was totally wired on god-knew-what. She was strong and fast and ... her eyes were fucked. Something was wrong with her mouth and that was all Sophia had time to take in before the woman wailed out a pitiful sound and fell back, clutching her head.

That's when Sophia saw the blood across her forehead and seeping through her fingers. Looking down at her own hand, she saw it was also streaked with blood and broken glass from one of the small bottles of holy water Abi had given her earlier.

Christ – she'd smashed it into the woman's *skull.*

Scrambling to a stand, she started to run, adrenaline pumping, then stopped.

Keep going and get the fuck out of there! she screamed to herself. Except the *noise* the woman was making was ... out of this world and ... wrong. And eerily familiar. Which was also very wrong.

A god-awful hissing, bubbling, noise sounded, but it was the *smell* that got to her and ended all her function. Unbidden, her mind catapulted her back to that night twenty-two years ago, burning flesh permeating her sinuses.

Oh, god, no...

She was *there* – right back there in her mother's arms and—

"No!" *You're not there. MOVE your legs and run!*

She stumbled rather than ran, fire still dancing in her vision, completely veiling the bridle path in front of her. Whichever direction she'd tumbled, it led her to a dead end – a brick wall – no, a...

Chest.

One which might as well be made of bricks.

Blinking hard to rid herself of the illusionary deadly flames, she looked up from the chest clothed in a black T-shirt, and into the eyes of a man who ... maybe was also made of bricks. Or stone. Or marble – one of those beautiful, muscular, Greek deities carved in sleek, white, hard marble – his expression was so *still*, she briefly wondered if she'd tumbled into a statue, but then he blinked and his eyes...

Shone.

Gold.

And for a second she didn't exist. Or perhaps she existed

everywhere. Her entire body *surged* from the inside out like she was in a dropping elevator ... falling ... rising...

"Did you kill her?"

She gasped, suddenly realising she hadn't taken a breath in – how long? And then the drug-fuelled, hungry woman filled her mind, her head bleeding, bringing Sophia back to reality and the danger she was in with a jarring starkness.

RUN!

On instinct, she raised her arm to punch him, but he caught her wrist, nostrils flaring as he glanced warily at her bloody hand. Still in primal mode, she tried to fling her knee upwards into his groin, only to realise she literally couldn't move. His other hand formed nothing short of a vice against the small of her back, pressing her to him so hard there was barely room to... She met his eyes once more.

No. No room for anything.

"Did you *kill* her?" he repeated.

Kill her?

You murdered her.

Appalled at the possibility, she shook her head. "I..." Oh, god, she hadn't meant to. If she was dead, would she go to jail?

Before further words could form, noises brought the trees surrounding them to life. Still caught in this man's grip, they both slowly turned towards the sounds to see the darkness part in places and figures – *many* figures – take form. About eight large people – men? Definitely more than five. She *felt* their anger towards her, and all at once she guessed they were protective of that woman. Their faces were mostly cloaked in darkness, but of what she could see, they looked nothing short of monstrous – fiends on legs – and their *eyes* were—

"They won't stop until they kill *you* now."

And there it was – the very fear she'd been running from her whole life, right in her face. Only, in her nightmares, whoever chased her had petrol and a lighter. Sometimes a bomb.

"Get on my back, hold tight, and close your eyes."

"What?" Although she'd heard him perfectly well. But she was six years old once more, on her *mother's* back, clutching her neck, and because of that she couldn't move – *couldn't* go there again.

He let out some kind of annoyed rumbling sound that ran right through her bones, then he twirled her around in an instant. Before she could blink, his hand grabbed her between her legs and she was flung upwards behind him and there really was no choice *other* than to clutch his neck with her arms and his waist with her legs – not if she didn't want to injure herself. She heard herself squeal and then *did* close her eyes, more out of necessity than anything else. Wind slapped against her ears because – he was running? Although this didn't feel like being carted around on someone's back, this was more like sticking your head out of a car's open window as it sped down the motorway. She suddenly wondered if they *were* in a car and she'd blacked out or something because she didn't remember getting in.

Gripping him tighter, she buried her head in the collar of his jacket, using the motion to arrest the screams threatening to erupt from her lungs. Tears slipped past the corners of her closed eyes, turning instantly cold with the wind before they were whipped from her cheeks. But neither the wind, nor his collar, could do anything about the sounds of her family burning – *those* screams had never fully left her. They never would.

The wind had stopped. A heavy door shut behind them. She was either safe or about to die and she had no idea which it was.

"You'll be all right here for tonight."

She heard him. She didn't move – still plastered to his back. Couldn't move – her muscles had seized; her joints rigidly set into the death-grip she'd used to save her life.

"You gettin' down?"

She tried, but the smallest movement sent her trembling, her muscles wanting to cramp rather than relax.

"Okay, okay ... here..." He reached behind him, grabbed the far side of her butt, and swung her round like she was a dancer on a pole, until she was straddling the front of his hips, not the back. "Come on – look at me. You're okay now."

Her head no longer crammed against the collar of his jacket, but against the crook of his neck, she finally felt the first trickle of emotion infiltrate her senses – embarrassment. Raising her head, her gaze settled on his lips – full and symmetrical – before travelling past the groove above them, up the length of a strong, straight nose, interrupted only by a ridiculously sexy bump, and landing on his eyes. The gold glint was still there, but they now carried a far richer brown tone that swam around dilated pupils. Heavy-set eyebrows framed them, and waves of longish locks of dark brown hair fell just above them, finishing the look pretty damn perfectly.

Locks.

She didn't think she'd *ever* seen 'locks' on a man before, all soft and twisted, a bit like the fusilli she'd eaten earlier that night. And *just* like that, it all hit her like a freight train. *What. The. Fuck—*

"Oh, my god." She jumped off him. Leapt. And did a bad job of it too, her feet giving way as soon as they hit the ground.

He caught her by the elbows, those eyebrows arched up in what might have been bemusement. Or condescension at her total lack of finesse.

"What just happened?" she asked, half rhetorically.

"Take a minute first."

"I don't need a minute," she bit out, more harshly than she'd intended, but reality was closing in fast and she needed her control back. "I was attacked."

He watched her warily, still holding her elbows.

She pulled herself away, out of his grasp. "I'm fine – I can stand."

Observing her guardedly, he let her go. "Yes, you were attacked. And you fought back. And you won, from I could see."

"Won? I might have killed her. I didn't mean to hit her so..." Her words trailed off as the memory of the fight surfaced. Startled, she looked at her hand, caked red in blood, shiny shards of glass still embedded in her palm, the sting of the cuts finally biting now her shock was wearing off, and then she looked at the man – a complete stranger – standing in front of her. His neck was stained red from where she'd held him. What the hell had she done?

She reached for his neck in apology. "I got blood on y—"

Sophia didn't even *see* him move, but his hand was around her wrist before she knew it, his jaw clenching like it might break; his grip like steel. She all at once remembered that force against the small of her back, keeping her from all movement. There was nothing she could do when he pushed her bloody hand downwards, her strength simply non-existent compared to his.

This is what it's like to feel completely powerless. In confusing contradiction, heat rushed through her at the thought. Not the heat of anger, but something she was far less comfortable with – something she'd avoided at all costs since the utter failure that was Pierce.

"I'll shower it off." His tone was as hard as his closed fist around her wrist. "The kitchen sink to your right is where you can wash your hand." Without another word, he walked off. *Marched* off like he despised her.

Maybe he does. Or maybe he really hates blood.

He slammed a door shut, making her jump slightly, and it wasn't too long before she heard what sounded like a shower switch on.

Standing there, feeling like an idiot, embarrassment unfurled again. And indignation. And a low-level anger at being ... *discarded* so suddenly, although none of it quite matched her confusion at the entire evening since 10 p.m.

Shit – what time is it? Shaking herself out of her confusion, she looked around for a clock, noting she was in a large apartment with a minimalistic feel and not much in it outside of the bare necessities. Exposed brick, painted white, made up most of the décor. She had no idea where she was at all.

She found a large, round clock on the kitchen wall. Just gone eleven. And then a horrid realisation hit her. She'd left her bag exactly where she'd dropped it after the attack. Her phone, the keys to her house, her wallet and everything in it ... it was all gone.

Chapter Three

Panic rose fast.

After so many years keeping a tight rein on her identity and her entire past, to know someone else now had those details...

Relax, Sophia, they have your adopted name, not your birth one – that's all gone and there's no trace.

It didn't make her feel any better – not after literally being attacked. Her home address was also on her driver's licence. *And there's always a trace.*

"Damn it!" she cursed.

They'd let her keep her first name after the fire. It would have been far too confusing as a young child to change that on top of everything else. But her middle name, her surname, and pretty much everything else had had a massive remix after she'd entered witness protection. Could someone find out? If they had her current details, would they be able to track her if they suspected who she was? If they had the know-how?

Her imagination was galloping a little too fast to capture.

That woman tonight had nothing to do with the past – she looked around your age.

Sophia held up her hand to the ceiling light. It had mostly stopped bleeding, but small pieces of glass glistened on her skin – *in* her skin. She had to get to the hospital. No – her hand wasn't so bad – they had to get to the police.

Yes! That's what she'd do. They'd always protected her and they'd know what to do – she still had a number she could call despite it having been years. She had to tell them everything about tonight.

Feeling a bit more sure, she strode to the window and looked out, hoping to have some understanding of where she was. She swore under her breath. She couldn't see a single damn street light anywhere nearby – only far in the distance – which meant she was probably in the countryside somewhere. For the life of her, she couldn't recall how long they'd run for ... if they had even run. The whole thing seemed a bit like a blur now, and if she was being honest, she wasn't certain what she could tell the police about how the hell she'd gotten here, wherever 'here' was.

Turning back to the open plan apartment – all on one floor – she scoured it for a phone. Nope – no landline anywhere. And if that man had a mobile phone, it was probably on him, or in his jacket, which was likely in his bedroom now.

Why *hadn't* he taken her straight to the police station after the attack?

She now glanced at the front door. *Leave. Get the hell out now.*

Her heart thumped. She could. She *should*.

And what if those large men are hanging around outside?

She'd only seen shadows – a glimmer of monsters beyond them. Had she even seen right? Or had she filled in the blanks with her very active mind?

She turned towards what she assumed was the bedroom. The shower was still running. Where did this stranger fit into everything? He'd rescued her but ... had he? What had he even been doing there in the bridleway? She could be caught in a trap right now without even knowing it – she didn't *know* him. *No phone and no way to contact anyone ... you're here alone with him and no one knows it.* He could be part of the whole attack that had taken place tonight.

Okay ... *calm down.* She always did this when she started to panic – her imaginings went nuts. Nevertheless, she *needed* to go to the police. She'd been in danger before and could be in danger again and... She gulped hard at the thought that had just entered her head. *You might have killed someone.* She needed to explain her side of things before everything got out of hand.

The shower turned off.

Shit! Her mind made up, she half-ran to the front door as quietly as she could, grabbed the handle and—

"What the *hell* do you think you're doing?" His hand slammed against the door, making it impossible to open.

How the fuck had he got here so—

Her thoughts froze right there, along with her entire self as she swirled around – as angrily as she could manage in the midst of her fear – to face the person who was starting to feel like a captor, not a saviour. A captor wearing nothing but beads of water *everywhere* and a towel around his waist, and that needed to be the absolute last thing on her mind right now. Blinking to break her line of sight with possibly the most sensually chiselled torso she'd ever seen in her life, she forced her face into a scowl, hoping she looked at least a little like she could handle herself in this unknown situation. "So, I'm a prisoner here?"

He didn't look best pleased. "You're a prisoner out *there* until the sun comes up. They're looking for you right now and the only thing you've got going for you is my ability to out-manoeuvre them."

And then, she didn't need to pretend anymore; didn't need to search for her anger or strength – it was right there, fuelled by the fear and his strange cockiness. She barrelled into him, shoving him back with her forearms, careful not to touch his bare chest with her hands and more than a little annoyed she wasn't immune to how attractive he was. "Stand *back*," she snapped.

Surprised by her actions, he did.

"Do you care to tell me what the hell happened to me tonight? *Who* is looking for me right now? Maybe *talk* to me instead of grunting, giving orders, and disappearing because you're pissed off. Where *am* I?"

He seemed temporarily lost for words. "You were attacked."

Well, give the man a medal. "We've established that already. Where am I?"

"My ... home."

"And where *is* that exactly?"

"In the countryside beyond the west side of Winchester."

"The west side of..." From Emerson, that would have taken *ages* to get to on foot. "Did we ... get a lift here?"

He frowned. "What?"

She recalled the wind batting her face. "We got some kind of ride here, right?"

His frown deepened. Silence followed as he stared at her, as if trying to figure her out. "Do you ... know what attacked you tonight?"

"You mean the woman? She was probably a drug addict or something – and homeless. She said she was hungry."

The silence deepened and it irked her because the way he was looking at her made her feel stupid. *Why* did this man she didn't even know have the knack for getting under her skin and making her feel like an oaf?

Finally, he sucked in a breath through his teeth and turned away from her, running a hand through his hair – *wet locks* – in a somewhat fraught manner. "Jesus Christ..." And then he whirled back – fast – making her start; pointing his finger at her, accusingly. "You threw her off you!"

Yeah, that was definitely an accusatory tone. Was defending herself a sin?

"You used *holy* water."

Guilt rose fast at how she'd made that woman bleed – likely hurt her badly. He'd seen that – great. God, he'd even asked her at the time if she'd killed her, hadn't he? Fuck it to hell, there went her chance to speak to the police first without any witnesses. She *was* going to prison. "It was the first thing I grabbed – I didn't mean to hurt her that bad. I was reaching for my pepper spray and couldn't find it and—"

"*Pepper spray*?" he spit out. "Fuck!

"What?! What's your problem?"

"You have no damn clue."

Wow. She hadn't thought she could feel even more angry, but there it was. He didn't know a thing about her. "Fuck you!" She turned and reached for the door again, only to have him block her exit as fast as a cheetah on steroids.

"You're going nowhere 'til the morning."

She went to slap him – not really her style, but he was *right there* in her space and she wanted him *away* from her – and, of course, he grabbed her wrist again because for some reason she couldn't seem to outspeed him when it counted.

"I told you to wash the blood off your hand." He'd all but snarled that, clearly pissed off with her.

She tried to yank herself from his grip, but couldn't. "Careful now – your caring nature's showing through." She had *no* idea why she'd said that – baiting some guy ten times stronger than she, wasn't the brightest idea – but her fury had maxed at his reaction and so had her confusion. She still felt none the wiser about anything that had happened.

Before she knew it, she was being dragged towards the sink.

"Hey!" she protested to no avail. "Stop it!"

She was practically thrown across its rim, his frame behind hers, pushing her stomach into the cold ceramic and arresting her escape.

"Ow! You bastard!"

He turned the tap on with a shove of his hand. Water rushed out and before she could fight him further, he thrust her red hand under the stream.

"Ouch!" The water bit, the force of it so strong, it splashed everywhere.

With both hands and not too gently, he scrubbed her right one, using his thumbs and fingers to dislodge miniscule shards of glass, and all it did was shred her half-healed skin. Fresh blood seeped bright red.

She cried out and gritted her teeth, tears erupting at the agony, and then she was crying. Sobbing at both the smarting of the hand and her utter defencelessness at being *man*-handled.

He stilled behind her, the water smacking the sink, and her weeping, the only sounds to fill the room.

With a quiet curse, he turned the water off, red still dripping from her hand onto the smooth white of the basin. One of his wet hands circled her waist. "I'm sorry," he whispered. "I'm so sorry." He let go of her hand and reached for the faucet again.

She shook her head, trying to pull back, but he pressed his cheek against hers from behind, the hand around her middle now stroking her gently.

"It's okay; it's okay..." The water streamed more gently this time. He turned on the hot tap too. "I'm sorry," he repeated. "I'm going to warm this up and go slow. I've got soap. I was a jerk – we'll go gently so it doesn't hurt so much."

She didn't have the energy to argue, all her focus on trying to manage the pain in her hand and control her crying. Resigned, she let him do whatever.

He kept to his word. Finally letting her waist go, he tended to her hand with both of his under a much more soothing flow of water that was just a little hotter than warm. He worked with an almost excruciating tenderness, being mindful of any sliver of glass he spotted, pulling it or squeezing it out, washing the soap off, then starting again for any areas he'd missed.

Her sobs finally quietened to just an occasional gulp and shake of her shoulders.

The tap went off and he opened a drawer for a clean kitchen towel. After folding it lengthways, twice, he turned her around, moving her with care. He wound the tea towel firmly around her palm. "I'm going to have to tie this tightly, all right? So it'll probably hurt for a second. But I think the bleeding will stop quickly just like it did before. We'll keep your hand raised and we can take the towel off in an hour or so and swap it for bandages."

She met his eyes. He looked sincere and ... yes, she thought she saw regret there. She nodded, then hissed when he knotted the towel, but the pain didn't last too long this time, just like he'd said. After a while it became a dull throbbing.

He led her to the brown sofa in the living area, and once she was seated, threw a blanket around her. She wasn't sure where he'd gotten that from.

He knelt in front of her. "I'm going to get changed. *Please* stay here. When I come out, I can make you a hot drink and then we can talk about what happens next. All right?"

She could feel the tears she'd cried crusted on her cheeks. She really wished she hadn't shown that kind of vulnerability in front of him, even if she'd been in pain. "You hurt me."

He exhaled, sharply, looked away, and then back at her, determination in his gaze. "I know – I'm sorry. You wound me up tight."

She had the smallest amount of strength left to muster up a glare.

He sighed. "I didn't mean it was your fault, just that... Look, I'm *not* going to hurt you again. I'll be just a few minutes getting changed. Please be here when I return."

After a pause, she nodded.

He might have attempted a smile – she wasn't really sure what that expression on his face was. "What's your name?" he asked.

She tried to ignore the soft curl that had just fallen across his brow. And the fact he was kneeling at her feet in a bath towel. "Sophia."

"I'm Daniel."

She wasn't sure if he meant to brush her leg with his hand before he stood up.

"And I'm going to make sure that whatever happens next, you're safe."

Chapter Four

"Sweet Sophia..."

Fire danced all around her, its heat menacing. She wished she could make it do what she wanted it to do, but it was always wild and chaotic. Instead, she cried, her wails and sobs chaotic, too.

His hand glided up her wrist, his thumb circling the pulse there, once, but his hungry eyes locked onto her neck, seemed to hesitate, then fell to her tummy behind her dress. He bunched her dress in his hands.

"Stop it!" she screamed.

"Now you behave. You have something very special and your job is to let me have it, do you understand?" His grip tightened and he wrenched her dress up—

She lunged at him, eyes snapping open in nothing short of terror. Escaping ... escaping the sudden pain, the fire, and heat, and...

In the recesses of her mind, she saw a man. A horrible man with brown hair and eyes and a sick, sweetly smile which...

Gasping for air, she blinked, repeatedly, as she clutched ... a T-shirt. Slowly coming back to herself, she grimaced and moaned as a pang shot through her right hand, still wrapped in a tea towel. Reality hit like a ton of bricks.

"All right, easy now." That was Daniel. This nearly-stranger's name was Daniel and he was *not* the man from her dream. He was on his knees by the sofa – had caught her as she'd flown at him.

"Sorry. It was a nightmare."

"I could tell."

She stared at him, guarded, her slumber falling away rapidly, and then quickly pushed herself from his chest, scooting back onto the sofa while cradling her hand. "I haven't had it in a long time. I'm sorry I leapt at you; if I hurt you."

"You didn't."

She couldn't believe she'd fallen asleep after everything. How long *had* she been sleeping? The nightmare had left her feeling nauseous. Who had that man been? Was that a memory? Or had she made him up?

She took in Daniel properly. He was dressed now and no longer wet. "Why were you gone so long?"

He raised an eyebrow. "I wasn't. Just five minutes; ten before you woke."

She'd fallen asleep in five minutes?

"You must have been exhausted, and I smell alcohol on your breath. I made you a coffee. It's black though – no milk. Do you want it?"

That was a curt way to offer her a drink. (And so wonderful that he probably thought she was drunk.) She stared at him in question, but he seemed genuinely unaware of his own bluntness.

"Er ... I guess. Yes. Thanks."

"Right." He stood so swiftly, it made her flinch. By the time he'd returned with her mug, she'd managed to calm and harden herself. The hardening was necessary – god, she couldn't go having nightmares and losing control of herself in a stranger's apartment. She had to keep her mind alert.

He placed the coffee on the table to the side of the sofa.

"Thank you."

"You're welcome."

She cleared her throat. "My handbag's gone. Everything was in it – my wallet, house keys... I need to go to the police as soon as I can."

He pursed his lips, then said, "There are better ways to

handle this than the police."

Of course. She sucked her bottom lip between her teeth in annoyance. "How did I know you were going to say that?"

"It's true. The woman who attacked you – she wasn't homeless. She was..." His jaw clenched. "Part of a gang."

"A *what*?" That sounded bizarre to say the least. "A gang?"

Amazingly, and she had no idea how he did this, he fidgeted – it was something almost imperceptible in the way he stood – *while* he held himself still. Too still. She didn't think she'd seen anyone do that before. And it screamed to her he was lying.

"A gang in the town of Emerson?" she asked, incredulously.

"Yes. That's why I was there in the bridleway. I was tracking them – they're new to this area and I don't know what they want or why they're here."

Lie, lie, lie, lie. But it probably wasn't wise to let him know she didn't believe him.

"And who are you? Are *you* part of a gang?"

"No. I work alone."

"So ... you're a private investigator, or something?"

He paused. "Something like that. And believe me when I say the police don't know how to handle these people. In fact, if this gang finds out you've alerted the police, they could retaliate." He actually sounded like he meant that, despite any lies.

She breathed out, slowly, and turned to take a sip of her coffee and almost coughed it up. Fuck, that was the *worst* coffee she'd ever tasted in her life.

Not wanting to be rude, she forced herself to swallow it. When she turned back to face him, he was staring at her so intensely she actually looked herself up and down. "Did ... I spill it down my face?"

He blinked; took a step back. "No." He turned away and strode the length of the living room, then back again. His wrought pacing reminded her of an agitated tiger desperate to flee its cage. "This gang moves at night – only at night. You'll be safe as soon as the sun comes up but not before then – not if they have your address."

They can get to you in your house. "Oh, my god." She paled.

"Only because they'll know where you are, but they won't break in, don't worry."

"Don't worry? How can you be so sure?"

"It's not their style."

"Criminals can't change their style?"

"These guys won't. Really, they *won't* break in. I suppose they could burn your house down, but that's highly unlikely because of the ruckus it would cause. Historically, that doesn't work for them."

Burn her HOUSE down? Her mouth fell open as the worst day of her life played out before her.

He obviously noted her reaction – it wasn't exactly subtle – and gave his nose a small wrinkle in uncertainty. "I'm sorry, I was trying to be comforting."

Her gaze hardened. "*Comforting*?"

Sighing, he muttered something she didn't quite catch. Then, he glared at her, warily, like the next thing he said might trigger Mount Vesuvius.

You did just jump him in your sleep. She wondered if she'd been shouting or flailing before that.

"Look – I get that there's a lot you don't know and that I'm not telling you. It's not because I'm trying to trick you. It's because the less you know the safer you'll be. It's like ... it's like a police investigation in some ways – they'll never give you all the information for your own safety."

That she understood, at least. Police investigations were a thing she was used to. "Okay," she nodded, slowly. "I can maybe deal with it from that angle. But what happens now?"

He stopped pacing and sat down on the other side of the

sofa, angling himself so he was facing her. "Do you have a spare set of keys to your house? In case you get locked out?"

"Yes. Buried under the soil in the flowerpot by the door." Should she have told him that? Knitting her eyebrows together, she glanced at him in mild irritation. Did he *have* to be so good looking and bloody odd at the same time? It was a perplexing combination. She decided she was going to blame that entirely for the fact she kept saying things she shouldn't around him. And throwing herself at him in semi-conscious states.

"Good. It's best for you to stay here tonight. An hour after sunrise, at about quarter past six, there'll be a car outside for you. The name of the driver is Les – he'll introduce himself to you. He'll take you back to your house."

Stay ... here. She looked around, weighing all her options in her head. Her goal was to come out of whatever this was alive. "So, in the morning, I get to go home? And that's it?"

"That's it for tomorrow. You're safe in daylight."

"What about tomorrow night?"

He hesitated and she wasn't sure she liked what that implied. "I'll be in touch about tomorrow night. Until then, you don't have to worry about it. Do you need to be somewhere tomorrow?"

She shook her head. "I don't work on Sundays." And then realised she'd just gone and given *that* away too – divulged something else to him about her plans and potential whereabouts. She had no idea she'd be so shit at being held hostage.

You're not a hostage.

But she sort of was, because where the hell else could she go right now? It was like he'd kidnapped her without kidnapping her. And saved her life at the same time. He was a really hot, curly-haired, life-saving kidnapper with subtle, persuasive charm and strange, erratic mood swings.

They're called serial killers, Sophia.

"That's good – it'll give time for your hand to heal. We can bandage it up now if you like."

"What about my handbag? I'm going to have to phone my bank tomorrow to cancel my cards. I'll have to report my driver's licence missing. I'll need to change the locks."

"Do what you have to. If those guys – the gang – took your bag, they're unlikely to spend your money or steal your identity. But they will use all information they can to track you. Especially if you killed their woman."

She swore under her breath. Despite her potential serial killer situation, she felt crippling guilt that she might have killed another person. "Do you think she's dead?"

He frowned at her question and seemed to pick his words carefully. "Usually, an attack like yours would not kill someone like her, but..."

"But?"

"When we left the area, she seemed ... incapacitated by what you did." He was keenly studying her expression now, curiosity colouring his. "Do you mind me asking why you were carrying holy water in your bag? Is it something you carry often?"

Great! He thinks I'm a religious nutcase. "It's such a silly story – it was just a thing I was given. I didn't even know what I was going to do with it. Put it in the kettle or something." She tried to laugh at that, but it fell short. "I didn't mean to hit her with glass – with something so lethal."

"Don't worry about that – I highly doubt you're going to be a suspect in anything. I doubt the police will even look for one, to be honest. The gang have a way of making their own kind disappear – even after death. They really don't want to be found."

"You really think so?"

"I know so."

He'd said that so sincerely, it actually calmed her somewhat. Living life behind bars just wasn't on her bucket list.

"I ... erm ... wondered if you were perhaps religious?" he continued to press. "Because you were carrying holy water around, I mean." He glanced at her intently again.

He *did* think she was a religious nutcase. But the way he was waiting for an answer to that question was more than unnerving. Maybe *he* was the religious one looking to recruit her into his cult or something. *Nip that one in the bud right now, Sophia.* "Oh, no. Hell no. I'm not sure I've ever believed in God."

"Never?"

She shook her head, nervously but adamantly. If religious cults were his thing, she was so not going to be his next victim. "If one exists, he's kind of cruel, don't you think? Letting all kinds of horrendous things happen to good people – innocent people. Children..."

She couldn't tell whether he looked more relieved or confused, but that seemed to be the end of that conversation, thankfully.

They fell into a brief silence. Then he gestured to her hand. "Let's get this tea towel off."

"Okay." She held it out in front of him and he loosened the knot, gently, then stared at her bare flesh ... and stared. This guy was *definitely* a starer.

"That's... that's healed up nicely," he said, before looking at her sharply.

Was that a bad thing?

Serial killers like to see their handiwork, Sophia.

She shut off her mind – it really wasn't helping. "Yeah – it's not bad. Wasn't sure it would fare well with the number of cuts I had from the glass. Still hurts a little, though. If I ball my fist, I think I'd split the skin."

He continued to stare at her. "Best not do that, then. Do you think you need bandages?"

She shook her head. "It's not bleeding anymore – I should

probably let the air get to it."

"Do you usually heal so quickly?"

She met his gaze, genuinely surprised at that question. "Do you think that's quick?"

Both eyebrows went up. One hit the bottom of a twisty lock. "Do you *not* think so? Have you ever been around anyone else who was injured to compare?"

Why the fuck was this guy so *weird*? She went with it and the whole outlandish conversation because scenes from *Psycho* kept popping into her mind. "No. I don't think so. I've never really thought about it before."

"Have you had any big injuries before tonight?"

She felt her own shutters come down as distant flames danced in the recesses of her mind. "No," she said, curtly, then caught herself. "Um, only once. But I was six and don't remember anything about it."

He paused for a bit too long, and she got the impression he was soaking up her reaction; soaking up *her*. "Well, it's all good. Your hand will be back to normal in no time."

Another pause.

She looked around, awkwardly. "So, I'm sleeping here tonight?" Might as well get to the crux of everything that was scary and awkward. She mentally slapped herself, hard, for adding 'and sexy' to the end of that last thought. She'd have Stockholm Syndrome before she knew it.

"You can have the sofa or my bedroom. It's up to you."

"Your b-bedroom?" *Yes, stuttering is great. Do let him know outright you find him attractive.*

"I'll be elsewhere. Despite my earlier actions, I am actually capable of being a gentleman."

"Elsewhere? Do you mean you're going out?" Did she want to be alone in *here*? What if someone else stopped by? One of his equally strange, less nice, I-promise-I'm-not-in-a-gang friends?

Perhaps he read her mind; perhaps her face said it all. "I have some things I need to do. I'm not expecting anyone and I promise you'll be safe here. Just don't let anyone in. I'll be back before you leave."

She picked at a loose thread on her jeans.

"Sophia—"

She blinked at his calling her by name. It *did* sound confounding coming from him – like he knew her or something.

"I know it's a big ask for you to trust me after everything that took place tonight, but I promise you, I don't have any bad intentions and I don't want to see you get hurt. I *do* want to know more about the gang we ran into tonight. I'll even keep you updated on what I find if you like."

She raised an eyebrow at that. "Selective information, you mean. You'll only keep me updated on what you choose to." If there was even any information there to find.

There was that fidgeting while standing still thing again. "I'll definitely let you know when they've forgotten about you, or if they move on. I'll let you know when you're safe again."

"I hate this," she blurted out before she could stop herself. "I hate feeling like I always need to look over my shoulder. I thought I'd..." She breathed out in frustration. "Never mind."

There was a pause, and then, "Hopefully, it won't be for long." He'd said that quietly.

She said nothing, but nodded, and another silence followed before she broke it. "I'll take the bedroom if that's okay – my neck's a bit sore from the way I was lying earlier."

His gaze stayed exactly where it was on her face; flickered to her neck once – or she thought it did – and then, suddenly, it was gone completely. After so many minutes of his focus *on* her so uncomfortably, his sudden withdrawal was ... almost desolating. "No problem." He was on his feet, gathering his things – keys, jacket – and left his bedroom door open all the way for her.

"It's in there." He gestured through the doorway. "Take a shower if you need and make yourself at home. I need to go – I need to eat. I'll wake you at sunrise." He slung his jacket over his shoulder and headed out the door.

Chapter Five

"The window! Go out the window!"

It was so hot. So hot she wanted to take her skin off so she couldn't feel the heat. She knew she was crying with fear, but her mum was crying too. And screaming. Fire was loud – not quiet. You could hear it eating everything it touched.

"Mummy..." Her voice got lost in the roar of the flames – the same flames that blackened the walls; the window sill... They hurt her eyes. She squeezed them shut and buried her face into her mother's neck from behind.

"Gerard! I can't get out!"

"Throw her!"

Her mother's sobs became louder and uncontrollable. Her whole body was shaking under her frame as Sophia piggy-backed her.

"Deborah!"

She heard her dad coughing hard.

"Sophia, baby ... come here." With a bit of struggle, she moved her around so she was carrying her on her front. Her mum's necklace came into view – a shiny gold cross with a man on it that she knew was supposed to be Jesus. It had always scared her a little.

She'd asked once why she wore something that looked so painful – that was an image of someone dying. Her mum had explained it wasn't about death – it was about resurrection – and that she'd explain it properly to her one day when she was a bit older. The pendant now looked a bright orange with the fire all around them. "Look at me, sweetie ... look at me."

She did. "I'm scared," Sophia said, quietly, not able to stop her voice shaking.

Her mum heard her and fell silent. Tears streamed down her face, but she managed a small smile. She felt her hand stroke her cheek. "I love you so much. I always will." It looked like she was trying not to cry again. Her mouth was moving – she was saying things – telling her something with that look on her face that said she needed to listen carefully, but Sophia couldn't hear the words. And then, her mum clutched her tightly to her and pressed a kiss against her cheek. Into her ear she whispered, "Do you believe in miracles?"

Holding her mother tightly, she nodded against her hair.

"Good. You're in God's hands now."

A quick pain ran through her body as it was jerked – hard – away from her mother's embrace. The heat was suddenly gone. Cool air enveloped her as the night sky greeted her, every star winking in welcome as she flew ... floated ... fell...

Whether it was her own scream or her mother's that chased her towards the ground, she couldn't tell.

The scream carried into the room as she threw herself up to sitting, tossing the covers off her. "Oh, God..." Breathing hard, it took her a few seconds to place the past back in the past. Her skin was hot and clammy. The events of the night rushed back, and along with them, where she was. A glance at the small alarm clock on the bedside table that wasn't hers, told Sophia it was 5:30 in the morning. Two nightmares in one night. Damn it to hell. After *years* not having any.

She'd given herself a pat on the back after Daniel had left, for keeping her cool. She'd hidden her anger and frustration – played how she felt right down. She'd wanted to get home as fast as she could – surround herself with every familiar thing – and had even thought of sneaking out after he'd gone, but instinctively, she somehow knew he'd know. And she already knew she was no match for him in speed or strength. It became clear to her that 'escaping' wasn't going to happen easily, so she'd reluctantly resigned herself to waiting until the morning and following his instructions, as ridiculous as they'd sounded. Despite loathing her situation, she genuinely didn't get the impression Daniel was going to hurt her. He confused her, though. On the one hand, he was almost charming and he had a reserve about him she found appealing and felt a certain resonance with. It was somewhat Victorian the way he contained himself emotionally. On the other hand, he could be rude and an arsehole, and paradoxically sported a huge *lack* of control at unpredictable times. And she couldn't figure out his triggers.

After careful consideration, she'd decided to leave the bedroom door open, despite stripping down to her underwear to sleep. While she didn't want him seeing her unclothed, she didn't at all like the idea of not knowing what might be happening behind a closed door in this strange place.

Well, you're still here. He's had the chance to tie you up, rape you and kill you, and he hasn't done any of those things.

The utter silence from the living room area and kitchen indicated he wasn't back yet. Another look at the alarm clock told her she had about forty minutes before her lift got here, and she was *itching* to get home. She was also itching from her drying perspiration making his cotton sheets feel scratchy.

Without thinking on it further, she got out of bed and silently padded to the adjoining bathroom, ignoring her earlier flashes of *Psycho* and that infamous shower scene. She'd spied shampoo and soap earlier and his towel had been strewn on the floor – it would do until she got home.

She *did* shut the bathroom door, then she took off her underwear, relieved herself, flushed the toilet, and got into the shower. The hot spray was heaven, and she sighed in relief. With satisfaction, she noted her hand was no longer smarting. Apart from a couple of small scabs, it looked like everything had healed well – and apparently, quickly. That had thrown her when he'd asked if she'd ever seen anyone else injured. Because she hadn't. Sure, lots of kids had gotten cuts and bruises from falling over when she'd been at school, but they were always whisked to the nurse's room, plastered up, and she'd never paid any mind to how long her classmates had taken to heal. It had never occurred to her she might "heal quickly" as Daniel had put it. Was that weird? She had no idea. It didn't seem like a bad trait to have, even if it was.

She looked down at the one scar she had on her body between her left hip bone and pubic bone. The doctors had told her she'd sustained the wound after being thrown from the window, although they couldn't tell her what caused it. It was suspected she'd caught it on a tree branch falling, or perhaps a splinter from the damaged window sill as she was thrown. She couldn't remember anything about it, but sometimes, it still hurt – an ache deep inside her she couldn't get rid of. Her only physical reminder of that night.

She soaped herself down quickly after shampooing her hair, allowed herself just enough time in the shower to feel warm through, and then switched it off and stepped out onto the floor mat, reaching for the towel she had straightened and hung up earlier. She dried herself as well as possible, then wrapped it around her before opening the bathroom door.

The continuing silence greeted her. As quickly as possible,

she put all her clothes back on, then gave her hair one last pat down before hanging up the towel.

She heard the front door open and shut. It irked her that she felt relieved at his return. *Fabulous, the Stockholm Syndrome is already here.* She shook her head and reminded herself that serial killers generally didn't let their victims sleep without restraints or have showers whenever they wanted. Whatever Daniel wasn't telling her, it probably wasn't because he wanted to hurt her. She decided to level up and act more freely and casually around him. Last night she'd been in shock. This morning, she felt more herself.

"You're up," he called out. It wasn't a question.

"Yeah – I woke up at half-five, couldn't get back to sleep and figured I'd take a quick shower. I hope that's okay." She made her way into the living room.

"Of course." He looked her way.

Her stomach somersaulted and for the life of her she didn't know why. It couldn't just be his attractiveness – she'd come across attractive guys before and her insides had behaved.

"Les will be here soon."

"The driver, right?"

"Yes. And I got you something."

With curiosity, she made her way to him and the box he held out.

Opening it, she took out the object inside. "A mobile phone? Is this new?"

"Second-hand, actually, but not that old a model. You lost yours last night. Figured this might come in handy until you get another. There's a charger in there too, and it's all paid for, so you don't have to worry about that. I wrote your number in the lid here, and my number's already programmed in. It's ready to go."

"Your number?"

"So I can reach you. About tonight."

"Right." Her heart fell. Ugh. She'd forgotten to ask further about what the nights would mean for her with some *gang* scouring the streets for her. Seriously ... a 'gang' in Emerson of all places? She didn't buy it. But she *had* seen the state of the woman, and those men that later appeared had definitely seemed menacing. That's all she had to go on.

He nodded once. "I'll call you."

She almost laughed – those three words sounded like the end of a one-night stand. "Bet you say that to all the ladies who stay over."

Fuck. Her joke fell flat. So much for free and casual.

He stared at her with a bewildered look on his face, and her cheeks burned.

"Sorry – it's a ... morning after joke. Not ... suited to ... this situation." Her words fell to ground. All of them. She exhaled sharply, then turned on her feet to grab her jacket from where she'd left it on the couch.

When she turned back with jacket and phone in hand, the first ray of sunlight streamed through the small break in his living room curtains, strewing a golden beam across the floor between them. Unbidden, a memory from her nightmare flashed into her mind: her mother's crucifix pendant, glowing against the flames. She'd forgotten all about that pendant until that dream.

She found Daniel staring at her with an intense longing – at least she *thought* that's what she saw. His expression was now blank. But it was *her own* startling reaction to his gaze that threw her for a loop. Her insides were doing wicked things again.

"Les is here," he said, suddenly.

It was her turn to look bewildered.

"I heard his car."

Really? She hadn't heard a thing. "Okay. Well, then, I'll just

... um..."

He didn't move a muscle.

Right then. Having embarrassed herself enough, she decided not to ask if he was seeing her to the door. She was a big girl. "I'll let myself out." She turned and strode away towards—

He was in front of her all of a sudden, opening the door.

What the—

"Wait," he snapped.

She waited, somewhat whiplashed by his movements.

And she waited.

He was staring at her again, but this time, his stare was unreadable.

"Yes?"

He caught himself. "Um ... look, after you get home, don't invite anyone in, okay? We don't know who's who until I can get more information about this gang."

She wasn't expecting anyone over, except maybe... "The locksmith might want a cup of tea."

He pressed the door shut, blocking her exit, just like he had last night, irritation swimming across his features. "He can drink his tea outside."

He was worried about the locksmith? Come on now! She had her comeback all ready, her own irritation climbing fast, but reined it in at the last minute – she *really* wanted to get home and this was wasting time. "Fine. I won't invite anyone in."

He looked at her, not believing a word, still blocking her exit.

Her irritation gave way to curiosity. Before she could stop herself, she took a step into his space, her chest meeting his, her face an inch from his own. She saw his pupils dilate and herself reflected in them. She wondered if hers did the same – if he could see himself reflected in hers. "I can't figure you out at all." She'd intended that to come out in a sassy tone, all boss-lady like.

She failed. Her throat betrayed her, and her words tumbled out all husky.

His gaze fell to her lips as if trying to catch those words. "Likewise," he replied, softly. Very softly. And then he looked confused and ... almost wounded. It got to her in a way she couldn't explain.

"I won't invite anyone in," she repeated, and meant it.

His gaze snapped to hers – their eyes locked.

With a blink, she stepped back, unsure what odd exchange had just taken place. Had she just ... *succumbed* a part of herself to him? Which part exactly?

"Thank you," he replied, in earnest, clearly grateful. He opened the door.

She had to get out of here. She had to get home. With a deep breath in and a mental slap to shake herself out of *whatever* this was, she nodded, turned, and left.

It was just shy of seven o'clock by the time the black Range Rover Autobiography pulled up outside her house. Les was a gem and the highlight of her night and morning, and she was no longer finding Daniel scary in any way – just puzzling.

An elderly, jovial man, Les hadn't stopped talking for nearly the entire trip, his London accent – with a mild Estuary dialect – filling the car with life. "Those were the days." He was recounting a part of his childhood growing up in East Anglia. "I'm *just* about old enough to remember the last horse-drawn cart in my area delivering milk and coal – Bob, that was the coachman's name. Yes, that was it. I was young, mind, when we moved away from the country and nearer to London, but that's a whole other story."

She couldn't help but smile at his exuberance – it was much

needed after last night. "I sort of wish we had more time – I'd love to hear about it."

He switched off the engine and turned in his seat, his blue-grey eyes twinkling. "Oh, I'm sure I'll see you again, Miss Sophia."

"Just Sophia, please. And I was under the impression this was a one-off lift."

"Oh, you were now, were you."

"Hmmn, sounds like you might know something I don't. Tell me, do you give lifts to Daniel's lady friends quite often?"

He laughed and it sounded like Christmas had come. She suddenly realised how much she'd missed the sound of laughter living alone – or *at all* in her life, come to think of it. It had been a rather serious life. "Oh, not for a very long time now, ma'am. Not for years."

Years? Her nosiness piqued. "You've worked for him a long time then?" She'd pegged Daniel for around thirty-five. He must have been young when he started his business.

Les nodded with something resembling pride. "Indeed I have. He's a good boss. And a good person. I wouldn't work for anyone else."

That was quite a statement. "I don't imagine many people can say that about their employers nowadays."

"Perhaps not."

She hesitated, then asked. "Did he tell you *why* you're driving me home?"

"Ah – about the lovely lot you ran into last night. He did."

"So, I suppose he tells you quite a bit, and he obviously trusts you. Are you part of his ... investigation team?"

He studied her, his expression a little more serious, but the corners of his eyes still crinkled in a kind of happiness she wished she had. He seemed to contemplate something before speaking. "I ... know Daniel better than some. I daresay better than most.

Before I worked for him, he saved my life."

She must have looked as surprised as she felt because he chuckled.

"But I don't work for him because I feel I owe him. I work for him because he has a good heart and he's climbed some impossible mountains to gain that goodness. Oh, yes, he can be difficult to say the least, and he keeps himself somewhat isolated, but those more awkward traits of his are not without reason. That I have the privilege to drive you home today, Sophia, means you managed to stir the goodness in him, and for someone like Daniel – with the things he's had to overcome – that's not just something he needs. It's an actual miracle."

"Do you believe in miracles…?" came her mother's voice. She blinked a couple of times to clear the uncomfortable memory. "I … don't know what to say." That was far more information than she'd been expecting and whatever information she *had* expected … well, it hadn't been that.

"Best say nothing then." Les smiled. "Let's get you into that home of yours now – you've been through enough for one day." There was a finality to his tone that told her the conversation was over. At least for now.

"Oh, please, don't get up, I can let myself out. Thank you so much for the lift."

He nodded at her. "It was a pleasure, ma'am. But I will walk you to your door – I have my orders."

Orders?

Predicting her silent question, he added, "To make sure everything's as it should be before I leave you."

"Of course." She didn't argue. Les was clearly loyal to Daniel and would completely ignore any protest on her part.

They walked to her front door together, and he waited patiently while she hunted for her spare key in the depths of her flower pot. Pulling it out, she rubbed the soil off it and unlocked the door. Stepping inside, she turned to Les. "Do you want to come—"

"Ah, no, no, ma'am – you mustn't be inviting anyone in, not even me."

She rolled her eyes. *He told him about that too, did he?* "Well, I'll take a quick look and let you know if anything's out of place."

He nodded and waited and she did just that. Everything looked fine, smelled fine, and all the rooms were empty. The windows were locked shut and even her bedsheets were in the same state of disarray she'd left them in on Saturday morning.

Making her way back to the front door, she smiled. "Everything seems as it should be."

"All right then, Sophia, I'll leave you be. Take good care of yourself."

"You, too, Les. And thank you again."

With a final wave, he left and she closed the door, feeling so very glad to be back home, but also strangely ... alone.

Alone hasn't bothered in all your years. Why now?

Daniel's face filled her mind – his nearness; his expression just before she'd left him. Les' buoyancy still stirred her senses, too.

She sighed and kicked her shoes off. *You're tired. You just need to process everything that happened last night and you'll be able to move on.*

As odd as it seemed to have another shower, being in *her own* bathroom and smelling of her own soaps and moisturiser appealed. Her skin would *love* some moisturiser. And after her shower, she had some phone calls to make.

Chapter Six

"Hello?"

"Hi, Dad."

"Sophia! What a wonderful surprise."

She pulled a face out of guilt at not phoning them enough. "I'm sorry it's so early, but I was hoping you were still a morning person."

He laughed. "You know me – up with the roosters. Your mother's still in bed, though."

"How are you and Mum?"

"Very good. Can't complain. To what do I owe the lovely sound of your voice, honey?"

"I'm sorry I haven't phoned in a while."

"Don't you worry – you're a grown woman and you flew this nest a long time ago."

"It just took a bit of time for me to settle down here after London and—"

"I said not to worry about it. It's good to know you're independent and well."

"I am. I really am, but, erm ... I was wondering if you still had all my documents from when I was a child?" She didn't need to elaborate – he knew exactly what she meant.

"Of course. We'd never throw that away. I think it's all in a box in the loft."

"The police records, too? And birth certificates?"

"Everything was all placed together, I think, yes." He paused. "Are you all right?"

"Yes – yes, absolutely." She didn't want to worry them, so she sent a silent apology for the little white lie she was about to tell. "I, erm, was out last night with a friend and we had a great time, but I got a little tipsy." She laughed. "So, silly me went and left my bag in the toilet of the café we were in, and half an hour later, when I realised I didn't have it ... well, it wasn't there anymore."

"Sophia—"

"I know, I know, it's not like me to do that kind of thing. I need to call the bank later, get my locks changed, and I doubt I'll need any of the details from my past – there's no need for them now – but I just thought I'd feel better having it all with me. In case I ever did."

"That's understandable."

"I know it's Sunday, but I was hoping there might be a private courier who could deliver it by the end of today? London's not too far from Hampshire."

"Oh, there probably is – everything's at the tip of your fingers nowadays, isn't it. It's quite a large box though."

"I'll pay for the transit."

He tsked down the phone at her. "Don't be daft – it's no problem. I'll speak to Jeanette when she's up and we'll get it sorted."

"Thank you so much." She paused, hesitating over asking her next question. Jeanette and Michael had been the most wonderful parents anyone could have asked for – they *were* her parents as far as she was concerned – and she didn't want them to be concerned or get the wrong idea, but her nightmare ... it had awakened a memory she'd forgotten and the memory had gotten under her skin. "Do you and Mum know much about my birth parents?" She held her breath and waited for his reply. She'd never once asked this question before because it brought up too many things she'd always been trying to put behind her.

"Sophia ... I can hear your worry in your voice. It's all right to ask – we knew you would one day – thought it would be sooner, to be honest. We know what the police told us and what we read about, which is pretty much all in the box we're sending out to you today."

"Okay, thanks. I just ... had a dream last night – sort of a memory really. One I'd forgotten, and it made me curious."

"That's normal, honey."

"I know. I dreamt about – erm – a necklace my mum wore that night of the fire. I had completely forgotten about it, but after remembering, I think she wore it quite a lot. It was a crucifix. It led me to wonder if my parents were religious at all? I wasn't sure if you'd know."

There were a few seconds of silence where she wondered if he was pondering over the question. "You know, if I remember correctly, I do think there was a church mentioned – or something like a church. They might have been quite involved in the church community. Roman Catholic, I think – I'm pretty certain it's in the documents you'll have later – but I don't recall there being anything particularly unusual about that or we'd have remembered. Your parents seemed well liked and much appreciated within their own circles – I'm pretty sure that came up during the investigation while they were ruling out suspects."

"Thanks, Dad. I'll just wait for the courier to bring me everything. I'm not sure why the memory's bothering me."

"Sophia, honey, you can't shut yourself off from the past completely. It might be considered unhealthy *not* to know about your parents and everything about your first six years."

She fell silent. Hadn't she told herself last night that she *wanted* to remember? Maybe that was why she was holding on to the suddenly resurfaced memory about the necklace – she was finally ready to know.

"We're always here for you – you know that, don't you?"

She smiled and welled up. "Of course I do. I wouldn't be here at all without you and Mum."

"Now, come on. You're strong in your own right and you'd

have found your way regardless."

"Thanks, Dad. Say hi to Mum for me, okay? I love you both."

"We love you, too. I'll send you a message when we've arranged the delivery."

"Oh! Wait, I forgot – I need to give you a temporary number. My mobile was in the bag that disappeared."

After waiting for him to get a pen, she read out the number. "I'll let you know if I change it again."

"Okay, honey. Have a restful Sunday – I'll be in touch."

They said their goodbyes and Sophia hung up. The mobile phone's home screen told her it was 08:42. After a moment of indecision, she flicked through the pages of her address book – grateful she also logged all her contacts manually, such was her distrust of technology – until she found Abigail's mobile number. It rang out to answerphone, so she waited for the beep.

"Hi, Abi, it's Sophia. I hope you got home okay last night. Listen, I know it's Sunday, but I remember you saying you'd swing by this way to get your car this morning and ... ugh, I was attacked last night walking home. I am completely fine, by the way, but I lost my bag because of it and the keys to the library were in it. I'm so sorry. Um ... let me know if you need me to do anything – I'll pay to have the locks changed, by the way," she added, feeling terrible about the whole thing. "Call me if you can." She repeated her new number then said goodbye.

Her head was spinning. Breakfast was definitely in order.

"Would you like a cup of tea?" She felt marginally bad for having *not* invited the locksmith in, and a tad annoyed she *also* felt duty-bound to keep her word to Daniel.

Luckily, he didn't seem bothered and he hadn't asked to used the bathroom. "Nah, it's okay, luv. I'll be finished in fifteen minutes."

"Thanks so much for coming out on a Sunday."

"We work all days – break-ins and emergencies happen all the time."

"Of course." Not quite knowing what else to say, she felt a semblance of relief when her new phone rang. The ring tone was straight from hell, though – her ears might be bleeding. She'd have to change that as soon as possible.

Abi was at the other end. "Sophia – what on earth! I couldn't believe your message. Are you all right?"

"Abi, hi. Yeah, I'm fine, just tired."

"I can be over at yours in half an hour if you like. And I do have spare keys."

"That would be great. Hey, listen, I have the locksmith here – do you want me to ask if he's free to change the locks on the library today?"

"Probably not a bad idea to get it over and done with."

"Okay, hang on..."

She dropped her phone on the table and went to talk to ... ah, she couldn't recall his name.

"Yep, my next client's not until two o'clock, so I can swing over right after doing yours."

"That would be amazing."

"Can't promise I've got the fittings for it, but I can at least take a look."

"Perfect – it's only the main entrance that needs looking at. Thank you so much."

She raced back to let Abigail know the news and they agreed to meet at the library instead, in half an hour or so. Having that sorted, she went to grab another handbag from her wardrobe and filled it with whatever she might need, including her new phone. Digging into her underwear drawer, she pulled out her spare credit card – the one she never used and kept at home for emergencies.

"Do you need paying today?" she called out to the locksmith.

"Nope. I'll write you an invoice after the work and you pay the company within fourteen days."

"Add the library's lock to my account, okay?"

"No problem. All right, luv, I'm all done. Here's your new set of keys." He showed her the new mechanism, tested the lock, and then they were off to the library. Since he couldn't take passengers in his work car, she agreed to meet him there in fifteen minutes on foot.

She'd thought nothing of it until she neared that same bridle path. Forcing herself to calm down, she approached it cautiously. *What if they're here?* That 'gang'.

Daniel said they're only out and about at night.

Yeah – but she wasn't convinced at his whole gang story, either, so it didn't make her feel better as she began to walk down it.

Might as well search for your bag – see if they left anything behind. She wondered again if she should go to the police. *Maybe you'll know the answer to that after you've inspected the crime scene yourself.*

She shivered. Thinking of it as a crime scene didn't sound nice.

Far too quickly, she reached the spot she'd been attacked. Taking a deep breath in, she readied herself, and then looked around, aware of her heartbeat sounding like a goddamn drum in the silence of the thicket.

With disbelief, she stared hard at the area. It was *immaculate*. No signs of a scuff or anything out of place at all. "You've got to be kidding me," she muttered. *You're going to bring the police here and show them what exactly?*

There was no sign of her bag. There was no sign of *anything* having taken place. Christ, she couldn't even see any footprints or messed up foliage.

The sun emerged suddenly, and one of its rays through the canopy caught something that glistened under some blades of grass. Making her way to it, she crouched and saw it was a shard of glass. *From the bottle of holy water.*

Feeling somewhat relieved she hadn't imagined the entire event, she gingerly reached forward and picked it up. Yes – she was sure it was from the bottle.

Reaching into her bag, she pulled out a packet of tissues, clumsily tugged one out, opened it, and put the shard in it before wrapping it up and slipping it into the inside pocket of her bag. She was just about to hurry along when something else caught her eye from where she was near the ground. This didn't glisten, but it was very white amongst the greenery.

Inching forwards, she carefully picked the object up and frowned. *What the hell is this? It looks like...* It looked like a tooth, only...

Repeating the entire process with the tissues, she placed the "tooth" in the centre of the soft, thin paper, and stared at it, perplexed.

When she'd moved in with her adopted parents they had had two tortoiseshell cats – one called Bubble and the other called Squeak. She had delighted in stroking and spending lots of time with both of them, finding their company both loving and therapeutic. They were her first introduction to cats (and pets in general) and she'd been quite intrigued at how their canines were literal fangs. Cute, small fangs. At the time, she had only thought of fangs as something a lion or tiger might have – a *big* cat – or a scary animal like a snake.

This, lying right here on the tissue, looked like a fang. Far larger than that of a domestic cat, but certainly not as large as a lion's. She racked her brain, wondering what else it could be, but it had *roots* like a tooth.

That is definitely a tooth. A fox's tooth? Do foxes have fangs?

Wrapping it and also placing it in her bag, she tried to push all her questions to the back of her mind and hurried along the bridleway, finally letting out a sigh of relief when she was out the other side. Picking up speed, she rushed towards the library. Her mind felt knocked sideways. Bits of her nightmare kept fleeting into it – memories which demanded recollection – and the sense of expansion it created felt thorny, like she had to make her way through a maze – carefully. *A maze you created yourself to block it all out.*

On top of that, all the questions kept piling up ever since she'd been attacked. *And ever since you laid eyes on Daniel.*

Between the memories and the questions, she might well be giving her old counsellor a call.

After the locksmith had gone and she'd placed the invoice in her bag for damn near £500, she approached Abigail who was testing the new lock once more. "All good?"

"Yeah, it's great."

"I'm glad I could get it sorted."

"Are you going to tell me what happened last night now?"

"Ugh, I don't even like to think about it."

"Wait..." She pulled her key out of the open door. "Come inside for a sec. I need to grab some food I left in the fridge – mine is ridiculously bare."

"Mine too. I need to fit a supermarket trip in at some point." After shutting the door and locking it behind her, they made their way to the staff room, Abi leading the way.

"What did the police say about the attack?"

The golden question. She hesitated, not knowing how much information she should be giving away. Should she tell Abi about Daniel? About how he'd just appeared out of bloody nowhere and whisked her off to his apartment? "Thing is, Abi, I was just at the bridle path where the attack happened, and it's clean as a whistle. There's no sign anything happened last night at all, so I don't even know what I'd say to the police."

She turned to her, aghast, as she opened the fridge. "You didn't call the police?"

"I—"

"What if someone else gets attacked?"

That made her feel all kinds of shitty. She decided to play the whole thing down for now. "It was *one* woman that attacked me and I think she needed help. She looked like she was homeless or on drugs. I managed to get away and lord knows what happened to her, but she likely needs a doctor or something. I reckon someone's bound to have met up with her this morning – she didn't seem to me she'd last much longer without some kind of care. So I figured I'd just forget the whole thing."

"But she's got your bag and everything in it."

"All of which will be useless to her except for the £15 in cash. I hope she managed to get herself some breakfast or something with it."

"Jesus Christ, Sophia." Abi shook her head in wonderment as she put a carton of juice and a tub of whatever food she had in there, in her rucksack. "You're a bloody saint. No way in hell I'd be able to just forget it."

A loud bang sounded from the basement.

They both froze and stared at each other.

"Anyone in today?" whispered Sophia.

"No – it's Sunday."

Concerned, Sophia turned to head out the staff room.

Abi caught her arm. "Where are you going?"

"To check out what made that noise. We can't just ignore it."

Muttering something under her breath, Abi followed her. "I

hate it down there," she said, quietly.

"You can wait up here – I'll go see."

"No way – I'll go with you."

They descended the old, original stone stairs onto the lower level. The steps dipped in the middle with age. Sophia remembered reading that this library, before it opened its doors to the public in the late-1800s, had been a church, although she couldn't recall exactly how old. The mid-sixteenth century was her guess, but churches were often built on even older sacred ground dating hundreds of years before that. Some of the old arches along the walls upstairs still remained. "This building has amazing architecture considering it's not even that big."

Abi looked at her like she was insane. "That's what you're thinking about right now?"

They had reached the locked door at the bottom of the stairs. "Look, I'm nervous too, okay, but the door's locked, there's no back entrance into the basement, and it was probably just something falling. Do you have the key?"

For a minute, she wondered if her colleague was going to lie in order to avoid going in, but after a pause, she pulled her massive keyring out. "It's this one, I'm pretty sure." She held up an old fashioned key that looked like it had seen better days. Sophia didn't have a key, so had only been down here twice – once on the day she was shown around, and once a few months ago to quickly grab a spare chair for a customer. Never long enough, either time, to explore and look around properly.

Sophia took the key (and the keyring), fit it into the lock and turned it. "Does the local authority ever come in here?" This was a Grade II listed building under fairly strict instruction regarding its upkeep, but she didn't think she'd *ever* seen anyone inspect the building or come downstairs. Abigail had been employed to manage the library for the past three years, but Sophia herself had only been here twelve months.

"I have no idea, to be honest. I think some building inspector came down here once, like, two years ago or something. We never, ever use the books in here for anything and no one at the council seems to care about them. They gave me all the keys as a matter of course when I started working here – in case of emergencies – but said to not worry about anything down here. So I never venture this way."

"Well," reasoned Sophia, finally opening the door after a bit of a struggle, "this could be considered an emergency, especially after having to get the locks changed upstairs."

A gust of musky air greeted them, the smell of paper and leather on it. The wooden door hadn't opened quietly, but moaned a little on its hinges. Excitement stirred in the pit of Sophia's belly – god, this was just ... it was everything she'd studied and wanted to be immersed in before life and living kind of got in the way. *This* was history. "Wow."

"Yeah – wow. It looks pretty empty. Can we just go now?"

"Give me a minute."

Abi huffed in annoyance, but didn't protest further.

Old books lined pretty much every shelf – mostly wooden shelves, but there were a couple of blocks of newer metal ones. And these were *old* books from what Sophia could make out. Higher up, on the wall to the left of the door, a huge broad sword hung. Further along, a family shield of some kind. "What's kept down here?"

It was a rhetorical question, but Abi answered it anyway. "Records, I think. The history of the town – maybe the county. Old land deeds. There's probably a people directory somewhere."

Resisting the urge to explore the books, Sophia focused on why they'd ventured here. "Okay, I'm going to look down all the aisles and make sure everything's all right – see if I can figure out what made that noise. You can wait here if you want."

"Like hell am I waiting here alone." Abi followed her.

They started in the aisle nearest to them and walked up each one. The basement was as large as the whole first floor. This was probably going to take a couple of minutes, at least. While Sophia scoured every corner, she also sneaked glances at the books themselves, trying to figure out what they were. It looked like they were mostly non-fiction and reference books. Almost none of them had dust jackets and some were bound the old-fashioned way.

One minute later saw them towards the back of the basement where the covers and spines looked different again. "Oh, my goodness, look." Sophia reached for a book on a shelf higher than her head.

"That looks crazy old. That whole shelf does. You should probably wear gloves to touch it."

"Maybe, but it's not sealed or anything. A bit of air gets in here through these vents above the windows, see?" The windows themselves could not easily be opened, the bottom half of every one positioned below street level. "You're right, I don't think anyone cares about anything down here – I'm shocked." Her attention went back to the book. "Look at this." She was pleased she'd spotted it and estimated correctly. Inside, there was no printed text, but pages of *handwritten* sentences and some drawings – a lot of it faded. "This must be from at least the early 1600s – maybe earlier."

"Really?" asked Abi, incredulously.

"Most books were printed after the mid-1500s, although, I think this is a choir book, so it could be newer – makes sense if this used to be a church. I think some of the more complicated lettering couldn't be printed until later, but handwritten books had pretty much completely died out by the end of the 1600s." Carefully, she put it back, and pulled down a huge tome the next shelf along. "Jesus, look, this one's leather."

"We're supposed to be inspecting the room," snapped Abi.

Oh, right. "Sorry, just let me look at this one."

Her colleague rolled her eyes and crossed her arms.

Sophia opened the large, heavy book and let it fall on whatever page it wanted to, the pages themselves brown with age. The *smell* of the book was insane. "The black ink's so old it's browning around the edges. There's red ink in here too. All of it's handwritten and not as faded as the other, so I think this book has almost never been opened." There was no title on the cover or the spine. "Abi, we could be the first to read this in *centuries.*"

"That's great," came her sarcastic reply.

Sophia was too enraptured to take it to heart. "Listen to this." She squinted and read out what she *thought* it said in the low light of the room, stumbling over the elegantly scripted words every now and again – even translating a word or two from her recollection of the Latin and older languages she'd studied. "Harry is gone and I dare not guess his fate. He is in the arms of God, or in the arms of the fiend that bade him into her bed." *You're in God's hands now...* She shook away her mother's final words to her, unnerved they'd entered her mind now. "I fear for his soul and I can tell no one. But I know. I know the upyri that hide in the dark and thrive in the cold mountains of the east. I know the lust they conjure in human flesh."

"Upi-what?"

"Upyri."

"What does that mean?"

"I'm not sure."

Abi sighed. "It sounds like the medieval version of a Mills & Boon novel. Can we *please* go now, Sophia."

Reluctantly, she nodded and placed the book back. She really didn't want to though. "Are we allowed to borrow these books?" She had no idea why they weren't in a museum somewhere.

"I don't know, I've never asked."

"I'm just going to check the last two aisles."

"I'll wait here since we're nearly done, but hurry up – I'm really fucking cold."

Yeah, it was a bit cold down here. She sped along the last two sections looking for anything untoward and resisting the astronomical urge to look through every single thing she laid her eyes on. She almost tripped over the book on the floor. With a smile, she picked it up. "I found the culprit," she called out. "A book fell – probably from quite a high shelf." It was a much more modern publication. She glanced at the title: *Churches and Gargoyles of Hampshire.*

She couldn't for the life of her figure out where it had fallen from. It looked more like it belonged upstairs than down here. She couldn't see any gaps between the books it could have been housed in, so she stuck it in her bag to take upstairs. She'd hunt for the Dewey number later – it looked like it should have been logged with their normal stock but got misplaced, then forgotten about. "Okay, I'm done." She made her way back to where they'd been standing.

Abi wasn't there.

"Hey! Where are you?" She let her gaze fall across the entire breadth of the room, then spied a movement – her view of it mostly blocked by bookshelves – by the door. *Should've guessed she'd be scurrying out as fast as she could.* She hurried over there. "Abi!"

A hand grabbed her arm.

With a shriek, she spun and *almost* attacked the wide-eyed Abigail behind her.

"It's me!" her friend cried, both her hands up in surrender. "Where did you go?"

"Fuck, Abi! Where did *I* go?" Then she turned to the door, confused. "I thought I saw you by the door?"

"I was waiting for you where you'd left me."

"No – you weren't there."

"Erm, I think I was."

Sophia stalled, then looked towards the back of the room where they had been. Had she walked down the wrong section? It was entirely possible with all the shelves. "Sorry – I guess, I got lost. Let's get out of here."

"Yay – finally!"

And even Sophia had to admit, she breathed a little easier once they were back on the first floor.

Abi unlocked the front door and they both stepped out into the sunshine. "I'm starving after all that. I might just grab a pub lunch or something – want to join me?"

But Sophia didn't answer. Her stomach churned at the figure now strolling up the path towards them. "Fuck it – what's *he* doing here?" she asked under her breath.

Abi followed her gaze and pulled a face.

Pierce smiled and waved.

Well, that was Sunday ruined.

Chapter Seven

"I wondered if you were open on Sundays," he said, cheerily, as if he hadn't cheated on his wife for twelve fucking months ... seven years ago.

Sophia scowled at him and his stupid blond hair, beaming under the sunlight. She used to love that stupid hair. "It's a library – of course we're closed."

"You're at work though?"

"Just sorting out a staff ... thing." And why was it any of his business anyway? "What do you want, Pierce?"

"I, er..." He looked at Abigail, then back to her. "I would really like to talk to you, Sophia."

"It seems I was too subtle yesterday – I have nothing to say to you."

"Anna and I divorced four and a half years ago."

She folded her arms over her chest. Damn it. She had not expected to hear that. "I can't say I blame her for wanting out."

Abi cleared her throat. "So ... I'm going to wait in my car for you, Soph. Don't be too long, okay? We don't want to miss our thing."

"Don't worry – I'll be quick."

She walked off to give them some privacy – and probably to feel less awkward.

Pierce was staring at her far too intently, his brown eyes a softer shade than Daniel's, yet she'd much rather be staring into Daniel's right now. Hell, that last moment they'd shared had felt like much more than eye-gazing.

What? She gave herself a mental slap. *Where had* that *thought come from?*

"Sophia, please, I—"

"You broke my heart. Okay? You don't get to waltz back into it. And worse than breaking my heart, you broke your wife's. And even *worse* than either of those things, you broke your *children's* hearts."

"I should have told you about her."

"No, Pierce. You should *never* have been with me while you were with her. Jesus, we did all this half a decade ago. Look, I'm hungry and I had a bad night. I would really like to catch a bit of sleep today, so if you don't mind—"

"Why did you have a bad night?" The *care* in his voice was exasperating. And he'd asked that in the way he'd always used to whenever she was struggling with something – like he was going to take all the weight off her shoulders. She'd ended up crushed under the weight of a family she'd unwittingly stolen.

"Damn it, Pierce... It's none of your business."

"Something big happened – I know you, I can tell."

She sighed. "If I tell you, will you just leave?"

He frowned a little, obviously annoyed that him being let into any part of her life came with conditions. "I don't want to leave."

"Go ask someone else questions then—"

"Okay, fine – I'll go. I just want to know you're all right, I still *care* about you."

"You haven't seen me for six years."

"I've thought about you almost every day since."

Hell ... she was too tired for this today. Too tired to put barriers up when she remembered how he *felt* when she trusted him.

"What happened last night?" he pressed. He knew her too well.

Had known. You've changed, Sophia. And he never changed enough.

"Someone – a homeless woman, I think – attacked me as I walked home, but I'm *fine* before you get all protective about it. I'm not hurt"—*anymore*—"and it's all over now."

"God, Sophia." He went to touch her arm, but she stepped back.

"Leave now, please. I've got Abigail helping me and she's been great. We need to head off."

He hesitated, then let out a long breath, knowing he'd need to keep his word if he wanted any hope of any reconciliation with her.

Which isn't happening, right?

"All right – I did promise."

Your promises mean nothing.

He reached into a pocket inside his jacket and pulled out a business card. "Please take this. It's my number. Call me if you need anything. I can't imagine you want to be alone after last night."

Had she not just told him she had Abi? "I'm not alone. And when I am, I *like* being alone."

"Take it anyway."

She did just to shut him up and stepped past him towards Abi's car.

"I meant what I said: I never stopped thinking about you."

She *hated* that her tiredness made her feel like collapsing into him – his arms; his chest… "Until yesterday, I hadn't thought about you in years."

He flinched.

She ignored his reaction and didn't look back, getting straight into the passenger seat of Abi's car once she'd reached it. She refused to feel bad about what she'd just said because she *had* to end this before it even started.

Abi brought the engine to life. "You okay?"

"He's divorced now."

"Hmmn, yep, I got that loud and clear. Where do you want me to take you? Do you want to go supermarket shopping together?"

Fatigue crept into the edges of her mind. "Sorry, Abi, can you just drive me home? If I walk, he'll follow me. I'm wiped out – I need to sleep."

"No problemo."

They headed off towards the main road, and Sophia did everything in her power not to glance at Pierce standing exactly where she'd left him.

Didn't keep his word, after all, did he? He didn't leave.

Uh ... eeew ... what the—

Sophia grimaced as she surfaced from sleep, that *noise* just the most horrible thing against her pounding head. Absent-mindedly, she reached out with her hand towards the screeching, until it landed on an object at the far end of her bedside table.

The phone.

"All right, all right, shut the fuck up."

What a vile ring tone. She scowled at the screen when she remembered she hadn't programmed anyone's numbers into it yet. "Hello?" she answered.

"Hi, Sophia, it's Dad."

"Oh ... Dad, hi."

"Honey, are you okay?"

"Er, yeah – just asleep."

"Ah, that's why I haven't heard from you, then. I texted you three hours ago about the courier – your box is getting delivered to you between seven and eight o'clock."

"In the morning?"

"No, honey, it's still Sunday – tonight."

Finally, the day's events cleared in her mind. *Oh, god.* How long had she been asleep for? "What time is it now?"

"Nearly six."

Shit. "Okay, I'm up – I can't believe I've wasted the whole day."

"You obviously needed the rest. Anyway, I wanted to make sure you'd be in, so I hope you didn't mind the call."

"No, not at all. Thanks, Dad."

"Okay, honey. Speak later."

They said their goodbyes, and Sophia pressed a hand against her growing headache as she stood. She almost fell as a wave of dizziness took her, and that was when she remembered she'd eaten nothing since breakfast. Great. All she had was a shitty one-person ready meal in the fridge, but it would have to do.

After throwing on her clothes, she made her way to the kitchen and put the oven on to pre-heat. Her stomach growled. And then her phone screeched again from the bedroom where she'd left it. Cursing, she went back to get it. It turned out one number *had* been programmed into her phone after all. *He told you that last night, didn't he?*

She answered the call. "Hi, Daniel."

"Hi." And then there was silence.

"Are you still there?"

"Yes – what's wrong?"

"Er ... nothing. Why?"

"You sound dazed."

"Oh – I was asleep until five minutes ago and I have this headache brewing." Her stomach growled again.

"And you're hungry," he added.

"You heard that?"

"Your stomach making itself known? Yes, I did."

Really – she hadn't thought it had been that loud.

"I'm coming around later with food."

"You are? You don't have to do that, I'm about to stick a"—she glanced at the packet and squinted to read what it was—"chicken and bacon penne meal in the oven."

"A ready meal?" He didn't sound impressed.

"Are you judging my food, mister?"

"Yes, I am."

She smiled despite herself. "I didn't have the energy to go shopping earlier, what with changing the locks, cancelling all my cards, the adventure in the library, and then running into my cheating ex ... yeah, I just wanted to get home and sleep."

Another silence.

She waited. The oven's pre-heat timer beeped.

"I'll be there in a couple of hours, maybe less."

Did she care? Did she want him over? Did she have a choice? She winced at the shooting pain her brain sent her. This wasn't going to be a fun argument right now.

He must have sensed her hesitation. "It's not safe alone at the moment, and I figured you wouldn't want to sleep at mine again, so I'll come to you. Also, I have news about last night," he added.

"Fine," she sighed. "But I'm eating this delicious and fulfilling ready meal now."

She thought she heard him chuckle. Or maybe it was static on the line – she couldn't tell. She wasn't sure he ever laughed from the little she knew of him. And before she could think of anything else to say, he'd hung up.

Huh – not even a goodbye.

She put her meal in the oven, then went on the hunt for a hair band, putting her hair up in a loose ponytail once she'd found one. She grabbed her bag from the sofa, wondering if she should start tidying up now, then halted at the weight of it, groaning when she realised why her bag was so heavy. She'd forgotten to put that book she'd found back upstairs in the stocktake pile.

Taking it out of her bag, she placed it on her coffee table. Pierce's card fell out as she did so. Glaring at it, annoyed, she picked it up and put it on the coffee table, too. The number on it was not the same number he used to have – yes, she'd memorised it and yes, she still remembered it. At least she did now she was thinking about it. She hadn't completely been lying when she told him she hadn't thought about him in years. At least not since she'd left London. He was one of the reasons she *had* left London.

Bugger the tidying. She'd do it later.

Half an hour passed quickly and five-day-old, pre-packaged

chicken and bacon penne tasted bloody lovely when you were hungry, and in fact, it turned out she was close to starving because she was sorely disappointed when she'd licked the last bit of sauce from her spoon.

The next hour was spent cleaning up for her impromptu guest. When her doorbell rang, her heart sped up. Which was stupid. She was clearly frazzled from the busyness of the morning and Pierce and his inconvenient presence. *It has absolutely nothing to do with seeing Daniel again.*

When she opened the door, she was met with a slightly surly nod from the courier. "Oh, the parcel!"

"Yes, ma'am." He pushed the large box from his trolley onto her doorstep. "Sophia Jameson?"

"Yes, that's me."

"Can you sign here, please?"

"Of course. Thank you for delivering on a Sunday."

"It's my job."

He's a barrel of laughs. "Well, thanks anyway." She went to lift the box, but it was awkwardly large and ridiculously heavy. "Do you think you could—"

"No can do. We're not allowed inside houses."

"Oh."

He turned, got into his car and left.

"Right then..." She tried again, but only managed to get it halfway across her doorway. It was now leaning, slightly tipped, on the lip of the bottom of the door frame. Maybe she could swivel it and—

"If you take the food, I'll take the box."

Startled, she looked up and ... yeah, there it was. The somersault of her stomach as her eyes met Daniel's. "Where did you come from?" He was standing to the left of her doorstep under the shade of the roof. She looked around him wondering how the hell he'd gotten there without her even hearing him approach. Had he come up the side? How, exactly? And she'd have *seen* him if he'd come up the drive – her focus wasn't *that* taken up by the box.

"Here." He handed her some plastic bags of...

"Ooh! Hot takeaway?"

"Chinese."

"I *love* Chinese."

"Good." He half-smiled. Attempted it, anyway.

Still more polite than the courier.

She took the food and stepped back. "You'll need to be careful, the box is extremely—"

Stuffed with feathers, apparently. He lifted it up like it was nothing more than air, albeit a bit awkwardly because he had remained to the left of the doorway in the shade. Clearing his throat, he hesitated, then asked, "Do you ... want me to come inside your house with this box?"

Bemused, she glanced down to where the box had been, and then back at him. What had they *just* been having a conversation about? "Is there somewhere else you want to go with the box?"

Irritation flickered across his countenance.

She hid a smile. *Don't be petty, Sophia – he bought you Chinese takeaway.* "Yes – please come inside my house with the box." She turned, let her smile form despite rolling her eyes to the heavens, and wandered into the kitchen to get plates and cutlery.

Chapter Eight

There were various breeds of vampires, all with different strengths and weaknesses; all with different abilities. The Bratvashka were amongst the oldest vampires in existence. Hailing from the east of the globe, they had moved south in their early years, and many say they inspired copious legends in Romania and its surrounding countries, from Russia to Hungary. In more modern vampire circles (modern spanning the last five or so centuries), they were somewhat feared, but also considered more myth than actual.

It is said that about two and half thousand years ago, for reasons unknown, the Bratvashka were nearly wiped out. As a result, they retreated to the northern mountains of the eastern regions, using solitude and the freezing, uninhabitable terrain to lie low for however long was necessary and eventually grow their numbers once more.

'However long was necessary' turned out to be right up until the present. And as far as Daniel knew, right up until last night, when a crazed female from their breed decided to pounce on a human being living in a quiet village in Hampshire.

Vampires liked the solitude. Choosing quiet villages to call home was not unusual at all and most of the time, everyone remained clueless about their presence because vampires did not mingle with humans for one very good reason – two if you counted the blood thirst: vampires were terrible at hiding their strength, their speed, and all the things that came to them very naturally. The ones that made the often poor choice to try and integrate with human society soon found themselves at the end of a stake, or burnt to a cinder, or beheaded, or if they were lucky, run out of town. As much as vampires could kill people quite easily – and half of them really wanted to – there were far more people in existence than vampires. *Far* more. And when people decided to group together for any mission or purpose, they were deadly themselves.

The Bratvashka were here. Daniel was ninety percent certain of it, but he had no idea why.

"Yes – please come inside my house with the box," called out Sophia, somewhat teasingly (and a little sarcastically), as she disappeared from view.

On a normal day, he'd say he was an idiot to be here, asking her to invite him in and all, but with the Bratvashka making a rare appearance... If it *was* them, all the rules were about to change.

He gently kicked the door shut behind him and followed her into the kitchen where he saw her pulling out the takeaway boxes. "Where would you like me to put this?"

"On the coffee table out there would be great – thank you. And thank you, again, for this." She signalled to all the food. "You're eating with me, right?"

He rarely ate the food that humans did. "I'll have a little, thank you."

The coffee table was only a bit larger than the box. He had to move a book and business card to its very edge to fit it on. On another glance, he picked up both the book and card as he made his way back to the kitchen. "Interesting bedtime reading you have here."

She looked up from spooning food onto plates. "Yeah, gargoyles – my absolute favourite bedtime companions."

He raised an eyebrow and she laughed.

"Kidding. I brought it home by accident – it was meant to stay at the library."

"That's where you work, right?"

Her forehead creased as rice went on plates. "Did I mention

that to you last night?"

He ignored her question. "I thought you might be thinking of doing some structural work on the library, what with this business card on top of the book."

Now, her face darkened. "No way. Remember the cheating ex I mentioned? That's his card. He just happens to be a structural engineer – or an engineer of some sort anyway. Something to do with buildings." She shrugged, and it irked him. A lot. She still had feelings for him.

He put the book and card down on the kitchen counter. He had no business caring about her life at all. Except the way he'd 'happened' upon her was a strangeness he couldn't rid himself of. He had *felt* like he'd needed to venture into that bridleway – almost as if he'd been pulled by a magnet. It wasn't usual. He was the one used to being the magnet.

He also liked her. At first, it was all primal – the way she'd smelled and looked, and even the way she'd fought. She'd bested a vampire while drunk and *that* had captured his curiosity once he'd realised she wasn't a half-breed or anything otherworldly. That she, in fact, was fully human and seemed to know nothing about vampires at all.

There'd been something striking and elegant about her from her rich, red-brown hair to her almost amber eyes. But this wit and feistiness she was carrying today (her more natural self after recovering from last night, he assumed) was also something he'd seen under the immediate fear and aggravation from being attacked. She had a nature he admired. More annoyingly, it seemed she also had a nature Les admired, for he'd gone on about how lovely she was for damn near an hour after he'd dropped her off this morning and made his way back. Les never said a bloody word about any of the ladies, men, or others he'd chauffeured in all these years.

He decided to change the subject for his own sanity. "Do I

remember you mentioning an adventure at the library?"

"Right. The library has this amazing basement filled with the most historic books – seriously, they should be in a museum. Anyway, no one ever goes down there and its door is always locked. We heard a noise, though. Of course, we went down to check and ... well, actually, nothing happened so this is quite a boring story, but it *felt* like an adventure at the time. That book"—she pointed to the one he'd just put down—"was the culprit, by the way – the noise creator."

"Gargoyles can be like that if you wake them from their sleep – or so I hear. Can't say I've met one myself."

She lifted up two plates and grinned. "Dinner is served and smells divine! Follow me." She headed out of the kitchen and into the dining room. "I usually never eat in here 'cause it's just me – it's nice to use this room for a change."

He pulled up a chair as she put the food down, along with the cutlery. "I did say I'd eat a *little*." Her portions were massive.

"Oh, I'll eat your share if you don't finish it – I'm famished!"

He tried to look and sound and feel like this was all a normal occurrence for him. The last time he'd sat down to dinner with a woman—*with a family, Daniel, remember?*—had probably been over sixty years ago. He *craved* this and hated himself for it. No wonder Les had liked her – she was a little bit like Amelia in her manner.

"Would you like a drink? There's water, squash, or wine."

He smiled. "You choose – I'm happy with anything."

"Well, if you don't find it boring, I'll start with water – I don't want my headache to get worse and I had enough alcohol last night."

She tucked into her food, and he tried to look like he delighted in it all. She moaned when she swallowed and yeah – what a great idea it was coming here.

He looked at his plate to divert his attention. He was already aroused – not just by her sexiness, but the sense of home and companionship.

But you can untangle yourself, can't you, Daniel? You'll be fine – you've done it more than once before. It didn't kill you then, it won't kill you this time.

The other half of his brain seemed to disagree. *It nearly did kill you, you optimist. You vowed Amelia would be the last.*

"This is sooo good... So, you said you had news about what happened last night? Do you know who that woman was?"

"Yes ... erm ... well..." He could *feel* her gaze. When he met it with his, he could see she was contemplating him deeply. "What is it?" he asked, stirring his Chow Mein and wondering how long he could get away with not eating.

She narrowed her eyes at him, although didn't seem to be annoyed, took a sip of water, then said, "You're not really a private investigator, are you?"

About seven ways to start a sentence entered his mind at the same time and he had no idea which to choose.

"I'm not mad," she continued. "I think you mean well, and I think maybe you saved me from a whole heap of trouble last night. And Les thinks the world of you."

He dropped his fork. "Les."

She laughed, lightly. "Yes, he had a lot to say about you."

He *did* drink water and reached for it. "I'll bet he did. Can't keep him from talking once he gets going about something, and you're the kind of woman he likes to talk to."

"Oh, I am? And what kind is that, exactly?"

He smiled. "Intelligent, elegant, polite ... are you enjoying this?"

She grinned. It was infectious.

"Les is great. He has my back in his own way."

"Yeah, I got that. I like him a lot, too."

"I'll set you both up if you like – he's into comedies, prefers pubs to high-end restaurants—"

Now she laughed loudly, and he found himself grinning back.

"You see," she mused, "I knew you had a sense of humour in there somewhere."

"I'm aware I didn't leave a brilliant impression on you last night, and I regret I hurt you – your hand." *Which looks remarkably healed.* "I'm sorry about that, and I hope the food makes up for it a little. It's not an excuse, but just like yourself, I was also somewhat ... hyped up after the events of last night. I needed to..."

"Release energy?" She was squinting at him again in that thoughtful way. "The way a cat goes a bit berserk after it's hunted a mouse it failed to catch."

He stared at her, suddenly wondering if she *knew* what he was. But that would be a first, and highly unlikely. "That's ... actually a very good analogy."

"I saw this in you last night – even amid all the craziness – this 'gentlemanliness'. There's a refined side to you." And there was definitely admiration there. She liked him, too. This was very bad.

There was a pause as she ate more of her dinner. "Do you have a surname, Daniel?"

"I do. It's Evans. Yours?"

"Jameson. So, Daniel Evans ... if you're not a private investigator, what are you, exactly?"

"It's hard to explain. Will you accept that I'm a good Samaritan and something of a vigilante? One who prefers to work nights as that's when all the madness tends to happen."

"You don't seem like the vigilante type."

"Which means?"

"You seem far too smart for all that, and not revengeful in the slightest."

He paused, not really wanting his mind to meander into the past and its old wounds. "I ... used to be – vengeful that is. A long time ago."

"Why?"

"Amelia."

She studied him in silence as she chewed. "You loved her?"

He nodded. "She was murdered."

Genuine empathy shone in her eyes. "I'm so sorry." And after a pause, "I know what that's like in a way. Not a boyfriend, but my parents and grandparents were all murdered – although they never caught the arsonist. Burnt alive. All in one night."

He was rarely taken aback, but this woman had a knack for that. "That's awful. Were you young when it happened?"

"Six."

The age Les had been when you took him under your wing.

A longer pause ensued until Sophia took them back to last night's events. "What about this 'gang'?" She'd said that word as if she didn't believe it.

He couldn't blame her – it had been the best he could come up with on the fly. He decided to try and be as honest with her as he could. "They are a group of people referred to as the Bratvashka."

Perhaps she was expecting another poor attempt at a misdirection. Intrigued and surprised, he had her full attention. "That sounds ... Russian?"

"Around that area, yes, but the etymology of the word, I believe is very old. They are mafia-like in their movements and arrangements. Close-knit; familial."

"And what are they doing here in Emerson of all places?"

"I wish I knew – I'm asking around. The Bratvashka rarely make an appearance anywhere. It's said they've been around for ... centuries." He wasn't sure he could get away with saying millennia. "But they became secluded a very long time ago. This is the first I've heard of their emergence into ... modern society, shall we say."

Sophia fell silent as she finished the last forkful from her plate.

He apologised for his lack of hunger.

She waved his apology away. "It'll keep – there's enough for three days. I'm really grateful, thank you."

More silence. She seemed disturbed.

"I didn't mean to make you worry by telling you about them."

"I'm going to be honest, Daniel, I don't know what to believe about all this. About you."

"Me?"

"Yes. I've been lied to before and it doesn't sit well with me. How did we get to your apartment last night?"

He froze. Damn it, he was hoping she'd maybe have been too drunk to question it. "You ... don't remember?" he pressed. "What *do* you remember?" He had no idea what the fuck he was going to say, but as luck would have it, the doorbell rang.

She looked at him, startled. "It's nearly nine o'clock."

He looked at her in warning. The sun had mostly set. "Expecting anyone?"

"No. No one ever comes here." She got up to answer it.

He halted her with a hand on her arm. He felt her skin *rise* under his touch as if her blood responded to his. "Sophia..."

She glanced at him, her lips slightly parted, and then at his hand.

He could feel her arousal. It matched his. But nothing could be done about it.

She moved her gaze to his eyes once more and held it there.

He hoped she sensed his sincerity when he said to her, in as serious a tone as he could muster, "Don't invite them in."

♦

He was just as perplexing as last night. Attractive to a dangerous degree, but perplexing. She knew she was getting to see his more calm and collected nature today – the insanity of last night behind them – but then he would do a hundred and eighty and come out with the weirdest things. An old and rarely spotted Russian mafia-type gang in Emerson? So dangerous she couldn't invite people into her house? He'd *sounded* like he'd meant it, but it also sounded like bollocks. If he *meant* the bollocks, he might actually be delusional. And she hadn't considered before this moment that he could be mentally challenged in some way – she didn't know him at all.

But when he talked about other things – Les; this Amelia he'd lost – she *knew* he was being honest. His dark brown eyes had softened when he'd mentioned Amelia, the depth in them, startling.

There was something a little old-fashioned about his manner (when he wasn't being all unpredictably beastly, anyway) – in some ways it was that similar kind of maturity that had had her attracted to Pierce. Well, that had turned out terribly. And in another similar vein, she couldn't help feeling she needed to stay far away from Daniel. He'd break her in his own way. There were lies there. She could all but smell them. And yet... there was *something* about him that made her feel ... she wasn't even sure of the word. There was a rousing of the body and soul. It felt like a part of her *knew* him.

And for all his reservedness, he could be intense – the drowning kind of intense.

So, yes – he was definitely perplexing.

She opened her front door, trying to ignore the fact he'd followed her to it and was now ... she could only call it *hiding* behind it. This was protectiveness gone mad.

The boy from next door stood in front of her. She couldn't remember his name, but he often played in his garden. He looked about ten or eleven. "I'm really sorry," he said. "My football just went over your fence. Can I come in and get it?"

She looked at the sky. The sun had set a short while ago and while it wasn't totally dark, it was dark enough to make playing football a bit of a challenge. "You've been playing in the dark?"

He shrugged. "Mum said she wants alone time, and Dad drank too much so he's asleep on the sofa. There's nothing else to do."

Poor boy. The only way into the garden was through the house – she had no side entrance – so she stepped aside to let him in. "Why don't you—"

"Nice story, kid." Daniel stepped out from behind her.

What the hell?

The boy looked startled, and then angry.

And suddenly, she wasn't entirely sure who to be confused at: Daniel with his inappropriate manner directed towards a child, or the child who was *glaring* at Daniel in a truly scary way. He wasn't just angry, he was furious.

Daniel was out the door, *charging* towards the child, before she could say anything, *and* before she could catch the door slamming shut behind him.

She yelped as it banged in her face, completely bewildered. When she came to her senses, she yanked the door back open to find herself staring at an empty porch.

Where the hell did they go? What just happened?

"Daniel?" She didn't say that loud enough and it was because she felt a little stupid, and suddenly very vulnerable at... *Being lied to again, Sophia. You're being lied to again.*

Yep, it was the same feeling she'd had when being with Pierce *before* she'd known he was still married. With hindsight, she'd been able to pinpoint all the times she'd felt uncomfortable or strange or subtly gaslit. God she'd been an idiot. She couldn't do that again.

Blinking back tears, she shut the door and went to clear up all the dishes, her anger slowly taking over. She knew Daniel would be back and he *did* come back about fifteen minutes later. She'd left the door unlocked for him.

He walked in, glanced at her apologetically, but she was done. "Please leave." It sucked that she'd told *two* men to leave her life today.

He stilled.

She saw his face fall; his whole demeanour wilt. That *thing* she couldn't place about him – the same thing that made her *want* him and *like* him – tugged at her, but she pushed it away right along with the memory of sleeping in his bed last night. She knew his scent. She'd become as crazy as he if he stayed. "I can't do this. I'm sorry. I have no idea what happened just then, but I can't *be* with someone where I'm constantly feeling *doubt* about all my thoughts and instincts. I've done that before and it's destructive."

"Sophia—"

"What just *happened?*" she asked angrily. "That boy is my neighbour, and he's just a child."

"He's not just a ... look, it's not what you—"

"Tell me what happened, Daniel. Or go."

"We found a way to get his ball back."

"Wow." She shook her head. "You must take me for an idiot."

He sighed, not even trying to look convincing. "Okay, we didn't. I can't explain what happened – if I could tell you about it, I would."

"You know, that's so funny – that's what my ex said when I called him out on being married the *entire year* we were together." Damn it. She forced herself to calm down. "And I know this isn't that, okay? We're not together, and this isn't that, but—"

"I like you."

She crossed her arms against his sincerity. Why couldn't he be honest about the other things?

"I'm attracted to you and I think you are to me, too. But I *am* here on business and nothing can happen between us."

"You're flattering yourself and I don't want you here on business. Like I said, I second-guess myself because of the way you are, and it makes no difference if it's business or pleasure, the outcome is the same: me going nuts. You need to leave now – please don't make me ask again."

He stared at her for what seemed like an age, his gaze smouldering with need and regret, and just when she thought he was going to let his guard down, he turned and left.

Just like that.

Feeling more than miserable, she locked the door behind him, then fell back against it. What exactly had she been expecting? God, she really was a fool. Seeing Pierce had got her so mixed up, her heart had conjured some make-believe date with Daniel when he'd phoned unexpectedly and said he'd pop over with food.

What she *needed* to do was find her independence again – where the heck had that disappeared to in the last twenty-four hours?

Her eyes landed on the coffee table and the box on it – the box he'd carried like he was bloody Hercules. A tear tickled her chin before it fell on her chest. Was she crying because of the box's painful contents, or because its journey to her coffee table brought up yet more strange and unanswered questions that made her feel lost.

Everything in that box brings up strange and unanswered questions. And does the loss of a family and home stolen from you ever lessen?

She'd spent an age finding footing within her life and putting crap behind her – successfully, so she'd thought. Feeling lost was something she'd overcome twice – once after the fire and once after Pierce. Both had been a form of 'home'.

She grabbed scissors from the kitchen drawer and made her way to the box. Slicing it open across the tape, she opened a flap and then another. To the left, a smaller box lay inside, also sealed. Someone had written 'documents' on the top of it. To the right of the box lay many other things she was going to have to take the time to look through. A shade of green she recognised caught her eye, though. Reaching for it, hand trembling, she pulled out a scarf that had belonged to her mother. God, she *remembered* her wearing it.

She held it up to her nose and breathed. Vague memories of old times surfaced. Fresh tears streamed. She remembered her mother's hugs. And, oddly, there was a flashback to last night on the bridle path – large figures emerging from the shadows; the unearthly noise that woman had made after she'd hit her ... merging with the past: high ceilings; a church – something intimate; something known.

She put the scarf back and wiped her eyes. *More questions.* She needed a coffee. Then, she was going to have to face the box.

"Yes, I'm certain, Les – he confessed. He said he was specifically asked to get an invite inside her house. But he had no clue who spoke to him or who turned him – they weren't a very caring sire. They left him ravenous. He had to drink from his own parents and had no idea why, or why they died after he did."

He heard Les' breath hitch at the other end.

"It takes at least twenty-four hours to transition which

means they did this to him last night around the time Sophia and I were in the bridleway, possibly earlier." Daniel switched the phone to his other ear so he could better position himself to survey Sophia's house. He was frustrated at how crushed he'd felt at her throwing him out.

What were you expecting – a date? You invited yourself over.

"There's no way it was a coincidence," he continued. "The boy was targeted *because* he was Sophia's neighbour, and an innocent-seeming one, being a child. If I hadn't been there, she would have let him in. She isn't safe, but I have no idea why. Her killing of their woman wasn't even a significant one as far as I can tell. I can buy that a more uncouth cluster of vampires would waste their time hunting her down for it – for the fun more than anything else – but the Bratvashka? They surely wouldn't bother with something so trivial. They hold themselves in high regard and always have some greater purpose or mission as far as I can tell. If they *planned* their trip here because of Sophia, there are likely other surprises for her in store."

"Daniel, you know my views on this."

He sighed. "It's not an option."

"Because of my mother? God rest her soul, but she died sixty-three years ago. You vampires are the worst at moving on."

"I'm not putting Sophia at risk by telling her everything."

"She's clearly already at risk and you can't watch her twenty-four hours a day. Call Jacque."

He stiffened at the name, but conceded, "I already have."

"Good. You both need to put your differences aside. If this is really as big as you're starting to believe, it's not something you should be handling alone."

"I'm not alone – I have you. You can help me to—"

"I'm old, Daniel. An old man now. I can't do half of what I used to and I'm much too slow to be safe at my age."

"I know." His throat closed. Vampires didn't cry – it was

physiologically impossible – but they felt the tears regardless. Thinking about Les no longer in this world was a looming sorrow.

Sophia hadn't closed her curtains yet. She hovered over that box on her coffee table looking as sad as he felt.

"Tell her, Dad."

He closed his eyes, fighting against the never-tears. Les rarely called him Dad nowadays and what a beautiful word it was – one he was privileged to know the meaning of *because* of Les.

"She's clever, that one. She has a strong mind, I can tell. She can take the truth. My mum could and Sophia can. And if those Brat-vamps really are after her for some reason unknown, she may be the only one who can find out why. The reason is likely *about* her."

"She told me she lost her original parents in a house fire when she was six. Can you look into that for me? See what you can find? Go through the witness protection portal."

"I can do that. Although *asking* her might yield you better results."

"She *is* strong," he agreed. "Strong enough to maybe cope with knowing, but I'm not sure *I'm* strong enough to cope with her knowing."

"Balderdash."

Daniel smiled despite himself. "I'll be losing you far too soon, Les."

"Which is why you need someone else there with you now. I was your humanity after we lost Amelia. There needs to be someone after me. Don't undo all the hard work that got you here – that got you the closest to human you could possibly be."

Sophia was crying at whatever she had in her hands from that box. He wondered what was in there – he'd never got a chance to ask. Instead he'd ruined her evening by being himself and doing the things he needed to do. *Like drive a stake through a child's heart. Yeah, go on – tell her the truth*. He was crying, too, somewhere inside his body.

The pull he felt towards her had knocked him for six. If he told Sophia everything, would there be a small chance they could be in there crying together?

You old romantic, you, chided his inner voice.

The world had changed a lot in sixty-three years. People and women had changed a lot in that time, too. "I'm not sure I can be what she needs – I'm *not* human, Les. You know my needs."

Daniel heard him chuckle. "I'll wager I know you better than you do. You raised me, and you raised me well. You were everything I needed, and you're strong enough for whatever comes your way. Sophia came your way last night – for some reason she's been brought into your world. Do whatever you feel you need to do, Dad, but consider using the four centuries of wisdom you gained and telling her the truth. Let *her* decide if she can take it. Let *her* decide if you can be what she needs."

Chapter Nine

This was far more painful than she'd thought it would be. Sophia held the gold crucifix pendant in her hand and couldn't quite contain herself over *touching* one of the very last things she had seen on her mother. It had taken her right back to that moment, and even some moments before – ones she could barely remember, but she *did* remember this necklace on her mother.

Everything she'd pulled out of the box had stoked something long buried, and she didn't know if she could carry on sorting through it all. Not tonight.

Now sitting on her sofa, she stroked the pendant with her thumb, somewhat absent-mindedly, as she asked herself, very candidly, if she even *wanted* to remember all the things she had forgotten. She'd dived into that damned box as a way to distract herself from Daniel, and Pierce, and yet another confusing day, but now ... she was spent. This was probably enough for now.

Sighing, she dried the last of her tears and rose to her feet. She put the scarf and an array of other things she didn't want to think further on, back into the box and shut its lid. But she kept hold of the necklace, its heavy cross comforting in her hand, as if her mother's essence was still carried on the gold it was made of.

A strange awareness prickled her skin. She stilled on the spot, letting her senses hum, then looked towards the window. It was dark now. Her curtains were wide open and her lights were on.

Someone's watching you.

Daniel, perhaps?

He might well be – she wasn't fully certain he'd have left, having harped on about her needing to be safe – but what she sensed felt ... different to how she felt with Daniel. She felt...

'Hunted' is the word you're looking for.

Yes. With Daniel, she felt excitement (even if a nervous one), a weird familiarity, and arousal. Now, though ... she really didn't. She felt weak.

The nightmare she'd had on his sofa flashed through her mind all of a sudden: that man tearing at her dress as she'd sobbed.

With a shiver, she blanked that from her mind, strode to the window and pulled the curtains shut as fully as possible, making sure no gap showed between the two panels. Inside, a part of her lamented. To be back at this place where her paranoia stirred and she was doing a double-take at every damned direction she looked...

No – you're not at that place again. This is a blip. You'll never be at that place again.

Undoing the necklace's clasp, she decided to put it on. At about two inches long, it wasn't a small crucifix – the weight against her chest felt calming; a solid, steady presence she needed.

Okay ... put the dishwasher on and go to bed. Get a proper night's sleep and everything will feel better in the morning – it always does.

She was about to do just that when the doorbell rang, making her jump.

If that's you, Daniel, I am not in the mood.

But when she opened the door, it was two policemen who took up her porch. *Oh, god!* Her heart thudded. Her first thought was they'd found out she'd killed that woman.

"Miss Jameson, is it?"

"Uh..." *Shit!* "Yes. Can I help you?"

They held up their badges. "I'm PC Brummel, and this is Detective Thomson. We're sorry it's late, but saw your lights on. We were wondering how well you know your neighbours next door." He pointed to the house on the right – the one the boy lived in.

A feeling of nausea rose in her gut. "I don't know their names – they're not very social – but I see them sometimes. We say hi."

"Have you heard any strange noises coming from the house in the last day or two?"

"No. But I was out all of yesterday and last night, too, and today I've been in and out. Are they all right?"

"Not really, Miss Jameson. Can you just take a look at this for me?" The police constable held a screen towards her on something that looked a bit like an iPad. "The house across the road caught this on their door-cam." On the screen, she saw the back of the boy from next door as he rang her doorbell. The image was a bit blurry, and small, but definitely him. She saw her answer and speak to him, and then she saw... "What was that?"

"I was hoping you could tell me." He rewound it and took it through frame by frame while paused.

She saw Daniel emerge from behind her, and then it was like some white blur took up the whole screen. When it had cleared, her door was shut and no one was on the porch.

"We know you and the man with you spoke to the boy, and then suddenly, he's not there."

"Er ... yes. He came over to get his football – he said he'd kicked it over the fence. And then..." All her options sped through her mind. What the hell did she say when even *she* wasn't sure what had happened? "It was so weird – it was like this gust of wind just took the door and slammed it. It shocked me. By the time I'd gathered my senses and opened it, he was gone." And so was Daniel, but the camera hadn't actually caught Daniel speeding out the house because of that distortion. Hell, *she* hadn't even seen him speeding out the house – just felt it on a gust.

The two policemen didn't look too convinced, but she was only lying a little – she couldn't *actually* tell them what had taken place, and the very odd and annoying 'thing' she felt for Daniel made her feel uncomfortable about landing him in it.

"Who was the man you were with?"

A private investigator would bring up shitloads of questions. A 'friend' sounded too vague and like she was hiding something. "My boyfriend."

"Did the boy say anything else to you?"

"Actually, he did. I asked him why he was playing football so late in the dark. He said his mum wanted to be alone and his dad was drunk – asleep on the sofa, I think. He never did come back to get his ball." Come to think of it, she hadn't even checked to see if his ball *was* in her garden.

"And you don't know where he went after he disappeared from your door?"

"No. I was expecting him back at some point – I thought you might be him, actually."

"Well, the boy is missing – we can't find him. His parents though..." The two policemen glanced at each other. "They're not drunk or asleep, Miss Jameson. I'm afraid they're dead."

She needed sleep sorely, but currently wasn't certain she'd get any at all tonight – not after that news. Murdered. Her neighbours had been *murdered*. Within twenty-four hours, this quaint town where nothing happened had seen the appearance of – if she were to believe everything at face value – an elusive Russian gang she might have pissed off, and two murders. Both taking place within five minutes of her home. *Next door*.

The lowest common denominator? That would be her.

Sophia shivered for maybe the tenth time in the last twenty minutes and wrapped her arms tighter around herself where she was sitting on the living room couch, her lights still on, because she did not remotely want to go into her bedroom, alone in the dark, only to tumble into more nightmares.

Restless, she got up, poured herself a glass of water from the fridge's water tank, and made her way back to the couch, grabbing the 'church and gargoyles' book she'd unwittingly stolen from the library – anything to distract herself from *two people murdered next door*.

The police had said they'd be in touch again if necessary. She had caved in and told them about the possibly homeless or drugged woman she had seen in the bridleway last night because her consciousness would not let her keep it to herself if that woman had anything at all to do with the people who had murdered her neighbours. But she had also lied. She had lied to the police – which she had never in her life done – and left out most of the attack. She said the woman had got testy asking for cash, but that Sophia had managed to leave quickly (and absolutely had not smashed a glass bottle into her skull). She *had* mentioned she thought the woman might be Russian, just in case that happened to lead the police to a Russian gang in the vicinity that may or may not exist. She'd left out anything to do with Daniel, even though she had no clue why on earth she was protecting him. Or perhaps she was protecting herself and her own past, not wanting to have to go there again with the police or anyone. She hadn't even told Pierce about the fire. To date, Abi and Daniel were the only two who knew. *Why did you even mention it to Daniel?*

Ah, yes. He'd told her someone he'd loved had been murdered. It had lowered her defences.

Frowning at how *easily* she seemed to succumb to that man, she tried to make herself comfortable in the folds of the sofa, flicking through the book half-heartedly until she landed on a chapter that looked interesting:

GUARDIANS OF HEAVEN AND HELL

In all of history, it has never once been recorded what the purpose of gargoyles is. While popular during the gothic period as decorative water spouts, they were also featured in Ancient Egyptian and Ancient Greek times, such was their cultures' reverence for animals and beasts. In the churches of Britain and Europe, gargoyles first appeared in the twelfth century, and while their practicality for flushing away water remained, they also became symbolic for being evil and demonic guardians of the secrets of whatever church they donned, and/or noble protectors of the same.

We would like to mention a more obscure theory put forward by Edward Theon who was among the inner circle of John Dee, occultist and advisor to Queen Elizabeth I. In the latter half of the 1500s, Theon adamantly recorded that he had unlocked the gargoyle's true role as guardian of the angelic realm, fervently defending the lineage and knowledge of all fallen angelic beings in the hopes they may one day find themselves back to The Kingdom of Heaven. Theon's work was both supported and funded by Dee; Dee himself obsessed with communicating with angels and uncovering angel lore. Theon stated that one pair of winged gargoyles for every angel fallen would sleep within stone until called by the blood of that angel to fly them home. He professed that all fallen

> angels were in danger of becoming upyri, thus losing their heavenly wings, and only the strongest could resist the surging of blood in their veins that lured them to the gates of Hell. Gargoyles were fashioned to be hellish-looking creatures guarding the gates that would return them to Heaven, for it was said a fallen angel would love the face of a demon before the face of God.

"Upyri." That word. Sophia had seen it that morning in that huge leather tome in the library.

Intrigued, she went straight to the back of the book to see if there was an index or reference list, or anything to explain what the word meant. There was – on page 128. She'd just flicked through to it when the phone beeped.

Glancing at the illuminating object, she placed the book face down on the open page and picked it up. It was a text from Daniel: **I'm still here.**

Sighing, Sophia replied, **I thought you might be. Did you see the police?**

Yes. And heard.

She asked the next question before she lost her nerve because she sorely needed to feel trust for this man who had so bizarrely entered her life and seemed here to stay for the immediate future: **What happened to the boy after you both left my house? Do you know?** She refrained from outright accusing him – her heart felt he was a genuinely good person; her mind thought she'd finally lost the plot after all these years. She hoped to god he wasn't some serial killer. She didn't *feel* in danger when with him, but does anyone who might bump into a murderer before he (or she) shows his true colours? Had the couple next door trusted their murderer?

It took longer than she'd like for his reply to come in: **I do. I took him to a safer place than the one he was in.**

She frowned. She felt that was the truth, but he'd picked his words carefully, and she wasn't sure what to make of them: **Should I be telling that to the police?**

There was another pause before his next message: **I'd rather you didn't as it would make things more difficult, but if you did, I would not hold it against you.**

Again, she let out a sigh, about to put the phone down – not wanting to drag out the conversation – when he added: **Wait.** And then: **I'm staying out here tonight. I'll watch your house. I'll protect you. If you need anything, call me.**

Of course it entered her mind to ask him back inside. And, of course, she didn't because it would either lead to more confusion or, with chagrin, she had to admit the possibility it may lead to lots of sex. And with that body of his she couldn't get out of her mind? Probably very fulfilling sex. Daniel had the air of someone who, she was sure, would be thorough when it counted and deep in all the right places.

Oh, this had to stop. She was literally getting turned on *right now* thinking about it – *barely* thinking about it. It had dawned on her today she hadn't enjoyed a man's touch for six whole bloody years, and with that more primal side of her reawakened through Daniel's presence and Pierce's re-emergence, she might not have the strength of will to deny it; to deny *him* if she invited him back.

She put the phone down, pushing out of her mind the *knowing* of what Pierce's hands felt like and the *wondering* of what Daniel's could do. Picking the book back up—*yes, focus on ancient, winged stone beasts instead, Sophia*—she acquainted herself with page 128, scanning it for... There it was: *Upyri – from the Old East Slavic language.*

Sophia sat up, suddenly intrigued. Old East Slavic was, or used to be in ancient times, a region of what Russia was now, didn't it?

> While the direct translation of the word is unclear, it is believed to have its roots in 'upiór' (a demonic being from Old Slavic folklore) or 'upír' - to thrust into; to thrust violently; someone who thrusts or bites.

Well, that went and bloody did it. Her insides leapt in ferocious, wanton response to the words on the page as a salacious image of Daniel 'thrusting violently' immediately clouded her vision and clenched her in other places.

She groaned (or was that a moan) because that was *not* how she wanted to go to bed. Alone. *Just pleasure yourself and get it over and done with*. Yeah, really, she might just do that. She tried to bring herself back to the more studious aspect of her reading and couldn't.

Slamming the book shut, she got up, irritated and *needing*, and very uncharacteristically, she suddenly imagined herself opening the curtains and working herself up to a frenzy right here on the couch knowing Daniel was watching outside. Her mouth went dry.

Unbidden, her gaze landed on the phone. She could *so easily* ask him to come in. And he would.

Fuck.

No. Just no.

Letting out a shaky breath, she decided she was done for the night. She turned off the lights and made her way to the bathroom, brushed her teeth, took off her necklace, got changed, and finally got into bed.

Daniel was watching her. She was safe.

Her logical mind told her neither of those claims necessarily meant the other was true. Nevertheless, she felt safer than she had earlier, and *refusing* to indulge her lust, she kept her arms tightly crossed atop her chest, hands clamped firmly under them as she lay on her back, closed her eyes, and allowed herself to drift off.

She knew it was a dream. For a start, the house she was in was a mish-mash of her current home and the flat she'd rented in London. Secondly, she was in bed, naked, with Pierce, and it was seven years ago and today all at the same time.

Pierce had always been a slow lover, wanting to devour every inch of her with care, and he was slow now, lazily circling a nipple with a finger before tracing a line down towards her belly button.

She sighed both in satisfaction and fierce want, her dream mind thinking it was all right to switch between the two every now and then. But her *awake* mind had not completely disappeared – it was also in the fray, laughing at her behind her back (she knew it was) because she'd brought this on herself by going to bed sexually frustrated.

"Mmmmm ... Pierce," she mumbled. "Go lower."

His smile was far too quiescent for the fire in her belly; for the erection against her side.

"What are you doing?" she half-complained, his fingers now drawing circles just above her pubic bone.

"Taking my time. I've missed you."

"Good. I hope you sobbed like me."

"Would you believe me if I told you I did?"

She lifted her hips, trying to encourage his hand lower. "Make me believe you."

He grinned, but didn't speed up, and her awake mind laughed again. *You're going to be begging for this orgasm until the end of time.*

Pierce suddenly shifted his weight and two strong hands grasped her thighs, pulling them further apart. She moaned as his head found its way between them. God, yes! He'd been *so* good at this. But he stopped just before her, his exhaling breath driving her near-to-bursting clit insane. "Tell me you forgive me."

What? "Pierce ... please." Yes, she was whimpering. Her dream self was not beyond that, it seemed. She tried to move herself towards him and that tongue she knew would give her the sweetest gratification, but his grip on her was strong and she went nowhere. "I need you to forgive me."

Why couldn't she move. She was all but thrashing, yet imprisoned. He couldn't be that strong.

He shifted again, the breadth of his torso finding its place between her legs as he rose and loomed over her. *Not* Pierce, but Daniel, his eyes lit gold just like in the first second she'd seen him, and her moan this time was a deep, wild one because *this* man moved her insides in every direction possible with his presence alone.

Her arms were pinned above her head, his strength and speed as indomitable as ever. The intensity he stared *into* her with would brand her for all time. "Forgive me," he pleaded, hoarsely, and then he *thrust* and he was in her – completely, wonderfully, and painfully. A pain that bit and bade her tighten around him instantly and savagely in a claim of her own – so tight and so *hers*. He was *hers*. She cried out in ecstasy, the promise of *everything* sitting deep in her centre where the fire coalesced; where only he could reach.

"Forgive me," he implored once more, his voice as manic as his motion, "for I was borne of violence."

Bright white and gleaming, teeth grew, he grew, fire grew, and caught somewhere between blissful awe and searing heat, he sank into her neck, razor sharp, brutally, breaking her and *into* her more deeply than any had before.

She bolted upright in a tangle of sheets, in terror or euphoria she couldn't quite tell. Her hand flew to her neck as she gasped for breath. *Holy fucking shit!*

She'd *never* had a dream like that before.

You went to bed tight as a knot – what did you expect?

Er ... not *that!*

Still shocked out of her system, she was somewhat dismayed to find herself soaking wet between her legs and ... *not* fulfilled. *Damn it.* She hadn't actually orgasmed. With a small whimper (because this coiled-up pleasure going nowhere actually hurt now), she placed her hand against herself wondering how horrendously desperate it was to start a Monday morning bringing herself off, and froze. Her eyes widened fully. *It's Monday!*

And she'd been so stressed out last night, she'd forgotten to set her alarm clock. *Oh, no...* Looking at it now, she grimaced and leapt out of bed. She was *so* late for work.

Chapter Ten

She was relieved to see the library as quiet as it always was on a Monday morning. She rushed in, probably looking as crazy as she felt judging by the look on Abigail's face. "I am so very sorry, Abi. I overslept. It was another insane night."

"I know. I heard."

She stalled, confused. *Abi knows about my dream?*

"It was in the morning paper. I can't believe you're here at all. I tried to phone you and got the answering machine."

Okay, unless she was in bizarro world, there was no way her dream could be in the newspaper.

Abi shoved the local paper in front of her and right there on the front page was *her* talking to that boy on a still from the door-cam. The headline read, PARENTS MURDERED IN THE NIGHT.

"Oh, my god!" She'd wondered who the two people were approaching her this morning when she'd left the house, but she'd been so late and frustrated, she'd pretty much snapped at them and then half-ran to get here. *They must have been reporters!* "Can they do that?" she squeaked. "Can they put my photo in the paper without my permission?"

"The police? For a case? I dunno – I guess, if it helps them catch the killer. Or maybe the reporters paid the door-cam's owner a huge sum of money to use it."

Wonderful – her neighbours were selling her out!

"They do mention you're not a suspect and that the photo is solely to help find the boy in case anyone's seen him."

Like that would stop people judging the level of her involvement.

"Sophia, are you all right? What the hell happened?"

"I don't know any more than what's in here." She ran through what had happened last night the same way she had with the police, leaving out Daniel and anything she felt would be best not known. This was starting to become messy. With the police asking questions, there was no way she could let *anyone* know things she hadn't told the police.

But a new, horrible uncertainty was stirring: she was standing outside her front door in that shot – everyone now knew where she lived. With everyone nosing into her life because of that picture, could they uncover her past? Who she'd been? What had happened? My god, if they could, would *that* then be all over the paper? She swayed where she stood.

Abi noticed and rushed to pull up a chair. "Sit down right now. Sophia Jameson, you need to head home and get some rest, which is what I said in the message I left for you. Forget work today."

She shook her head. "I'll just go crazy alone with all the thoughts in my head. I'd rather be here."

"Even if it means people might whisper about you? It's a small town – more like a village, really. You know how it gets."

She must have looked utterly miserable because Abi gave her a hug and then changed the subject. "I don't know if this is going to cheer you up or piss you off, but"—she gestured to an area on the counter and Sophia noticed for the first time a bunch of flowers sitting on it, still in its cellophane and tissue wrapping—"those arrived for you this morning."

"Surely not from nosy well-wishers!"

"I doubt it – they literally arrived first thing, so my guess is they were ordered yesterday."

Annoyance rose. "Which means it's from Pierce."

Abi shrugged. "There's a card with it."

At least it got her mind off making the front page news. She made her way to the flowers, opened the card, and sighed, her face clearly giving everything away because Abi said, "I guess he *really* wants you to know he's divorced now."

She threw Abi and unimpressed sideways glance.

"What does the card say?"

She read it out. "Dear Sophia, I hope you'll find it in your heart to forgive me." She felt the heat rise to her cheeks when she remembered he'd made an appearance in her dream last night – before Daniel in all his marvel – and had asked for exactly the same thing. "I want us to have a second chance. I left an envelope with the florist for them to deliver along with the flowers. Please open it. And please forgive a mistake I made seven years ago that I deeply wish I never had. Yours, Pierce."

"And here's the envelope." Abi handed it to her.

"I can't believe this." She ripped it open and pulled out a few sheets of paper.

After she'd been silent for too long, Abi butted in with, "What does it say?"

"They're a copy of his divorce papers. He wants me to know he's not lying and that he *did* divorce his wife, and he wants for us to start over in complete transparency and honesty."

"Wow... I mean, I know he's a jerk and all for what he did back then, but he's really going all out here. Do you love him?"

"I ... maybe I *did* – back then. We never said those words to each other. I thought about saying them, but with everything that happened to me as a kid, there's this detached side to me. I guess what I'm trying to say is, I don't *know* if I loved him, and I don't know if I didn't. I don't know if I would know if I'm in love. I just don't let people in that way. I never even told Pierce about the fire."

Abi seemed genuinely shocked by that. "You didn't?"

"No. It ... it was history. It happened to someone who wasn't me. At least that's how I felt at the time." *That's how you felt until two nights ago when all hell broke loose.*

"Do you want to try again with him? That's the only thing that matters, really. And if he's promising complete honesty and—"

"I don't know." She shoved the letters back in the envelope. "I really don't. There's nearly twenty years between us. While that didn't matter to my twenty-one-year-old brain, it matters a lot now. I just want to forget about this for now."

"Okay, I'm done. No more questions."

What was left of the morning went by smoothly and quietly. A total of five people walked into the library, and Sophia was grateful that meant she wasn't on the receiving end of whispers and glances. Work helped keep her mind off everything, from the murders, to the forgiveness flowers, to Daniel and his inexplicable hotness (and oddness), to the pent-up weight inside her abdomen that mockingly reminded her she *needed* an orgasm before something ruptured.

Suddenly remembering the book she'd brought back, she quickly went to get it from her bag in the staff room. On a whim, she opened it at page 128 again, trying to remember where she'd ended her reading—*oh, yeah - at 'thrusting violently'*—when the sentence below that one caught her eye.

> Upír is widely considered to be the origin of the word 'vampire'.

Everything fell into place and she laughed. Subliminal perception at its finest! *Vampire.* She would have seen that word last night without taking conscious note of it, and then her very creative brain had conjured it into being courtesy of Daniel and all his mysteriousness.

Her neck suddenly warmed right in the spot he'd dream-bitten her. *It had felt so real.*

But it wasn't real because it was right here in black and white: *vampire.* And vampires were not real. However, she *had* had an awareness of them in films and books when she'd been a teen – she'd forgotten that until just now. Clearly her mind had not. She had found the concept of them alluring, taking comfort in the similarities between the vampire's aloofness and aloneness, and her own personality. People did that, didn't they? Connected to perceived heroes on the screen to help them find the hero within.

Feeling relieved that hard logic had a proper place in all this, she pushed aside the smaller part of her mind that had started to join the dots ... *he's fast, he's strong; refined yet untamed; he disappears at sunrise and likes to stand in the shade with heavy boxes he can lift without—*

"Sophia?"

"Huh?" She snapped her head up from the book.

Abi looked at her over her glasses and Sophia suddenly wondered how long she'd been in the staff room. Damn – she'd been daydreaming.

"He's here," she said urgently.

Sophia almost dropped the book. "Daniel's here?"

"Who? No – Pierce. Who's Daniel?"

"Oh. No one. Pierce is here?"

"Yep, and I have more bad news." She scrunched up her face. "I totally forgot to tell you, but the council phoned first thing this morning and said they were sending someone over to look at the building because an inspection was due – weird, as we'd just been talking about that yesterday. Anyway, they never tell me who they're sending, just that they're sending them, and it turns out that someone is Pierce."

What?

"He's not just here to see you. He's here to see everything from the basement to the roof."

♦

Daniel wandered from his bedroom, his body feeling like lead. He knew Les had let himself in at some point in the morning because he'd smelled him the moment he'd awoken. With a yawn, he spied him sitting on the breakfast stool and greeted him.

He shifted on the stool and cast him a look up and down, that forever twinkle in his eye. "You look like death."

"Is that better or worse than undead?"

"A shade worse. The eyes on the last potato in my cupboard look prettier than yours."

"Thanks." Daniel put the kettle on for coffee. He rarely drank it, but he'd bought more in case he needed to house Sophia for further nights. Today, though, *he* would be the one indulging. "I had a dream. It woke me."

Les' eyebrows shot up – because vampires didn't dream. *No* vampire dreamt and none of them knew exactly why, but Daniel had always assumed it was another physiological anomaly – they had no past and had no future; they weren't alive and dreams were for the living.

"More like a nightmare, really," he added, disgruntled.

"Have you ever dreamt before?"

"Not for four hundred and twenty-eight years. It would have been nice to be welcomed back with a happy one."

"What was it about?"

He wasn't going to go into the insanely erotic details. Christ, he'd woken up thinking he *was* alive for all of three seconds. He wasn't even sure he'd dreamt that vividly when human. "I was with Sophia. We were close. I lost it and bit her. Brutally. I was monstrous about it."

Les got up and made his way to the cupboard. Opening a door, he reached for the coffee.

"What are you doing?"

"Making you a cup – that's what you put the kettle on for, isn't it? Well, I know how it's supposed to taste better than you."

He wasn't going to complain. Instead, he sat where Les had been. "Thank you."

"It's not unusual for our fears to surface in our dreams."

"And if I were a human being, I'd completely agree with you. But I'm not. So why now? Why am I dreaming now for the first time since I was human?"

"You're asking me?"

"Rhetorically, yes. If you have an answer, even better."

"Do you know of any other vamps who have dreamt?"

"Not a single one."

"Well, my old man"—that was his little joke: Daniel was his 'old man' (despite him looking three and a half decades younger than Les) and also very, very old—"the only answer I've got is the one staring me in the face; it looks like a beautiful brunette."

Daniel glared at him.

He chuckled. "I'm not actually joking. She's here and everything's different for you now, and I'm betting it's the same for her: you're here, and everything's changed for her. I believe it's called attraction. Or destiny. Or something along those lines. I tend not to question those things."

He chewed his lip in thought. "I admit I'm very attracted to her and I like her a lot, but emotionally, it's not like it was with Eliza or Amelia. It doesn't seem enough to be able to conjure a dream about her when I'm not even supposed to be able to dream. I'm not convinced she's totally human, Les."

"Because she made you dream?"

"That. But also her aroma is ... I can't explain it. The difference is so subtle, I wasn't even sure I could trust it, but in addition to everything else... It's *not* like that of human women. And then there's the healing."

"Healing?"

"On Saturday night, she'd gotten her hand all cut up with glass fending off that vampire. When I saw her hand last night, it had healed pretty much completely – there wasn't even any scarring. Do you know any human that heals like that?"

He seemed to think on it for a second, then shook his head. "Lots of cuts on a hand, from glass, would probably take at least a week to heal for most."

"Exactly. And the even stranger thing is, *she* didn't seem to have a clue it was odd. Didn't blink an eye over it. Didn't acknowledge it and I doubt she'd even have noticed if I'd said nothing about it."

Les placed his coffee in front of him and he picked it up, gratefully. It was official – this stuff smelled good even to the dead. Les asked, "Is it because she's always healed that way? So it's not unusual for her?"

"I assume so."

"If that's the case, and she *is* something other than human, it means—"

"She has no idea. No one told her."

Les let out a long sigh. "That makes her a sitting duck. You're one as well if you're trying to protect her blind. There's every chance the Russian vamps—"

"Bratvashka."

"I can't say that bloody word—there's every chance *they* know what she is and that could be why they're after her. You need to tell her what's going on. Time is not your friend here."

"I'm starting to think you're right, but how do I even begin to tell her about me and the existence of vampires, when she doesn't even know *she* might not be fully human? It could tip her over the edge. Did you find out anything about her past? The house fire?"

"I'm still looking – I did this thing called sleep last night, then got here an hour ago. I'll start on it now."

Daniel nodded. "You know where my computer is."

"That's why I'm here – it's a damn sight faster than mine. Have you heard from Jacque?"

Having to think about Jacque ruined the good vibes of the coffee completely.

Les tilted his head as he studied him. "You're the only person I know who can *actually* mimic thunder with your face."

"No, I haven't heard from him," he curtly replied.

"How long have you been holding this grudge for? Two hundred years?"

"Two hundred and six."

"Well, it's time to forgive and forget."

"Not happening."

"You don't have a choice. You've been solitary for too long and the dog's mess is flinging in all directions. You need him on your side, and the one time I ever met him, he seemed genuinely regretful of what he did."

Daniel snorted, disparagingly. "He charmed you into liking him like he does with everyone and everything."

"I know how it all works with you vamps, thank you very much – your charm and your hypnotism – and that isn't what he did. *You* taught me the better of your kind were not too different to people. Well, people make incredible mistakes they regret. He regrets it."

"Then he can atone for it for a few more centuries." He wasn't budging. The wound was still there.

Luckily, Les always knew how set his stubbornness was. He changed the subject. "You should go back to bed soon. I've got a feeling you're going to need all your strength for whatever's ahead. By the way, I picked up the local paper." He pointed to his couch. "I left it over there. Sophia's made the front-page news."

That was *not* good. He could see the photo gracing the front of it from here – the back of the boy on her doorway; her facing both the boy and the lens of whatever camera had captured the scene.

"*You* didn't get caught on camera, did you?"

"I'm not sure. I did step out behind her before leaving with the boy, but no camera can catch us when we're at our fastest." There were no exceptions – when sprinting, vampires created distortions in front of any camera.

It was all spiralling: the attack, the murders, and now everyone knowing where she lived in that tiny town ... it was like those hunting her were trying to flush her out of her safe, cosy life. "Shit," he muttered, tearing his gaze from the paper.

"Shit indeed, my old man. Shit indeed."

Abigail was with Pierce on the far side of the library's main floor. He was pointing at the old arches, clipboard in hand, saying goodness knew what about them. Abi had promised she'd show him around everywhere but the basement – she didn't want to set foot down there again. So, Sophia was going to be the one taking him down there.

So far, she'd successfully avoided him, but the half an hour she'd been spared since his arrival hadn't inspired her in any way, shape, or form into conjuring up a conversation or knowing what she was going to say.

And here they came.

Damn.

Trying to settle her speeding heart, she took a breath in, then attempted a smile, after all, he had bought her the hugest bunch of wildflowers – her favourite kind – and had gone that step further to prove his sincerity. She was nowhere near wanting a committed relationship at this point, and certainly not a messy one, but she couldn't deny that the wound he'd left had never fully closed. She'd liked him a hell of a lot and it was a bloody shame last night's dream was playing small havoc with her mind today.

"Sophia," he greeted as they arrived at the events counter where she stood; no small amount of feeling in his voice.

Abi cleared her throat as she handed her the key to the basement, having taken it off her giant keyring. "Pierce was commenting on how beautiful the architecture is in here, just like you did yesterday."

With a half-scowl, Sophia grabbed the key off Abi, not appreciating being verbally placed in some agreeable position alongside him, as if they had a world of things in common.

But you do have a world of things in common.

"Right, then," she addressed him, as formally as she could, "I'll show you downstairs." Refusing to meet his eyes, she turned and led the way, acutely aware of his presence behind her. "Thank you for the flowers," she said, when they were halfway down the steps. "They're beautiful."

"Hopefully still your favourite. I knew they were yours the moment I saw them."

She cursed herself for blushing. "You really didn't have to."

"I wanted to. Did you also get the other envelope?"

Half of her really didn't want to talk about this, but there was no way around it. "I did. Look, Pierce, I appreciate your candidness and—"

"Honesty, Soph. I want honesty between us. I meant everything I said. I can't take back the mistakes I've made, but I can start again the way it was always meant to be and make it right this time."

They reached the bottom and she pushed the key into the lock, grateful to have the door as a distraction – something to do – as she stumbled her way through this brambly conversation. "And your honesty is appreciated. I have to be honest, too." He followed her inside and she shut the door, not wanting their private matters to reach customers upstairs – or Abigail for that matter. "I don't know if I'm ready for commitment, or a relationship at all."

On an almost sigh and a meaningful tone, he said, "What rush is there? Unless, of course, you're seeing someone already, and perhaps it's rude of me to hope you're not, but I couldn't leave here, and you, without making my feelings clear, regardless."

"Oh ... er, no, I'm not seeing anyone, but—"

"So there's no hurry. And *I'm* in no hurry." He took a step towards her, but she carried on walking towards the centre of the room. It didn't deter him. "We could take things as slow as you like and in your own time, but Sophia, we were so bloody good together, I can't walk away from a second chance with you – not if there's any way this could work."

She felt dizzy. He was everything she remembered – all the wonderful bits before the horrendous truth came out – warm, determined, practical, and still handsome despite the last six or seven years. "Pierce, I'm twenty-eight. You're – what now? Forty-seven?"

"Just turned."

"What if I want children?"

"I don't feel old and I enjoyed fatherhood enough. I would have children with you, Sophia."

Oh, Christ. She didn't know why she hadn't expected him to agree to that. She'd just assumed with two teens (or were they young adults now?) of his own, he'd be thankful for the respite and want to start enjoying these more freeing years. She didn't even know if *she* wanted children. To be honest, whenever she thought of herself in some future life, it was always only her – and maybe a cat or two. No husband, no kids... She'd never thought she could offer them much having no history to give them; no heritage or family identity. "Oh..." was all she managed to say in reply.

An odd, cool breeze passed over her, and she blinked, wondering if one of the windows was open.

Pierce didn't seem to notice. He put his clipboard down on the single large desk positioned to her right. "I know I've been the bad guy in your mind for the last six years and I deserved to be, but despite my cowardice – which is the truth of it, really; that's what I was – I was with you for a year and longed to be with you for more. You were *not* a one-night stand, or some 'bit on the side', god forbid. You were not my mistress. You meant the world to me. I handled things appallingly because I was a fool, too frightened to lose everything, and I lost everything anyway. The past few years, I accepted my lot. I paid my dues. And I let you go – inside, I mean. Or at least, I thought I had. I wasn't going to chase you and beg you to listen after what I'd put you through. And then I saw you here on Saturday, out of the blue, and it was like a blessing from above; I saw a chance to make things right."

He'd made his way to standing right in front of her. She hadn't noticed, far too enraptured by his words. For all her avoidance of his gaze a moment ago, she couldn't look away from it now. He lifted his hand, hesitated, and then brushed a few loose strands of hair, escaped from her ponytail, tucking them behind her ear.

She tried not to – didn't mean to – but her eyes fluttered closed on a small intake of breath at his touch.

Encouraged by her reaction, he cupped the side of her face and... Yeah – *this* was what it was like to be touched by a man. She'd forgotten. She remembered now – the warmth; the sense of shelter it brought. Somewhere within, she knew it wasn't enough – *something* was missing from this connection, as beautiful and solid as it was – but his lips found her forehead and she heard herself sigh; his touch was lighting fires. Wicked dream fires.

"At the very least let me make it right," he mumbled, his tone hushed with a clear need to it. "Even if you choose to walk away, let me make it right."

"Yes," she whispered against his palm, not entirely sure what she was agreeing to, but knowing he damn well *should* make it right, and then his lips were on hers.

She grasped his shoulders, his face, and it was *she* who pulled him to her and against her, needing more; yielding her mouth, her tongue, herself.

He moaned, and not breaking their kiss, she was half-carried to the desk where he propped her, sitting. "You. Feel. Amazing." Three words too many, he was back to kissing her wildly and with abandon.

She returned in kind, the hungry knot inside her demanding an outlet for its twelve hours of forced patience.

His hands were everywhere and she didn't mind one bit. He squeezed her hips, her waist, the back of her shoulders, and then his thumbs were rubbing her breasts and nipples before hurriedly seeking a way into her blouse or under a hem or—

She smiled. "It's a dress, there's no way into it without being out of it."

He returned her smile, lazily, muttering something incoherent because his mouth was now against her neck, and she froze. He sensed it and looked up. "Are you okay?"

She nodded yes, but no, she wasn't; more than flustered by the spot on the side of her neck where a scorching heat had suddenly bloomed. *Daniel's spot*. Which was ridiculous because dreams were only dreams, and vampires and their bites were not real things; nevertheless, she guided Pierce to the other side – her right side – with a "please don't stop" tumbling out of her lips.

He obliged, but every ministration was becoming urgent. He

pulled up her dress and she lifted her backside in agreement, helping him with the task. He stopped when the bottom of her dress was over her hips, his brown eyes wonderfully stormy – a desert storm – as they met hers. "I'm going down on you, beautiful."

Dazed and desirous, she nodded. Hell, she needed to come like she needed air.

He was on his knees in one second, his hands pulling down her underwear.

An icy breeze brushed the back of her neck and she faintly heard a ladylike giggle. "Pierce, did you hear—" Her question ended on a cry of pleasure as his mouth found her centre. "Oh, god!" *Jesus, it's too good.* "Please make me come." She was too tightly wound to care about her insanely wanton outburst, visions of her salacious dream taking over her mind as he worked her with his tongue.

Only vaguely, out the corner of her glazed eye, did she see a shape – an object hurtling through the air. Even if she'd been coherent, there wouldn't have been enough time to say a word or stop it.

"*Aaaarrgh*!" Pierce cried as he was knocked off his knees.

"Oh, my god!" She leapt off the desk and hurried to his side where he'd landed, trying to pull her knickers back up as she half stumbled getting to him. "Are you all right?"

He clutched his head where the book had hit him, wincing in obvious pain. She spied a bit of red.

"You're bleeding. Let me see."

"God, it hurts. Was that a book?"

"It must have fallen from a shelf."

"We're not near any shelves."

"Please just let me see. What if you get concussion?"

"From a book?"

Footsteps sounded from outside. *Uh-oh.*

Sophia stood and hastily readjusted her underwear and dress.

Abi's voice reached them from the other side of the door. "Hello?"

"Abi, hi – we need some help."

Her colleague opened the door and walked in, nervously surveying the room, clearly not happy to be in the basement again. "I heard someone yell."

"A book fell on Pierce's head."

"Really?" She glanced at him still clutching his head, then grimaced. "That doesn't look great. There's already a lump and it's going purple."

"Can you take him up to the first aid kit?"

"Sure."

Sophia and Abi both helped him up, ignoring him when he tried to wave them off. "I'm all right."

Abi used her 'manager voice'. "I need to put it in the accident book, so you're coming with me anyway."

"My clipboard," he murmured.

Sophia grabbed it from the desk and handed it to Abi. "Pierce, please just get the injury seen to," urged Sophia, squeezing his arm. "I'll speak to you later, okay?"

He nodded, then let Abi guide him out of the basement, leaving Sophia standing there, alone and bewildered. Very bewildered. And her body felt stunned. She wondered if she might have permanently petrified her vaginal muscles for good after that interruption.

Imperceptibly, she heard – or *thought* she heard – laughter ripple around the room. But she shook her head to clear her hearing, and it was no longer there. The book was, though – lying on the floor a few feet way. Bloody thing. Had she seen it *hurtling* or had she imagined that?

Cautiously, as if it might leap into the air of its own accord, she approached it. It had a dust jacket, just like the other she'd found on the floor yesterday and also looked like it belonged amongst the books upstairs rather than down here.

Picking it up, hesitantly, she turned it over to read the title on the front, and didn't know whether to laugh or cry: *He's Not the One: Your One-Stop Guide to Choosing the Right Man*.

Chapter Eleven

"What. A. Day!" exclaimed Abigail, locking up after the last customer left – not that they'd had many today and that was a relief after everything that had happened. "Has Pierce texted you?"

"No." He had promised he would to let her know he got home safely since he'd refused to go to the hospital. Having never wanted to hear from him again, to the tryst in the basement, to needing him to call so she knew he was okay, Sophia marvelled at how quickly and bizarrely her life had changed in a short space of time. "I'll try and call him later tonight. Abi?"

"Yep."

"Why exactly do you dislike going into the basement so much?"

"Seriously?" she threw her a look. "Can't you *feel* how strange it is down there?"

"Sort of, but I like old buildings and books, so, I dunno – maybe I don't feel what you feel."

"It's not just that it's old. It's cold, it's too quiet, and then sometimes, because it's so quiet, you also *hear* weird things. Like when you're alone in a house and it creaks a lot – but it's not just creaking down there, it's just ... *strange*."

"Well, I wasn't going to say anything, but I *thought* I heard someone laughing down there earlier. Is that what you mean?"

"*Laughing*?" She looked aghast. "I don't think I've heard that."

"Do you think it's haunted?"

"The basement? It wouldn't surprise me. I think my parents' house is – the one we're going to on Friday. It's one of the reasons I moved out as soon as I could. Oh! You're still coming on Friday, right? With everything going on, I forgot to—"

"Yes! I want to – *especially* with everything going on."

She sighed in relief. "Thank god – I don't want to face that party alone. Anthony's going to be there, too, but he'll be ignoring me most of the night so as not to draw suspicion our way."

"That's horrible. Why invite him, then?"

"I didn't. Part of this party is like a fundraiser event – there will be a few churchy people there. He was invited through his order – I think his bishop will be there. I am *so* glad you're coming. The car's picking us up straight from the library, okay? We should probably change here before we go."

"Sure." She couldn't imagine being at a party where she had to ignore her own boyfriend and vice versa. Although the whole 'being with a married guy for a year without knowing it' made that pale into comparison. "So, going back to the basement – and your parents' house, I guess – do you *believe* in ghosts?"

"I suppose I must do." She shrugged. "Never given it much thought, but I've never doubted it when I've felt that spooky vibe, you know?"

"But have you ever seen one?"

"Nope. And I don't want to. I'd freak out. Okay, I think we're all done here. You ready to go?"

"Yeah – let me just get my bag." She hurried to the staff

room, now pretty much certain that what she'd seen *was* a book flying at Pierce. But she was still a step away from believing a *ghost* had given him concussion. Why? To what end? Did it just like to play and had a bit of a sick sense of humour?

She'd brought the book it had thrown upstairs with her – it was lying next to her large handbag, on top of the 'church and gargoyles' one. *Churches and Gargoyles of Hampshire* and *He's Not the One.* Two books left by the supposed ghost.

Maybe the books are for you – nothing to do with Pierce at all.

But why would a ghost be trying to give her messages?

Rolling her eyes at her ridiculous internal conversation, she placed both the books in her bag to take home. Maybe she should actually read them – god knew she needed help in the love department.

Making her way back out, she smiled at Abi. "All ready."

They headed outside and said their goodbyes. Only when she neared the bridleway again, did she start to feel anxious. Not only at the previous attack that had taken place there, but at whatever news reporter might be waiting for her at her front door. *And the dead neighbours next door to you.* Oh, god, she hoped *their* ghosts wouldn't be making an appearance.

Her phone rang and she jumped, its shrill ringtone sending birds flying. It was Daniel. "Hi. Your timing is impeccable."

"It is?"

"I'm walking through the bridleway – the ringing scared me half to death."

She could practically hear him frown. "Why are you still walking that way? Do you have a car?"

"I do, but I live so close to work, it seems daft to drive. Besides," she teased, "it's still light outside." That was supposed to be a dig at his 'you're not safe when the sun goes down' obsession, but she wondered where her sense of humour had gone when she suddenly found herself taking it seriously. The image of Daniel with fangs erupted in her mind and she shivered (with fear or with want?) and then abruptly stopped mid-stride.

"What?" he asked, sharply, at the other end of the phone. "What is it?"

"What do you mean?"

"You've stopped walking."

"How did you... Nevermind." She really didn't want to know – she was going loopy as it was. She'd stopped because she'd completely forgotten, until this second, about the strange tooth she'd found just a little further up. The one that looked like a fang. But she didn't want to mention it – not here and not to Daniel for some reason. It was already insane she was starting to consider fantasies were real – dream bites and ghosts – she didn't need Daniel encouraging her with his own peculiar insistencies.

Yeah – you keep telling yourself none of it's real. Annoyed, she shut off her mind. "Is there a reason you called?"

"I saw you in the paper."

"Oh." She picked up her stride again, wanting out of the bridleway as soon as possible.

"You need to stay at mine tonight – you're not safe at yours."

She made a small noise in protest, but didn't know what to say. He wasn't wrong – two people had been murdered and somehow, she'd ended up 'involved' (and her jury was still out on the whole Russian gang coming after her issue) – but she didn't want to leave the safety and comfort of her beautiful house.

"I know you don't want to be here, but I don't know if I can protect you well enough there."

"How are you even protecting me?" She hadn't meant that to come out the careless way it sounded, but she consistently felt out on a limb trusting him, despite the fact she did – for reasons unbeknownst to her.

"I *can* protect you physically if it came to it."

Like he had the first night. She couldn't deny the attributes he had when it came to strength and speed.

"Sophia," he continued, "I have this feeling the shit's going to hit the fan very soon." And he sounded resigned about that. "So just please try to put up with this for a few more nights – that's all. I don't think it's going to be long before we have answers and understand what's going on."

"You're saying that like it's a bad thing."

There was a too-long pause before he said, quietly, "Sometimes, ignorance is bliss."

She didn't have time to register how she felt about that statement because she spied two people hovering on her driveway as her house came into view. "You've *got* to be kidding."

He waited for her to explain.

She continued, "I'm guessing those are news reporters on my driveway. They were there this morning, but I ran past them because I was late for work. Persistent, aren't they?"

He said nothing, and then asked a question she'd have found bizarre just two nights ago – not anymore it seemed. "Are they standing in sunlight?"

"You really need me to answer that question, don't you?"

"Indulge me."

She sighed. "It's mostly cloudy here right now. But they're still standing in daylight. Does that count?"

He mumbled something she didn't catch. "Is there another way into your house?"

"No."

"Why don't you—"

"Daniel, I am *going* into my house. I'm going to *talk* to the wanna-be paparazzi I have to barge past – swiftly and curtly – and then I'm going to lock my door and *not* invite them in, okay? That's all I'm giving you. I've had a crazy day as it is – a *ghost* tried to knock out my ex earlier – and that's all the supernatural stuff my brain has the space for right now."

Silence.

Then, "You saw your ex today? The cheating buildings guy?"

"*That's* what you took from what I just said?"

He exhaled sharply. "Fine. I'll text you the time Les is picking you up."

"Goodbye, Daniel." She hung up.

As she neared the two people, she noted they *were* the same two who had tried to speak to her that morning, and insanely – *stupidly* – she felt relieved at the recollection that this morning, they *had* been standing in the sunlight.

What was Daniel *doing* to her! She was starting to *think* like him. If she wasn't careful, she'd be in an asylum by the end of the week.

Her shower was a quick and jittery one, knowing there were potentially still reporters hanging around. She'd shut all the curtains in her house as soon as she'd raced in, double-checked she'd locked her door, and was starting to think maybe a night away would be all right if it meant she had a semblance of peace.

Making her way into her bedroom, unclothed and carrying her towel, she saw Daniel had already texted: **We can't wait until dark. Les will be at yours at six thirty.**

That was only in half an hour!

I need more time. Everything's going too fast.

I'm sorry – we don't have it.

I need to pack. There are things I want to take in case

everything goes pear-shaped. The box you helped me bring inside needs to come with me.

She absolutely was not leaving all her personal and private documents behind. She couldn't guarantee they were safe here.

There was no reply for a while, and then: **All right. You're likely being watched and it's important we're not followed. Leave everything you want packed in the car in your back garden – I will take them and get them to the car. After I have, wait five minutes, then leave out the front and get into Les' car – you'll see it. I'll meet you both at my place later.**

But there's no way into my back garden. I'm surrounded by neighbours.

Leave that to me.

What was he going to do? Jump fences with boxes and bags? And suddenly, she was certain that was exactly what he was going to do. They were going to have to have a *serious* talk about everything this evening. *No more evasiveness with the truth, Daniel Evans!*

Are you ready for the truth? asked her more sensible self?

She ignored it and dressed at lightning speed, packing her overnight bag as she did so. She didn't need much, just the box, her handbag – everything important was already in it – she dug her passport out and threw that into the overnight bag, too...

She stopped when her gaze landed on her mum's necklace which she'd left on her bedside table last night. It hadn't seemed appropriate to wear it to work, after all, she wasn't Catholic or religious at all, and that was definitely a necklace that made a statement. But she couldn't bear it if something happened to it.

After a moment of hesitation, she put it on, then pulled a light polo neck sweater over it. Her toiletries went into her bag last.

That was it.

Glancing into the mirror, she dashed some balm across her lips, and threw that into the bag, too, trying to discard the feeling she wasn't coming back. *Of course I'm coming back.*

Her bedside clock read 18:25.

As quickly as she could manage, she reached for her phone and sent Pierce a text, glad she'd programmed his number into it before he'd left the library. **It's Sophia. Did you get back okay? How's your head? Please let me know you're safe.** She wasn't going to add a kiss, and then told herself not to be so stupid – the man had gone down on her earlier – and typed, **Xx.**

When he was feeling better, she needed to set the record straight with him. What had happened earlier had been one massive mistake and she should never have let it happen – she'd been turned on and blind-sided by two denied orgasms.

Three now.

As much as she had probably loved him, she was a different person now with different needs. Not to mention, he knew nothing about her – not really. Abigail's surprise at her not having told Pierce about the fire ... well, that had woken her up a bit. Made her see how she'd kept her own huge secret from him.

She grabbed her overnight bag, made her way to the back door, and placed it in the garden, glancing around nervously. Was she really being watched?

One attack and two dead people? It's not out of the realms of possibility, is it? Someone knows your past.

Not until this moment had that reality sunk in: someone actually *could* be trying to finish the job they'd started twenty-two years ago. *Finish you off, you mean.*

She headed back inside, clumsily dropped her huge, heavy box onto the floor – the entire said past in it – and pushed it with her feet all the way to the back door, managing to get it over the plastic ridge along the bottom of the frame and into the garden, next to her bag.

Huffing a little from the effort, she almost screamed when she turned around.

"Sorry," said Daniel.

"Where did you *come* from?"

He shook his head, looking up unhappily. "I need to be quick."

She looked up, too, wondering what he was seeing. All she saw was heavy cloud covering. It didn't look like anyone would be enjoying a summer sunset tonight.

By the time she looked back down, Daniel had gotten her bag on his back, carrying it like it was a rucksack, and the box was in his arms like it didn't weigh a tonne; like it weighed nothing at all.

She stared at him, every question she had in her eyes, and she wondered if he could read her single thought, because it rang loud and clear in her mind: *What are you?*

He met her gaze, looked like he wanted to say something, but said, instead, "We'll talk about it all tonight. I promise." And he meant it. There was depth in his look and bottomless emotion. It was hard to pull away from that stare of his; in fact, it was as if it pulled her in, its own history limitless, taking her down timelines of *him* and everything he was. And in a split second she saw both ethereal beauty and monstrous viciousness – two sides of the same coin; two sides of the same face.

Her breath hitched and he heard it. He shifted the box and with a single hand, cupped her face. Fire lit her skin where he touched it. An inferno bloomed on the left side of her neck as the veils between dream and reality faded a fraction.

"Five minutes, then head out the front door," he whispered, somehow making that instruction sound like the start of some passionate and illicit rendezvous.

She nodded. Did she move otherwise? Did she blink? She had no idea what happened, but the only thing that lingered was the feel of his skin against hers. Daniel, himself, was gone.

Les had insisted she sit up front, next to him in the passenger seat. Fifteen minutes into the drive and she didn't feel any calmer. Instead, overwhelm was closing in. Her breathing felt slightly ragged and she sensed she was on the cusp of something life-changing and permanent. Her mind had reached the end of its limit, only to discover it could go farther. But farther meant acceptance. There always reached a point in any challenging situation where acceptance was the only door you could walk through if you wanted to get to the next level.

A women's skin had burned with holy water; she'd found an elongated, sharp tooth on the ground where she'd burned; the side of her neck kept flaring from a dream bite; she'd almost had sex with Pierce earlier; the library she worked in was haunted; her mother had religiously worn a crucifix for reasons currently unknown to her; and Daniel was a...

That's where her mind stopped working. That's where the door was. It wasn't one she was willing to open – not just yet. Perhaps not ever. Because if *this* was the world she found herself thrown into, what exactly did that mean for her? What did that make her?

Maybe – almost definitely – Les had picked up on her mood because he kept looking at her every now and then, his lovely chatter from last time, not nearly as much or as buoyant. Still, he tried. "This can't be easy for you, love. But if anyone *can* help you, it's Daniel. You can trust him."

She didn't doubt she could. It was rather that trusting him

came with questions. Far too many questions. And a great big door she didn't want to open.

She looked out her open window instead. The sky looked as stormy as she felt inside, the heavy clouds from earlier, darkening. The smell of rain was in the air and the wind was starting to bite. They pulled to a stop in traffic.

Les scrolled through his Sat Nav screen. "I can't see what the hold-up is; there aren't traffic lights on this stretch of road."

"Let me see." She half stood against her seatbelt, leaning as far as she could out the window. She felt a spatter of rain on her cheek. "I think there are police up ahead – some kind of road block."

"Police, you say?"

"Actually, I'm not sure. I don't see police cars, just two normal cars – both gunmetal grey. But there are two men moving down the traffic talking to all the drivers."

"What do they look like?" Les asked, his tone darkening.

"Long coats. One of them's got his hood on and they're both wearing sunglasses." She turned to Les. "They can't be undercover if speaking to everyone. Police never dress like that, do they?"

But Les was already dialling through on the phone propped up on his dashboard.

His call was answered immediately, Daniel's voice at the other end.

"We've got a situation on Hardrock Road, near the Henley junction. Road block. There's no room for me to turn and I'm getting the sense I really need to."

"On my way." The line went dead.

Les nodded to her open window. "Roll it up."

She did.

He locked the doors.

Her heart was in her throat. "What's going on?" Although

she already knew. Deep inside, she already knew. Those large men that had appeared after she'd bested that woman had looked the same way – large, long coats – she was certain they had.

"A meeting we're not going to be able to avoid," he answered, grimly.

"What do we do?"

"Meditate."

"What?"

"Slow your heart rate right down if you can."

In two minutes? There was no way she was going to be able to do that.

"Don't suppose you've got any more of that holy water in your handbag?"

"No."

"Shame. The glove compartment – inside it, you'll find four wooden stakes. I have my own set down here in the door's storage hold. If you need to use them, aim straight for the heart and you've got to strike bloody hard – use all your strength. Missing the heart could cost you your life."

She stared at him, agape.

Les smiled, and she didn't know how he managed it, but it did actually reach his eyes. "Sorry, Sophia. This wasn't the way Daniel wanted to break the news to you. But I've got a funny feeling you're not quite as surprised as you could be."

"I ... I..." She didn't know what to say. What came out of her mouth was the unfiltered truth. "I don't know if I'm ready for this."

Those men were three cars away from theirs.

"One thing life's taught me: you're always ready, no matter what."

Hand trembling, she opened the glove box, pulled out one of those wooden stakes and hid it behind her where she sat, her back pushing it against the cushioned seat. "This is crazy."

"It's going to get crazier."

"How will I know they're ... I mean, they could be actual *men*. Normal people. I'll *kill* them if I stake them."

"Oh, you'll know, don't you worry about that. It will be clear as crystal. Okay, we're up next. When they knock, only open the window a fraction – don't give them easy access inside. We're surrounded by people and it's rare vampires play up in front of so many – they prefer a low profile."

Oh, my GOD, he actually said it. He said 'vampires'!

"Make them get testy; make them lose their temper."

"*Make* them lose their temper?"

"Believe me, it's easier to kill them that way than when they're acting all sweet."

These guys really didn't look like they could act sweet if they tried.

"And *don't* look directly into their eyes. Some of them have a way about them – it's hypnotic, like they're trying to get inside your mind before they go for you. But I don't think they want you dead, Sophia, or you already would be. I don't know what they want you for and let's hope we don't find out today."

The men straightened up, done with the car in front.

Shit!

There was one man – or *vampire* – on the left and one on the right, both huge and effectively trapping their car between them as they approached. She couldn't see their eyes for their shades, but she knew they could hear her heart beating. Knew it the way she knew—

She gasped.

"Sophia?" Les' urgent whisper was barely audible.

"I'm okay, it's just..." Her hand was already cupping the left side of her neck, the heat in it rising. "Daniel's here," she whispered back.

Les nodded, not even a query in his eye (unlike her who had a thousand and not a second to ponder any). But she did think she saw relief there. Or maybe he was just mirroring hers.

Les and herself received knocks to their windows simultaneously. After swapping a look and a nod, they each rolled their side down a couple of inches. The rain was coming down much harder now.

Sophia attempted a smile at her interrogator. "Hi! Is there a problem up ahead?"

Shades or not, she could feel his stare pierce right into her.

He ignored her question. "ID please."

"I'd like to see yours first. You don't look like police to me." Inner-Sophia praised herself for her flat, steady voice. Sensible Sophia was shaking her head and already signing her death warrant.

Les made no sound. It seemed he wasn't jumping in – he was letting her lead the conversation.

"ID now – both of you – or we're breaking this window."

"Thus proving you're not the police." And she had *no* idea where this 'I have a death wish' version of herself had come from. Probably from the terror she was trying to hold at bay. Les had said to piss them off, but it turned out – despite her fear – she was getting pissed off herself. No matter the threat or danger, being spoken to so obnoxiously always got under her skin. So, her mouth took on a life of its own. "And I *have* no ID on me – it was stolen two nights ago; my new cards haven't arrived yet." *So eat shit, vamp-Rambo*. Because, apparently, that's what they were: vampires. *Vampires, vampires, vampires...* She had to keep repeating it for it to stick. It was too unbelievable. Yet, to disbelieve it was to deny *everything* her intuition screamed.

Both men stared at each other across their heads.

She felt some comfort in the hard wood behind her back, although another small comfort suddenly made itself known – not Daniel's presence like she'd half expected from her phantom bite, but a different, no less comforting heat, slowly emanating from her mother's crucifix resting on her chest under her sweater. She'd forgotten about it until just then. It was entirely possible she was imagining it, her mind needing to create strength from somewhere, but it only grew hotter against her skin when the man by her window pulled his shades down.

Les let out a cough – in warning she assumed – but she remembered his advice half a second too late, her eyes already locking with this man's icy yellow ones, drawn to them against her will. Daniel's eyes had been similar, hadn't they? Only they'd been warm and gold, and *that* had felt like a mutual connection or attraction. This was different. He was *pushing* his way in. And it wasn't unfamiliar. *Someone's done this to you before.* But no clear memory surfaced, and there was no time to try and pick her brain apart.

Her ire rose, peaking higher than it had a few seconds ago. Was he expecting her submission? A surrendered invitation into her mind and body? What compelled her to do what she did next was anyone's guess. There was no coherent thought – it was more like a *knowing*. She unclasped her seatbelt, ignoring the way Les shifted nervously.

She let the fire of the necklace travel through her until it met with the blaze in her navel; all that coiled sexual energy, stoked repeatedly for twenty-four hours, needing an outlet, badly. She rose and met his gaze, at level, through the gap in the window. Whatever she did, she did purely instinctively, *pulling* him in – not pushing back.

The vamp's eyes flickered in surprise as she *held* his stare in a mental lock – held his *mind*. He was going nowhere.

Come on in then – that's what you wanted, wasn't it? Have a good look around. She might have said that out loud, she wasn't sure. The crucifix felt on fire – just as hot as it had been against her mother's chest that night, licked by flames and death. She *felt* the fire all over again, now surging from deep in her abdomen, upwards; then *saw* it leap into her mind and join with his. "Come get it."

He burst into flames and screamed.

The manifested fire in front of her shocked her out of her state, and bewildered, she fell back into her seat. *What the hell?*

Les suddenly moved – faster than she'd have thought he could – opened his door and drove it hard into the guy standing by it, who was clearly caught off-guard by the spectacle of his friend running around in the middle of the road, burning.

Burning. "Oh, my god..."

Commotion ensued. Daniel had appeared next to Les, the man he'd attacked with his door now gone. The burning man screamed again, this time because a stake went flying into his chest. *Had Daniel thrown that?*

People were yelling and shouting down the length of the road, pointing to the dying flames now fading into a pile of dust and embers on the ground.

Sophia was virtually catatonic. That man had just—

Les got back in the car, Daniel straight after him, leaping into the back seat. "Let's go!" he yelled.

Les wasted no time, jerking the car into motion. Sophia yelled as she went nearly head-first towards the windscreen, forgetting her seatbelt wasn't on – her arms saved her head.

"I've got you!" She was pulled back by powerful hands and found herself, all of a sudden on Daniel's lap. "Go, go!" he yelled as he held her. His grip was strong – a strength she needed.

Had she ... set a man on ... fire?

"I've got you," Daniel whispered in her ear as the car took off, finally speeding down the road in the opposite direction, before turning left into a lane she was sure they were going far too fast along. Les handled the vehicle like a pro, though.

She barely registered it; felt none of it. Shaking with adrenaline and fear, and a searing heat in her abdomen, she understood Daniel was stroking her where he held her, trying to calm her coiled state – understood it, but didn't see it. All she saw was the past – twenty-two years ago – the pendant on her mother's chest, looking bright orange with the fire all around.

"Look at me, sweetie ... look at me." Her mother's eyes held hers, so soft, yet so determined. "You need to listen to me very carefully, Sophia. Listen. You are so special – your blood is special; your destiny is great. There are people who will try to steal it all – some with good intentions, and some only for themselves." Her eyes welled up and fresh tears streamed. "Sophia ... others yet, will see you dead for the things you are capable of. Miraculous things you must never be afraid of. Never. Your power is big, but however it manifests, you are a healer of souls – remember that. You are *a miracle."*

And then, her mum clutched her tightly to her and pressed a kiss against her cheek. Into her ear she whispered, "Do you believe in miracles?"

Holding her mother tightly, she nodded against her hair.

"Good. You're in God's hands now."

Chapter Twelve

In the wooded valley in Wales where Daniel had lived at the turn of the seventeenth century, Aspen trees had dominated the lush green hills he'd called home. When the wind blew through Aspen trees, their leaves trembled and shimmered. He had always thought the tall, bright trees stunning; their aesthetic fragility belying their remarkable ability to regenerate – especially after fire or shock.

Those trees were what came to mind now as he carried Sophia through his front door, Les not far behind. He'd *had* to carry her – she wasn't fully present and speed was of the essence. And she was trembling – tiny little shivers that were barely perceptible, but he'd felt every one as he'd held her in the car. He also felt her strength, as buried as it might be at this precise moment.

Daniel placed her on the sofa in the exact spot she'd sat two nights ago. Had it only been two nights ago? He put his hands on her thighs, rubbed gently, and said, "You're safe now and I'm not going anywhere. Let me speak to Les, I'll be right back."

Her eyes flickered *almost* in his direction and he decided to take that as acknowledgement of his words.

Les was standing near the door looking unsure as to what he should do, and Daniel knew this man a part of him would always see as a boy – *his* boy – was concerned for his safety and trying not to show it. He genuinely liked Sophia. But no one had been prepared for her sudden show of pyrotechnics.

"Les, she's going to be all right. Take the upstairs apartment tonight – I don't want you home alone. You have the keys?"

He nodded. He wasn't going to argue. "Her things are still in the car."

"I'll get them later." The car was safe and hidden in the underground garage. Daniel owned this entire block of flats where he lived. Built to look in keeping with the other houses along the road, the block was only four floors high, containing eight flats in total. Rarely did he rent them out, but owning the whole block – leaving lights on in various rooms at various times –

made it look like others occupied the building, and vampires never lived in dwellings with humans. It offered him a disguise of sorts.

Les' gaze travelled to Sophia on the couch.

Daniel softened his tone and brought it right down so Sophia wouldn't hear. "I'll be all right. I don't sense she's a danger to me, and I need to help her overcome this."

Les met his eyes and nodded again, but said nothing.

"Try and get some rest if you can. We'll all be relieved when the sun comes up."

Another nod – he was on autopilot.

"Please call me if you need anything."

He finally cleared his throat. "I will." With another glance at Sophia and a small smile at him, Les let himself out the front door.

Daniel waited, listening to his footsteps ascend the stairwell – he never took the elevator – and only moved away from the door when he could no longer hear them.

Making a swift stop to the kitchen, never taking his eyes off the anomaly on his couch, he poured a glass of water. Taking it to her, he knelt before her where she sat. It seemed to be where he often ended up: kneeling before her on this couch.

She wasn't totally gone – there was movement and understanding. She reached for the glass he held out, her movements small, and took a sip despite her trembling; despite her teeth clanking on the rim of the glass as she drank.

He took the glass back and placed it on the side table. Resuming his position, he placed his hands on her thighs again, her blue jeans still sporting fading droplets of the rain they'd gotten caught in.

Her stature was small and hunched, her arms across her abdomen in a self-protective manner. She didn't flinch or try to move away. But she also wasn't meeting his gaze, focusing her stare, instead, on a spot to his left.

"Sophia. Look at me."

When there was no reply, he repeated his words.

A small shake of her head, and then a whisper. "I can't."

Slowly, so as not to scare her, he reached up, grazed her chin with his fingers, then turned her face towards him. "Please."

She closed her eyes, her face creasing with fear.

"You're not going to hurt me."

She let out a small sound, half-sob and half-whimper. "I don't want to hurt you."

"You're *not* going to hurt me. Look at me. Come on."

Her eyelids fluttered open, wetness around them.

"I love it when you look at me," he said, going out on a limb. "Whether it's in anger or desire. And I can take it, Sophia. I'll take it either way. Please look at me."

She finally did, the teary sheen to her hazel eyes tinting them golden-amber under his ceiling lights. Like a frightened rabbit, she stared and waited, and only on realising he wasn't about to catch fire, did she let out a shaky breath. "I killed him."

"Actually, I killed him."

"I set him on fire."

"But it was still I who killed him. And he wasn't human, Sophia. Nor was he 'good' in the way we use the term – those two vampires were part of the Bratvashka I've been researching. Whatever he wanted with you, I very much doubt that was good either."

"Daniel..."

He stroked her cheek, then dropped his hand back to her thigh. "Yes, darling?"

"What am I?"

He gave her a small smile. "I very much wish I could answer that question. I don't know. But I'd like to help you find out."

She suddenly pulled back, her hands clutching her chest.

"I'm sorry. I forgot." She sounded mortified. "Stay back." She scooted away from him, burying herself into the back of the couch, and reached under the high collar of her sweater. Only when she pulled out the object did he understand.

He forced himself to remain nonchalant in the face of the crucifix she unclasped from her neck. Vampires could usually fairly easily stand religious crosses and other such symbols that might be aimed at them, but he could feel the torridness of this one. He wondered its origins for it to emanate such a threat.

"It was my mother's. I can't wear it anymore." She tossed it across the room, flinching as she did so – perhaps not really wanting to treat such a meaningful item that had belonged to her mother in that way. It landed near the far corner.

"It's okay."

"No. I think it maybe ... it *helped* me make that man burn."

"Sophia, we can figure this out together. Let me help you."

She shook her head, almost vigorously. "I can't. It'll happen again."

"Once we understand it, we can—"

"No, no, no ... it's inside me – right now, it's..." She faltered, letting the silence reign.

"It's what. Tell me."

"The burning's still there, like a knot. Like a ... snake about to strike."

"Where? Show me where it burns."

She met his eyes again.

"You will not hurt me. I know you won't."

A single tear fell, and another response rose in its shedding ... one he knew well: hot need.

A look passed between them.

"Where does it burn?" he repeated, quietly.

Tentatively holding his gaze, she placed a shaking hand on

his, then brought it up towards her and placed it on her abdomen, where she'd been guarding. "Here."

Briefly, he closed his eyes, letting his own trembling breath out as the scent of her desire tinged the air. This woman... The *feel* of her.

Her heat seared him, his own navel awakening to everything she might offer.

When he opened his eyes, the look in hers had darkened; glazed over with want.

Still gripping his hand, she moved it downwards, pressing him between her legs. "And here," she whispered, her voice thick.

He could see his gold irises in her pupils' reflection – it was one of the myths about vampires that had always been false: they absolutely had a reflection. They just rarely liked to look at it.

His teeth ached. He wasn't going to be able to keep his fangs from emerging. "And would you like me to help you with that?" He curved his hand against her.

She moaned, softly, and nodded. "Yes."

Christ, he might burn after all, just not in the way they'd witnessed earlier. "I won't hurt you. And I won't bite you. You *tell* me if I'm hurting you, do you understand?"

"Yes."

He drove his hand under her, grabbed her backside and hauled her forward, off the sofa, until she was straddling his lap where he knelt on the floor.

The whimper that escaped her on contact with his erection was pure music.

He let his hands wander up her back, enjoying the way she curved under them. "You know," he said huskily, "when a vampire's hungry, especially if for too long, that can feel like a burn too – a hollow burn that can only be satiated by blood. But with some patience and discipline, flesh can fill the hollow in a different way. At least for a little while."

Her hands found either side of his face, her own hunger clear to see. She stroked his bottom lip with her thumb.

"Tell me what you want, Sophia."

He needn't have worried she might be too scared to express herself, nor that shyness would rule her actions. She ground herself against him, gasping at every sensation, her beautiful eyes wild with lust; her need overriding all. She dropped her forehead against his.

Dear god, this was a beautiful kind of bliss he hadn't had for a while. "Tell me."

"I want you to hold me down – hard – don't let this thing in me escape. And fuck me 'til you drive the burn out."

His groan was swallowed by her kiss, and then everything was kisses – frantic and feral and driven by one single goal: *drive the burn out*.

He flipped her over on her back. Hands went everywhere – his and hers – buttons ripped, zips pulled until their teeth split; she yanked his trousers down and he tugged at hers, bringing her underwear down with them. "Fuck..." He inhaled her scent, drinking it in, knowing his canines were on full display.

Her eyes only darkened with desire on seeing them.

Her hands slid up the taut muscles across his navel; she teased every swell and flex with her delicate fingers as they rose towards his chest.

He drew her up enough to pull her sweater off, taking her bra with it, both the garments going over her head. He stopped at her wrists where he wound them tight.

She moaned as he pushed her back down, his full weight on her as he held her arms above her head, relishing in the feel of her bare skin against his. She tried to move her hips; tried to rub herself against him, but he had her feet, her legs, her thighs, her entire body pinned.

A cry escaped her, desperation driving it. "I don't want to hurt you," she blurted out, manically. "It's there … too much … the fire … I'm—"

"It's going nowhere. Open your legs." He released his weight just enough so she could move them.

Her legs came up around him.

"Wider."

She obeyed, and hell if that wasn't one of the most erotic things he'd ever seen in his four centuries.

He brought himself back down on her, positioning himself, readying himself, *forcing* all his energy away from his fangs and into his cock because the need to bite her – drown in her blood – was excruciating.

With his mouth against her ear – not her neck – he entered her as hard and fast as she'd asked for; his groan just as carnal as hers.

"God … don't stop," her broken voice pleaded.

He groaned. Whatever this was – a need to heal; a need to satiate – he wouldn't stop until she shattered beneath him.

He moved inside her, once, and every part of her yielded like the tide to the force of gravity. *Christ…* "Forgive me, Sophia," he whispered in her ear, giving into the possessiveness that tore through him, hotter than anything she'd conjured today. It was beautiful to feel it again after all this time. "I'm going to fuck you like you're mine."

She tightened around him at that – deliciously and completely – gasp after gasp tumbling from her lips as he did exactly as he'd promised, driving them both to ecstasy and over the edge of only god knew where.

Chapter Thirteen

Light. That was how she felt on surfacing from the deepest sleep she'd had in an age and a day. Sophia moved, lazily stretching her body, still emerging into awakening. Wow, she felt ... completely unburdened, every joint loose and malleable, every muscle worked; every cell regenerated. A moan of satisfaction left her as she stretched again, enjoying each sensation.

"Keep making those noises and I'm taking you all over again."

Her moan ended on an intake of breath at Daniel's quiet, throaty voice, the events of the night rushing back to her. *Fuck me.*

Yes, he had. Four times if she recalled ... complete with four orgasms she hadn't known were possible. Who the hell orgasmed four times in one night? Apparently, she had, and the night wasn't over judging by the darkness encasing the room. The alarm clock on the bedside table said it was just before two in the morning.

Her eyes searched Daniel out, landing on a tantalising silhouette by the window. Even in shadows, his physique was beautifully defined. She rose onto her elbows to see him better.

The silhouette moved, growing, until it depressed the bed and his hauntingly beautiful, dark face came into clear view, sporting that rugged 'just fucked' look. She genuinely couldn't help the noise she sounded at full appreciation of the sight before her.

With a gleam to his eye, he climbed up her body until he was lying on top of her, laving slow kisses across her shoulder.

She sighed. "How you feel against me is crazy. It's like your skin makes mine alive."

"The feeling's mutual," he muttered, sliding his tongue along her chest.

"Is it a vampire thing?"

"Partly."

She made herself comfortable on the bed and ran her fingers through his hair, delighting in doing so now as much as she had a few hours ago. His hair was bloody gorgeous. Unable to resist him any longer, she grasped his face and pulled him up to meet her, eye to eye.

His look was one of deep contemplation that had obviously taken a serious turn. "Sophia," he said, quietly. "Tell me about the scar near your hip." He kissed her nose.

"It's nothing. The doctors said I got it escaping the house fire. I don't even remember how it happened."

He looked at her for what seemed like an age, seemed like he wanted to say something, but then maybe changed his mind. His frame relaxed against her and his next kiss landed on her lips. She stretched again, this time relishing in the firmness of his body on hers, skin gliding against skin.

Sophia smiled, languidly, into his golden eyes, hooded as they were from his sensual response to her. His teeth were out – his fangs – but only slightly. At some point in the night she had noted they could be coaxed out and often emerged at various lengths.

With a sexual hunger she had no idea she was capable of, she reached down between them until her hand found its prize.

He grunted as she took his hardness and teased it.

It worked. His fangs grew and who would have thought that could be such a fucking turn on, but it was. She wondered if she looked as greedy as she felt for him.

"What are you doing?" he asked, although she was pretty sure he already knew the answer.

She was staring pointedly at his teeth, desire already

blooming through her centre. "I have so many questions," she confessed. Among them were the questions about setting that man – or vampire – on fire. But she didn't want to think about that now – what that meant for her; what that *made* her. Other questions took precedence in the pruriency of this moment.

Reaching down, he took her hand and moved it, leaving her disappointed only for a second, and then he was sliding inside her again, and by god, nothing compared to this feeling. Although, her experience of men and sex was not vast – not at all – there had only been one other before Pierce and he had been a clumsy teen 'first'.

He teased a whimper out of her as he settled fully inside her.

Biting her lip, she tentatively laid one finger on his left canine, the tip of it looking as sharp as the tip of a pin. The phantom bite on her neck scorched; its own ache demanding a fulfilment she instinctively understood. She hadn't told him about her dream and how he'd bitten her in it. "Does it hurt?" she asked. "If you were to bite me, I mean. Would it hurt?"

"Do you want me to bite you?" he asked, both his guttural tone and further hardening within her, very clearly expressing how he felt about that. But there was also a guardedness surrounding his question; and a sorrow on his features.

She toyed with the idea of telling him he already had – in her dream state anyway. That she felt that bite as a real entity that affected her in very real ways. But she didn't – not while that sorrow glinted in his eye. She didn't want to scare him away; lose *this*, whatever this was. She had no idea what this was between them, but she knew the thought of it taken from her felt like a loss she couldn't bear – not now, anyway. Not while her life was fire, attacks, and death. And later? She had meant what she'd said to Pierce: she was in no place for any commitment. The future felt as uncertain now as it had after the house fire. So, she didn't answer him. "I asked first."

Contemplating her, he seemed to come to a decision. "Place your finger on the very tip of the tooth, but don't press – just hold it there." He bared his teeth to give her easy access.

She tightened around him as she followed his instructions – didn't mean to, but it was insane how aroused she was.

After a few seconds, a clear bead of fluid emerged from his fang onto her finger.

He pulled back and she brought her finger closer to her face to inspect it in the near dark.

"That's our venom," he said. "It's equal parts anaesthetic, aphrodisiac, and paralytic. Some vampires can also use it in a healing capacity, although I can't say I've ever mastered that. Every vampire excretes it at the point of biting and we can control how much of it we release. Too much kills you, and quite quickly too. The more monstrous among our kind bite brutally and violently; the benevolent ones amongst us will take great care to make their prey feel as little pain and as much pleasure as possible. We don't have a name for this substance – it's simply referred to as 'the vampire's bite'. Feeding – the taking of blood – is the act that follows it and is, in many ways, separate to the bite. For example, I could slice you with a knife and feed on you, and the bite would not be needed or relevant."

"Then why the need for the bite? For this liquid?"

"It's primordial. We've existed for as long as humans have existed, and in prehistoric times when there were no tools or the understanding of how to use them, our bite was a necessary weapon. It is, however, still the *cleanest* way to either feed or kill. It can be swift, and it need not be messy."

She felt entranced by it all. It was fascinating. "So, there are bad vampires and good vampires?"

"For want of better terminology, yes. And none of this nonsense about having no souls, please – we all have souls and we can choose what to do with them, much like humans can. What we *do* have is extremes – extremes of emotion and sensation. We are sensory creatures. The extremes make it difficult for most vampires to walk that benevolent path; makes it too easy for us to succumb to basic desires for both comfort and satiation.

"There's never been a poll – but, to give you an idea, we'll say that ninety-five percent of all vampires are just average: they are neither good nor bad, they just live more so by their instincts – their more animalistic qualities. But they can be debated, bargained, and reasoned with. They just want to lead quiet lives and will rarely harm a human unless threatened.

"Out of the remaining five percent, half overcome all baser instincts and become what you might call good or benevolent, and the other half prefer the power that aggression and strength gives them, becoming heinous, violent, and potentially evil beings."

"And you? You're a 'good' vampire?"

He smiled. "You're asking me this *now*?"

"I was the evil one last night."

The smile disappeared in an instant. He pushed himself deeper inside her, rising up before her; placing his forehead against hers. "I don't bring evil into this bed, Sophia. You are anything but."

She bit her tongue to stop herself sounding out at the feel of him. She wanted to learn more; was drinking in all his words of this world she never knew existed but was starting to make fast sense – the most perfect sense.

"No vampire is born without hunger and the teeth to kill for food. I was not created a 'good' vampire – none are. I learnt to be that way because I"—he paused—"I had a good creator who taught me well – a caring one. And because I wanted to be that way."

"How old are you?"

"Four hundred and twenty-eight."

She let out a sharp breath, calculating the years in her mind. "You became a vampire in—"

"1597. And I was born human thirty-five years before that."

She took a moment to process it all. "Are all vampires human first? Who was the first vampire?"

"As far as I know, all vampires are turned from human, yes. And we have as many myths about our origins as humans have about theirs."

"In that churches and gargoyles book, there's something about fallen angels becoming vampires? I think in the book they're called *upyri*."

"It's one of the origin stories, yes."

The questions just kept forming. "If you bite me, will I turn into a vampire?"

He brushed her nose with his. "No. It's actually very hard to create a vampire – not all attempts are successful. You would have to die to become a vampire – drained of most of your blood until your heart stopped, but only for a few seconds, after which, your blood is replaced with the blood of your creator. Your heart is re-started by your new vampiric blood."

"So vampires have a heartbeat?"

"We do. That's why staking it works. But it does beat differently to that of humans – a different rhythm; very much slower – about once a minute. We breathe, but it's merely a bodily function – air is not needed for our survival. And we do not age, but of course, can die in various ways."

She was all in a spin with this whole other world that existed.

Daniel rested on an elbow and looked at her in thought. "Let's put the main misconceptions about vampires to bed straight away: we can walk in daylight for a short while as long as it's overcast, but direct sunlight kills us in an instant – it's partly the strength of the UVB rays – so you'll almost never see vampires in daylight, it's just too risky. UV blocked windows do protect us to an extent – for example, in cars – but only for a couple of hours; long drives are impossible when it's sunny, and sunscreen doesn't work for us at all. That's why our curtains at home are always drawn during the day.

"We're not demons – we're merely a different species and humans can be as demonic as anything else. If you destroy our hearts with something big enough, you kill us, hence the stakes. If you cut off our heads, you kill us. Fire can kill us, too, if not put out straight away. That's it, though. Crosses, holy water, burial grounds, churches, and religious artefacts rarely do a thing to harm us – your holy water trick was an exception." He looked at her, meaningfully. "*You're* an exception to be honest."

"Wow." She might actually be dizzy lying down. "You mentioned a creator..."

"The one who turns you. Also called a sire, or a maker. There are a few names."

"Have..." She almost didn't ask – wasn't sure she wanted to know. "Have you ever created a vampire?"

He stared at her, a glimmer of hurt flashed through him, then he kissed her. "No, I haven't. I need to feed soon, Sophia. I won't be gone long."

Feed?

Feed on blood. Blood from another human. *Oh, my god!* Blood from another *woman*?

The jealousy was stark and unforgiving and she'd never felt it before. It rose in her like a viper and before she could stop herself, she clamped her legs around him, her body knowing way before her mind she wasn't letting any woman near this male, and like hell was he 'biting' any woman with that aphrodisiac-paralytic venom thing, giving her pleasure doing so.

Her phantom bite *seared*.

Daniel laughed. It was the first time she'd heard him do so and it was a deep, intoxicating sound she'd have found endearing had it not been aimed at her childish, uncontrollable feelings. She'd *never* felt jealous over any man before.

His next kiss was near ferocious, consuming her completely as he began to thrust inside her, his lips found a spot under her jawline, and then her neck, and then right on that damned spot he'd dream-bitten her. Did he know?

She keened, the want almost unbearable – the want for him to slide inside her in *every* way.

"I'll not take your blood – not when we don't know what you are. But by god, I want to."

"Daniel." *Fuck.* She could feel her next orgasm stirring and the river of jealousy raging through her was heightening every sensation. *Who* had she *become*?

"Say what you feel," he demanded, his need as bare as hers. "Tell me."

Were these the extremes of emotion he was talking about. Except *she* wasn't a vampire. But the unforgiving truth was, she was no longer sure she was entirely human. Whatever she was, he'd unlocked it – somehow – and it was both extraordinary and dangerous ... and *painful*.

"I can't help my need to feed, Sophia."

She whinged in protest; clamped him hard and his thrusting grew fast and urgent.

"God!" she cried as the mother of all climax's loomed, and it loomed *with* the jealousy, both like serpents entwining. Sensory creatures, he had said. She didn't recognise herself, and yet—

"Fucking say it. *Say* it."

With a cry, she grabbed him; pressed her nails into his shoulders and neck. "Fuck you, you *bastard*, don't you *dare* take another woman – you're mine; you're *mine*."

His shout of release outdid hers.

Tears welled in her eyes at the sheer fervency of what they'd just shared.

Daniel was panting against her ear, both of them needing more than a minute to find composure again. "Fuck ... you're amazing. Listen to me carefully, Sophia ... the intensity of ... *this* ... when a vampire takes your blood – when you take theirs – it becomes ten times more. It's all-consuming, do you understand? I won't drink from you until we know what you are and what that means. And humans really shouldn't drink from vampires, so I won't offer you my vein. Even if it turns out you're more than human, you need to be ready for such a connection. If you ever are." He drew his head up and kissed her, gently. "I want to stay"—he pulled himself out of her—"but I need to feed."

"Daniel, please..." She grabbed his wrist and the damn tears slipped. It *was* too much.

"Shh, shh, shh." He placed a finger on her lips, then kissed her again. "I mostly feed from donor bags. From the blood bank. I'll not feed on any man or woman tonight." He dropped another kiss on her cheek, then was gone.

Chapter Fourteen

"There are various connections a vampire can make. There is the sharing of blood like we have already talked about – this can be practical and does not have to be sexual – but a bond is formed nevertheless. Sharing can be vampire-to-vampire which is very common, or vampire-to-human which is very rare, and both have different effects.

"When between vampires the blood is shared both ways and lasts merely days, but in that time, you can feel each other's

presence, know each other's location, even each other's emotions.

"Sharing blood with a human almost never happens because when a human drinks a vampire's blood, the effects are permanent. The vampire will have a connection with the human forever – feel their presence and emotions as I've already discussed – it's quite an invasion of privacy for the human and a huge bind for the vampire. It's also unequal, because when a vampire drinks a human's blood, the human gains nothing from it, and all the vampire gets is food.

"Another form of connection is the siring of another. Siring requires huge commitment from the part of the sire for it takes at least a century to nurture a newling vampire into its full potential, and the progeny is completely dependent on its sire. The relationship is intricate, and not equal for that first century. This is why its best if great love exists between sire and progeny; at the very least there must be great patience and understanding.

"Lastly, there is the Surging. Also called the Blood Surge. But this is unheard of nowadays. So unheard of, it's a thing of legends, much like Excalibur is in your Arthurian stories. A vampire must be able to extend their fangs beyond three inches to create a Blood Surge. So, inevitably, it is a male that Surges a female and not the other way around – females' just don't get that long. I don't know any male vampire with fangs that long either. I believe the tip penetrates the subclavian artery, through the shoulder – usually we feed from the carotid through the neck. The blood flowing through the subclavian artery is said to be purer and richer before it reaches the carotid, its effects longer lasting – especially if taken from the left side, directly form the aortic arch; it's richer in oxygen. It's called a Blood Surge because of the way the blood is said to pulse into the mouth from that point – like an ocean wave moved directly by the beat of the heart itself. But a Surging is a forever deal. With other types of blood sharing, one vampire can choose to leave the other, no matter how difficult that may be. But with a Surging,

it's a permanent bind to the vampire that Surges your blood, and it's not a bind that any vampire wants – certainly not a female one – because you are, in effect, owned. What exactly that means – what a Surging leads to – has been lost in history.

"Nevertheless, vampires can be as romantic as humans, and there are fairy tales – if you want to call them that – we have written about the Blood Surge; a love-beyond-death tragic romantic fantasy trope – it never gets old for some. There are also horror stories written about it – ones of complete possession and enslavement.

"So, you see, Sophia, blood is everything to us – food, life, lust, and love; it's the origins of where we come from and it's what we want to become. Don't ever give or take it lightly."

That was how Daniel had left her – his parting words this morning because she had wrestled with the jealousy that had risen from nowhere last night, defying logic and sense; unfamiliar and abhorrent. Jealousy had never been her way. Strong emotions, in general, had never been her way, come to think of it.

"Don't get involved with a vampire then," he'd teased, but he'd also been serious.

Sophia looked up at the sun as she stood outside the library, its already warm rays dissipating all darkness. Her skin delighted in the feel of it; its life-giving light. She knew without a doubt she did not want to be a vampire. But could she be with Daniel as a human? (And until they knew what she was, she *was* still human.) Could she stand the intensity and overwhelm?

After Daniel's feed last night, he had returned with everything she'd left in Les' car. He had also paid a visit to her house, used her car keys, and had returned with *her* car so she would have more freedom to get around without relying on Les, especially if she was going to be staying at his a while. She'd been grateful. She had driven into work today and had promised to return home straight after so they could continue their investigations into everything taking place.

They had talked until the early hours, of her past and who she might be. They had delved into her box and been sorely disappointed at finding nothing that might give any clue to her seemingly supernatural abilities: healing fast, and spontaneously combusting a vampire. She hoped to god that particular ability was limited to only vampires, and the not-so-nice ones, at that.

The box had not left them completely empty-handed, though: she had learnt that her family name at birth was Auclair.

"French?" she had asked in a daze. She'd had no idea of her French heritage. "Sophia Auclair." She'd repeated the name a few times and had felt nothing – no connection to it. Daniel had reassured her most children so young rarely connect with their surnames the way they do with their first and certainly don't understand the meaning of heritage until much older.

The home that had burned in the fire had not been far from here, in the next county over in Sussex, nestled to the west of South Downs National Park: Laycroft Manor. A large, eight-bedroom abode surrounded by ten acres of land. They had even owned a portion of the cemetery belonging to the church in the adjacent field, and although Sophia had the most vague sense of having known the cemetery, no memory had surfaced.

After days of memories springing up out of nowhere *so clearly*, to have none on finally emptying the box had felt like a loss.

"Don't force it," Daniel had said. "A lot has happened. It will come."

The crucifix had stayed where she'd thrown it. She wasn't ready to put it on again, and it seemed wrong to wear it in front of a vampire – one she'd slept with, anyway, and could develop feelings for.

Back to the feelings – the all-consuming, freedom-destroying feelings.

She sighed and made her way up to the front door, trying hard to make herself fit into this world the same way she had yesterday.

A part of her found that awfully funny because the truth was she'd never fit in anywhere anyway. She'd always assumed it was because of the fire, being placed in witness protection, and all those early happenings. Not once, until now, had she considered it could be because she wasn't fully human.

Just act normal. It's not like you've sprouted horns.

Abigail was already in, cleaning shelves. "Oh, hi – you're earlier than usual."

"I drove in. I'm actually staying with a friend out near Winchester for a few days. Didn't fancy staying at mine after the murders."

"I don't blame you one bit."

They had half an hour until opening. "I forgot to give you the key back to the basement yesterday after the fiasco with Pierce. Do you mind if I spend a bit of time down there before the customers come in?"

Abi looked at her like she actually *had* sprouted horns. "If that's your idea of a fun time, you go for it."

"I just fancy the quiet, that's all."

"Have you heard from Pierce?" Abi asked.

Worry rose at that question. "I haven't, and I feel weird about that. He pursued me so relentlessly, and now to not hear from him at all ... I'm a bit concerned."

"He actually left a message on the answering machine yesterday, about half an hour after leaving here – I only checked the messages this morning though, sorry," she said meekly, pulling a face. "He left his clipboard here and wondered if we could mail the sheets on it to him – he left the address he's staying at. I was going to take it to the post office at break time."

"Wait ... what's the address?"

"Somewhere in Brentley."

"Brentley's only about a twenty-minute drive away. Why don't I take it on my lunch break, that way I can also get peace of mind he's all right."

"Sure – it's in the mail pile."

"Thanks." She looked through and found it. "Just call me up from the basement if you need me before opening."

"If I hear screaming down there, I'm not coming to rescue you!" she called out behind her.

Sophia laughed. "I'll let you off since you came to Pierce's rescue yesterday."

"Very hesitantly, I might add."

"I'll be fine – I can rescue myself."

So ... how did one begin to speak to a ghost?

With the door firmly shut behind her, Sophia looked around the basement, then up at the ceiling, and then into all the corners she could see. She found nothing that resembled a ghost. She'd *felt* it last time, though, hadn't she? A cold breeze. And she'd heard it.

Clearing her throat and feeling more than a little stupid, she walked into the middle of the room, near where she'd been standing yesterday with Pierce.

Sitting while he pleasured you, actually.

Guilt rose sharply. Because of Daniel. Even though Daniel and her had *not* been any kind of item at that time.

Yeah – this 'all-consuming' lifestyle really wasn't going to be all buttercups and roses, was it?

You don't have to say yes – he gave you an out.

Oh, it was far too late for that. It had been too late the second she'd laid eyes on him – she knew that now. He'd literally *calmed* her fire-starter mode with all the sex. Throw in the supernatural stuff and where the hell else was she going to go?

She cleared her throat. "Um ... hi, erm, library ghost." *That doesn't at all sound ridiculous.* "Sorry – I don't know your name. But I do know you're here, and I'd like your help if you want to give it. I'm *asking* for your help. Please."

She waited.

Nothing happened.

"I need to know more about vampires and how they live – the truth – not Hollywood make-believe stuff. I need the real deal. Can you help me with that?"

Not even a creak from the wooden shelving.

One speck of dust floated before her eyes and that's all she got. Letting out a breath of resignation, she headed back toward the door. *You'd been expecting what, exactly? Another concussion?*

THUMP.

She squealed and turned, the noise so loud it echoed for a few seconds.

That was a book falling, wasn't it? *Yes, it was!* Heart thudding, she started racing up the aisles, scouring every inch of floor for it. *There it is!*

It was an older one – no dust jacket – probably late 1800s. She picked it up, cautiously looking around as she did so, and when she felt safe no object was about to fly at her, she looked for a title. Gold lettering embossed the front: *The Ideologies of Edward Theon.*

Edward Theon ... where had she heard that— "Oh! John Dee's friend – the angel guy." She wasn't expecting the ghost to reply, but she was sure a cool breeze passed by her.

Her wristwatch told her she only had fifteen minutes before the library opened. She'd have to be quick. Perching herself right there on the floor, she opened the book. It was a good five minutes before something significant caught her eye:

Theon feared retribution - imprisonment or beheading - for his assertion that the vampyre and the angel were of the same cloth. The church denounced his so-called findings vehemently, and yet, he claimed to have a growing following from a Catholic branch that called themselves the Resurrectors. They supported his assertions, pitting them against the status quo, and later, as a subject of the church's persecution.

Edward Theon and the Resurrectors believed that the first vampyres were fallen angels who would thirst for blood - their carnal penance for having rejected the light of God - and the fallen ones who could not resist the temptation of the blood, over and over again, grew the tool with which they would forever be bound to blood - their feeding teeth. The sacrifice for this tool was their wings.

Now wingless and bloodthirsty, the fallen ones became the first vampyres and along the folds

> of time, became capable of creating other vampyres, shunning the last of their angel traits, for angels cannot create life, not even undead life.
>
> On the first vampyre borne of its own creator, the vampyre came into its own, no longer angel, but demon.

Wow. She should really read this alongside the other book and make notes. A quick look at her watch told her it was three minutes until opening. There was more in this chapter about the Resurrectors.

Feeling a little guilty, because she was fast becoming a book thief, Sophia tucked the hardback into her bag and stood.

"Thank you," she called out to the ghost, and then, after a pause, "Do you have a name I can call you?"

After a few seconds, she heard and saw a small book slide out just a few feet along. She went and caught it before it could fall out: A very early edition of *Jane Eyre*, by Charlotte Brontë. A further noise, and another book slipped out to her right. This one she had not heard of: *The Countryside Adventures of Miss Jane.*

She held both books together, staring at them. "Jane. Your name is Jane?"

A cool breeze fluttered against the nape of her neck.

With a smile, Sophia put both books back. "Pleased to meet you, Jane. I have to go now, but I'll return. Thank you again."

65 Longdale Drive. Her Sat Nav wished her a nice day after reaching her destination.

Turning her engine off, she picked up her bag and the envelope for Pierce and got out of the car. The house looked like one of those Airbnb rentals judging by the coded safety box she could see attached to the wall near the front door. It made sense. He had said he was around for two weeks on a work assignment. *Should have told me your work involved the library, Pierce.* Although she hadn't exactly been welcoming on seeing him, or let him get a word in edgeways.

With a sigh, she walked up the driveway, hoping he was in so this wasn't a wasted trip, and also wondering if now was a good time to break things off completely with him – not that anything had *really* started; just some needed sexual release in a basement. Sans the release part.

Sophia knocked on the door and waited. After a few seconds had passed, she also rang the doorbell. Glancing at his windows, she could see all his curtains were shut – across every single one. She frowned. She remembered Pierce as someone who always opened his curtains first thing to let the morning sun in.

The light's not so welcome if you have a sore head from a concussion, though, is it?

Peeking to her left, she spotted the side access gate open, leading to the garden. *Might as well look – you drove all the way here and you don't have long before you need to be back.* She walked down the side, noting the curtains were also drawn along those windows and also the ones at the back of the house.

Worry stirred. He might *actually* be hurt, especially if he never saw a doctor after that injury.

Sophia stilled when she saw the back double doors into the house were ajar. Approaching them with caution, she glanced inside, into what looked like the living room, and saw no one. "Hello?"

No reply. The house suddenly seemed far too silent.

"Pierce? It's Sophia." She stepped inside. His briefcase and jacket – the one he'd worn yesterday and on Sunday – lay on one of the sofas. *At least I know I've got the right house.*

Her worry for him rising, she strode across the living room and into the hallway, calling out once more for him to no avail. If he was feeling bad, he'd be lying in bed, which she assumed was upstairs, so that's where she went. "Pierce?" She really didn't want to shock him with her arrival; wasn't entirely comfortable with the fact she'd walked in uninvited, but his welfare trumped her discomfort.

The room directly opposite the top of the stairs was the bathroom, the second along was an empty bedroom, which left a third, the door half open. The curtains were drawn in every room and even across the windows on the landing, making the whole house dark – his bedroom, if this was it, looked the darkest.

She pushed the door fully open. "Pierce?"

She could see someone on the bed, lying on his back. Clearly this was Pierce – she'd recognise him anywhere – but ... she stood rooted to the spot. Something was off. Really off. "Pierce?" That came out as barely a whisper this time, and to her alarm, she realised she wasn't expecting a response.

Oh, god.

Taking one slow step at a time, she made her way closer to him. He was deathly still, the emphasis on the word *deathly*. His chest did not move. "Oh, no..."

And then *she* moved, stumbling towards him. He wasn't dead – couldn't be! She'd seen him just yesterday. If she could do something to—

With a gasp she pulled her hand right back from where she'd just laid it on his. His skin was cold as ice. And pale. With a kind of blue-green tinge, so apparent now she was next to him, it could be seen in the dim light. Was that normal? Did that mean he'd been dead for a while?

Call an ambulance. Call one now.

Her tears surfaced as she delved into her bag to reach for her phone, and then stopped again because something crucial was out of place; she just couldn't figure out what it—

Oh.

Her gaze landed on his head. Stepping closer, she leaned down to make sure she wasn't missing something. Yesterday, his head had suffered a cut and the bruising had been horrid. There was not a trace of bruising now, or any injury at all.

Maybe he heals as fast as you.

Her eyes were pulled to a spot on the right side of his neck – the side facing her – where two small, neat puncture wounds stared back at her.

"Oh, *shit*! Oh, no."

A shuffling sounded from *under* the bed, and then a hiss. With a yelp, she leapt back, but not before she was attacked by something *scurrying* out – something small, naked, and wiry with arms of steel.

On instinct, she kicked – hard – getting whatever the hell it was right in the face, which pissed it off because it hissed louder and bared its teeth.

Aaah – the teeth – there they were.

It lunged at her again, and she blocked it with a duck and a swing, having no bloody clue what she was doing, but doing it anyway. It went nuts. It *was* nuts. She got a good look at it for a second. Forget tall, dark, and seductive – this creature was some hairless, wrinkled, ghoul from hell, looking like it had crawled out of some mine, or cave, or—

She screamed as it sank its fangs into her ankle. *Shit* it was fast. And that *hurt*. If that was the same 'venom' Daniel had shown her, it was already setting her veins on fire.

Something blurred before her eyes in fast motion, blasting a gust of wind through her hair as it did so. Whatever it was ripped the creature from her leg, and she let out another yelp because it hadn't let go of her willingly.

All she saw was blond. Long, blond hair. Everything moved too fast. She couldn't focus on it anyway because she could already feel the paralysis setting in across her ankle and foot.

The creature suddenly landed by her, to her right, a stake embedded in its chest. Still alive, it scowled, then looked positively grief-stricken, then let out a yowl that hurt almost as much as her ankle, and then it disappeared, nothing but dust in its place. And a wooden stake.

The 'blond hair' – dark blond – was suddenly in front of her, tugging her trouser leg up sharply. The deepest blue eyes she'd ever seen met hers. They belonged to a sleek, strong, and masculine face, and she caught her breath – not because he was attractive in that charming, vampiric way she was starting to recognise (he *was*), but because a memory tried to surface. A really strong one. It *didn't* surface, but she *knew* it was there and it had everything to do with those eyes.

"Take a breath," he said. "This is going to hurt." And then he clamped his mouth around the wound on her ankle and sucked.

She yelled.

Christ!

He didn't let up, spitting out what of the venom he'd gathered and sucking more out – spitting and sucking. Five or six times he did this, and she was battling stars, the pain was so intense.

He glanced at her through his long, silky tresses. Strangely it made her think of Daniel's locks and she found herself wondering, in her disorientated state, if 'designer hair' was a vampire trait. "Nearly done."

The next time he sealed his mouth around the wound, the sensation was different. She could feel him licking it with his tongue – not sucking or drinking, just licking. Coating it, she assumed, with – well, she wasn't sure she really wanted to know what, but it felt better in an instant, the burn of the venom all but gone, and she could feel her foot. The paralysis was wearing off.

The man spit one last time, wiped his mouth, and got up. He held out his hand to her. His attire was just as elaborate as his eyes and hair – a purple, velvet jacket encased a white shirt with quite the large collar, tucked into fine—*were those silk?*—maroon trousers she wondered how on earth he kept intact if he went around sparring with little monsters on a regular basis. It was clear he was well-built beneath all that grandeur. "You'll be fine." He spoke curtly. "The sooner you stand, the better."

She took his hand. The connection was instant and very unlike the connection she felt to Daniel – her attraction to Daniel was intense, but had been physical from the start. This was – deeper. Deeper of its own accord. She couldn't place it.

"You can't stay here – more of them will come."

Them. She looked at the pile of dust on the floor. "What was it?"

"Just another vampire, ma chérie. There are many types of vampire."

Her face must have looked a picture because he smiled, bemused. And then it fell from his face as he reached into the inside pocket of his jacket and brought out another stake. He handed it to her.

She looked at it like the weapon it was.

"You have to kill him."

"Kill wh— Oh!" She shook her head, horror mounting. "No."

No trace of amusement was in his tone now; just a semblance of sympathy. Only a semblance. "It's the kindest thing you can do for him now. After his transition, he will become like them."

Like those hairless goblins? Oh, god! That was too horrible to contemplate. Tears welled and fell in an instant as she turned to look at Pierce. "Can't we heal him or something?"

"Non, ma chérie. His transformation is nearly complete. If you don't do it, I will. But I thought I'd offer you the choice at least. Intimacy is a precious thing not to be given away."

She tore her gaze from Pierce and back to the man – no, the *vampire* – standing next to her. "Intimacy?"

He met her eyes.

There was that memory again – it pushed against her mind, almost painfully; more so because she could not unravel it.

This time his features held not just sympathy, but a profound knowing that triggered fresh tears from her. "There is nothing more intimate than being the hand that slays a loved one."

She tried to hold it together as she looked at the stake; tried to imagine herself sinking it into Pierce's heart, and couldn't hold back a sob. This was *not* something she was ready for. "I'm sorry. I just can't."

He nodded. "Look away." He moved past her towards the bed.

She did as he instructed, wanting to scream; to grab him and pull him away from the man who had still made her laugh, hope, and want, and possibly *love* despite his vices.

She *heard* the stake go in.

She clamped her hands over her mouth to hold back the sobs and failed.

Job done, the blond vampire walked past her towards the door, then hesitated, turned back and after a moment, tenderly grazed the side of her wet cheek with his hand. "I am truly sorry.

My advice is to go home to Deiniol, let him take you in his arms, let him comfort you, love you, and help you forget – at least for a short while. He's good at that."

Stunned, she gaped at him. Did he mean *Daniel*? "How do you—"

"His scent is all over you." He turned once more and made his way to the bedroom door. "Tell him Jacque will drop by soon and that I did receive his message. I have information he's looking for." He stopped in the hallway, then stared at her, and even in the dark of the house she could see fathomless emotion amid his evocative blue orbs, slightly aglow.

His final words to her were both pained and ardent. "You're very lucky, ma chérie. He used to be mine."

PART II

Jacque

Chapter Fifteen

When she walked into Daniel's flat, he was pacing a hole in the carpet. His head whipped around at her entrance and he was on her in a second, her back against the closed door. "What happened? What the fuck happened?"

"Daniel—"

"I sensed something was wrong – I have no idea how – but with no blood shared between us I couldn't place you. I phoned the library and no one answered. The sun's *streaming* outside and I couldn't hunt for you."

Abigail was terrible at answering the library phone. She'd had to phone her mobile to get through to her. Luckily, after she'd recounted the events to Abi (she'd told her she'd found Pierce dead and had left out everything else), she'd been suitably shocked and absolutely fine with Sophia taking the afternoon off.

She'd come straight back here, not knowing what else to do. She welled up with tears anew and Daniel noticed. His hands came up to her shoulders, his eyes burning with concern.

"Pierce is dead."

He let out a sharp breath. "I'm sorry. Sophia, are *you* all right?"

"I don't know."

He led her to the sofa. It seemed to be the spot she ended up when things went wrong. "He was lying there as if dead and then I noticed the bite mark. A vampire tried to turn him. It was still in the room – a horrible looking thing that was like a hairless goblin, or something."

He frowned. "Carry on."

"It attacked me." She looked at him. Intently.

His expression didn't change. Instead, his nostrils flared, just slightly.

"You know, don't you. You know who was there. You can smell him on me."

His brown eyes darkened almost impossibly.

"He saved my life. Said he was going to drop by soon to see you; that he had information."

Daniel inhaled, closed his eyes, and then let the breath out, interlocking his fingers as he rested his arms on his legs. "I'm glad he was there for you." He'd pretty much bitten that out, his frustration clearly audible.

"Who is he? Who is Jacque?"

He sat back on the couch, his jaw clenching. "What did he say to you?"

"Does it matter? I want to hear it from you, Daniel. I want to trust you and know you if we're even contemplating sharing a connection in any way."

He stared at her. "So he *did* tell you."

She sighed. "He said you were once *his*."

He reached for her. "Sophia—"

"No, don't. I don't care, okay? If it's past, it's past, and it's none of my business, but you're four centuries old and I am *dwarfed* by a history you have that I will never be able to touch. And Pierce is dead." Her face crumpled as she cried. "And all I want to do is fall in your arms right now – into everything we were last night – but I don't *know* you at all, and I don't even know myself because everything's changed, and Pierce is dead. And that man you belonged to gave me the chance to put a stake through Pierce's heart and I couldn't, so he did it himself and I *heard it*," she sobbed. "I heard it go in." She was gone – a blubbering mess having held it together in the car all the way here.

"Sophia..." Daniel pulled her into his arms.

She didn't protest this time, but sobbed into his chest for a good ten minutes as it all sank in.

He said nothing, letting her cry. After she stopped, he didn't let her go, nor did she move.

After another few minutes, he kissed the top of her head. "Killing him was the best thing you could have done for him, I promise."

"That's what Jacque said, too."

"What was Jacque doing there?"

"I never got a chance to ask. That goblin vampire bit me."

Daniel stiffened.

"Jacque sucked the venom out, killed Pierce, and then left. It all happened so fast."

Another minute passed, then Daniel squeezed her tighter. "Jacque is my sire."

Numbly, she pulled herself back to see his face. "He made you?"

Daniel nodded. "The relationship between a vampire and his or her maker is a complicated one. There's the bonding from having shared blood in the first place, but there's also complete dependency, almost exactly like a baby has on its parents. The moment you wake, you're hungry and your senses are sharp and so incredibly heightened, but also chaotic. You're overly sensitive to everything and don't even understand what your senses are telling you half of the time. You need and yearn for food, guidance, affection, love, and your maker is the one you give yourself wholly to for all those things. There is no other choice. Choice only comes later when you've grown enough to learn that it can be different, much like when a teenager sees the world they really want – enough to leave home.

"Jacque was everything I had and for two centuries I was accepting and happy. We were happy."

"Were you ... lovers?"

He let out a long breath, as if wondering how to answer that question. "Not ... exactly. But you must try to understand that for a vampire, everything is about the blood. Blood is both food and identity, so you become territorial over it; you defend it possessively and fear to lose it, hence the out-of-proportion jealousy you've gotten a hint of. Sexual attraction is an independent entity to blood, but when blood is shared between vampires – in any capacity – it creates a need to guard that bond and sometimes the lines can become murky."

She raised an eyebrow. "Daniel, yes or no?"

He faced her and held her gaze. "If you're asking if we were lovers, the answer is no. If you're asking if we have ever shared sexual encounters, the answer is yes.

"Jacque has always been detached when it comes to affairs of the heart. In terms of sexual attraction, I've never directly seen him with anyone. But I assume he's been with both men and women during his many years – that's not unusual when you live long enough, even without the blood aspect. You experience everything. I was not attracted to him when I was human. But the blood of your sire inside you... Like I said, it's complicated."

"I can deal with complicated – I just want the truth. I told you I can't be with someone secretive – not after Pierce."

He nodded, and continued. "In 1819, I met a woman called Eliza Hampton. She turned my head. She was not much like the other ladies around at the time. She was outspoken, funny, intelligent, very attractive ... to cut a long story short, I fell in love and that love was returned. She discovered I was a vampire, and she was not frightened, but fascinated. In the end, she wanted to be turned, and I wanted to turn her. We wanted to belong to each other and our love shone everywhere we went. I have often wondered if Jacque hated it because it meant he'd have to let me go – that our time together was up – because..." Daniel sighed. It was a long and sorrowful sigh. "He turned her first."

"My god." She didn't have to be a vampire to see the

devastation in that.

"I was stricken, Sophia. I do not have words for what I felt, but it was the end of Jacque and I. When Eliza awakened, it was Jacque she reached for; Jacque she needed."

"You think he did it to hurt you? To hurt you both and part you?"

"I have always assumed so. I came home one day and it was done – Eliza was in transition. He'd turned her – just like that. He didn't speak to me about it first and never gave me a reason. The betrayal cut deep. But he also hurt himself, because I severed him from my life in every way I could, and apart from the occasional necessary formal conversation for societal upkeep, I have not spoken to him for over two hundred years."

Sophia studied him, aware she was 'feeling' him in ways she had not before; unsure if that was down to last night's connection they'd shared, or more. "It must have been difficult to pull away from your sire."

"I was suicidal for a while. I became reckless, putting myself in situations where I might be staked or beheaded or anything to end the misery. But I pulled myself out in the end."

She wanted to know more. She wanted to know about Amelia – where she fit into it all; where Les fit into it all – but she was exhausted and hurting. "Thank you," she said, instead. "Thank you for explaining."

He smiled at her and brought his hand up to stroke her hair. His touch was divine. "I *am* glad he was there to help you. I was going crazy inside these four walls not knowing how to get to you. Jacque has tried to apologise to me over the course of the last two centuries, but I cannot forgive him and I do not want to hear the details of what took place anymore; coming home and seeing it was enough to gouge a wound that's never healed."

"Why do *you* think Jacque was at Pierce's place?"

"I think he followed you there because of me. I put word out to him a few days ago that I thought the Bratvashka were around and I could do with speaking to him about it – part of that societal upkeep thing I was talking about. He might already have been around for a day or so, observing our interactions before making himself known – especially given our history. He's wary of pushing me further away."

"Can you not feel when he's around?"

"Only if I concentrate on doing so. But I won't – I don't want to. That hurts too. So I shut it out. I shut *him* out."

That sounded so damaging. She said nothing, but leaned in and kissed him instead. He returned it in kind, and before he could pull back, she levered herself up and straddled his lap, deepening the kiss, tongue sweeping over tongue. "I want to shut out Pierce's death for a while," she mumbled against his mouth. "Maybe we can help each other out."

He smiled against her lips. "That's an invitation I'll not turn down."

And kisses became touch, became movement; became the sensual friction of flesh as all memories and all losses were abandoned for the next hour.

Les had joined them for dinner. The remnants of steak and chips sat on one end of the table while the rest of it was covered with newspapers from around Hampshire and the surrounding counties. Les had uncovered that the increased number of 'random' attacks and deaths – the ones with an air of 'vampire' about them – were not only confined to Sophia's vicinity. They were happening within a thirty-mile radius of where they were.

"Does this mean it's nothing to do with me after all?" she asked.

"Your house is bang in the middle of those thirty miles; I'm afraid you're very much a crux of things; we're just no closer to knowing why." Les passed her a typed sheet of paper. "I ran your family name, Auclair, through some searches. While the main channels don't bring up anything too unusual, the dark web did."

"My family name is on the dark web?"

"My dear, anything that is taboo, hidden, supernatural, or criminal is on the dark web."

She looked at the sheet he'd handed her.

"The name is tied to a radical Catholic group called the Resurrectors."

"Oh, I've heard of them! I have a book, but I haven't read that part yet." She stood to retrieve it from her handbag. "There was some interesting stuff in here about the origins of vampires being tied in with angels."

Daniel let out a small huff. "An extremely outlier theory – even the church denounced it."

"That's what this book says, and that they also shunned and later persecuted the Resurrectors. But think about it – the surname, my mum's crucifix – maybe my parents and grandparents were part of the Resurrectors group."

"I think that's highly likely," Les agreed. "It seemed the Resurrectors believed in the vampire's angelic origins, and also that, because the vampire descended *from* the angel, there would one day be a vampire that would rise back into its true angelic form, paving the way for all vampires to return home in their original make up."

"Home?"

Les shrugged. "Heaven, I'm guessing."

"That's the reason for the crucifix." Sophia glanced at it, still on the floor in that far corner of the living room. "I asked my mum about it when I was little – why wear Jesus dying on the cross? She said it was about resurrection, not death."

"Many Catholics believe that."

"Right, but if my mum was one of these Resurrectors, her words would have held different meaning. I remembered more things. After burning that vampire, I remembered my mum saying something to me about my blood being special and that people might want to steal it."

Daniel swore softly under his breath. "I don't want to be disrespectful, Sophia, but it all has the markings of fanaticism. These Resurrectors sound like the kind of cult who might sacrifice an innocent child to save mankind, believing it a justified means to an end."

Sophia's stomach turned. Her mother *had* thrown her out a window. But that was because she'd been trying to save her from a fire, wasn't it?

She felt Daniel tense in his seat. His nostrils flared, and she swore she felt his body heat rise despite there being a foot between them. She was about to ask him what was wrong when another voice joined the conversation. "And your point would be so valid if you hadn't staked a child just two nights ago to save a lot of potential future deaths."

Jacque stood in that same corner of the living room the necklace was lying.

They all sat there, stock still, looking at him.

Sophia then glanced at Daniel. God, the air between the two men was as heavy as iron. And heady with anguish. "Daniel, the boy – does he mean my neighbour?"

His eyes flicked to hers, then back to Jacque. "I'm sorry, Sophia. He had been turned, just like Pierce."

"How the blazing heck did he get in?" asked Les, darting his eyes around the living room.

Jacque's eyes bore into Daniel's as if waiting for *him* to answer that question. Which he did. "Different vampires have different skills. One of Jacque's is ... mist."

Sophia's mouth dropped open as she swung back around to

Daniel. "Mist? As in ... *what*? Like in Bram Stoker's book? He can turn to *mist*?"

Daniel looked away, pensively. "Yes, it's rare amongst us, but exactly like that. He can seep into any building through its gaps and cracks."

Jacque took one step forward out of the shadows, his piercing gaze still on Daniel, his voice low and implausibly sensual. "I can seep into anything that offers me an opening."

A thick and heated silence followed as Sophia's mind threw her an image of exactly what that meant.

Les gathered his papers and stood. "Well, that's me out of here for the night."

What? No! "Les," she hissed.

He was already half way to the door, key in hand. "I'll be one floor up if you need anything."

"*Les.*" She rose from the table and all but accosted him at the door. "You're leaving me alone with these two?" she whispered.

He opened the door, and although his look was apologetic, it was nowhere near sorry enough. "Been here before, done that before, and I'm old, luv – way too old for this shit. I daresay a little bit of your femininity might not hurt the situation. You'll be fine – keep your wits about you." The door shut and he was gone.

When she turned back around, Jacque had made his way to the dining table, her mother's pendant resting on a purple silk handkerchief he held in his hand. Daniel was avoiding his gaze with gusto and they were really going to have to have this out if she was going to survive any amount of time with this tension in the room. Part of her had felt angry about what Jacque had done to Daniel, but it had been over two centuries ago – surely lessons had been learned – and he'd gone and saved her life earlier.

And she was not unaffected by *either* man's presence – Daniel's she was fast-learning the ins and outs of. Jacque's was a riddle.

He placed the handkerchief, with the pendant, in the middle of the table. "Can you feel that? The enmity for our species emanating from the metal?"

"Hard not to," replied Daniel.

Jacque looked at her and beckoned with one finger. "Come."

Before her mind could even protest that autocratic command, her feet obeyed. *What the fuck?* Did that kind of subtle dominance come with the age of the vampire? Why was it so hard to resist it? To even initially *notice* it used upon her?

Very inappropriately, her brain chose that moment to remind her she'd done the same thing in the throes of lust last night when Daniel had demanded she open her legs wider for him. Equal parts arousal and humiliation coursed through her at her badly timed recollection.

Daniel noticed the shift in her – his eyes flashed to her, although she couldn't read his expression.

If Jacque noticed, he didn't give anything away. "Objects have no power on their own," he stated. "The power comes from the strength of its bearer, or, in your case, the strength of the lineage the object is tied to."

"The Resurrectors?"

"Yes. Your family were Resurrectors – your mother's side, especially, has a stronger ancestral tie to the group. This is what happens if I touch this crucifix." Before anyone could stop him, he lay his palm upon it. They *heard* his skin singe.

Daniel flinched.

Smoke from burnt flesh rose towards the ceiling and Sophia wrinkled her nose against the memory that smell conjured.

"Stop." Daniel gripped Jacque's wrist.

Their eyes locked, and Jacque lifted his hand. Now looking at Sophia, he slid the handkerchief and crucifix towards her. "Pick it up. If you look down the side of the pendant, nestled between where the two arms of the cross meet, you'll see a catch. It's small, but it's there."

In surprise, she studied him, but he looked dead serious. She picked it up and did as he instructed. She missed it the first time – the catch was almost imperceptible. "I think I see it."

"Flick it. I'm not sure which way it goes."

Meeting his eyes again, he nodded.

It was hard to grip the catch, it was so small, but she managed to get her thumbnail against it. It took a couple of attempts, but she finally felt it give under her push and—

She shrieked and almost dropped it when two wings came flying out, one on either side of the cross.

"Good," said Jacque. "Place it back on here."

She put it on the silk cloth, all three of them peering down on it. The arms of the cross were completely obliterated by the metal wings. The dying man had become an angel.

"The resurrection. The ascension back to heaven. The vampire becomes the angel once more."

Daniel spoke first. "No wonder the church went ballistic. Are you telling me the Resurrectors believed Jesus Christ was a vampire?"

"No, no, no, look more closely at the figure on the cross."

Only Sophia dared to put her head down close enough. Daniel obviously didn't want a burnt nose.

"Look very carefully," pressed Jacque.

After about ten seconds, she gasped. "He's got fangs. Either side of his mouth are the smallest etchings, and there's no blood falling from the crown of thorns, but there *are* two blood lines that trail down the sides of his mouth."

"Exactly. Two bloodlines. That of the angel and that of what the angel became: the vampire. This is not Christ on the cross, this is a vampire hidden in the guise of Christ so the Resurrectors could wear the symbol and hide their beliefs in front of everyone. Now"—he moved the handkerchief an inch towards Daniel—"lay your palm on it."

They both stared at him like he was joking.

He wasn't. His tone dropped to the most seductive, caring whisper she'd ever heard from anyone's mouth. "Deiniol Evans, lay your palm upon the cross."

Daniel's breath hitched and Les was wrong – whatever passed through the two males at that moment was *way* beyond her and nothing her presence had any say in.

She suspected if she had a sire, there might be a similar flow of whatever this was. She really wasn't sure she ever wanted to experience it. All-consuming was an understatement.

Without dropping his gaze, Daniel lifted his hand and placed it on the pendant.

After a moment of absolutely nothing happening, his breath whooshed out in relief.

Sophia shook her head in wonderment. "The wings have taken the power of the cross away."

"Not the wings, but the *belief* in them," replied Jacque. "This pendant now becomes a symbol of the rise to heaven; the symbol of the forgiveness of all sins – even the sins of vampires. And that," Jacque concluded, his gaze still firmly on his progeny's face, "is the power of forgiveness."

Chapter Sixteen

"Oooohh, Anthony!" The naughtiness was electrifying. Anthony had come to the library straight from his session today, still in his cassock and collar. She'd shut the library an hour ago and Abigail didn't have long before he returned to his church for his 7 p.m. mass. She hadn't been expecting to see him today, but he'd phoned her just four hours ago, shortly after she'd received the horrendous news about Pierce, telling her he'd desperately missed her and he needed to see her as soon as possible.

With his mouth sucking on her bare left breast, she felt his hard-on against her thigh as she leaned back on the table in the staff room. Third base had still not been reached, but she'd acquired four more bottles of holy water and she couldn't complain about how second base felt. Over and over again.

"You are definitely a creature of God, Abigail. You're stunning."

She sighed as he moved his attention to her other breast.

"Are you *sure* your friend said she wasn't going to be back today?" he mumbled against her flesh.

"Sophia? Yes, I told you – she had an emergency. Not even sure she'll be in tomorrow if you want to visit again?" she asked, hopefully.

"But she's still going to the party on Friday, right?"

Frowning slightly through her lazy lust, she pulled her head up to stare at her illicit boyfriend. He'd mentioned Sophia more than once tonight. She sort of wished she hadn't told him about the fun she'd had with her Saturday night. Everyone always latched onto the idea of her having a friend as if she was lonely and dependent on others. Just because she worked in a library and had never been as popular and outgoing as other girls. It was so annoying. "She said she was, but honestly, I wouldn't blame her if she didn't after what she's been through today." She gasped as his tongue flicked her nipple.

"Make sure she comes, Abigail." He looked up at her, his dark brown eyes imploring. "For *your* sake. I can't stand the thought of having to act like I don't know you on Friday, or you being there alone, having to put up with that."

She sighed, partly over how talented he was with her breasts and partly because she couldn't shake a niggle she had over the party. It just wasn't going away, but she had no idea what the root of that niggle was.

It was Anthony that had suggested she ask her work colleague to go with her – just over a week ago he'd brought it up. She'd been more than surprised. She wasn't sure she'd even brought up Sophia's name – she rarely talked about work with him – but he'd told her some from the church had been invited, himself included, and he didn't want her there with no support given he'd have to ignore her.

"Especially with the bishop there. We have a ceremony planned for everyone – even if I *could* be with you, I wouldn't be able to due to the planning and then the ritual itself."

"Ritual?"

He gave her boob a last kiss and pulled himself up, much to her disappointment. "Part of the ceremony."

"But surely not everyone there is going to be Catholic?" Her parents were. And quite strictly so. It was part of the reason she'd wanted out of that house as soon as she could. That and the sometimes strange atmosphere of the grand stately home. She loved them – well, not so much her mother – but she had needed her freedom and independence, and to be able to live a life *away* from under their often disapproving noses. It had not escaped her that her rather wanton interactions with her priest-in-training might very well be *because* they would disapprove – a huge metaphorical 'fuck you' to them because living on her own, she *could* do what she wanted and they had no say.

"The ceremony is for those who align with it."

"Oh." That seemed obvious, yet it had sounded strangely cryptic when he'd said it.

She sat up and pulled her bra straps back on, adjusting the band around her, and then put on her blouse. "Am I going to see you again before Friday?"

"I'm not sure. I'm to speak to the Right Reverend Colin Faramount as soon as possible to get my schedule for Friday. Until then, I won't know how much time I'll need to prepare."

She had no idea who all these people were and often forgot after he told her. There were too many names and titles. "Is he the one who ... er..."

"My mentor, Abigail. He's the bishop for most of Hampshire."

"Aaah." Yeah – no idea.

He smoothed his cassock down after he'd gathered his satchel. "It was so good to see you, Abigail." He flashed her his cheekiest smile – she adored that smile, dimples and all. "I've missed you. Let me know if Sophia can't come on Friday, all right?"

Honestly, it was almost as if his reason for seeing her was solely to make sure her colleague was coming – it was weird.

"I'll be fine either way, Anthony. It's my parents' home after all. I'm certainly not going to force her if she's grieving." She had told him about Pierce's death, but only because he'd asked about Sophia's whereabouts as soon as he'd arrived – he hadn't wanted her to spot them together. Still, it felt like he'd asked about Sophia a lot today. If he were anyone else, Abi would have wondered if he secretly fancied her, but he hadn't even met her.

"I just want you to have a good time on your birthday.

You're special to me, Abigail."

She returned his smile. "You're special to me, too. You know..." She studied him, trying to gauge his potential reaction to what she was about to say. "I read that most churches, even Catholic ones, are all right nowadays with priests having wives; even committed relationships if it's been going on for a few years. Is that something you might consider speaking to your bishop about?" She really didn't want this to be a secret for too much longer, as fun as the secret was at times.

His smile faded, and he drew her in for a kiss and a hug. "I told you from the beginning this thing between us can't be known."

"I know, but it's been three months now and it's more than a 'thing', isn't it? I mean, I really like you."

He squeezed her harder. "And I *adore* you." He dropped a firm kiss on her lips. "I have to go now, I'm sorry. I can't be late for mass."

"Okay." She tamped down her disappointment. "Let me know if I can see you before Friday."

"I will, as soon as I know."

She walked with him to the front and unlocked the double doors, refraining from sighing out loud when he peeped out of the door and looked both ways and all around before practically tiptoeing out of the building.

Locking up after him, she finally let out that sigh and went to gather her own things. She'd text Sophia later to see if she was coming in to work tomorrow. She could hold the fort if not. *Poor Sophia*. What a terrible week for her.

Her mobile phone rang as she turned off all the lights. The landline for her parents' house flashed across her display. "Hi," she answered.

"Abi, darling!"

"Mum, hi. How are things?"

"Good, sweetie. I just wanted to make sure you have everything you need for Friday. The chauffeur's name is Brian. He should be picking you and your friend up from the library at around six o'clock."

"That early? I'll have to close the library an hour before I should so we can get ready." And then, she paused. "How did you know I was bringing a friend?"

Her mother made that dismissive noise she always made when she thought Abi was being silly. "You mentioned you might weeks ago."

She had? She couldn't remember.

"And I was so glad you did," she continued. "I never hear you talk about your friends."

"Well, there's a chance she might not be able to come after all – she's had a personal emergency today and depending on how it—"

"Oh, Abi," her mother cut in, sharply, on an intake of breath, "no, no, she *must* come."

"Er—"

"It will be a wonderful evening and it will help her get her mind off her problems, I'm sure. Plus, it's your birthday." Then, after a pause, "And I've already given the caterers the exact number of guests."

"I'm sure one less won't—"

"You *must* let me know if she can't come so I can let them know straight away. But try and persuade her if you can."

What the— first Anthony and now her mum? Were they all maybe in on a birthday surprise for her? She didn't think Sophia had ever met her mum, or Anthony, but it *would* be like her to reach out and offer some kind of surprise. However, it was definitely *not* like her mother to agree to it.

As odd as her mother was acting, her mother's demanding nature was extremely familiar, and birthday surprise or not, she really didn't want to encourage it. "Fine." It was time to end the conversation. "Say hi to Dad for me, okay?"

"I will, darling. Call me if you need anything before the big night."

"I will. 'Bye." She hung up, not wanting to be rude, but she suddenly couldn't wait to get back to the comfort of her own home. What a bloody weird hour it had been.

She was about to head out when she heard a clatter near one of the shelves in the fiction area. If that had come from the basement, she'd have run out those front doors as fast as possible. But she'd never felt fearful of the bright, airy upstairs. Knowing she'd forget to look for it in the morning, she made her way over to see if anything important had fallen and eventually spied a book on the floor in the horror section. *Of course. My favourite section,* she thought, wryly.

Picking it up, she pulled a face at the blonde, buxom lady portrayed on the front cover, screaming as she ran from some shadowy figure behind her who emerged from a gloomy looking mansion. *Murder at the Stately Home.*

Abigail snorted at the title and slipped the book back where it belonged. Knowing her, if she *had* to be around her mother for too long, that was exactly how her night was going to go.

Daniel had disappeared to feed early (and she suspected to get away from whatever Jacque-induced emotions were churning through him). Jacque had disappeared because he'd gotten a phone call he had to follow up on. Both men had told her they'd be back within two hours, and Sophia opened a living room window to breathe in the fresh air.

Jacque had told them he'd looked into the Bratvashka's appearance. They considered themselves law-keepers, even if working on the fringe. He didn't think they were responsible for murdering Sophia's neighbours, the attack in the bridleway, or the random killings around the county. The Bratvashka just didn't kill that way.

He had then inspected the fang she'd found and concluded that the woman in the bridleway had been a 'common' vampire – unlikely one of the Brastvashka, although the vampires with her may well have been the Bratvashka observing Sophia's movements. 'Common' vampires were your 'average Joe' vampires, turned from human, that made up most of the vampiric population.

Most of the other attacks all had the hallmark of the Hupogeios species of vampire – the very same that had attacked and tried to turn Pierce – a race that lived underground, never mingled with human beings unless to feed or turn, and had little in the way of an evolved vampiric system of rules. They were primordial beings still very much led by their basic needs and instincts. They only came to the surface in such numbers when chaos or some kind of dark energy attracted them. He felt they were responsible for most of the 'random' attacks in that thirty-mile radius around her, but not the child next door to her.

Turning a child was a vampiric no-no, and generally, vampires stuck ruthlessly to their rules because to break them could topple an already delicate system that kept them alive (or undead) and unseen. Since the child had told Daniel he'd been *instructed* to enter her home, Jacque felt a common vampire had sired him – one who wanted to get at Sophia and didn't much care for vampiric laws. Who the hell that would be, Sophia had no idea, but she all at once remembered feeling watched that night and shivered at the thought.

Sophia's phone sounded. She turned away from the window and dipped into her bag to pull it out. It was from Abigail: **Today went well. I hope you're doing okay. Let me know if**

you need tomorrow off too, it's never that busy on a Wednesday and I'll be fine. I'm so sorry you're going through this. xx

With a smile, she hit reply: **You're amazing, thank you. I think I'd like to come in – keep my mind off things. I just needed this afternoon off because of the shock of it all. xx**

Of course. I totally get it. And if you decide to back out of the party on Friday, that's okay too. Xx

No way. I'm going to need a highlight to get me through the week! We are going to the party :)

Abi replied with a smiley face, and Sophia put her phone away.

The box with her history in had been placed along the left wall of the living room after they'd looked through it. Glancing at it now, she felt a strange sense of belonging she'd never felt before, but the confounding realisation was that it did not come from the box or its contents – it came from being here. It came from Daniel; it even came from Jacque and the mountains of knowledge he clearly had, and the mystery of the pendant solved. It came from the inevitable need to unpack her past and identity, and the fact she wasn't doing it alone. It came from an intrinsic understanding they seemed to have of her.

Her thoughts turned to Pierce, and a lump formed in her throat. She'd had to sneak out of the house and leave him *not* turned to dust owing to his incomplete transformation, with a gaping hole in his chest. She *couldn't* be seen with him given her picture was already in the paper because of the murder of her neighbours. She wondered if he'd been found yet. She wondered if his ex-wife and children had been told the news.

A motion near the window pulled her out of her thoughts,

but her startlement quickly turned to awe and intrigue as a purple haze floated in, condensing, eventually filling out and up before it solidified completely. Jacque stretched his shoulders and neck out, then nodded to her in greeting, looking slightly bemused by the expression on her face.

"How do you *do* that?" Feeding, bonding, turning, all-consuming jealousy and need ... she'd gotten a handle on those, even if not comfortable with them, but *mist*? It was still daylight outside, although the sun could only be seen from the gaps through trees from this side of the apartment. "Do you avoid being burnt by the sun if you're mist?"

"Oh, I can still get burnt," he smiled. "But only one particle at a time."

That ripped a hearty laugh from her and his smile became a grin which was more than bewitching. He placed himself on the sofa next to her, arms stretched out across its back, the ankle of his right leg crossing his left at the knee, all with the air of royalty. His expression was one of self-satisfaction with a hint of haughty, and Sophia had to clamp down another laugh as her heart found a soft spot for the resplendent male beside her – she'd seen the same expression on her cat.

"You're back early," she said instead, although she failed to completely keep the laughter out of her voice.

"The information I was given turned out to be swift. A couple of months ago, I was invited to an event taking place this Friday evening – the estate hosting it has a history with the Auclairs. I wasn't going to attend, but given your appearance in my life, perhaps I should."

"My appearance in *your* life. And here I was thinking you appeared into mine."

His smile faded a fraction, a mild sorrow seeping across his features. "Perhaps after learning more about me, that perspective might change, ma chérie. In any case, I was trying to find out more about the estate itself: Bannerman House."

"Wait ... out near Arundel?"

"I believe it is."

"I've been invited, too."

He raised an eyebrow. "Well, that *is* interesting."

"Not for any strange reason, though. My work colleague, Abigail – the house belongs to her parents. I get the impression her relationship with them is strained. She didn't want to go alone, so she invited me."

"Not for any strange reason?" Now, both eyebrows were raised. "You are a *direct descendant* of the Auclairs and the estate has a history with them."

"Can't some things just be coincidence?"

"Along with two of your neighbours and an ex-lover dead within sixteen hours of each other? Non, ma chérie, I don't think so."

"Why do you call me that?" she snapped back, annoyed the one good thing she was looking forward to might be thwarted.

His smile returned, along with that very strange sorrow, but he said nothing. He just looked deeply into her; *intensely* into her.

"Why have *you* been invited?" she asked, mostly to break his gaze. It was still frustrating she had no idea why he, and his eyes especially, seemed so familiar to her. But when she tried to dig out the reason, it was as if her mind blocked the pathway to it; like when forcing yourself to remember a dream just pushes it further away.

Her question broke nothing. He continued to hold her gaze and try as she might, she couldn't pull away from it. *Bloody vampires.*

"Because, Sophia, I have a long and complicated history with the Auclairs."

A sudden memory bloomed and she couldn't tell if it was

triggered by what he'd just said, or by the blue of his eyes; the same, unearthly blue as the sky in her vision now. The most beautiful golden gates towered against the sky; birds she'd never seen before – there were iridescent ones and translucent ones – flew with such grace it brought tears to her eyes, and a gust of wind took her. A gust of wind created on the wave of a wing – a huge, white wing...

She took in a breath as she came back to the room, although she hadn't completely landed. Jacque's eyes still held her there, wherever that beautiful place was, his expression so filled with an unfathomable peace that a swell of love washed over her. And she knew, all at once, he'd seen it too; he'd *been* there, too.

The front door opened and Daniel walked through. And stopped dead in his tracks.

She wasn't sure what he saw from his perspective – although her leaning towards Jacque with her hand on his thigh, such was the pull of his stare, probably didn't help – but his fangs emerged in a second.

"Oh, great," muttered Jacque, and that's all he had time for before Daniel lunged.

The sofa went backwards and Sophia shrieked as she went with it. The two vampires had already flown off it, catapulting across the living room from one side to the next, a literal blur as they sparred.

"Stop it!" she yelled. Which made not a blind bit of difference. Only random gusts of wind as they flew by her clued her in on where they tumbled to next. "You're acting like *children*!"

For a moment the blur stopped and she saw Daniel on Jacque – their faces red; the veins on their temples popping – his hands full of his collar while Jacque held him off, his own teeth bared.

Daniel roared. "You couldn't help yourself, you bastard!"

"Deiniol, your head's as soft as your heart."

"She's not yours!"

"She's more mine than yours."

Really? "Standing *right* here belonging to myself, thank you!" she shouted.

She was ignored. The blur resumed as they threw each other across the room.

With her own small, very human growl, Sophia stormed to the dining table, grabbed her crucifix, folded its wings back in, then raced towards their forms as best as she could holding it out and hoping to god they were fast enough to stop themselves crushing her between them. *Or* actually getting burnt.

Their shapes took form in front of her and stilled. Clutching each other, they both side-eyed the crucifix.

Sophia didn't waste her moment. "*Never* have I seen such a ridiculous display in my life. And you both think you're going to protect me? *You*"—she swung the pendant towards Daniel and he flinched—"did *not* see what you think you saw and even if you did, this is the *least* mature way to handle it this side of the galaxy. And *you*"—she swung it towards Jacque who blinked—"should not be taunting him given what you did to him two centuries ago, and *both* of you are old enough to know better."

They didn't move an inch.

"Let each other go *now*."

They both dropped the other. Jacque sniffed and folded his collar down. Daniel took a step towards her. "Sophia—"

"Nuh-uh-uh." She thrust the cross in front of his eyes.

He inhaled sharply and took a step back.

"This is going around my neck now"—she put it on and did the clasp up—"and it's not coming off until *I'm* good and ready because guess what – I'm not *either* of yours." And with her own angry hiss to seal that proclamation, she stormed into the bedroom and slammed the door behind her.

Chapter Seventeen

She loved the cemetery because it was quiet and beautiful. Grown-ups argued so much when they were alive. No one argued when they were dead. And the dead didn't hurt you.

Sophia wasn't supposed to wander out this far on her own even though she could see her house perfectly fine – she really wasn't that far away from it. But it was also darker now. The sun had set. She hadn't noticed. She only noticed now.

Mum and Dad had told her several times to always watch the sun go down from inside the house. She usually obeyed, but she wasn't enjoying the party at the house tonight. Relatives were visiting; some of them didn't like her. She heard them arguing, and she was sure they were arguing about her, too, even though she didn't understand everything they were saying.

She didn't want to go back, but she'd stayed out way too long, so she started to run towards the house, knowing she'd be in big trouble if they found out. She crept under the fence where the cemetery ended and found the path that would lead all the way to the house. A loud fluttering noise and an eerie, high-pitched squeak, heightened her fear.

Legs appeared in front of her. Sort of floated to the ground. Legs with big, black shoes at the end of them.

With a small whimper, she stopped and looked up. They belonged to a big man – way bigger than her daddy – with black hair and a scary smile. She didn't like his smile at all. His eyes were also black – so black they looked a bit like holes in his face.

She blinked and stepped back. It was like the holes were trying to push their way inside her so they could make holes in her own head. That was also scary, but it made her feel angry too.

"What's the hurry, sweetheart?" the big man said with the smile that was not a real smile.

She said nothing. She didn't want him to know where she was going, or that she lived in that house. But her eyes betrayed her – she couldn't help but look towards it.

The man noticed. "Aaah – you're Sophia Auclair, aren't you?"

She clamped her mouth shut.

"I've heard a lot about you." The holes he had for eyes seemed to gleam. Then, he got down on one knee so he was the same height as her (nearly, anyway). He was trying to act like a friend, but Sophia knew he was only pretending. Friends didn't try to make her eyes and head hurt like he was.

The angry feeling she had billowed and got hotter, like a fire churning in her belly – lower than her belly – and if he didn't stop it now, she knew it would get so hot it would need to jump out of her. That had nearly happened earlier today. "Stop doing that," she warned.

"But Sophia, sweetheart, I only want us to be friends." He laid his hand on hers.

She hissed at him. Or maybe it was the fire inside her that did.

He looked astounded for a moment, and then laughed. It was a mean and greedy laugh. He looked like he wanted to eat her. "So it's true. It's true what they say about you – about your blood."

She didn't know what he meant, but it didn't matter because her blood was roaring in her ears, boiling all the way up because of the fire. She hissed again, and this time, he grabbed both her arms hard. It hurt a lot and she was sure she'd have bruises.

He opened his mouth and two of his teeth grew long – really, really long.

She wanted to run, but couldn't move because of his grip, but also because of the burning feeling inside her. If she moved, she'd explode. She needed *to explode.*

The man suddenly grunted and jerked, and then he sort of fell apart in front of her. He was no longer holding her tightly, but she still couldn't move. She was shaking. The burning feeling wasn't going away.

"Didn't bloody like him anyway," someone said. Another man. The one who had made the bad man go poof. "Sophia, your mother sent me to find you."

She wanted to speak, and she wanted her mum to know she was okay, but she was scared if she opened her mouth, the fire would come out.

"I'm not going to hurt you. Sophia, look at me. I can help you."

A small whimper escaped her. It scared her. Any movement she made scared her.

"I can help it feel better inside you. But you need to look at me."

With every effort she had, she looked at the man in front of her, also kneeling, also smiling, but this smile was a real one, not a pretend one. She looked past his mouth and met his eyes and … held on. Held onto the blue colour that looked like an ocean and felt like water pouring over fire. He didn't push like the other man; he pulled. Pulled her in and she wanted to go wherever he was taking her. She did feel better – a lot better. Better than she had been all day, and every hot bit inside her was no longer hot.

She smiled back, happiness bubbling up instead of fire.

That's when he blinked and looked away. She was almost disappointed, but the happy feeling was too good to feel sad, so she wasn't sad. In a wave of gratitude, and following that happy feeling, she wrapped her arms around his neck in a hug.

He let out a small laugh and lifted her up as he stood. "I'm going to carry you back to the house, all right? Your mother was worried."

"Will she be angry? I didn't mean to stay out so long."

"I'll have a word with her. Don't worry about it."

She liked him and she felt safe. She didn't even feel this safe when Daddy carried her.

"I thought I was going to explode the bad man," she confided.

"Ah, no big loss, sweetheart. I exploded him first."

She giggled at what he'd said, but also put a hand over his mouth.

He glanced at her, looking a bit worried, but she didn't think he was really *worried. "Sorry, that was a bad joke, wasn't it?"*

She shook her head. "The bad man called me sweetheart."

"I see. How about I call you something else. Where I come from, we sometimes call our favourite children 'ma chérie'. How does that sound?"

She giggled again. "It sounds funny."

"Funny good, or funny bad?"

"I like it," she nodded.

"Good." They reached the front door of her house. "Well, ma chérie, shall I knock, or do you want to do it?"

"Me!" She was never usually tall enough to reach the lion-head knocker, but with him carrying her, she could.

"Go ahead."

She lifted it, feeling strong because it was so heavy, and knocked.

Sophia woke with a start, blinking back tears.

Knocking...

"Don't forget, don't forget..." she whispered. Her hand went straight to her head, then dropped to her heart. "Jacque." The dream – no, the *memory* lingered. It wasn't fading away. And there was more – she knew there was more.

Knocking...

In the dark, she stared toward the door.

"Sophia ... please?"

Daniel was knocking on the door.

The evening's events came back to her. She'd stomped in here, furious, and had fallen asleep – hadn't meant to, but the emotional day from finding Pierce to – hell, *everything* – had obviously got the best of her.

Pulling herself out of bed, she went to open the door.

Daniel stood on the other side of it looking more than forlorn.

She cocked her head at him. "What time is it?"

"Ten o'clock."

She'd been in here two hours. "You could have just walked in – it's your bedroom."

"I didn't want to invade your privacy after what you said." He looked warily down to her chest.

So did she. Ah – the necklace. She reached behind her neck for the clasp.

"You don't have to take it off. I mean, if you feel safer with it on."

She rolled her eyes. "I'm not *scared* of you, Daniel. I was angry because of the way you were both acting. It was completely unnecessary. I don't want to wear it anymore." She moved past him into the living room and placed the cross in her box of belongings. "Is Jacque here?"

He shook his head. "He thought it best I iron things out with you first. He'll be back tomorrow evening."

She couldn't hide her disappointment.

Daniel obviously noticed because *he* couldn't hide the scowl that briefly crossed his face.

She scowled back. "Nothing happened between us."

"I know," he replied. "He said before he left and I believe him."

"Did he also tell you what he told me just before you walked in?"

"No. He said he'd brief all of us on more of what he knows tomorrow."

Damn it. She couldn't wait until tomorrow – not after that memory. "I know him, Daniel. He was there in my house when I was a child. Just now I had a memory while I slept. I don't remember everything – it's so frustrating how I don't – but he also knew my parents. I think he was a friend of the family or something. He told me he had a history with the Auclairs, but didn't elaborate because that's the moment you walked in."

Daniel stared at her in silence. After what seemed like an age, he sighed and sat down. "I'm not sure what to say. I know a bit of his history before me, but he never once mentioned the Auclair name. I didn't know. But why didn't he say? He's been here for a few hours today – why not just spit it out?"

"I'm not sure. Maybe he didn't want to hurt *you* any further given your reaction when he's around me."

He had the decency to look a little sheepish.

"I know there are more memories of him, I just don't know what they are."

"I suppose we ask him tomorrow, then."

She nodded, then went to sit next to Daniel. "When are you both going to sort things out?"

Silence.

"He obviously wants you to forgive him."

"He *turned* someone I loved and wanted to sire myself. What he did was despicable."

"I agree. And I don't know what drove him to do it, but if it was anything like what drove *you* to attack him today..." She let that sentence hang. "I think he has a good heart."

Daniel glanced at her through furrowed brows. "You haven't got all your memories of him yet."

"True." She suddenly hoped beyond hope she didn't come

across a bad one. If she'd felt *that* happy and close to him on that night she'd recollected, any betrayal she learned of would be hard to bear.

Shuffling closer to Daniel, she lay her head on his arm. "I'm sorry I shouted at you both."

The side of his lip turned up. "And I'm sorry I behaved badly."

"Is Deiniol your birth name? That's what Jacque calls you, isn't it?"

He nodded. "It's Welsh for Daniel. After living for so long and travelling so much, and then the English language becoming so much more dominant, it just became easier to use Daniel. But Jacque has always called me Deiniol – it's how he knew me."

They sat in the quiet of each other's thoughts for a while, reminiscing of times gone.

"I've never felt so much before, Daniel. I've been somewhat detached from the world and from people my whole life. I adore my adopted parents, but also remember the day I met them; not really had any close friends. I'm not sure I've ever loved, or really know what love is. I thought it was because of the fire and having to grow up without my family, or because of witness protection, or losing the first six years of my life ... but it could be because *I'm* different, couldn't it? Because I might not be totally human? Could it be because I'm not supposed to be around humans at all? After all, I feel more being with you, and even Jacque in that memory, than I ever have with any person. Even the crippling jealousy that flashes through me is more than the detachment I've carried."

He leaned in and kissed her cheek.

"I blamed Pierce for everything that happened between us, but now, I wonder if I sought out a man I couldn't be with because I didn't know how to be close to anyone." She turned in her seat to face him. "It was different with you from the moment

I saw you; from the moment I *touched* you. You made me *feel*. Am I supposed to be with a vampire?"

"I have no idea, Sophia. I don't know what you are. But vampires do have some choice, you know. I've been with human women as well as vampires."

"Amelia?"

"Yes."

"Did you share your blood with her?"

"I did. I was already in love with her and willing to make that commitment. With her being a human in my world it allowed me to know when she might be in danger."

"Like you sensed earlier today with me."

"I don't know why it's so strong between us when we have not shared blood."

"Except..."

He looked at her, his eyes slightly glazed with want. "Except?"

"Two nights ago, I dreamt you bit me; that you drank from me. Right here." She palmed the spot on the left side of her neck. "And I can still feel the bite. It heats up when you're near, and it burns when another man interested in me is too close."

He looked startled. "I dreamt the same two nights ago. It confused me because vampires can't dream." And then his gaze darkened. "Who's been interested in you?"

She ignored that last question, sucking her bottom lip in thought. "I think I pulled you into my dream. Just like I pulled that vampire into my eyes in the car; just like Jacque can pull me into his to calm me. I had already met you and I wanted you, so I pulled you into my dream."

"You could be right. You're an anomaly, Sophia. I can't answer any of your questions, but it seems Jacque may have a lot of answers."

She stared right back at him, studying his features. "I felt like

I knew you from the moment I saw you. But I also felt like I knew Jacque the minute I saw him."

"As far as I'm aware, I've never met you before. But ... I do share your sense of familiarity – I felt the same way when I met you."

"Tell me about Jacque," she asked after a while. "About where he came from."

Daniel took in a breath and leaned back on the sofa. "I don't know too much, to be honest – he never spoke much of his own past – but I do know he was a soldier; often in battle from one place to the next."

That surprised her. "In *that* outfit?"

Daniel laughed. "At the end of the 1500s, I owned land in a wooded valley in Wales, within the Brecon Beacons. It was rich and abundant; farming was successful; food was plentiful; my family was happy."

"You had a family?"

"I did. A wife and five children – four girls and one boy. The oldest was fifteen. It was a time of relative peace when a tall, broad man with long, wild, dark blond hair and eyes the colour of the bluest forget-me-nots wandered onto my land." He chortled at the memory. "He looked like no one around our way. He introduced himself as Jacque Aubert. His last battle had been, I believe, against the Spanish Armada."

"Even though he was French?"

"Mmmm," Daniel nodded. "Human origins, to a vampire, are not always as strong as their sire's origins and over time you become quite worldly, discarding things like nationality. And before you ask, no – I have no idea who sired him.

"Jacque was ... restless. He didn't know what to do with no mission to be a part of. I'm not even sure on his exact age, but he did talk to me of being in the Knights Templar, and they were active around a thousand years ago."

"A *thousand*?"

Daniel smirked. "Perhaps you can see how it is he took to the frivolous fashion of the modern era given he may well have lived centuries, if not millennia, in armour and practical attire.

"He needed a place to stay and we needed help on the land, and we never turned soldiers away. He stayed for a year, glad for the focus of physical labour – I had no idea he was a vampire. He worked at night or in the shade. At first I felt disconcerted about that, but he would often travel into the mountains and he never failed to bring back a large kill – sometimes more than one – and we had feasts and enough meat for storage over the winter. So, I ignored the strangeness of his hours. It didn't matter as long as he did the work – it was good to have another male my age around. He also respected my family's presence and our personal and work boundaries." He laughed. "I'm certain my eldest daughter fancied the pants off him.

"One night, after he had been with us a year, we were attacked. Jacque was on one of his travels into the mountains. It was vampires that attacked us. The bubonic plague had wiped out so much of their food source, forcing them to move further from the cities, into the country, looking for anyone untouched by the disease.

"When Jacque returned, my whole family was dead."

"Daniel ... I am so—"

He waved her off. "It was over four centuries ago." But he took a moment before continuing. "I was alive by a thread, only because I had been by the well, away from the house. I was the last one attacked and Jacque's return interrupted their feed. Jacque in battle is formidable – he killed them all – five of them if my memory serves me. But too late. Too much of my blood had been drained. His choice was either to leave me to die, or turn me."

"He turned you."

"He did. And until what he did to Eliza, I was thankful for it. I grieved the loss of my family immensely, for decades, but found an entire new world. He taught me everything I knew about being a vampire. We had a peaceful life for two hundred or so years. But times change. You have to change with them. Towns change, districts change, governments change, and we could no longer stay nestled in our beautiful valley. We sold up and moved. The world grew bigger; I met others, like Eliza, remembered how it felt to love, and wanted more. You know the rest."

The air of the room was thick and heavy with the centuries that had no voice.

"But Sophia, his history with your family line, I know nothing about. His history with *you* was after I had removed myself from his life, and I know nothing about that either. The only person who can tell you is him."

Sophia needn't have worried about being late to the library. Abigail was not in yet when she arrived, which was very unlike her, but she took the opportunity to gather herself and her bearings. Her world had been turned upside down and completely transformed. She was no longer the same person she was yesterday, or the day before that, or the day before that. The only thing keeping her sane was that she had been here before, to this point where everything was taken from her and she'd had to start again. It was a weird reassurance knowing she wouldn't collapse under the weight of it all. The thing that scared her most was the fire she knew she was capable of igniting, but she now knew *two* things that calmed it: sex with Daniel and that odd hypnosis with Jacque.

She picked up the mail from the floor as she walked in, most of it junk, and one addressed to her – hand delivered.

She opened it.

Stay out of the shadows today, ma chérie.
Stand only in the sun.
We will speak later.
Jacque.

His handwriting was as elaborate as his clothes, the tail of the 'q' on his name trailing elegantly under the whole note. With a small shake of her head, she popped the note in her bag and *had* to assume he meant it metaphorically because there were very few places inside the library where the sun streamed.

The door opened behind her and Abigail walked in. "Hey, you."

"Abi!" It was genuinely good to see her after the flying testosterone of last night. They shared a hug and Abi asked her how she was.

"All in all, I'm fine. Just sad."

"You're a star for coming in today – you didn't have to." She looked incredibly tired and Sophia told her so. She shrugged. "Oh, I'm fine. Didn't sleep too well last night, but I think it was because my mother phoned earlier in the evening."

The morning continued on with chats and jokes so *normal* Sophia almost forgot vampires existed. Almost.

"Here," Abi said at break time as she held out two bottles of holy water. "These are for you – I got some last night." She winked.

Sophia laughed. "Third base?"

"Nope, but close."

This time, Sophia gladly took the bottles knowing exactly how useful they could be. They went straight into her large handbag.

An hour before closing, when the library was virtually empty, Sophia asked, "Do you mind if I go into the basement for ten minutes? I still have the key, and you can have it back today by the way."

"You can *keep* the key, honey. I'm not going in there unless forced to."

"I'm just in awe of the books."

"Go for it. I've totally got my hands full with the one customer sitting over there."

Sophia smiled and thanked her, and was halfway skipping down those stone steps before feeling apprehensive. She liked Jane, the ghost. At least, she did so far. But she never quite knew what book was going to be thrown at her next – metaphorically or literally.

Once inside, she swung the door shut behind her, but stalled a few feet into the room. Something felt different. But she wasn't sure what. "Jane?" she called out. "Are you here?"

She thought she felt a flutter of a breeze, but it was very slight and very distant. Maybe she was preoccupied. Maybe ghosts had down time, or slept, and she'd gone and interrupted her. "I'm sorry if it's a bad time. I ... don't really know if there's a good time. I'll be quick. There's a vampire called Jacque Aubert." She felt a twinge of guilt saying his name – prying in this way. But three times she'd received information from this ghost that had felt both neutral and beneficial. Out of everyone in her life right now, the ghost felt motiveless. "He may be at least a thousand years old – is there any information you can give me about him?"

Nothing rattled. Nothing thumped. Nothing moved. Sophia waited thirty more seconds, and then let the tension leave her shoulders. She couldn't tell whether she felt disappointed or relieved. *Nevermind. Worth a shot.*

But there *was* a sudden noise. She spun her head towards a

gust of wind that rattled one of the windows which lay slightly ajar. A bird fluttered somewhere outside and a single white feather hovered high in the air, just inside the window where the wind must have blown it in. Entranced, she watched as a speck of light from the sun momentarily caught its barbs, giving the feather an almost iridescent aura as it slowly glided down. Too late, she asked the crucial question, her eyes flicking back to the ajar window. *Who opened the window?*

A loud fluttering sounded *inside* the room. And a high-pitched squeak.

Startled she spun. "No." *That* noise she'd heard before – that night leaving the cemetery. Searching for the source of the sounds, her gaze landed on movement in the corners of the ceiling, near where the exposed timbers crossed. *Bats.* About six of them.

Had they always been here?

No way. I'd have noticed.

Pierce would have noticed.

He wasn't really focusing on the building at that point.

A creak, and a bang, and a book tumbled towards her with force, its cover and pages flapping wildly until it landed in front of her, open, at the beginning of a chapter page. Its heading read **RUN.**

Chapter Eighteen

That word acted like a starting pistol. She sprinted to the door only to be attacked by a flurry of wings. Shrieking and trying to protect her face, her hand found the door handle and—

Solid form.

Most of the flapping had stopped and a man stood before her, right in front of the door, with black hair, the smile of the devil himself, and eyes so black they looked like two holes in his—

"No." *God, no.* "You're dead. He killed you." Her six-year-old mind was reeling with the sight, warring with what was memory and what was reality.

Above her to the left, there was a distortion to the air, and one of the bats billowed out into another man, landing on his feet as he concluded his transformation. He looked *just* like the first man. Four more bats followed suit, all six vampires finally circling her, carbon copies of each other.

She backed away, but there was nowhere to go. Her back collided with a chest belonging to carbon copy number four or five. Her arms were grabbed and pinned behind her back, his strength formidable.

"What species of vampire are you?" It was small talk she didn't need or want to know the answer to – well, maybe she was a *little* curious – but keeping them talking meant she stayed alive for longer.

They didn't stop smiling – it was creepy as hell. "We are most commonly referred to as the Nocturnes," said the one in front of her.

"Are you always bats, or – you know – maybe swans?

Squirrels?" Spewing gibberish gave her brain time to think of escape. Unfortunately, no actual plan came to mind. She could scream for Abi, but she didn't want the poor girl to end up dead.

The one before her chuckled, humouring her. And then the one pinning her arms said, "Shall we take it in turns now or take her back to the lair?"

Lair?? Oh, HELL, no. Panic set in. "I have nothing you want."

"You have everything we *all* want." The one in front of her took one large stride forward and grabbed her face. He widened his mouth, his fangs protruded, and this was the part where Jacque had staked him.

The six-year-old in her screamed for him. Silently, anyway – she wasn't saying much with her face imprisoned in that hand.

He forced her head over to the right and bared her neck. "I do wonder," he whispered against her ear, his breath trailing down her neck, "what sunlight tastes like."

Squeezing a tear out as she shut her eyes, she braced herself for the inevitable. What she heard instead was a yelp and a thud and then *lots* of yelps and thuds.

She was released as the vampire behind her took cover, head over his face as hardback books went flying in his direction – in *every* direction.

Thank you, Jane!

She ducked, hit the floor, and belly-crawled as fast as she could towards the door.

Her ankle was grabbed, and she was dragged back, spun over, and with a roar, carbon copy number two—three?—had her pinned under him.

Not waiting for him to best her, she grabbed *his* face this time, avoiding his fangs, and rammed her two thumbs into those soulless eyes.

He wailed, snatched at her arms, and she briefly wondered if they were about to be ripped out of their sockets, when a purple haze formed between them. She could have cried with relief, but oomphed instead when the full weight of Jacque's body consolidated on hers *while* it jerked as he kicked the vampire away.

The vamp went flying the whole length of the basement.

All at lightning speed, Jacque spun, grabbed her and rolled with her, with no time to spare as four vampires *threw* themselves where they'd just been. Then he was off her and on them. The fight was a blur. The basement door flew open, but it wasn't Abi who walked in. Another woman clothed in biker gear and leathers and the biggest damn grin on her face, strode in like she owned the place, whipped out a stake from somewhere on her person and drove it into one of the blurs around Jacque. The blur solidified for two seconds, then poofed into nothing, the stake clattering on the ground where it stopped a couple of feet from Sophia.

Jacque leapt onto the wall, and before she could blink, the broad sword hanging near the door was in his hand. *That* was when she all at once saw the warrior Daniel had been talking about. With a holler, he landed back on the floor and god knew how he did it, but he drove the length of the whole fucking blade into *three* of the vampires while the other lady was fighting off the fourth.

The three bodies skewered on the sword shrieked out the most piercing noise that had Sophia wincing, then they exploded – not into dust, but into bats. Lots of bats that raced towards the window and escaped through its gap.

Jacque's eyes finally met hers.

"Look out!" she cried.

The vamp he'd kicked off her earlier landed on his back and they both tumbled to the ground in a stalemate of strength and viciousness. Jacque was against the floor, on his back, trying to ward off a broken table leg, sharp end pointed at his chest. At least it wasn't a blur of nonsensical speed. She could *see* this fight.

Sophia dove for the stake on the floor and leapt on carbon copy number one. *Literally* leapt on him, her knees trying to find purchase on his wide back. The heart was just a bit to the left, right? Ramming the stake in with all her might, she refused to think about the sound it made, the feel of flesh breaking, or the vibration of wood scraping bone. And just in case all her might wasn't good enough, she threw her own weight on the stake too. It slipped into him more; some weird 'popping' sensation rippled up the wood and through her hands, the vampire made that high-pitched shriek that had her grimacing, and then there was nothing but air beneath her.

Oh, no!

With a yelp, she fell right onto Jacque.

His arms came up around her. "Are you all right?"

Not knowing how the hell to answer that, she looked at him, astounded.

His gaze was fierce with worry, anger, something that looked like pride ... and something else she couldn't name.

"*Whoooop*!" the woman hooted, as the last vampire dissipated. She pulled back her stake and tossed it in the air in victory before catching it. "That was the most fun I've had in *ages*."

The basement door opened. "Sophia, damn you for making me come down here! Is everything okay? I heard—" Abigail stopped dead, and her eyes widened impossibly at the sight before her. Her hands went to her mouth, then dropped back down, her mouth still open. "I'm going to lose my job," she whispered.

Sophia took in her surroundings for the first time since all chaos ensued. Books lay *everywhere* – some of them *must* have been damaged – the desk in the middle of the room was broken, chairs were knocked over, two shelves at the far end of the basement had fallen, a broad sword caked in blood lay on the floor along with two stakes, three piles of dust, and a crazy biker chick stood in the centre of it all, smiling from ear to ear like this was the best day of her life.

But it was Sophia who Abi's stare landed on, a flash of anger darting across it. "*More* boyfriend problems?" she snarked.

Boyfriend what? She snapped her head back to Jacque. Having taken everything else in, she'd failed to include the spectacle she must also look, meshed against him on the floor, legs entwined, his arms around her— "No! Abi, no, no, no." She tried to jump off him, but for some reason, couldn't.

His arms remained exactly where they were.

She slapped them. "Get *off*."

"Oh – sorry." He released her.

She jumped to her feet. "Abi, I can explain." Except she really couldn't explain.

Abigail waited.

"Er..."

"That was the *best* rehearsal ever, guys!" threw in the woman she still didn't know the name of.

Everyone glanced at her in bewilderment.

"Romeo and Juliet. I'm so sorry," she continued, "Sophia had no idea we were coming – we surprised her, too."

Oh, so she knows my *name?*

"But Friday's nearly here and we needed to go through the play again for the party."

Whoa! Jacque told her about the party at Abi's house? She wondered how much this woman actually knew.

Jacque, now sitting up, threw her a look of warning.

She totally ignored it. "Our original Juliet dropped out, but we can't cancel last minute and it was suggested we speak to Sophia about stepping in and—"

"Oh, my god!" That was Abigail, anger taking over all her features now as she addressed the woman. "Did my *mother* put you up to this? She did, didn't she?"

"Well..." started the woman.

And Abigail took the bait, nodding. "She told you not to say anything, right? This is her way of making sure Sophia comes to the party no matter what. Unbelievable!"

"She's *very* persuasive," the woman agreed.

Jacque shook his head at the ceiling.

Sophia tried to gauge Abi's reaction. "Abi, I'm so sorry. I'm—"

"*Don't* apologise for her, she's a narcissist and she knows it – it's always about her and what she wants and she tramples over everyone to have her way. I'm so sorry she's dragged you into her life like this."

"We're happy to tidy this up for you right now," the woman consoled.

"Now? We're closing in forty-five minutes."

The woman waved a hand in the air. "We'll have it done by then."

Abi looked around the room again. "You will?" she asked, disbelievingly.

"Yeah – no problem. Sophia, we'll meet you at your car when we're done?"

Oh, you will? Eyebrows raised, Sophia looked at Jacque.

There was something of an apology in his eyes, but he nodded.

Abigail's shoulders sagged in what Sophia assumed was relief. "Oh ... if you're sure, that would be amazing. Thank you."

"Okay, great," added Sophia, although she really didn't know if it was. "I'll be up in one minute. I'm just going to ... find out exactly what your mother wants my part to be in this er ... play and then it will all be sorted."

Abi looked at her and sighed, her face scrunching up in embarrassment. "I'll bet you haven't even met my mum, right?" She looked at Sophia who shook her head. "I knew it – she orders everyone around, even remotely, and sends her cronies in to do her dirty work." She gestured at biker chick as she said that, and biker chick cocked her head, maybe contemplating what being a 'crony' might entail. "If this is some kind of weird birthday surprise you got roped into, you can say no. *Absolutely* you can say no. I hate my mum for this. She hasn't pulled something like this in ages, and I should have known the way she was harping on at me yesterday about *making sure* you came on Friday."

Jacque's head turned sharply at that. He studied Abigail.

"Abi, don't worry about it." Sophia hoped her tone was reassuring. "Just give me two secs."

"Okay." Abi nodded, then she addressed the other two. "Thanks for tidying."

"Happy to," said the grinning woman, and then Abi disappeared up the stairs.

Jacque stood, dusting himself down and rearranging his cuffs. He stared at the woman, then made a half sucking, half tutting noise in mild disapproval. "Went out on a limb there, didn't you?"

"Saved your arse and you're welcome."

Jacque harrumphed.

"We're not *really* going to put on a play, right?" asked Sophia, softly, dreading the idea. She couldn't act for toffee.

"Nah. Would be fun, though," shrugged the woman as Jacque picked up the broad sword, inspecting it with approval.

The woman smiled again, all white, dazzling teeth, as she approached Sophia. She was *actually* quite dazzling – she could see this now everything was over and she had the ability to look properly at a normal, human pace. Her eyes were a piercing blue – a much more grey shade of blue than Jacque's – her short hair was almost black, her skin a gorgeous ivory; she was well built, not tall, and despite the biker outfit, carried a classical beauty and elegance. She looked about Abigail's age.

She held out her hand in greeting.

Not wanting to be rude, Sophia took it. "Thank you for, well, helping to save my life."

"I'd have never heard the end of it if I hadn't."

Jacque threw her another admonishing look.

She was starting to like the bluntness on this woman. After having to uncover secret upon secret, it felt refreshing. "I'm Sophia."

She squeezed her hand, friendlily, as she shook it. "Oh, I know who you are Sophia Auclair."

"And you are?"

She almost wished she hadn't asked. "Eliza. Eliza Hampton."

Chapter Nineteen

An array of sensations were taking place low in Sophia's abdomen, some of which felt alarmingly like the burning she – or Daniel – had thwarted off whenever the hell that had been now: two nights ago? Three? Time was fast disappearing.

It didn't feel quite as bad or as uncontrollable as that, but the fight in the library had shot her adrenaline through the roof, Jacque's presence was igniting *things* in her that hadn't been there until her memory of him had surfaced (and she really wasn't ready to pull apart which feelings belonged to her six-year-old self, and which belonged to her adult self), her mind was still working through the new knowledge that some vampires could actually turn to bats, and the love of Daniel's life was sitting in the car behind her.

A car blasted its horn at her as she switched lanes a little too quickly.

"Awesome swerve!" exclaimed Eliza.

Jacque glared at Sophia from the passenger seat as he held his jacket up to his side window as a sun shield. "Only getting home alive will answer your questions," he bit out.

"It's not my home," she bit back. Home was long gone. The house she'd lived in four days ago was no longer her home, and her childhood home was proving to be more of a problem with every memory that surfaced, and Daniel's home ... well, she highly doubted she'd be sharing his bed tonight.

Oh, yes, and then there was the *jealousy* – that wonderful, not-at-all-inconvenient *dragon* of a feeling that ripped out the insides of all vampires and those who decided to be involved with them. She couldn't help the small growl that escaped her.

Jacque raised an eyebrow at her, then glanced back at the road, warily.

She accelerated to make it through the next set of traffic lights before they turned red and just about managed it.

Eliza made some kind of noise of approval at that. Two minutes and that woman would be reacquainting herself with the only man/vampire/person/being who had offered Sophia a world of understanding in ninety-six hours.

Better learn a new way to not set things on fire, Sophia, 'cause that boat's just sailed.

But right now, that wasn't the worst part. The worst part was the confusion of the stabbing jealousy she felt. It was impossible to know if it was because Eliza was Daniel's big love, or because she'd been sired by Jacque. And *that* pissed her off big time.

Not bothering with signalling, she swerved into the driveway that led to Daniel's underground garage and pretty much raced its circuit all the way to her designated parking bay. Slamming on her brakes, she wrenched her handbrake up and killed the engine.

Eliza whooped and clapped.

Jacque let out a curse, aimed another glare at Sophia, then swung around to Eliza. "Up the stairs for two floors; flat number three."

She was out the car in no time, bubbling over with excitement. "Thank you so much for the lift, Sophia!"

Sophia depressed her seatbelt to follow suit.

Jacque's hand gripped her arm and pulled her back. "Wait, ma chérie."

She. Let. Rip. "You don't get to call me that *ever* again – I'm not *six* anymore!"

That muted him. *Wounded* him, actually. He reeled back a bit.

"You *lied* to me; kept things from me. You should have told me you knew me; knew my family. That was the *same* breed of vampire in the library as the one you killed near the cemetery that night. *Why* didn't you *tell* me?" Tears surfaced, unbidden.

He stared at her for an age, hand still on her arm which she finally shook off, then he took a deep breath in. "How much do you remember?"

The lie was on the tip of her tongue. She wanted to tell him she remembered *everything* just to see his reaction; just to see if he'd sweat more. It was the wounded look that stopped her. That, and, she had no recollection of anything else to back up the lie. "Just that night – it came back to me in my sleep. But I know there's more and I know you're part of it."

He was clearly relieved at her reply.

"Fuck you, Jacque," she seethed. "How *dare* you keep this

from me."

"You're going to know everything by the end of the night. I wanted to do this last night, but after the way Deiniol was, it was all wrong."

"And sending Eliza up there now, after how you took her from him, is going to make things better?"

He hissed in anger. "I *never* took her from him – not in the way he thinks, and I tried to tell him that before he left and again thirty years ago. His hurt was so great, he's never been willing to listen. Maybe he'll finally listen to *her*."

That, she had not been expecting. Her heavy breathing filled the car, all her adrenaline still pumping. "You didn't?"

"No. Eliza came to *me*. She was ill. She'd just discovered she had incurable cancer of the breast."

Stunned, she fell back in her seat.

"Did Deiniol tell you we have rules about turning humans? There are exceptions to every rule, but there are three we try to always follow. One: no children because it's too cruel to be forever young, unable to experience the world fully; we don't even share blood with children. Two: never turn a human without their permission – lesser vampires might, but we bloody don't; Deiniol was my exception. Three: no ill people, especially not with something like cancer. While we cannot die or become ill from human diseases in the same way, they *can* sometimes cause complications of the blood; anomalies that are difficult to predict. Cancer cells replicate and some do so very fast. It has been known for vampires to not be able to rid it from their own bodies after drinking cancerous blood. It does not kill them, but it's forever inside them as undead as the vampire it now inhabits, which makes it hard to form blood bonds going forward and to live a satisfying life as a vampire.

"Eliza was aware of this. They had previously discussed Deiniol siring her, but she did not want to harm his blood, and because she knew me well enough to know I'm not always afraid of breaking the rules, she asked me. I'm far older than Deiniol, so she was hoping my blood could take the disease without causing harm to myself, which it can – I was not harmed. She never told him. And I didn't tell him because I *knew* he would insist on siring her anyway and neither Eliza nor I wanted him to suffer as a consequence."

Something tickled Sophia's hand. She looked down to find it was her own tear drop.

"I was reluctant to turn her. A newling vampire needs to be nurtured by their sire for damn near a century at least, and I wasn't sure Deiniol would be able to cope with my part in that. But I knew how much they loved each other. I vowed in my mind to return her to him a hundred years later, but his heart has never healed enough to hear me out. Yesterday, and today, is the third time I've tried reaching out to him, and Eliza was strong enough to come herself today – to meet him herself."

She had no words. None at all. She just shook her head.

"And, selfishly on my part, I would like her there to calm him – to be his rock – after your memories return to you. And after he understands my part in your life."

She met his eyes, a realisation dawning. "How did you know I needed help at the library today? *And* at Pierce's place yesterday?"

He let the silence sit there, before replying, "You know how. But it would be better to learn these answers from your full memories rather than my words."

She gulped, her throat tight. "How will my memories return to me?"

"I will help you remember. I know how. But there is something you need to know first."

More? Dear god, she wasn't sure there was room in her for more.

"The Resurrectors have two branches, albeit both are very small nowadays. The first is a somewhat more normal expression of their religious beliefs where they simply celebrate the possibility of a vampiric ascension. The second is more extreme: they don't just celebrate it, they involve themselves in ways to make it happen; ways to make things just; ways to control the outcome they judge to be right. Your family was involved in the extremist branch – I am loathed to say that to you, Sophia, but it's important you know before we bring back your memories. It's not that they did not love you; it's that their beliefs and practices took over all things."

Good god... "I'm now not sure I want to know," she whispered.

He smiled a sad smile. "I think your memories will come regardless now, but it could take years if we did nothing to help the process. To consciously bring them out tonight, means we do it all in one go and you no longer have to wonder. It's safer to know it all now – those vampires in the library will not be the last. You've been attacked virtually every single day this week."

"I think they wanted me for my blood."

"They did."

"Do you know why?"

"Not completely, but I have guesses."

"I need to know why, don't I?"

"You do."

"Daniel will be all right?"

He glanced towards the door that led to the stairs of his apartment. "I think he will now. She'll keep him steady." He turned back to her. "I'm sorry if you thought you'd be the one to do that."

She met his gaze.

He meant it.

"He saved my life on Saturday night. It was the beginning of everything. I felt ... I thought..."

"You reached for him first. But I always knew you would – it was inevitable."

First? She didn't ask. She had a feeling she'd know what he meant by the end of the night. After a moment of hesitation, she asked, "Will *you* be all right?"

His smile faded a fraction. "I'm afraid I have no idea."

"Abi, darling, I have no idea what you're talking about." It was perhaps a blessing her mother couldn't see the face she was pulling down the phone. This was typical of her mother, to cause the chaos then deny it completely.

Abi wasn't getting anywhere with this conversation. "You could have cost me my job, and you're lucky you didn't scare Sophia half to death – *you're* the one that said you wanted me to have friends. I wouldn't blame her if she pulled out."

"She *must* come, darling, and so must you – it's your twenty-fifth birthday. Please dress up for the occasion – high-end dresses, darling – we'll be putting on a show."

That's exactly what she'd been talking about – the damned show! "I know – Romeo and Juliet."

"Is that code for something, dear?"

She sighed.

"Oh, and I *insist* you be part of the ceremony."

She froze. For a second, she wondered if her mother knew of her affair with Anthony.

"The bishop's going to be there – it's a once-in-a-lifetime event." Her mum sounded positively giddy with excitement. And she'd ignored every word Abi had said.

"I'm not religious."

"Everyone's religious about something, dear."

Abi sighed and finally conceded – it was the easiest way with her mother. Get through whatever it was, get it over and done with, then she could put it behind her. "Okay, fine, just ... no more surprises, okay?"

"Only the most prodigious surprises, darling," she replied, gleefully. "Some surprises are worth the new dawn they bring."

"Look ... can you see? Sophia, look." He held his hand out under the sun, his brown eyes lit with glee. "I'm not burning."

But inside, she was burning. She didn't want to cry again, but tears threatened to fall. "You hurt me," she accused. She tried to say that like she felt strong inside, but she didn't. She felt cut open. She looked at her wrist, her lip trembling. The wound had already healed from earlier, but the pain was still there.

"It was the smallest bite, little one."

"Don't do it again."

That made him angry. He was in front of her straight away, his face almost touching hers as he stared at her, seething. "I'm your uncle, Sophia, I'm your family. We brought you into this world for a reason and it's to save us all, so you will give me what I need."

She moaned; the scene changed. Fast forward – it was four days later... She remembered counting down the days.

"Sweet Sophia..."

He bunched her dress in his hands.

"Stop it!" she screamed.

"Now you behave. You have something very special and your

job is to let me have it, do you understand?" His grip tightened and he wrenched her dress up—

With a yell, she woke to a car horn beeping. Her car horn.

Sophia pulled her hand off the horn from where she'd slammed it in her sleep and tried to catch her breath. Exhaustion was an inconvenient companion. She'd be falling asleep while driving if she wasn't careful.

She was alone in her car, still in the driver's seat. Jacque had gone inside. She'd told him she'd needed a bit of time before joining everyone upstairs.

Before seeing Daniel and Eliza together as much as anything else.

The clock on the dashboard told her twenty minutes had passed.

It wasn't that she was not happy for Daniel – in a way she really was; it had been clear how much he'd loved Eliza – and the jealousy, despite feeling brutal, was something Sophia could push aside and deal with if she had to. Right now, it wasn't about jealousy; it was that she'd lost her lifeline. Daniel had helped her solidly for the last four days to come to terms with everything. Having to give that up felt more brutal than any amount of jealousy.

But there were bigger things at stake. Pierce had been targeted, and that meant others she cared about could be targeted if they didn't fix whatever the hell was going on. Her mum and dad – Jeanette and Michael ... it had occurred to her she might need to protect them somehow. It would devastate her if anything happened to them.

Time to get your big girl panties on and get this over and done with.

The memories might hurt, but if it meant she knew what she was dealing with, and those dear to her could be spared because of it, it needed doing.

Sophia gathered her things and got out of the car. The remnants of that last dream lingered and made her feel more than horrible inside. At the moment, it was just a vague recollection. After she got her memories back... She didn't know what it would be then; what *else* she would remember.

Pierce is dead. Abi could have died today if she'd come downstairs at the wrong time. No one is safe with you right now, so get up those stairs and fix it.

She locked her car.

Three deep breaths. *Slow your heart rate down.*

Another image came to her mind – the one she'd had yesterday of the beautiful golden gates amid a blue sky and soaring birds. It washed her over with a sense of peace and calm. She had no idea if that was a memory – it seemed too ethereal to be real. It was more the kind of beautiful thing you saw in dreams; good dreams that took you to wonderful places, not the nightmares she'd been living with.

She held onto the vision and let it soak into her until she swore she felt as warm as the gold on those gates, and then, she made her way up the stairs towards the apartment.

Chapter Twenty

Daniel and Eliza were deep in conversation at the far side of the living room, holding each other's hands, when she quietly slipped in. Les was tapping away on the laptop on the kitchen counter, and Jacque was nowhere to be seen.

Sophia made her way to Les, dropping herself onto the seat next to him.

He glanced at her with a wink and a sympathetic smile. "Good evenin', luv." And she was grateful he didn't beat around the bush. He pointedly nodded at Eliza and said, "The past always creeps up on you when you're a centuries old vampire, one way or the other."

Despite herself, she smiled. "She sort of bounced, actually."

He laughed.

"It's fine. I'll live. I've only known him four days."

"Living might well suit you better than being undead. And in those four days, you brought a spark to his unliving self, and don't you forget it."

She held back the huge urge to give Les a massive hug and changed the subject. "Are you hanging around for the 'bring back Sophia's memory' party or..."

He chuckled. "Jacque filled us in on the plan, if somewhat briefly – man of few words, that one. Unless you truly feel you need me"—he glanced at Daniel and Eliza again—"I was hoping to head off. I'm considering handing in my retirement notice this weekend."

"I don't blame you."

"I'm far too slow for all this and, you know, the vampires – they can hear my joints creaking, so sneaking up on them just doesn't work."

This time, Sophia laughed out loud and gave Les a playful nudge.

"I'm chauffeuring you all to and from the party on Friday, though. That'll be my last gig."

"Oh, I'm going with Abi."

Les raised an eyebrow. "I'll let you break that one to Jacque."

Jacque walked out of Daniel's bedroom at that moment.

He'd changed his clothes from earlier, now wearing just a simple pair of blue jeans and a slim-fit, white T-shirt. The more frivolous attire had gone quite a way to hiding his broad chest and shoulders and ... muscles. A lot of muscles. The T-shirt left little to the imagination.

Needing to quell her nerves, she brought her more rarely seen, sassy Sophia to the fore. "Are you afraid I'll fling things at your fancy clothes after all my memories return?"

The corner of his mouth went up. "I've already thrown away all the soups and sauces and hidden some of the breakables."

She rolled her eyes but returned the smile. "Listen, I'm getting a ride with Abigail to the party on Friday – her chauffeur's picking us both up straight from the library."

Les made a soft snorting noise behind her.

Jacque's smile became a frown. "Are you sure that's a good idea? According to your friend, it seems you're desperately wanted at that party and I'm not sure on why. Next thing you know, her chauffeur will be taking a detour and god knows where you'll end up."

"Are you serious? Her parents don't even know me."

"Her parents are involved with the Auclairs. You might be more known than you think."

She decided on a different tack – the last thing she wanted to do was let Abigail down after all the support she'd given her the past week and them *wrecking* the basement this afternoon. And she completely trusted Abi. If her parents had some issue with her and the Auclair family, she didn't for one second think Abi was in on it. "Then changing plans so suddenly will make them suspicious that I'm onto them. Why doesn't Les follow us from the library. That way, you'll know if anything happens to me."

It was a reasonable enough alternative. Jacque nodded. "All right, let's do that."

"Thank you." She felt relieved at not having to change plans on Abi. "Now all I've got to do is find the right dress on my one-hour lunch break in a tiny town full of charity shops."

Jacque shook his head. "Don't worry about that – it's sorted."

"It really isn't. Abi messaged me and said high-end labels only – it's one of those classy, expensive dos."

"I said I have it sorted."

The couple of the evening wandered up to the kitchen counter. They still held each other's hands. There was nowhere for Sophia to look, so she took a breath and met Daniel's eyes. Pure contentment shone throughout his features. While that now-familiar sense of jealousy rippled quietly in the background, she also found herself happy he'd gained something so monumental he thought he'd lost. She had an unsettling feeling anything from her past she gained tonight wouldn't be nearly as fulfilling.

There was a slight apology to Daniel's gaze as it held hers. He made a small gesture with his head. He clearly wanted to speak to her in private for a moment.

Not now. Not tonight with everything else going on. She threw him the most accepting and loving smile she could manage in the hope he'd understand she was fine and not about to get in the way of anything he and Eliza had, and then she turned to Jacque. "So, when are we doing this?"

He leaned against the counter. "You and Les need to eat. So we can have dinner first, or do it now and have dinner after."

"Oh, I've eaten," piped in Les. "And I'm shooting off in a mo."

Eat? Sophia's stomach turned at the idea. Her nerves were so big, she didn't think she'd be able to hold anything down. "Dinner after. Let's get this over and done with now."

Jacque nodded. "Okay, then. On the dining table."

"Um ... excuse me?"

He didn't answer, but the next she knew his hands were around her waist and she was moved four steps away and hoisted onto the edge of the table. He took his place in front of her.

"What—"

"This is the position we were in when your memories left you."

Stunned, she had no idea what to say, although a low-level anger did stir at quite literally being carried like a child. "I told you, I'm not six anymore."

His stare found hers and held it; his voice dropped a note. "Oh, I'm very aware of that, Sophia." The pause that followed was a beat longer than necessary, bearing far too many abstract notions to guess at.

"Good luck, all!" chirped Les as he let himself out, dissipating the thickness of the air before it started.

Everyone sounded their goodbyes.

Jacque glanced at Eliza who nodded and pulled Daniel back a bit. "We'll be right over here if you need us," she said.

His attention went back to Sophia. "It will help your memories if your mind can place you as you were twenty-two years ago."

Still feeling a bit put out, she nodded.

"I don't know *how* exactly your memories will display – it could be through your own mind and the things you heard and saw; there's a chance it could be through mine simply because of the way this needs to be. But regardless, I won't see what you see – it's still *your* mind. You're in control. And your mind will give you information in the way *you* need to understand what happened. Does that make sense?" He was waiting very intently on her answer.

"Yes. I think so."

He seemed satisfied at that, stared at a random spot over her shoulder, then took a breath in and turned his full focus on her.

"I need you to trust me."

She blinked, wanting to look away, some hidden feeling behind what he said almost too intense, but he didn't let her.

"I would never hurt you then or now." The sincerity in that statement was unequivocal. "I'm going to need you to let me take your mind on a journey – you need to give me the reins without resistance. That works far better if you trust me." He held out both his hands to her.

She swallowed a lump in her throat that had risen from nowhere. All she had to go on, where Jacque was concerned, was one memory. But in that memory, she knew she *had* trusted him. Hesitantly, she placed her hands in his and it was as if every single hair on her body rose on contact. It had also been like that at Pierce's place, hadn't it? When he'd helped her up from the floor – a depth to a connection she hadn't understood; still didn't. She met his gaze. "I trust you."

He nodded, and his eyes softened. "Just settle on my eyes now, Sophia. Don't look away – look *into*."

She did as he instructed and it really wasn't hard – Jacque's eyes were the epitome of what 'hypnotic' was supposed to be. She felt her mind relax almost instantaneously, so much so, she *did* resist on instinct alone.

"You're safe," came his voice – it could have come from the next room. "Just let me take you to where you need to go."

Need to go?

Her mind threw up an image with ease and she sighed into it, her heart more than joyous at those golden gates spiring before her, and she didn't know if it was Jacque's pull or her own mind that had her rushing through its bars, freely and familiarly. Inside the grounds of this palatial place, she felt like air and light; like everything belonged as one and *she* belonged – she was needed and wanted, and she was life itself. Life moved through her, and she moved through it, and everything was perfectly slotted to create everything that existed and everything to come. If she thought she didn't know love, this was it. This was surely it, but it was nothing tangible or earthly – it was simply there, existing, in and of everything that was and will be.

Too good was it to last forever, and all too soon she was pulled down, and down, and down, like falling into eternity and through time; awaiting a landing that never came, but instead formed around her as she entered a molecule, which became a cell, which became a body, a room, a year in a reality...

"Jacque!" she called out, happily, in greeting, as she put down her last chess piece on the board Daddy had bought her. She liked his name, even though it made her mouth tingle to say it because of the way she had to press her tongue on the first sound.

"Good evening, Sophia." He smiled and sat himself down opposite her and she giggled because that was a chair for children and he had a giant's body. Bigger than anyone else she knew, anyway.

"You'll break the chair."

"I most probably will," he agreed.

She knew he'd just been talking to her parents. "Is Mummy angry I stayed out after dark?"

"No. Don't worry, it's all sorted."

"Do you want to play chess?"

"Do you know how to play?"

"A little. Daddy taught me. He said it's like how he has to think about a courtroom."

He picked up a Queen and raised an eyebrow at the pink dress and lipstick on the wooden carving. "Do the people in court dress like this?"

She grinned. "I took the clothes from the dollies in my doll's house. I like dressing up the pieces."

"Well, I like dressing up, too. It daresay it makes chess more interesting. Probably a courtroom, too," he added.

"Are you family, Jacque? Like my uncles and aunts?"

"Non, ma chérie. I am ... a very old friend of the family."

"You don't look as old as Grandpa."

"Oh, I'm much, much older."

"Are you sleeping in the house like everybody else?"

"Only for three days."

"Oh." She felt disappointed. "Will I see you after three days?"

"I'm afraid I'm not sure. But part of the reason I'm here is to get to know you better, so we can spend a lot of time together until I leave, okay?"

"Yay! I'd like that. I like you much more than everyone else."

"Is that so?" He put the Queen back and moved a Pawn wearing a yellow jacket forward.

She already knew which piece she was going to move, so she did it, and then replied, "Yes. I like Mummy and Daddy, but everyone else just whispers about me. They think I don't know about it, but I do. And I don't think anyone really likes me very much."

After a moment of silence, he said, "I highly doubt that's true."

"It is true. And I like Uncle Hugo the least. He looks at me funny a lot." He also hurt her, which is why she'd run to the cemetery in the first place, but she didn't want to tell him that because it would spoil the happy feeling she had when Jacque was with her.

Jacque was so quiet, she looked up from her game to see if she'd upset him. He did look angry, but only for a moment, and then he smiled and said, "I'll bear that in mind next time I speak to Uncle Hugo." His voice sounded all icy when he said that, so she decided to talk about something else.

"Where are you from?" she asked.

"Lots of places."

"I mean the first place you're from – like the place you were born."

He moved another Pawn forward. "A place far away from here."

"What's it called?"

"It has many names."

"What does it look like?"

He sighed and sat back in the chair even though she was sure he would topple it over. "When you see it from a distance, it's like you're seeing a golden river falling from the sky. When you get closer, the shimmering water becomes the most beautiful and grand golden gates you've ever seen."

Oh! She knew this place. She continued for him. "And the sky is very blue like the colour of your eyes, and the grass is so green and also whispers to you, and the birds that fly"—she stood and raised her arms to mimic them—"it's like they're dancing when they're flying and then there are really *big wings – white ones—"*

"Sophia."

She stopped her bird dance and looked at him. He was no longer sitting back but sitting forwards, staring at her like she'd told him a surprise-secret – like accidentally saying what a birthday present is when she shouldn't.

"You know this place?"

She nodded, tentatively. "Was I not supposed to tell you?" she whispered, unsure.

"Of course you can tell me. It's just that a lot of people don't know this place. How do you know it?"

She walked around the table towards him because she was no longer sure she should be talking about it out loud. She tiptoed to reach his ear and placed her hands around her mouth so no one else would hear. "I see it in my head. I go there when I dream."

She pulled back and looked at him to see if he was angry. He wasn't. His eyes were all smiley.

"I usually keep it a secret because it's in my head, but if that's where you're from, we can share the secret, can't we?"

He nodded. "Yes, we can."

A tug ... a pull ... and on a gasp of a breath, she was floating and falling down time's tunnel once more; one sunset, one sunrise ... one day later...

"You're wrong!" Her dad's voice bounced around the hallway where Sophia was hiding. She wasn't always able to hide – usually Uncle Hugo found her – but she'd learnt that when grown ups were so angry and arguing, they rarely heard anything but their own voices.

She'd come to find Jacque after her breakfast to tell him about the kitten Daddy said he would buy her if she behaved and didn't go out after dark anymore. But she'd found him in Daddy's study along with everyone else – Daddy, Mummy, Grandma, Grandpa, Uncle Hugo, Aunty Fiona, and Aunty Rita.

So, she'd hidden in the far corner of the alcove under the stairs. She couldn't see much because she was crouching down, but her hearing was really good. Sometimes, she could even hear people all the way in the garden.

Aunty Fiona's voice sounded next. "She was never supposed to display vampiric qualities. We agreed no vampire DNA."

"And none was used." That was Daddy. "We're certain of that. Only the purest prayers and blessings with the smallest amount of magic."

"The fangs tell us otherwise," Aunty Fiona scoffed. "And magic has a habit of doing its own thing."

"Maybe we need to wait," said her mother. "She only started displaying them little over a week ago – that was why we called Jacque – maybe they'll disappear."

“She hisses, *Deborah, before she displays them,” said Aunty Fiona. “It’s diabolical.”*

“Darling,” said Uncle Hugo, “I thought you rather liked it when I hissed.” He said that in the sickly sweet way he always spoke. Sophia hated his voice. She looked down at her wrist where he’d bitten her yesterday afternoon, but the mark was gone, thankfully. He told her he’d hurt Mummy if she told anyone, so she hadn’t, but Jacque was not like anyone else she knew. He could probably stop Uncle Hugo hurting Mummy, so she still might tell Jacque before he left.

“Oh, Hugo, please. It’s different with you – we took you in after you were turned and domesticated you. You were a successful experiment.”

“And how’s your other experiment going, darling?” His voice dripped sarcasm. “That maternal gene kicked in yet?”

“For god’s sake, shut up the both of you,” Daddy said, sounding tired.

“Please, everyone, Sophia can still be a successful experiment,” came her mother’s soft voice. “The insemination was successful in every way, as was her birth. Everything until now has been like clockwork – we can’t abandon it all now.”

“She saw *a vampire last night, Deborah, for the first time. Hugo doesn’t count. God knows what he was doing on our grounds – maybe she attracts the beasts. Throw in her emerging fangs, and that’s bound to trigger something – some primal growth spurt. She’ll respond to the vile creatures.”*

“You respond quite well to my vile fangs, Fiona, darling.”

“Hugo, please!”

“And I haven’t heard your sister complaining either,” he added, silkily.

There was a gasp from Aunty Rita before Fiona rounded on her. They always *bickered. “You feeble bitch, always stealing my things! Is it not enough you take my clothes, my jewellery – you need to steal the cock from between my legs, too?"*

"That's enough!" That was Daddy's very *angry voice. "Can we please remember our manners and why we're here. Jacque, I apologise for my family's repellent verbiage. Regarding Sophia, please, we would love to know your thoughts."*

Everyone fell silent for a moment. When Jacque's voice came, he spoke deeply and softly. "I think you're all vile."

It was her mother who gasped this time.

"I've had no dealings with this family line for damn near five centuries and you dig me out of history for this? Never mind your filthy tongues, can you hear the way you're speaking about a child?"

Fiona huffed. "She's a monster, not a ch—"

"She's a child!" Jacque's voice boomed. "And a largely human one at that, in case you all missed her heartbeat. The rest, you brought on yourself, meddling with life and death and things that should be kept sacred. And on the first sign your perfect master plan shows a dent, you blame the child?"

"Jacque Aubert," her grandmother said. "Please calm yourself a moment to remember the Resurrectors' mission."

"The moment the Auclair house put their mission before sense was the moment I cut ties with this family line."

"All but one tie, Mr Aubert."

Everything went silent again.

"You would not be here were it not for our intervention five centuries ago and you vowed to repay that debt. Not until today has there been a chance to do so."

"Mother, what are you talking about."

"Deborah, I have a suggestion that might keep everyone happy. Everyone but Mr Aubert, perhaps, but once he's consummated his vow, he is fully released from this family line and we shall never bother him again."

"Go on," encouraged her father.

"Our daughter, Deborah, is correct – we do not give up on our

children when we were the ones who chose to bring them into this world. But Fiona is also right in that we need to safeguard both ourselves and the mission, and perhaps even the wider world from what Sophia may become if things do not go to plan. After all, we have *utilised the most powerful of magics. We need to buy ourselves more time to see if these less desirable qualities of hers overshadow her purpose."*

"It's not *her purpose," threw in Jacque. "It's yours."*

"We are all given to a higher purpose, Mr Aubert, even Sophia – even you. My proposal is this: buy us more time by taking her memory of everything she has so far become."

She heard her mother gasp again. There was a bit of murmuring, and then Jacque's protest. "That cannot be done."

"Yes, it can. I know your influence is powerful enough – it is recorded in our journals."

"Only on fully grown humans have I done this and only when deemed necessary – never a child and never one like her. The memory loss is permanent – there's no way back. What you're asking for is a violation."

"The alternative is to kill her, Mr Aubert. Would you rather do that instead? It need not be you – there are plenty within these walls who would like to see her dead."

"Wipe that grin off your face, Fiona, darling," said Uncle Hugo.

"No!" her mother cried. "Please..." She heard a shuffle and a scrape like her mum was getting out of a chair. "Jacque, please, I beseech you. She is my only child – I cannot lose her."

"Mr Aubert, it could be that the vampire in her still emerges, or it could be that after you stunt her memory – and therefore to some degree, her growth – she will keep her divinity and be able to fulfil her destiny."

Jacque said a few bad words. "Your mission is a myth, Elle Auclair."

"That is not for you to decide."

"And it is not *for you to decide Sophia's future."*

"Who should – you? Let me make myself perfectly clear, Mr Aubert, she is nothing to you. She is not your blood or your responsibility now or otherwise. She is ours. Her mother loves her. You have no dominion here other than the choice you make now. This is your chance to repay your debt to the Auclairs once and for all. Clear her mind of who she is or we will choose another route. You have two more days with us – take your time to think about it. Spend that time with Sophia and get to know her well so you know the extent of what you need to clear. If you choose to do it, it must be done before you leave. Let us know by the end of tomorrow.

"Gerard, we are done here." Her grandma's words were final. Everyone left the room one by one, and Sophia hugged her knees and kept as still as possible so no one would hear her.

Her mother's feet went past, her dad's, then Aunty Fiona's, Aunty Rita's, then Uncle Hugo's ... his feet stopped and turned towards Jacque's feet. "You know, Jacque, I'm not so bad at the old hypno thing myself. If it's too hard for you, I'd be happy to step in and—"

There was a big growl, and a whimper, and then Hugo's feet left the floor, scrambling for purchase against the wall. "You, Hugo Bassett, are a despicable creature alive or undead. It's been a long time since I spiked a man's head, but I swear on the gates of hell if you lay one finger on that child, I will decorate its entrance with that barren skull of yours."

Jacque's feet stormed off and Uncle Hugo fell to the ground, face red, and clutching his neck.

Pull ... tug ... another sunset; another sunrise ... the morphing of another room ... the dining room...

Dinner was finished. Everyone had gone to bed except Uncle

Hugo who had gone out. He went out often at night. Jacque was pacing up and down, up and down, up and down, and she didn't know what to say to calm him down because it was obvious he was upset. Maybe he was as upset as she was that he was leaving tomorrow morning. They'd spent every day together since he'd been here and played loads of games, and they'd talked lots, too.

An idea came to her. She got up and ran to the bookcase at the end of the dining room. She loved books. Although, this was the grown-up bookcase, but she was sure she could find something. Not wanting to take too long, she grabbed a book with a bit of very deep blue on the cover because it was similar to the colour of the sky in that beautiful dream place they both knew about. "Do you want me to read you a story?" she asked Jacque, excitedly, as she ran back towards him.

He lifted his head. He looked so sad and tired. "A story?"

"Stories always make me feel better." She stared at the book in her hand and frowned. "Oh, I think this is Aunty Fiona's book."

Jacque snorted. "She doesn't seem like the type that reads to me."

*"Well ... it looks a bit boring and it's called something weird, but most stories are good, so"—she put on her best storyteller voice and started with the title—"*He's Not the One: Your One-Stop Guide to Choosing the Right Man.*" She wrinkled her nose. What did that mean?*

Jacque laughed. It started slow, but then filled up the room, and Sophia grinned because the story was already working.

"Shall I read more?"

He couldn't answer for laughing, so she flicked through the book to find a good place to start. "There are some really strange pictures in here."

He was helpless now; had sunk to his knees, unable to stop, but he reached out anyway and took the book from her with a slight shake of his head. "It's okay, it's okay ... leave this one for an-

another ... day." Another laugh burst from him as he put the book down. "Your Aunt Fiona ... very much n-needs that book." More laughing.

She sat there, smiling, waiting for him to stop laughing.

When he finally did, he looked up and met her eyes – his were much happier than before. He let out a big sigh. "Come here, you." He stood up and took her with him, sitting her on the edge of the dining table. "I will miss you when I go, Sophia."

"I'll miss you too, but I won't forget you."

His smile faded a bit, but not completely. He let out another sigh, then said, "May god forgive me for what I'm about to do. Sophia ... that man who attacked you near the cemetery – do you remember seeing his long teeth?"

She nodded.

"Do you know what he was?"

She sucked on her lip, thinking about all the words her family used that they thought she never heard when they talked about her. "A vampire."

"That's right."

After a beat, she said, "Uncle Hugo's a vampire, too."

Jacque's face darkened. "You've seen his teeth?"

She shrugged. And decided not to tell him. She wanted happy Jacque back.

He mumbled a bad word, then said, "There are good vampires, too – not all of them are bad. I'm a vampire."

She looked at him, surprised. "Do you have long teeth?"

He nodded. "We can make them grow."

She suddenly smiled, relieved.

"This makes you happy?"

"A little. I think I'm a vampire, but I thought that made me bad. But if you're a vampire, it can't be bad, so it's okay."

"I'm not sure what you are to be honest, Sophia, but I do know you're good. And I know you're extraordinary." He glanced away,

and held still like she sometimes did when she was listening for things, then turned back and dropped his voice low as if he was telling her a secret. "I'd like to give you something that means I'll always find you if you're lost. It also means if you ever forget anything important, I can help you remember it again. It's..." He hesitated. "It's not normally something I would give you, but ... it's the only chance I have to keep you safe. And sometimes rules need to be broken."

"What is it?"

"A little bit of my blood – only a little."

She looked down at her wrist where Uncle Hugo had hurt her. "Do I have to give you my blood, too?"

"No. I will not take your blood. And you taking mine will not hurt you."

After a moment, she nodded. She knew Jacque would never hurt her. "Okay."

He smiled. It was a bit sad, but he said, "Thank you." His teeth grew then, and Sophia stared at them, intrigued. Carefully, he let one tooth puncture a vein on his wrist. Blood pooled fast. "Put your mouth around the blood, let it fill your mouth and then swallow, only once."

She did as he instructed. The blood tasted sweet and warm.

Jacque pulled away after she'd swallowed. The wound had stopped bleeding already. "Was that all right?"

She licked her lips and nodded with a small smile. "It tastes a bit like raspberry syrup, and it feels like sunshine in my tummy." Suddenly, she felt very brave. She wasn't scared of Jacque at all and she trusted him. She held her own wrist out. "You can have my blood, too."

Shaking his head, Jacque took her arm and lowered it. "Non, ma chérie, I will not drink from you."

"But how will I find you if you're *the one who's lost? It needs to be equal."*

"Oh, it does, does it?" he asked softly, amused.

"Yes. I need to look after you as much as you look after me." After all, she'd made him laugh with the book when he'd looked more miserable than Grandpa. "I know," she exclaimed all a sudden. "I can do something."

"What's that, then?"

"Will you let me look inside your mind for how to find you?"

A bit startled, he stepped back and studied her. "You can do this?"

"I did it once with Aunty Rita and she went so pale she almost fainted and asked me never to do it again. But I don't think you're like Aunty Rita and I promise not to hurt you."

She was worried he'd be angry or too afraid to do it, but he just looked curious. "Okay, Sophia. I offer you my mind."

Excitement bubbling up, she smiled and took his face in both her hands, moving his head until she could look properly inside his eyes, and then she did that thing that felt like pulling ... pulling his mind ... pulling anything else that was inside him. He didn't try to stop her like Aunty Rita, or get all panicky, but felt relaxed as he let her pull him. And then it felt like he travelled through her – all of his many years – and Sophia searched for the way to find him if he got lost. There were lots of images, but one was stronger than the others. It was of a man with dark eyes and dark, curly hair – very curly – that looked a bit like her mother's twisty hair after she put her small curlers in. The man smiled at her.

She smiled back. "Okay," she let Jacque go. "I'll be able to find you now."

He was staring at her like she'd told him the biggest secret in the world. "It's remarkable you can do that, ma chérie. You are more extraordinary than your family will ever know. Here, take my hands."

She put her hands in his.

"Remember the dream place with the golden gates?"

"Yes."

"Picture it in your head and look in my eyes."

She did.

"Now, let's go there together. Let me take you there..."

She smiled, enjoying that feeling of flying as his voice got further and further away ... it was easy to forget what her body felt like when she floated; to forget how everyone talked about her and didn't like her; to forget Uncle Hugo and how horrible he was; to forget ... everything.

Chapter Twenty-One

She'd often wondered what it might be like to have lived the life she was always supposed to live if the house hadn't burnt down; if her family hadn't died. Having no memory, she'd created scenarios – heartwarming family scenarios that had included non-stop happy days out with her parents; in parks, with ice-cream; paddling at the beach. What a lie. They'd all been lies.

When she was a teenager, she'd fantasised that regaining her memories might be an epiphanic experience. Everything would slot into place. The sun would burst through the constant cloud in her mind where the first six years of her life should be.

What burst through her instead, right now, was *feeling*. An overload of sensory sounds, sights, smells, tastes, and *feelings* that made every memory solid; every betrayal real.

The first thing she heard was the ragged sound of her breathing; the first thing she saw was Jacque; the first thing she tasted was his blood in her mouth; and the first thing she *felt* was—

She hissed.

Jacque squeezed her hands. "Sophia—"

No! Wired and wild, she haunched her legs up and flung them out. Her feet caught his chest and he went flying across the room as she somersaulted, backwards, off the table.

Her back hit the wall.

Her navel *burned*. And the burn was worse than ever because she could feel—

"Sophia!" That was Daniel.

"Daniel, wait." Eliza held his arm; held him back.

Daniel... Sophia's gaze settled on him and she reeled at the understanding that bloomed in her mind. *You called him. You pulled him.* She'd plucked him out of Jacque's mind and straight into her life—

"Sophia." Jacque was on his feet again, circling round to reach her.

—all so she could find her way back.

To Jacque.

It cut deep. Everything cut deep. "You took my memories - *you*." She accused him.

"I didn't have any—"

"You did what?" cut in Daniel, his tone one of shock.

Jacque held a hand up in defence. "I knew I could return them to her."

"Because you gave me your blood," Sophia whispered, all of her life jaggedly and rapidly falling into place. The jagged pieces tore.

A growl filled the room, but it wasn't Jacque's – it was Daniel's, his furious glare fully on his sire. "You fed your blood to a human?"

"I knew she wasn't solely human."

"You fed a human *child* your *blood*? When she couldn't even consent to—"

"It wasn't like that." Jacque's tone was low – a definite warning.

Sophia grasped her abdomen as old agony ripped through it, a final memory threatening to break through – *needing* to break through – that spot between her hip and pubic bone. *Just a scar ... just a scar...*

Daniel's next words – delivered in full attack mode – obliterated the safety of that illusion. "What kind of *depraved fuck* do you have to be to tear through the iliac artery of a child!"

Oh, god ... Daniel had seen it when they'd slept together – the scar. He'd asked about it. He knew what must have happened.

Jacque's growl now matched Daniel's and the whole apartment sounded like a fucking zoo. "*Think* for one damn second who you're talking to. I would *never*—"

"Daniel," pleaded Eliza as she put herself between the two males. "He did what was necessary for her at the time."

Daniel whipped round to face her. "You *knew*?"

And all hell broke loose. Voices escalated; anger furnaced; heat rose...

"Sweet Sophia..."

Fire danced all around her, its heat menacing. She wished she could make it do what she wanted it to do, but it was always wild and chaotic. Instead, she cried, her wails and sobs chaotic, too.

His hand glided up her wrist, his thumb circling the pulse there, once, but his hungry eyes locked onto her neck, seemed to hesitate, then fell to her tummy behind her dress. He bunched her dress in his hands.

"Stop it!" she screamed.

"Now you behave. You have something very special and your job is to let me have it, do you understand?" His grip tightened and he wrenched her dress up.

"Uncle Hugo, no!" She scratched his face. It didn't help.

"Your veins are too small. I need an artery."

"NO!" Her dress was pushed up to her chest.

He pulled her knickers down. "You're the only one who can stop us burning." His teeth went in deep.

She screamed. But it wasn't just sound that erupted.

Uncle Hugo screamed too, wrenching himself from her, his head on fire. He maniacally tried to swat the flames with his hands.

She screamed again.

The wall behind her uncle billowed out as if responding to her scream, and then combusted. Flames were everywhere, eating everything.

It was bad what she'd just done – she knew it was bad.

Uncle Hugo was still screaming when she ran from the room and sprinted up the stairs. She raced into her bedroom and dove under her covers. Sophia squeezed her eyes shut. Go to the golden gates ... go to the golden gates... *She used that image in her head as her only lifeline; sank into it; the only peaceful place she knew. Snuggling lower under her covers, she put herself there completely, wishing she was asleep; letting the sounds of the fire fade; the sounds of screaming fade; the sounds of her mummy and daddy, now downstairs, also screaming ... fade... All she heard was her breathing. All she saw were golden gates and blue skies. And a voice she liked. She couldn't remember who it belonged to, but it helped her drift off to sleep amid the heat and chaos... "Let's go there together. Let me take you there..."*

"A vow you made five centuries ago, doesn't justify—"

"It wasn't about the vow, it was about her *life*!"

"Oh, does that make you feel better telling yourself that?"

"You weren't there – you don't know!"

Sophia reached behind her, feeling her way, barely aware of

anything around her. They could fight it out without her here. She needed air; she needed the cold – anything cold. If she didn't get the hell out now, she was going to burn the place down.

Her fingers collided with metal; felt the shape of the door handle under them. She grasped it and tugged. The door opened, and she ran.

Never in her life had she run so fast – so fast, she couldn't even feel her legs. Motion took place around her, whizzing past at astronomical speed – trees, buildings, cars, people milling on street corners and outside pubs under the pleasant summer twilight, their cheerful chats and drinks no doubt spoilt by her crazed commotion.

She didn't know what the time was. She didn't know how long she'd been running for. When her chest began to hurt, she welcomed it – it was better than the other hurt. Better than burning.

It didn't register in her mind what exactly happened when she collided with something solid; solid and moulded to her frame as arms encircled her – lifted her – and took them both darting to the left and into a small shaded copse.

"Sophia ... Sophia, we are going to talk about this."

Blue eyes held hers through tears – her own – and not until that second, with the wind no longer whipping her face, did she realise she was sobbing. Uncontrollably.

"Please, Sophia," Jacque pleaded, his voice more desperate than she'd ever heard it. He had her by her arms and he wasn't letting her go. "There were no good choices I could make for you, so I took the best of the worst. If I'd done nothing and left you be, Fiona would have seen you dead, or Hugo would have done god knows what with you instead. Your parents might have loved you but they didn't stand up for you against your grandmother. I took your memories at their request because I knew it was the only chance you'd be afforded more years; more of a chance, and as long as they believed you were the answer to some sacred mission of theirs, they wouldn't hurt you. I *only* did it after feeling certain I could fix it at some point in the future and that's the only reason I gave you my blood. I was damned if I was going to leave you at their mercy, in the clutches of those witches you had for aunts and that abhorrent excuse for an uncle.

"And I *did* look out for you. The fire was unexpected, but I felt your fear and I came. I caught you when your mother threw you out the window. When you landed in my arms, you were unconscious, but alive. The fire brigade and ambulance came quickly – I left you with them and afterwards, I made sure you got a good home – good parents – fudged the files a little, but it didn't matter because I knew they'd raise you well. And they did. And I waited for the right time to bring your memories back, but you were happy in your new home, Sophia, happy at university, and you'd forgotten the mess you'd left behind and I started to wonder if I should leave it all alone.

"So, I did. I walked out of your life for good. Until a few nights ago when I felt your panic over your attack in the bridleway, but I wasn't in the area and arrived too late. When Deiniol called me a few hours later about that same attack, that's when I knew it was the right time to return. Please believe me." He brought her into his chest in an embrace that was everything she'd needed twenty-two years ago. "Sophia, please."

"He bit me," she whispered, her voice shaking. "Twice."

Everything fell silent. It was like the world collapsed, but she couldn't tell if it was hers or Jacque's.

"I wanted to tell you, but..."

His arms tightened around her. His tone gave nothing away, but it needn't because she could feel his fury in his muscles; in his controlled stillness. "Tell me now."

Her words sounded so ridiculously small, but they finally came out. "The day I met you was the first time. On the wrist. It was why I ran out the house and why I stayed out so late – I didn't want to go back. I felt like I was on fire inside in a bad way. I wanted to tell you; I wanted to but I couldn't.

"The second time was after you left. He wanted more. He said ... he said he needed an artery because my veins were too small."

Silence. And then the cutting of it with the iciest blade. "Where did he bite you?"

She blinked more tears out against his chest, but everything was easier now she'd said what she needed to. Keeping herself exactly where she was – this was not an embrace she was giving up easily – she reached behind her and took one of his hands, brought it round to her front and pressed it on the spot between her left hip and pubic bone. "The one on my wrist went away. This one left a scar, and it still hurts sometimes. Deep inside."

The low rumbling coming from his chest, against her ear, was both frightening and comforting. He returned his hand to where it had been behind her back.

"I didn't remember. I didn't remember the first time he bit me because my memories were gone. And the second time, I knew I wanted you there, but I couldn't remember who you were – you were just a feeling."

"Fuck. No, fuck no, no, no." He pressed her harder to him and she didn't mind.

"I screamed," she continued. "And I set him on fire, Jacque. I set everything on fire." A final sob erupted. "It was me who burnt the house down. I killed everyone."

The mumbled string of 'no' kept tumbling from his lips. "I felt your pain, and I came, but I thought it was because of the fire – I didn't know it was because—*fuck.* I never thought he'd do something like that under your grandmother's nose given how important you were to them. Forgive me. God, I'm so sorry. Forgive me."

She raised her arms to his neck and pulled him into a hug, burying her face into its crook. "Please don't leave me again."

"Never. Never. I'm never leaving you again."

PART III
Sophia

Chapter Twenty-Two

> **Abi, I'm so sorry. It's all gotten on top of me again. I feel terrible asking, but can I have tomorrow off? I'll definitely be in on Friday and I'm definitely coming to the party. Sophia x**

Of course! Friday's busier than Thursdays – I'll be fine on my own. Just take good care of yourself. You need a break. Abi x

She hadn't been able to face talking to or seeing anyone again – not Les, not Daniel and Eliza, and certainly not *being* in the same apartment as Daniel and Eliza. Not with the way she felt, all cut up and open and exposed.

Jacque had led her to her car – told her to wait just one minute. Thirty seconds later he'd returned with her handbag and overnight bag, taken the car keys from her, and half an hour later they were pulling up on a driveway she didn't recognise. But it was okay. It was okay because Jacque was here and she remembered who he was: the one good thing, lasting only three days, out of those first six years of her life. He was back.

Exhaustion had taken her – she'd slept for over half the journey, only stirring when the car engine was turned off. "Where are we?" she asked, her voice sounding hoarse.

"Mine. Further into the countryside, just half an hour out from Deiniol's place. There's a guest bedroom with its own bathroom. You won't be disturbed here and it'll be easy enough to take the 'A' roads into work on Friday. About a forty-minute drive into Emerson."

She turned her head to see him in the dark. "Thank you."

He nodded. "I'll take your things. Let's go."

The house certainly had a gothic air to it – Victorian and detached, it was surrounded by a gate and more than one majestic tree. Hedges formed as much of a boundary as the gate. "You own this?"

"I do. I moved here three years ago."

"I moved to Emerson three years ago."

"I know. And Deiniol moved to his place three years ago."

She glanced at him, not quite knowing what to make of that.

"I watched over you every day until you'd been with your new parents for a year, then I left, only coming back to check on you every now and then. The last time I saw you was at university. You were so well settled. That's when I knew you were all right – you'd make a good life for yourself. And I knew I'd feel it if you were in danger, so I pulled away completely. But I stayed close to wherever Deiniol was, partly for Eliza's sake. She wanted to be near him. But I also knew that if you needed me, you might somehow make contact with him first, although I wasn't sure how that would manifest."

"Because I found him in your mind. I pulled him to where I was living."

"Yes." He unlocked the front door and gestured for her to enter.

She couldn't help her intake of breath on walking through the doorway. Dark wood flooring stretched across the hallway and up the stairs, decorated with what looked like Norwich carpets or Persian rugs – perhaps both. Original wood panelling encased the sides of the stairs and some of the walls. Velvet curtains draped every window pane. But what piqued her heart rate were the artefacts inside the glass cabinet along the right wall as they walked in. Unable to stop herself, and despite her fatigue, she approached them with a giddy stride, her passion kindled. "Oh, my god. These are—"

"Originals. Not replicas. All of them." He came up behind her, a wistful smile on his face. "And I can tell you a story about every one."

"This is..." She caught herself before 'my dream house' left her lips, although the sentiment was true. When in her early twenties, she'd often wondered if there was a way she could pay rent to live in a museum.

"The cabinet's not locked," said Jacque. "Feel free to indulge. Come on, I'll show you to your room."

She had to force her eyes away from the cabinet as he led her up the stairs, but she lost all restraint the moment she saw the suit of armour on the upstairs landing. A small whimper left her as she – quite literally – fell to her knees before it. Her hands went straight to the chainmail; her eyes to the stitching of any cloth still attached. "Oh, my god! This is ... I think this is a hauberk." She needed to breathe. She felt dizzy. "Is this... no, it can't be, it can't be – is this from the tenth *century*?"

"Eleventh, actually. Although I last wore it in 1298."

Her jaw dropped. She stared at him, towering over her on the floor as she all but dribbled on the war suit, no coherent words forming, except, "You *wore* this?"

"Many times." He strode past the armour and her display of worship over it and opened the first door on the right. "Your room's through here."

Stumbling to her feet, she followed him into a simply decorated, but airy room with white walls and curtains and one dark wood wardrobe. A dressing table sat to one side, a floor-standing mirror next to it; the bed was a four-poster, again in dark wood, and the adjoining bathroom was also painted white, gold taps decorating the ceramic sink and bath. The shower cubicle in the corner was far more modern looking, but no less chic. This was *so* different to Daniel's place.

Jacque placed her bags on the bed. "I hope it's to your

liking."

"It's amazing." She smiled at him. "Thank you."

He smiled back and nodded. "Are you hungry?"

A sudden image invaded her mind of her sinking her teeth into flesh – blood – and drinking deeply. It was so unexpected and sudden, she took a step back in semi-shock, but caught herself quickly as the vision dissipated. "Er..." Her stomach growled.

A blond eyebrow went up. "I'll take that as a yes. Is there anything you don't eat?"

"No."

"I'll have dinner sorted in about an hour then. Oh, before I forget"—he went to the wardrobe and opened its door—"you probably don't want to think about this now, but there are a handful of dresses in here that would suit the event on Friday. Most were fashioned between 1910 and 1930, but they're immaculate – barely worn. Hand sewn to perfection. Choose whichever you'd like."

"1910 to 1930?" Her hand went to her heart – she wasn't sure why. To stop it falling out? To stave off a heart attack? To quell her excitement? And that wasn't a lie. Everything in this house excited her so much her tiredness had actually faded.

"The best time period for women's fashion in my humble opinion."

"But ... you own the dresses, too? *All* of this?" The artefacts, the armour... He probably took it all with him every time he moved. "Why?"

He seemed to contemplate that question until he finally answered it on a slight sigh. "I've been around a long time; I've seen civilisations come and go. It's easy to forget what 'was' in the passing of time; more natural to focus on what is here and now. The things I collect are reminders of cherished times. And perhaps reminders that, no matter how far I fall, I've still had a place in the world."

She had no idea what to say to that, but before the silence could settle between them too long, Jacque turned and left. "Dinner in an hour," he reminded her as he disappeared down the stairs.

Half an hour later saw her showered, moisturised, and standing, naked, in front of the full-length mirror next to the dressing table. Her eyes wandered to the bite on her abdomen, wretched, ugly thing that it was. Only now could she see it resembled a vampire's bite. The old wound had throbbed, stabbed, and burned at the point her memories had returned, but it did nothing now. Just sat there as a reminder of her helplessness and her family's betrayal – from every single member of her family.

She was still piecing together fragments of conversations she now remembered. Her mother had used the word 'insemination' regarding her birth. What did that mean? Did that mean she wasn't her mother after all? And her grandmother had been willing to kill her. Tears surfaced, but she quickly blinked them away. Grief was fast turning to anger.

Walking away from the mirror, she hunted through her bag for underwear, found a green, lacy pair and pulled them on, then, after a moment's hesitation, allowed curiosity to get the better of her and headed to the wardrobe.

The dresses were stunning. So stunning, it felt like a dare to put one on. *Just try one on quickly – only one. Might as well see if any fit well enough before Friday.* Because she didn't have a lot of time, she chose the one she felt might be the easiest to put on, and with the greatest care, slipped it over her head, trying her damnedest to push away the many questions she had about *who* had worn these dresses and how those women must have meant something to Jacque for him to keep their clothing.

Because his blood is in you, and now you know it and can taste it because you remember it – hello, unreasonable jealousy. Take a hike.

It was sleeveless and made of a dark brown silk material, with pearls sewn in to frame the shape of the curve of the chest down to the ruched centre that hung low around the swell of the hips, making hers look more sensual and rounded than they ever had. Her waist looked deceptively tiny above the ruching. The V opening at the back went all the way down to the waistline, hugging her shoulder blades and sides to perfection, and the front... She gulped at her reflection. The V opening sat half as low at the front, showing much more cleavage than she was used to. The silk was thick enough to be opaque, but the way it hung around and off her breasts made her blush where she stood. There was no way she could wear a bra with this.

But there was no denying its sensuous sophistication.

Gotta be French.

Her phone sounded a text message. Pulled out of her thoughts, she went to get it from her handbag. It was from Daniel: **Let me know you're okay. Thinking of you. Would love to meet you tomorrow if you're up to it – during the day is fine. There's always a shaded spot somewhere. Tell the bastard if he hurts you, I'll stake him. D x**

She shook her head and smiled: **I'm fine. He's looking after me well so far. Let me know where and when tomorrow – I took the day off. Xx**

He'd clearly been hoping she'd agree because the answer came back straight away as if he already had it prepared: **10am at the War Museum on Worthy Road, north of Winchester. Most of their parking is in the shade and the edge of the building is covered by the roof all the way around. No one**

ever in there that time of the morning. Free entry.

Okay. See you then. X

The display screen told her it was nearly 10 p.m.

A scent caught her completely unawares. It carried on the brief draft that billowed under the door and rose up after colliding with her bare feet.

Somewhat entranced, she opened her door. A wave of whatever was for dinner hit her square in the face – that was a delightful aroma in itself – but it wasn't what had captured her. Glancing to the right, down the dark, narrow landing, she spied an open window towards the end.

There it was. She caught a thread of the scent and followed it. The window was an older styled one with a pane that slid upwards. Slipping her hands under the ajar frame, she pushed the pane the rest of the way up, enjoying the way the night air encircled her and tingled her flesh. A hundred different smells grabbed her, so unexpectedly she swayed a little and held onto the frame for purchase. Closing her eyes, she instinctively sifted through them, searching for the one that had drawn her out of her room.

When she found it, she turned her head towards it and opened her eyes. Her sight and hearing sharpened in a way she'd not known before, although she did now recall she'd been able to hear remarkably well as a child. Her vision cut through all the shadows and greys, immediately able to define every shape with perfect precision until she zeroed in on a creature strolling down the unpaved path beyond the front garden.

It was a fox. It had a rabbit by the neck and even in the near dark, fifty metres or so away, Sophia could see the red that matted its light brown fur from where the fox had ripped its skin.

And it was the blood that had snared her.

A dull pain raced through her gums as she plotted, in her mind, the distance between herself and what she had, on some primal level, decided was her meal. Could she leap that far? Was she faster than a fox?

Not really in her body, yet able to feel the spring of every muscle and tendon inside her, she leaned her torso forwards, her focus never leaving her target as she lifted a leg and laid a knee against the sill.

She was hauled away, sharply, by a hand around her waist, her back colliding with hard muscle. An 'oomph' left her at the contact. Alerted by the noise, the fox looked her way and scampered off with its prey. Her first reaction was a growl and a hiss at her lost food. An attempt to kick herself away failed when she was spun and barrelled against the wall. Both of her arms were caught and pinned above her head; a flailing leg arrested mid-attack, and then Jacque's entire body imprisoned hers. She was moulded into his frame with nowhere to go.

"All right, all right..." His hand left her thigh where he'd caught her leg and encircled her waist instead. He pressed a thumb into her stomach. She gasped and her stomach growled, releasing the ache of her hunger a fraction. It was enough. Her *human* awareness finally returned.

"Let it go," Jacque muttered into her ear, his jaw against her cheekbone. "Let it go. If you want to sink your teeth into flesh, I'll teach you how, but it needs to be safe and it needs to be clean."

Mortification rose. *What* had she just craved.

"I'm sorry. I left you waiting for food a bit too long."

The last part of her conscious human self landed in her body with a jolt. It should have helped; it should have quelled whatever *inhuman* hunger had dominated her, but it stirred a new type of yearning – a very female one that had full awareness of the powerful male body pressed up hard against her breasts, her hips, and between her legs.

Releasing her arms, he cradled her backside as he swung them away from the wall and walked her down the landing, back to the entrance of her room.

Half in shock at her own behaviour, she didn't protest, but held onto his shoulders as her legs gripped his hips.

By her doorway, he motioned for her to release him, which she did, effectively sliding down his body until her feet hit the floor.

He didn't move away. With just the slightest of movements, he rubbed his cheek against hers. "You're doing just fine, Sophia. Come downstairs when you're ready. Don't be long. I'll feed you properly." Then, after a moment, "This dress looks stunning on you."

He walked away down the stairs, and she somehow, robotically, made it back inside her room. Unthinking, she ended up back in front of the long mirror and found almost a stranger staring back. Her hazel-amber eyes gleamed a light gold and ... she had fangs.

Catching her breath, she moved closer to the mirror and opened her mouth wider.

They were small.

Baby fangs.

But they were there, although already withdrawing now that bitter reality tore through any and all hunger. *This* was why her family had despised her.

She was a vampire.

Chapter Twenty-Three

Sophia changed out of the brown silk dress and into her own, more modest, pastel green summer one, before making her way downstairs towards the smell of food. She'd squashed down her embarrassment at her behaviour as much as possible, as well as the feeling of insecurity that cascaded through her at remembering the things her family had called her. Aunt Fiona's disgust at her fangs was particularly prominent in her mind—*she hisses, Deborah, before she displays them; it's diabolical*—as was her grandmother's nonchalance at having her disposed of.

Not only was she a vampire – or one with a human heartbeat, anyway – she was pretty certain she wasn't a very good one, unable to hunt or feed, unable to run as fast or be as strong. Throw in the occasional sudden shooting pains from Hugo's bite, made worse since her little episode upstairs, and her sense of worth was at an all-time low.

But unworthiness wasn't a feeling she wanted to best her – she had beaten it back after Pierce's betrayal; she would beat it back now.

There was movement in the dining room, so that's where she headed.

Jacque was pouring wine. "Just on time. I'm serving up."

Two serving bowls sat on hotplates, one filled with herbed potatoes and one filled with a mouthwatering type of stew, and they both smelled divine. She was a little in awe and very surprised at the layout in front of her. "You cooked?"

"Where you expecting something else?"

"Oh, no, I ... well, yes. I suppose I thought it would be a takeaway or something."

"A takeaway?" He sounded positively insulted by that.

"What in god's name has Deiniol been feeding you the past few nights."

She smiled despite herself. "This is *so* much better. I'm just surprised. I didn't think vampires ate food. Or cooked it for that matter."

"Most don't. Food doesn't sustain us and most vampires have no taste for it. But I'm not most vampires, and neither are you. Take a seat."

She did. "Um ... Jacque, I'm really sorry about what happened upsta—"

"Don't."

She glanced at him as he spooned the most drool-worthy looking meal into her shallow bowl.

"Don't ever apologise for what comes naturally. Or for your needs."

It hardly alleviated her guilt, but she let it drop in the face of all the hard work that had obviously gone into making whatever this was. "This looks amazing."

"Bœuf à la Bourguignonne. Done the right way."

She had no idea what the wrong way was, but she wasn't complaining.

"And without garlic," he added.

That piqued her interest. "Does garlic actually harm vampires?"

It was his turn to smile. "Not in the slightest. But it makes blood taste rather awful – in that sense, it does ward off vampires. If you're ever worried a vampire wants your blood, eat plenty of garlic – it really will keep them away. Dig in."

She didn't need to be told twice. More famished than she cared to admit, she grabbed her cutlery, balanced a bit of everything onto her spoon and—

"Oh, my god ... this is"—she swallowed, already spooning more—"this is more than delicious."

"Good."

"You made this in an hour?"

"No. It was mostly prepared last night. I was expecting to eat it on my own tonight, so it's nice to have company."

"You cook for *yourself*?" she asked, already piling up her third spoonful.

"I like cooking. You can make anything taste exactly as you want it to – it feeds my need for control."

She studied him, not quite knowing what to make of his answer.

"And," he continued, "much like all the artefacts in the house, there are stories in food – secrets of entire cultures that can't be learnt any other way."

God, the refined education in that statement ... his understanding of history and heritage was a turn on for her mind and no mistake. "And your culture? Is France where you lived when you were turned?"

He didn't reply. Just stared at her in contemplation.

She didn't know where to look, so she asked another question. "If food doesn't sustain you, do you feed – on blood, I mean – before you eat food, or after?"

"Most vampires feed once a day. I only need to feed about once a week."

"Oh." Les was right about him sometimes being a man of few words. He managed to answer questions, yet somehow, say nothing.

She was disappointed to see she'd almost finished her serving.

"Help yourself to more," he said, softly.

"Am I that easy to read?"

"Sometimes, yes. And also, no – not as easy as you might think."

After filling her bowl with seconds, she took a breath and decided to invite the elephant into the room. "Maybe, um, I won't need to feed that often, either." She felt like an idiot when that statement hung in the air, the whole thing so unfamiliar. She couldn't meet his eyes. Was it right to joke about it? Should it be something she welcomed into her life? "If, um, if I'm a vampire, that is." She shrugged. As if she didn't care that much about it, which was obviously ridiculous to everyone in the room including the elephant.

She reached for her wine.

"Your heart beats like that of a human, Sophia, and most of the time, your body functions as one. So food will sustain you. However, you have clear vampiric traits, which were stifled through the suppression of certain growth hormones when I took your memories."

She wondered what her expression looked like – if she appeared a bit simple – because he frowned a little and then went on to explain, "The hippocampus area of the brain holds your memory, but it directly modulates your physiology too, by affecting the hypothalamus-pituitary-adrenal axis. I'm sorry."

She put the last of her dinner in her mouth and tried not to look like she was staring blankly at him – human biology (although, was this vampire biology?) had never been her strongest subject. She got the gist, though.

"Now you have your memories back, those traits will reappear, but you may also go through something of a growth spurt. The vampire in you might be unpredictable while that takes place. You also have ... other qualities, that are neither human or vampire."

She sat back with her wine, her dinner finished. "I do?"

He nodded, slowly. "Your ability to pull another into your mind with your eyes – to call them to you the way you called Deiniol – is not a vampiric trait. Vampires push their way into you; they don't pull."

"But *you* pull. It's how you took my memories."

He held her stare, then continued. “It’s a … skill I retained. Your gift with fire is also not that of a vampire.”

“I’d hardly call it a gift.”

“It can be a gift if managed and trained.”

Manage it? She didn’t feel anywhere near being able to do that. “So, what am I? A dragon?”

He smiled and shook his head. “I don’t think so. Although they did exist.”

They did?

He stood from the table. “Come on.”

She got up, bringing her glass of wine with her, and followed him into the living room.

“Where do *you* feel that place is that we both know?” he asked. “The one with the golden gates and blue sky.”

“I…” She’d never actually thought to ask or seek out *where* it was. “I don’t know. It’s always seemed too perfect for this world, so I suppose I never thought to place it anywhere.”

“But if you could, where would it be? What one word does it conjure up for you?”

After another sip of wine, she placed the glass down on a side table and closed her eyes, bringing that place to her in her mind. She let herself go there; become one with it. It had always been so *easy* to do that. “Home,” she said, opening her eyes. “It feels like home.”

Jacque’s eyes were almost watery as they held hers. He turned around, grabbed the hemline of his T-shirt and pulled it up and off him.

Her breath caught in her throat – yes, at every single taut muscle that flexed under his movements, but that wasn’t what took it away. It was…

She approached him, his back still turned towards her. Two huge scars ran from the top of his shoulder blades, around each one, dipping inwards towards the middle of his back, and then outwards again until they ended near his hip bones. They were almost perfectly symmetrical.

It was a compulsion to reach out and touch them, as if she were led. She placed her fingers, gently, at the top of each one.

She heard him hiss at her touch; flinch a little. But he didn't move away.

She waited until he relaxed against her, then trailed her fingers down their length. Slowly. And closed her eyes, letting her touch be her sight: *golden gates, birds of grace, giant wings – giant, white wings – a tremendous turning that felt like the earth's crust splitting ... falling ... plummeting; and then pain. The darkest, most agonising pain that bore screams, and fear, the tearing of skin, and the corporeal tang of blood to fill the void that now existed where the gates once stood.*

"Sophia."

She opened her eyes, her fingers no longer grazing ancient scars but clasped in large hands. Jacque stood facing her. He leaned in and kissed her cheek; kissed her tear.

Her face was wet.

"What one word comes to mind now?" he asked, quietly.

She whispered it, and it was as if there was no ground beneath her feet. "Angel."

He nodded, once. "I have no sire. I was not turned. I fell to earth eleven, maybe twelve thousand years ago, and like almost all of us who fell, I lost everything. My fangs grew to feed my physical needs and I lost my wings until I became one of the first vampires to walk the earth. That origin myth is the truth."

Many things inside her clicked into place and made sense – fused a new part of her into existence – although she couldn't name what any of those things were. "The golden gates—"

"Are the gates of the angelic realm within heaven itself. Where I come from. And you are the first I've met in a very long time who's also been there – certainly the first human being to have *ever* seen it. I have no idea how, but you, Sophia, are part human, part vampire, and part angel."

Jacque's living room somehow managed to retain its cosiness despite being as regally fancy as any other room in the house. An unlit fireplace promised the warmest winters possible, and the floor-to-ceiling bookcase covering the entire far wall would have had Sophia all but glued to its sliding ladder at any other time.

Right now, though, she was taken up by the twelve millennia old male reclined on his nineteenth century bergère as she curled up on his lap. His T-shirt was back on. Touching the scars of his lost wings had shattered a barrier between them, and it wasn't one she could name. It left her feeling, paradoxically, more comfortable than she had ever been and equally as anxious.

"Why didn't you ever tell Daniel and Eliza about your angel origins? They must have seen the scars."

"I told them they were battle scars. It's safer they don't know." He ran his fingers softly through her hair, absent-mindedly, as she rested her head on his shoulder. "Safer that as few know as possible. I'm only telling you because the same origins are within you, somehow. Do you know how many have killed to possess the power angels have?" Something shifted in his demeanour, some deep-seated anger or hurt materialised, then quickly evaporated. "How many have done things even more terrible than killing?"

Instinctively and subconsciously, she nuzzled herself further into his chest to comfort him. "Does anyone know?"

"None alive today. The Templar Knights did – some of them anyway. There were two or three circles within the Templars. But none since then."

"Are there more like you?"

"A handful, yes. And some of the Bratvashka are of angel

origin, although, after their drop in numbers two and a half thousand years ago, probably not many now."

"How many angels fell?"

"I couldn't say. Although the Resurrectors believe it to be 144,000 owing to certain prophesies, which I have no doubt leave a lot to be desired in their translations."

She pulled back and levered herself up a bit. "Do you know how I was created?"

He met her eyes and shook his head. "I don't. Your family didn't divulge any of that information to me. I would tell you if they had."

"I was there that day you were all arguing in my dad's study. The day my grandmother gave you the ultimatum."

She felt him stiffen under her; practically heard his mind reel as he took himself back to that conversation. "You were?"

"I hid outside, but I heard everything. I heard my mother use the word 'insemination' when talking about me. Do you think I was ... I don't know – created in a lab, or something? Uncle Hugo said"—she flinched as his bite flared, but ignored it, closing her eyes to try and remember his words... *I'm your uncle, Sophia, I'm your family*—"we brought you into this world for a reason and it's to save us all, so you will give me..." She let the end of that sentence fall, not wanting or needing to bring that part alive.

She opened her eyes to look at Jacque.

An icy anger burned in his. "Don't *ever* take yourself back to him."

"It's okay." Although another sharp pang deep in her abdomen told her it wasn't. "I'm just trying to piece together—"

"I said don't."

"But it was why he wanted my blood – it could be important. He could have told others – those Nocturnes seemed very adamant I had something they wanted, and the one that night near the cemetery knew my name—"

"Sophia, stop." A dangerously possessive growl rolled into those two words, his eyes now gleaming their blue hue, but her button had been pushed, every memory wanting a resolution, and she couldn't stop talking even though some primordial part of her warned her, *begged* her, to do as he said.

"If there are other vampires who know about me, we have to —" She yelped as the mother of all stabbing pains barbed through her. She pressed into the spot below her navel to try an ease it.

Jacque shifted both himself and her on the seat, almost aggressively, so she was more upright. "Let me see."

"It's not fair," she bit out, shakily, her forehead pressing against his chest for balance, almost as hard as her hand pressed against the wretched bite. "It's not fair I have to feel it over and over again."

Something changed – some subtle air between them. She felt Jacque sort of ... seep into her thoughts. "Sophia, let me see the bite. *Now.*" His voice was as cold as his stare had been, his command etching itself into her brain. She found her obedience to it inexorable, her hand already reaching down to pull her dress up. Even as a part of her protested, she also found she *wanted* to concede to him. She'd been slowly spiralling as she'd talked, her own control on her mind and feelings, teetering. The frantic spiralling had instantly stopped the minute Jacque seeped in and took control. Not that that made this all right.

Caught between right and wrong, she gulped as another type of spiralling now sparked, distant, delicious, and low in the base of her spine.

He suddenly released his dominance – his hypnotic hold – or whatever the hell it was. He nudged her head with his. His voice was heavy with a hundred needs. "I'm sorry, I shouldn't have done that. I feel ... it's my fault he fucking bit you; I should never have... Please let me see."

She was somewhat shocked he held himself to blame for what Hugo had done. She also needed to see the scar for herself. The strength of the pain it exuded was frightening. What if something was ruptured inside her? What if it was bleeding? Was it possible for a twenty-two-year-old wound to split open?

"You're not to blame – I *don't* blame you," she said, her voice shaking. Moving herself with a grimace, she pulled her dress up to her waist, suddenly wishing she'd worn underwear that covered a little more than the sheer green lace she'd chosen.

About half a centimetre of the scar peeked over the top of it.

Jacque pulled down the top of her underwear until the entire scar could be seen. It was just a normal, fucking scar – healed and surrounded by white scar tissue; not red. Old, not new. "Why?" she asked, her voice quivering with revulsion. "Why does a vampire's bite linger?"

Jacque passed his thumb over the length of the scar.

That was not a predictable sensation. She gasped and *undulated* under his motion.

He held her around her waist, gently pressing her into him further. "It's okay. It's okay." He did it again – pressing his thumb in a bit harder this time, just like he'd done with her stomach upstairs. And again, there was some kind of release. The pain was still there, but so was an easing of it. "Bites don't usually linger more than two or three days. But this one was a traumatic bite. When that happens, it's sometimes as if the trauma holds the bite in place, keeping it there, enhanced now by your memories."

"Trauma? It feels like more than that."

He kept stroking it and kneading it. His chin moved against the top of her head, his voice tinged with guilt. "I would have done things differently if I had known what he'd— Sophia, listen to me..."

She tried to focus on his words, his actions softening everything inside her. All she wanted to do was float away.

"I can heal this. I can make this go away, but it's intimate. I wouldn't mention it – wasn't going to – but seeing you in pain... And I have to admit to being selfish: I want that bastard *out* of you."

She made a noise. She didn't know what it was, but she agreed. She wanted the same.

"Do you know about the vampire's bite? What it is and what it entails?"

She nodded against him. "Daniel showed me the fluid from his fangs."

He stilled for a fraction of a second, going rigid, an almost-growl erupting from his chest, but he'd quenched that reaction in the blink of an eye. Not soon enough, though.

Her own body, now relaxed, responded to his possessiveness. She exhaled sharply. Everything below her navel was starting to burn in a far more wanted and needed way.

"I can heal with that fluid," he continued. "But I need to bite the same spot. I need to inject the fluid in."

Everything warred within as the heat in her rose. Forcing herself back to earth, she opened her eyes and glanced down at herself, taking everything in.

She'd ended up kneeling on Jacque, each shin balanced on one thigh. His hand was under her dress, still stroking and stoking the infraction that marked her.

And she was wet.

Soaking between her legs.

She moved her face upwards, placing her right cheek against his.

His own breathing, she now noticed, was strained to a degree. And his irises glowed slightly.

She ran her right hand through his hair, cupping his head.

"I'm not ready," she whispered.

He froze; started to remove his hand.

"No." She grabbed it with her left hand, pressing it back where it was. "Please don't stop. What I mean is..." She had no idea how to put it into words. "I'm straddling two worlds: one of them is this very second, the other is twenty-two years ago. I've only had a few hours to make up those twenty-two years, and I haven't quite made the leap yet. I'm trying. But not yet. I'm sorry."

She felt him shake his head. His voice came quietly. "I said, never apologise for your needs." He pulled his hand out from under her dress, straightened it a bit, then replaced it on the same spot, over her clothing. "Let me know when you're ready."

How would that look and feel? She had no idea. Being with Daniel had been physical and intense, but also simple in some ways. The idea of intimacy with Jacque felt deeper than bottomless oceans. There was no 'casual' here. There was commitment made never-ending by towering golden gates and she couldn't even begin to fathom what was on the other side of that.

Chapter Twenty-Four

Sophia pulled into the car park of the war museum. Daniel was right, it was almost empty. She chose a spot in the shade near the also-shaded side of the building.

Her sleep had been dreamless last night. Her and Jacque had spoken until gone two in the morning about frivolous things as well as angels, vampires, and the event on Friday.

"You haven't called me ma chérie since—"

"You asked me not to. And you're right. It was a term of endearment suited to a particular time."

She agreed. But she missed the affection. On the tail of a yawn, she asked, "What term of endearment would suit now?"

He didn't answer for a while, and then said, "I'm going to think on that."

There had been no more 'intimate' moments. She'd been worried she wouldn't be able to sleep given her earlier sexually aroused state (and what had happened last time she'd gone to sleep in such a state), but she'd ended up drifting off on the sofa mid-conversation, and had a vague recollection of being carried to her room and put into bed. She'd groggily woken up enough to peel her dress off before falling into the deepest of sleeps.

This morning, she'd woken at half past seven feeling very rested and horny as hell. So much so, she didn't think twice about pleasuring herself into a satisfying orgasm, biting her lip hard to stop any noise from reaching overly sensitive ears.

Jacque had left a small, hardback book for her on the kitchen counter titled *Seraph.* The accompanying note said, ***Read this. It might be useful.***

He'd also left another note explaining where all the breakfast things were and that he would be in an important meeting out in Sussex from 5 p.m. until around seven – if she needed anything, it would take longer for him to reach her between those two hours.

She turned off the engine, wondering how much of a burden she was actually being by staying there. He shouldn't have to be thinking about what she might need every second of the day. While she appreciated his care, she was determined to stand on her own two feet somehow or another. Things needed to be equal between them. Knowing she might need to stay at his until at least after the party, she'd also resolved to speak to him about paying for food and some kind of board, even if only for a week.

She locked the car and made her way inside the museum, and there was Daniel in a section to her right, hands in pockets, browsing weaponry and ammunition from 1750 to 1850. He heard or sensed her before she needed to say anything.

He turned with a smile, and all the last traces of difficulty she was feeling melted away. Despite their bizarre situation, he'd been exactly what she'd needed for the last few days, and she considered him a friend, even if the more physical nature of their relationship had ended.

He extended his arms in greeting and Sophia rushed into them gladly, enjoying the way he lifted her off her feet with his embrace. "It's so good to see you," he said, letting her feet back on the ground only after a full fifteen seconds or so. "I was worried about you. I'm still worried about you, to be honest."

"Considering everything, I think I'm doing okay. See anything you like in there?" She nodded towards the weaponry.

"Oh, nothing I haven't seen before. There's always this odd sense of nostalgia though, when you've lived an era no one else who's still alive has. And I'm pretty sure that rifle right there"—he pointed to one of the longer ones towards the back—"belonged to a guy I knew called William."

"Are you serious?"

"Yep. It's got scratches and nicks in specific places – he used to tell me how those happened. Anyway ... times long gone. Come on, let's wander. Tell me how you really are."

They strolled slowly, pretending to study display after display. "Confused, mostly," she laughed. "I have fangs and a heart that beats every second."

"I noticed. The fangs showed yesterday just before you kicked Jacque across the room."

"Right. Well, I got my first hunger pangs yesterday over a rabbit in a field that a fox had caught."

"What did you do?"

"Jacque got to me before I could leap out the window."

"Is he treating you well?" He'd asked that a little coldly.

She raised an eyebrow at him. "Have you not forgiven him yet? Did Eliza explain what really happened when he sired her?"

Daniel sighed. "She did. It took a while for it all to sink in to be honest. When I opened the door and saw her standing there..."

"Had you not asked about her in all this time? Did you not even know if she was still alive? Or undead – I don't know – what's the correct term for being alive when you're undead?"

He laughed. "Alive will do. I didn't want to know, Sophia. You know how hard you find the jealousy? The possessiveness? The way it tears through you? I loved Eliza, but she couldn't be mine anymore – not wholly. I'd mastered those feelings – or I thought I had – until Jacque sired her." Then he let out another smaller, drier laugh. "None of us are completely immune to those feelings no matter how old we are. Did you know that's why a newling needs a whole century with their maker? To conquer all the sensory challenges so they don't become crazed vampires that topple society."

"Jacque did explain that to me."

"Hmmn, and most aren't lucky enough to have that kind of sire. If there's one thing I'm grateful to Jacque for it's his sense of duty in that regard. Eliza and I have turned out well."

"Do you still love her?"

"I do." He smiled, then looked at her. "But we're also getting to know each other all over again. In many ways she hasn't changed – still strong and opinionated and unafraid of goddamned near everything. But in other ways, she has. How about you? What are your feelings for Jacque now all your memories are back."

"Feelings?"

"Yes, feelings. With vampires, everything is about feelings. Eliza explained it all to me, by the way. Jacque had told her beforehand about his involvement with your family and what consequently took place so she could talk it through with me last night after I calmed down."

"He knows you well, then."

Daniel harrumphed.

"I..." She hesitated. "I don't know about feelings." And she sort of didn't want to think about them. It felt like a *hundred* feelings coursed through her last night and they had included various levels of confusion, arousal, devastation, hope, as well as experiencing the deepest care she'd ever received from anyone in her life. Because Jacque knew her needs before she even knew them. It was terrifying. And sublime.

"His blood is in you – *that* is not something I'm happy about given your age at the time and your humanness. It was impossible for you to consent to such an invasion of your privacy."

"He was given an ultimatum."

"I get that. I can appreciate the position he was put in, I'm just not sure I agree with his choice."

"I might not *be* here if he'd chosen differently. And I don't think I suffered for it. If anything, he's the one who linked himself to me to make sure I didn't get hurt – then or now."

"Listen, Sophia, I'm not going to drone on and on about this, but it is important you never forget Jacque's a vampire and all vampires are bound by blood."

"I'm sort of a vampire too."

"I know. But you're also human with a higher potential of

being harmed in all of this. He's already created a link with you by giving you his blood, and it's irrelevant how noble the intention might have been. Please think very hard about ever letting him drink *your* blood – that completes the sharing and it would seal the link. Whatever you feel about Jacque now will increase tenfold and it will be the same for him. I'm saying this because I *remember* what it's like to be human. I had a human wife and family. I remember it all. You need the sun, Sophia, and no matter your vampiric traits, a vampire's world is no place for someone who wants or needs to live a human life. Jacque is very old. I'm not sure he remembers what it's like to be human."

She bit her lip in thought. Jacque had *never* been a human. She really wanted to tell Daniel about the whole 'angel origins' thing, but wasn't about to go behind Jacque's back, not when she didn't know enough about this world. "No, he probably doesn't," she agreed quietly. There was a moment of silence as she let Daniel's words sink in. "He's always refused my blood though, Daniel, and he's never asked for it."

His eyes darkened and so did his tone. "That scar near your hip—"

"That *wasn't* Jacque." And she couldn't hold back her anger when she'd said that. "He would *never* do that."

Daniel took in a breath and seemed to relax. "All right. I needed to hear it from you. Thank you. Do you think you can trust him?"

"Do you think I can't? You spent two centuries with him – very intimately, I'm led to believe. And Eliza has, too."

"Intimately in one sense, but he's different with you."

"He is?"

"Yes. And Eliza's seen that, too. He may have sired us and taught us everything we know, but ... he's always maintained a detachment with us – the way a parent has to be detached enough to let their kids leave. He *is* detached by nature. At least he is with everyone but you."

"What do you mean?"

Daniel glanced at her sideways. "I saw his body language with you on my couch – he was *open* and he never is; and I saw the way he chased after you last night when you fled. Eliza's seen more including the state he was in twenty-two years ago after he took your memories, although he didn't tell her what that was about at the time."

Eliza had seen him *then*? The fuse of jealousy lit inside her, battling with possessiveness. She pushed both feelings away, refusing to let Daniel be right in any way about a vampiric lifestyle and all its suffocating emotions being a vice for her. What was she supposed to do? Deny part of who she was?

"She would love to meet with you this evening – I gave her your number. I hope you don't mind. I think she can explain it a bit more."

"Jesus, Daniel, it sounds like you're both *warning* me away from him. Of course I was initially upset when I got my memories back, but he saved my life twenty-two years ago and he's been nothing but attentive since I've known him – then and now."

"You're already jumping to his defence."

"Because he's done nothing wrong, not because he wants my blood and not because he wants to get in my—" She cut herself off, remembering he almost *had* been in her panties last night. But for valid reasons. And private ones she wasn't going to divulge. But it didn't mean anything anyway – vampiric 'things' and sensuality and sexuality all went together – she was learning that fast.

Her voice had risen on her last sentence, echoing a bit too loudly around the room. She took a breath in to calm herself. "Look, I know you're just watching out for me and I love that you are, but please don't worry. There's no need. I'm a clever girl."

Daniel smiled. "I know that. It's just ... this whole you and Jacque thing—"

"There *is* no me and Jacque."

He looked at her like she was simple. "There really is. And it carries a tinge of inevitable tragedy about it. And that breaks my heart," he ended, his tone hushed.

They stopped walking and she looked at him sadly. "There was *you and I* until yesterday morning." Her eyes filled with tears – she couldn't help it.

"Hey, come here." He swept her into a huge hug and kissed the top of her head. "I wanted to talk to you about that too."

"We don't have to talk about it," she sniffed. "It was one time and I've known you just a few days. And I can't feel your dream bite anymore."

He chuckled against her. "Apart from the 'dream' part, that's normal. Any sensations from a bite usually only lasts two or three days. And we weren't *one* time," he added, his tone dropping, a hint of possessiveness still evident over her and them. "It was many times. And being with you was the best I'd felt in *decades*. I mean that." He kissed her head again. "I need time with Eliza, though." He'd whispered that last sentence, almost as if he hadn't wanted to say it.

"I know." She pulled back. "I really do. You don't have to explain. In fact, you already did by telling me all about how you met her and what she meant to you."

He cupped her face, staring at her intently. "You *ever* need anything, you call me and I will be there."

"I know you will. Thank you, Daniel."

He stroked her cheek a couple of times then let her go and reached into his jacket's inside pocket. "There's something else I wanted to mention to you – a bit more business, a bit less personal."

"Go on."

He brought out a chunky envelope and gave it to her. "Open it later, not here. Les went through your old police reports again in case we missed anything. Something did flag up. It could be nothing, but it's worth being vigilant."

"What did he find?"

"Your statement was the only thing the police really had to go on at the time. You gave the names of all the people staying in your house when it burned down."

"I did."

"Have you always been sure about who was there?"

"Yes. There was my mum and dad"—she displayed her fingers as she reeled off her family—"Uncle Hugo, Aunty Fiona, Aunty Rita, my grandmother and my grandfather. That's seven people. If you include me, that's eight."

He nodded. "The police substantiated that with any DNA they could find, but the only conclusive DNA was from your parents' bodies. Most of the others were too charred to identify in any way, and we already know Hugo – being a vampire – would have likely left no trace in the end. Even a vampire's ashes turns to dust very quickly. So his remains were never officially found at all. Him aside, the rest of the bodies were identified by personal items carried on them, or near them that didn't burn completely. Your grandmother had earrings on. Your grandfather, a watch."

"Yes – I remember identifying those items for the police at the time, now that you mention it. They found Aunty Fiona's crucifix necklace, a more regular one, smaller than my mum's."

"And Rita?"

She frowned. "I can't remember."

"From the reports, it seems the police found nothing that belonged to Rita, and no remains either – no ash or otherwise – to indicate she had perished in the fire. However, they took your word for it because they also couldn't find her living – no one had seen her and no one claiming to be Rita came forward, so after a few years, they recorded her as having officially died in the fire."

"What? I ... Daniel, what are you saying?"

"It could be nothing – maybe she simply wasn't wearing anything that could have survived the fire at the time – but we can't rule out the possibility she may have got out. Your Aunt Rita may still be alive."

Eliza's text came through at midday: **Going to get a few more hours of sleep, but can we meet at five o'clock? I want to show you something. I can pick you up from Jacque's. Wear something trendy – no jeans. Eliza x**

What else was she going to do? Jacque was out tonight anyway. She replied with an affirmative, left her phone on silent because she assumed Jacque was asleep upstairs, and scribbled a note for him about what Les had discovered. She left the note with the documents in the envelope on the kitchen counter. He could go over it when he woke up.

She wasn't sure on how to spend the next few hours. In the end, she decided on heading to her own home to grab some extra clothes and other things she might need. She could also do with buying Abi a birthday present. Picking up her car keys and phone, she was about to leave when the exact same goddamned thing happened as last night – an aroma of blood imprisoned her senses.

Her entire body sparked with adrenaline. Her gums throbbed, and this time she *felt* her fangs break through.

Trying to get a hold of herself, she looked for the source of the scent, her eyes landing straight on the smaller kitchen window – ajar. It looked out over the garden, which she hadn't had time to explore yet. Now in daylight, she spied a cabin towards the end of it, standing in the shade, the tiny window of the cabin, also open.

Her heart pounding, her eyes already trying to focus on prey, she took a step towards the window and froze. She knew that smell. That was *human* blood.

Shadows moved against the cabin's frosted windows; faint sounds accompanied them. Her hearing took over, as sharp as it ever had been, and she cocked her head so her ear was positioned towards the gap in the window.

"Oh, god, yes, yes, yes ... harder ... Jacque..."

Oh, *shit.*

No way, no way, no way. But she couldn't now find a way to *switch off* her hearing.

"Aaaah! Aaaah!"

She had to leave *right now.* Cursing her supernatural auditory perception, she forced her legs to move, then had to catch the kitchen counter to steady herself as Jacque's deep moan caught her ear, that very low, male vibration igniting something deep inside her that simply wasn't safe to trigger – not now.

Jealousy was an astronomical understatement for what tore through her. She battled swathes of violent images – *of her own violence* – as she used everything she had in her not to race into that building and tear the head off whatever had its claws in *her* male. *Her* vampire.

My angel.

No, no, no, no...

She didn't know how she made it out the house, but she did. As soon as she felt the sun on her, she used it to remind herself she was *human*. Not a monster.

But by god. Everything hurt. *Everything* hurt.

She half stumbled into her car, started the engine, and drove home, trembling, hoping she'd get there in one piece.

She'd been crouched on the floor in the corner of her bedroom for half an hour since arriving home. She hoped Jacque's ability to know when she was in danger was limited to *real* danger and not this embarrassing agony that seared her because, god help her, if he barged in through her door right now she'd go for him. She knew that. She'd rip him apart – or try to anyway. And she didn't want to do that.

Hugo's bite was playing havoc with her, too, but for once, it wasn't the worst feeling traversing her. Blinking back tears, she continued to reason with herself, knowing logically that absolutely nothing of consequence had happened, but the vampire in her was a screaming child, throwing a tantrum, unable to understand reason. All it felt was pain, possessiveness, and loss. If all vampires had originally sprung from fallen angels, maybe that was the source of the torment and the reason for the unruly jealousy – the *actual* fall. Losing not just an entire world, but an entire self. To have your wings torn from you must surely be like having your soul cut in two.

"Fuck this for a game of laughs," she whispered to the room. She eventually pulled herself up with a grimace and proceeded to do what she'd come here to do. She found a spare bag of hers and filled it with some clothes, then decided to change now for her meeting with Eliza. She had no idea where they were actually going.

She put on a pair of black, faux leather trousers, a red crop top, and her favourite, short leather jacket. Black boots completed the look. She brushed her hair, deciding to keep it down for a change. Reapplying her lipstick, she felt a little better. More numb anyway. Numbness was better than whatever the hell that had been.

A few more deep breaths and she left the house. She almost stopped at the library to say hello to Abi, but she'd essentially called in sick, so it would be taking the piss to go in after dolling herself up a bit.

Instead, she parked up by the river, sat in her car and phoned her parents' house.

When her dad answered, she burst into tears.

Chapter Twenty-Five

Behold! A holy furnace of purification and protection: it burns, it burns! Defender of all choirs. Two wings to carry the sins of the immortal; two wings to resurrect those not dead; two wings to return to the throne of God. Forever light amid the dark: Seraph; angel who burns for every angel who turns.

♦

Eliza pulled them to a stop outside a huge manor house in the middle of nowhere. The lights were on inside. It looked like it was filled with people and she could hear music.

Eliza's car – and the cars of all vampires, apparently – had a laminated windshield and windows which were UV protected. They could ride in such cars in daylight without too much trouble, although Eliza had taken care to park under a thick, overhanging canopy of trees, like half the cars here.

Sophia's car only had a UV protected windshield (and vampire-flammable side and rear windows). That was why Eliza had insisted on driving.

Sophia had been appalling company during the twenty-minute journey. Having bawled her eyes out to her dad (obviously divulging nothing about vampires and the like), she had told him all about Pierce's death. She'd then taken another fifteen minutes to calm him enough so he was sure she'd be fine before hanging up. Talking to him had helped though – at least a little. It had made her feel human and safe as opposed to a bunny-boiler monster who was a walking firelighter.

Then, she'd driven back to Jacque's, only arriving at five o'clock on the dot because he'd said he'd be away at that time and she was certain she wouldn't bump into him. Eliza had been waiting for her on his drive.

And here they were.

Eliza switched the engine off and turned to face her in the car. "Okay, what gives. Is it me? I know you don't know me that well, but Daniel told me so much about you and I am absolutely fine, by the way, with anything that happened between you two."

"Oh, Eliza, please, no. It's not you. I'm so sorry. It's all of *this*, to be honest. The whole vampire thing and the ... feelings that come with the territory."

She nodded in understanding. "I did wonder. Daniel told me you got your first hunger pangs last night."

"Well, it's happened twice now." Although she wasn't going to go into any detail over that delightful second time she was still recovering from.

Eliza grinned widely and patted her on the knee. "That's why we're here."

"And where is here?"

"Here is where you're going to find your independence."

She stared at Eliza in question.

"You're a grown woman, but a baby vampire – through no fault of your own. You need to do some catching up. This is the perfect place for that."

"Erm—"

"It's a feeding house."

"A what?"

"One suitable for newlings. This is one of the places a sire brings their progeny to teach them how to feed – you know, the ins and outs."

"Did Jacque bring you here?"

"In the 1800s? Nope. I've only heard of this place by reputation and it only opened a few years ago, so it's my first time here, too. But all feeding houses have the same rules and structure – I learnt somewhere similar to this."

"Oh, god, I really don't know."

"It's safe and it's clean. All the humans are consenting donors – they *love* being bitten – and they have all the necessary health checks every six months. The vampires that run this gig organise the checks themselves. There is no better place to start taking your first steps, and I figured you'd want to, right? I mean, I'm a woman – not just a vampire – and I know how Jacque can be, all bossy and controlling even though it's 2025, not 1819. You *need* to stand on your own two feet as fast as possible."

Anxiety stirred in her gut. She hadn't found Jacque particularly bossy or controlling so far – although, she did recall he'd made some quip last night about cooking and control. *And the 'come here' voice he's used on you twice? The one you can never resist? The way he eased your hunger in a nano-second? The way he eased your bite? Is that maybe a bit too much power to let someone have over you?*

She frowned. She was pretty sure Eliza and Daniel knew nothing about what Hugo did to her. Absent-mindedly, her hand went to the bite. "Jacque told me the vampire in me might go through a growth spurt and be unpredictable, so I'm not sure going in there is—"

"Which is why you need to get your skates on. You'll be fine. I'm going in with you and I'm staying, and I'm taking you home afterwards."

"Jacque doesn't know you've brought me here, does he?"

She rolled her eyes. "This is literally the *safest* place I could bring you for feeding. If he has a problem with it, he's being unreasonable. One-day-old vampires come here. I'm surprised he didn't bring you here himself last night after your fangs showed."

"They first showed when I was little."

"That's even worse then – you've been deprived too long. Honestly, when it comes to you, Sophia, I think he's too attached to see things clearly."

She pushed away the memory of the erotic acoustic show she'd stumbled on earlier. "I really doubt that somehow."

"Yeah, right. You should have seen him when he felt you in trouble at the library. I couldn't even keep up – that's why I arrived late. Come on. Let's go in."

"This is such a bad idea," she mumbled as she got out of the car. But she *had* been thinking just this morning she needed to stand on her own two feet. And the way she'd *felt* hearing ... *ugh*. Her mind far too easily threw up the visuals her eyes hadn't seen. Maybe Eliza was right. "Eliza, the two times I got the pangs were totally by accident. I'm not even hungry right now."

"That's all normal. Just don't force it." She stopped walking and swivelled round to look at her. "Try to just *feel* it, okay? Everything to a vampire is sensual including food. It's like oysters down your throat, or that chocolate that melts *just* the right way, or strawberries and cream when you move it slowly around your mouth—"

"Yeah, okay, I get the idea."

She grinned. "But there are many types of pleasure for vampires, remember that too. Food is one kind of pleasure, but a very superficial one. It's *only* food. Throw in blood sharing or even love, and you have a whole different ball game. All you have to do is focus on food. Focus on the primal, most basic of instincts and the pleasure of having that instinct fulfilled."

Sophia sighed. "Right." She didn't even know if she *liked* blood, just that blood seemed to like to snare her unawares. "I've never bitten anyone before. I'm not sure I even know where the right vein is."

"That one's easy – you will absolutely know, I promise. When the hunger comes, all your senses sharpen and your hunter-vision takes over. It will be very clear where to bite and how to bite. And like I said all the humans here *want* to be bitten, so their blood's all pumping hard and ready; their veins are primed."

Sophia wrinkled her nose. That sounded kinda gross, not sexy.

Two bouncers stood at the front entrance to the massive house.

"Oh! I almost forgot." Eliza dropped her voice to a whisper. "You have a heartbeat, so just follow my lead getting in, okay?"

Eliza threw a large smile at the bouncers as they approached the double doors. Once in front of them, she let her fangs grow then slid her hand down Sophia's arm and threaded her fingers through hers. "Two tickets, please."

One of the bouncers looked Sophia up and down. "The human got a health check card?"

Eliza kept her voice light and silky. "It's her first time, boys. She's clean and only mine for the night – no one else is biting her. But I've given her a little taste of what heaven's like and she may sign up as a donor if she likes what she sees tonight."

Sophia threw her a stare – did she *really* just say something as cheesy as that? Eliza squeezed her hand in warning.

The bouncer seemed just as unimpressed as Sophia, but raised his eyebrows and seemed to take it in his stride. He handed Sophia a yellow bracelet. "Keep this on you all the time. No one else bites you, got it?"

"Yes, sir," she replied.

He took both their names – Sophia gave her surname as Jameson – then he stared at Eliza. "It's on you if she gets hurt."

"I accept all responsibility." Eliza winked at the bouncer as he took Eliza's money and let them through.

The music was ridiculously loud inside. "How exactly am I supposed to feed if they think I'm human?"

"They'll stay outside. There are so many people in here, no one's going to know. Put the bracelet in your pocket and relax. No one in here's going to bite you without your consent, so just say no if anyone asks to. Come on, let's go into the next room along."

The house seemed never-ending and more than grand.

"We're allowed anywhere on the ground floor, I think there are five rooms overall. But everything upstairs is private access only."

She looked at the staircase. It was a large and winding affair.

"A lot of the feeding happens just in front of everyone, but if this is like some other places, there are also little alcoves adjoining each room if you want a bit more privacy."

"Oh, my god," gasped Sophia as her eyes landed on a couple – a *few* couples; no, a *lot* of couples – literally *having sex* as they fed. Or were being fed on. Standing up, sitting down, lying down, *in front of everyone*.

"It's pleasurable, remember?" laughed Eliza. "But also superficial – to a vampire anyway. Sophia." Eliza turned her so she was looking at her face and not the insane orgy all around her. "Listen, to the human, the whole sex with a vampire thing is heaven. To the vampire, the human is *just* food – pleasurable food, but *only* food. We've developed a good relationship with some humans over the millennia we've been around: we give them pleasure with our bodies and our bite, and *they* feed us happily and often. It works. It means we can remain *good* vampires and not turn to violence and killing. But to a vampire, mind-blowing, out-of-this-world sex is not what you see in here – that kind of sex would be *wanted* sex; *soul* sex; blood-bonded sex; all-consuming love sex; usually with another vampire so the same level of need can be reached, but not always. You get the idea?"

She couldn't actually answer that, so she asked the question that was at the forefront of her mind. "Is this how you and Daniel feed? I mean, with others?"

Eliza laughed again. "Well, yeah, although Daniel's been feeding off donor bags for some reason I just don't get." She did sound quite confused by that. "But he did used to before I was turned. It doesn't have to include the sex, by the way – that's just down to who you're feeding on and whether it feels right to go with it."

"But ... but how do you deal with the jealousy? When you see him feeding off a human like *this*?" She waved at the undulating couples around her.

Eliza smiled sympathetically and pulled her into a hug. "It's *only* food, honey. But, yeah, the jealousy's a shitter, even when I was human, although it's so much worse as a vampire. I wish it never existed. It takes about a century to tame it. But it *does* tame."

She'd be dead in a century. She was stuck with it forever.

"The best thing you can do is go mingle. The human donors won't be able to hear your heartbeat, so feeding will be easy. Any vamp that hears it will just think you're a donor. Remember, this is a *safe* place. It's friendly and everyone's vetted. I'll be around and I'll take you home in a couple of hours. But go *learn* what it is to be a vampire. Go feel it and be it." She nodded with encouragement and then walked off.

Never had she felt so out of place in all her life. But she had learnt a few things about herself in a very short space of time. One – orgies and public sex just didn't do it for her. At all. She felt not even a hint of arousal at all the thrusting, mashing bodies, or moans of pleasure. Two – she was fast getting the impression that human blood maybe didn't do it for her either given that she could smell it very strongly (the air was literally tinged with it), but absolutely nothing was happening to her stomach, or her guts, or her loins for that matter. A great big zilch.

Trying not to look bored out of her mind, she strolled out of room number three and into room number four. More of the same greeted her.

"Hey, you hungry?" That came from a fairly handsome sandy-blond haired man as he walked by, stopping only because he'd noticed her standing there like a wallflower.

Come on, Sophia. He's not bad looking – mid-thirties maybe. Strong physique. Dive right in. "Oh, I've fed, thanks."

"Okay," he smiled. "Maybe next time."

She smiled back, then after he disappeared, she blew a strand of her hair away from her eyes by blowing upwards. Ha! She used to do that as a child a lot, she just remembered. She'd go cross-eyed doing it.

Christ, had she only been here half an hour? She had no idea where Eliza was.

She wandered out of room four and into the hallway. Someone else approached her. An elegant looking Asian woman this time, with an equally elegant smile. "Hi, there. Have you eaten?"

"I have, thank you so much. Maybe next time."

She nodded and politely left her to it, and the next moment she was alone, Sophia swung herself under the huge, winding staircase and leant on one side of its column.

No sooner had she hidden herself from view than two giggling women (they sounded like *very* young women) decided to stop on the other side of the column and have a gossip. "Did Jenna tell you about what the sex is like when a vampire loves you?"

Sophia rolled her eyes and bit back a curse at the mindless conversation she was going to have to endure.

"Jenna has a vampire who loves her?"

"No way, she's way too tame and fat for any vampire to look twice at her. That's why she practically lives in feeding houses."

Nice. A bitchy gossip. God, if you actually exist, get me out of here.

"But a vampire *told* her about it. You know how everything's, like, super sensual when you're with them anyway, right? Well, apparently, when a vampire is actually in love with you they can make you come with a kiss."

"Bullshit. No way."

"Yes way. She said they can make you orgasm without even touching you anywhere else – just by kissing you."

"You liar."

"I'm not lying."

"Then Jenna's lying."

"I believe her – she talks to enough of the vamps." And thank the heavens they started to walk away. "Anyway, my new aim is to get one to fall in love with me."

"Eew, but what if he gets all clingy?"

"Seriously, if I can orgasm without even having to take my clothes off, he can cling all he likes."

Their voices disappeared into one of the rooms behind her and Sophia let herself slide down to a crouch. Silence was fucking golden.

Looking at the underside of the wide, spiral staircase above her, she was ironically reminded of that time she'd overheard everything in her dad's study from under the stairs. She hadn't wanted to be seen then and she didn't want to be seen now.

Unfortunately, this wasn't quite as private a hidey-hole as that one had been. Still, as long as she stayed this side of the column, she could only really be seen by those leaving room five. The other four rooms were mostly hidden from view. As long as she didn't have to listen in on any more inane conversations, she was staying right here for the next half hour at least.

Closing her eyes, she breathed in and out a few times, wondering if she actually *could* slow her heart rate down now she had vampire traits. *Yeah, look at you hiding. Some vampire you are.*

She wasn't sure what caught her first – the scent or just the *feeling*. Or perhaps it was his footsteps. Yes. That was it. His footsteps. And she knew they belonged to a 'he' because her hearing was suddenly primed. In her mind, eyes still closed, she homed in on the sound of his steps and pieced together a visual: male, large, wide and confident strides; a long coat maybe, because there was a soft flap and rustle as he strode.

As if a window was suddenly opened, his aroma billowed around her and she saw—

Her eyes flew open on her soft gasp. *Golden gates.*

Half-drugged by his scent, she pushed herself up from her crouch, her back still against the plaster of the staircase's trunk.

Her fangs were out. The tips of them sat on her bottom lip. And *something* ran through her. Was it arousal? It was something *like* arousal, but it ran deeper. She'd had the same feeling before when she'd taken Jacque's hand at Pierce's place.

Intrigued and simply called to look, she walked around the safety of the column until she'd found her mark.

With red hair that hung above his shoulders, and jovial pale blue eyes that looked like they dropped women (and maybe a few men) to their knees, he strode across the hallway like he owned it. A suede duster jacket rippled over black jeans and leather boots, and hugged a dark maroon shirt to a large and well-defined chest.

Oddly, Sophia could suddenly recall the taste of Jacque's blood in her mouth as if she was swallowing it anew. *My angel*, she whispered in her mind. She'd whispered it to Jacque, but the man turned his head and his eyes met hers. It was as if everything slowed to a stop, even though it didn't. Still walking, his gaze wavered from pleasant, to mildly surprise, to strangely bemused, finally ending on the slightest of frowns. All of them almost imperceptible.

She wondered if he was about to veer course towards her when a presence appeared from above.

"Ronan."

The man glanced up to someone – another male – who Sophia assumed was on the stairs. "Aah, bout ye, Manuel?" With the quickest motion not visible to the person above, he glanced back at her and signalled, with a flick of his stare, for her to get back to her hiding place.

She did, understanding the hidden implication of danger.

"I thought you'd done a runner." The other man didn't sound amused.

"And miss your boss eating my head off on this fierce mild evenin'? Never. Let's get this over and done with."

His buoyant Irish brogue didn't fool her. She could feel his anxiousness like it was set in her own bones although she wasn't entirely sure why. She made a mental note of how he was the only vampire she'd heard so far to have a strong accent. Daniel's English just sounded neutral, and Jacque had the faintest accent that most would simply assume was French because of his name, even if it wasn't.

Ronan – that's what the man had called him – walked on and up the stairs.

She waited until he'd reached the top and was out of sight. And then followed.

There was only one floor above the ground floor as far as she could tell – and maybe just the roof above that one. The upstairs landing was expansive. The white marble flooring up here matched the floor below. The whole house had an air of both grandeur and hardness.

Her hearing still primed, Sophia let it lead her to the voices coming from the third room along. Its door was ajar, but with the music pounding away below and everyone in their zoned-out aroused state, she doubted even vampires would hear the argument in progression. She also suspected that in a place like this, everyone did what they were told. If the rules stated that upstairs was out of bounds, she couldn't envision anyone breaking them and risking an end to their enthusiastically given supply of erotic food – probably at other feeding houses, too, if word got around they had a troublemaker on their hands.

Walking as quietly as possible, she made her way to the edge of the door, made sure no one else was around, and looked through the half-inch crack where the hinges met, taking a chance her heartbeat would go unnoticed amongst the music, the palpable anger, and all the other humans in the house.

Three large men – most probably vampires – had Ronan boxed in against the large table in the room. The room itself, from the little she could see of it, looked like it was used as a meeting or conference room.

"I think it's really fucking convenient every time we send him on this mission with *good* information, he comes back with sod all. It starts to look like he's *protecting* the project, doesn't it?" That was Manuel – she recognised his London accent from downstairs.

Ronan started to protest, but the man standing directly in front of him held up his hand. He looked the most menacing of all three. The tallest and widest, he had slicked back dark hair, a short beard, and two diagonal scars across his face. When he spoke, his slight accent was indistinguishable. "Perhaps Mr McLaughlin needs a reminder of what *permanent* scars feel like, no?" He gestured to his own face, and then placed his hand, far too gently for his words, on Ronan's neck; stroking it where it dipped into his chest. "It's been too long since his powerful, indestructible body really knew fear, hmmn? Or perhaps"—he stepped in and leaned right into Ronan, making him grip the edge of the table for balance as he tried to move back—"I could spend some time with it myself. I do enjoy carving my mark into a fine male physique; outside and inside."

"Joseph." Ronan attempted a calm tone even in the face of the macabre violence she could feel oozing from this Joseph guy. "Project Veil is one in a million. It is literal salvation for those who believe in it. It's *going* to be guarded with the same ferocity as every holy relic anyone ever sacrificed themselves for. My inability to get close to it is not indicative of my incompetence."

"Fuck this tosser, Joseph," seethed Manuel. "He hired that goon, Iain, last time. He almost wrecked the whole damn thing – almost got us all killed, and here he is making more excuses. I reckon he's *got* his hands on what we want; he just wants it for himself."

"Is that the truth, Ronan?" asked Joseph, silkily.

Manuel and the other bloke who hadn't said a word yet, both stepped further into Ronan's space, caging him in. He wasn't getting away – none of them were small men.

Sophia scanned the hallway for anything that could be a weapon.

"You know it's not. That Iain was a fucking gobdaw, it's not my fucking fault he came highly recommended, likely by someone as shite as him."

All she saw was a forgotten bottle of whiskey on a console table, half full. Other than that, the landing was bare. The doors to the other rooms were all closed. They'd damn well hear her opening a door.

"See this?"

She turned back to the gap to see Joseph placing a hose on the table. Next to it, he put a small bottle that looked similar to the ones Abi had given her.

Joseph resumed his too-intimate position against Ronan. "Tell me, Ronan, are you a fan of colonic irrigation? With holy water? Last time I eased this tube into a vampire, he screamed so hard his throat bled as much as his insides." He stood back and looked at the others. "Strip him. I want full access."

Ronan was spun with a growl – his or Joseph's she couldn't tell – and slammed face down onto the desk. His duster jacket and shirt were both ripped off him with a brutal strength, confirming to Sophia these were definitely vampires – not humans. He swung back in an attempt to attack, but his left hand was swiftly smacked onto the desk and a stake went through it.

Sophia jumped.

Ronan screamed.

And then Sophia's eyes widened as his struggle gave her a clear vision of his naked back for a few seconds. Two scars, identical to Jacque's, lined it. It bolted her into action. She had no bloody idea what she was going to do, but she prayed on the only two things she had going for her: a bottle of whiskey and an erratic human heartbeat which she hoped would hide anything she might use to her advantage.

Leaving the crack of the door, she made for the bottle and picked it up, its lid already off, and dabbed some of the whiskey over herself, then took a swig of it for good measure, swishing it around her mouth before swallowing with a grimace. She'd always thought it was the rankest of spirits.

She ran a tongue along her teeth. Her fangs had disappeared the moment her attention had been taken up by what was going on in the room. *Good – stay hidden.*

Readjusting her bra a bit, she pushed her breasts up more and her crop top down until there really wasn't much left to the imagination.

Another scream sounded, and refusing to think for any length of time about what she was *actually* doing, she barged into the room, letting herself fall into it with a stumble, hoping to god reeking of alcohol would make her bad acting acceptable.

"Ooh!" she exclaimed with a giggle. And then took in the scene around her as if seeing it for the first time. She let her eyes widen. "Ooooh!" she repeated. "This isn't the bathroom, is it?" She feigned dizziness; stumbled two more steps.

"Damn it," muttered Manuel as he hastily shut the door and locked it.

All eyes were on her, even Ronan's in his compromised position. His belt had been removed, and it looked like his back might have been lashed with it, but that's as far as they'd gotten. The third man sat on his right hand, on the desk; his left was completely caked in blood. She could *feel* Ronan's gaze but refused to meet it. It would distract her. She waved a hand around at the room and everyone in it. "Is this a bondage thing?" she asked in awe. "I have *always* wanted to try that shit out."

"Get the fucking human out of here," hissed Joseph.

She ignored him and zeroed in on Manuel who had his back to the door as he stared at her. His eyes glinted ever so slightly as they roamed her face and then her cleavage. *Checkmate.* "Oh, but no one's even fed on me yet." She ran a finger over a vein that ran across the top of her left breast.

Like a moth to a flame, he followed her finger. His tongue darted out to lick his lips.

"And here I am, looking at all this, and"—another little stumble—"*you* big boys, and, well, I'm kinda ... wet between my legs now." She made a point to look at Manuel's crotch as she said that.

"Manuel." Joseph's temper was about to snap. "She's already seen too much. *Dispose* of her."

"Er, Joseph," said the vampire sitting on Ronan's hand. He was also taking her in with hungry eyes. "Word gets around to all feeding houses that we snuffed a donor, we're not going to be able to do our work as easily."

"Anton's right," agreed Manuel, his tone now a shade more threatening as he drank her in from head to foot. "You're probably too drunk to remember anything anyway, aren't you, honey? And after I've had you ... you're not going to remember your own name." He went straight to his belt buckle.

She put on her sweetest smile. "So I get to do the bondage thing too?"

"Oh, yeah, baby. While I'm feeding off you and fucking you."

She giggled and drunk-stumbled as she made her way, backwards, towards the desk, not taking her eyes off Manuel. "That's great, big boy," she purred. "Because there's a game I *really* love to play."

"Oh, yeah? What's that."

"It's called Simon Says. You're Simon, and I have to do exactly what you say. Kinda like you're my master and I'm your slave."

"Sounds good to me, princess." His button was off now. His zipper coming down over his very obvious bulge.

"But there's one rule – the game always has to start the same way otherwise you forfeit the chance to make me your slave."

"And what's the rule?" he asked, his voice now tinged with a hoarse edge.

Sophia slid herself onto the edge of the desk, sitting. Ronan was pinned next to her on the left. She leaned back suggestively, parting her legs. "You have to look deep into my eyes and say,

'Let me in.' Think you can do that, big boy? Like you're the bad wolf, wanting to eat up the little piggies?"

Manuel chuckled. He sounded so fucking sure of himself, half of her wanted to laugh too. "That your little fetish, princess?" He grabbed her hips with a growl as he mashed his erection between her legs, grinding her into him.

She held herself together; pushed away any and every ounce of disgust because she had *one* chance to get this right. She ignored the way his hands felt around her; ignored the way Hugo's scar stabbed her. "Look at me and say it," she whispered. And she actually needed to hear him say it. Maybe it eased her conscience. Maybe killing him would be more acceptable if he was the one who had asked to come in.

His starving, dark orbs met hers as his grin widened. "*Let. Me. In.*"

She smiled. "Okay, then."

In truth, she had no idea if this would work – she'd never bloody done it on purpose before – but she had a plan B. Plan B was to reach behind her, yank the stake out of Ronan's hand and drive it into Manuel's heart. As it happened, plan B wasn't needed.

Sophia grabbed his face, locked his gaze with her mind, and pulled, and she didn't waste any time over it. She knew exactly where she wanted to take him and rushed him there with alarming speed.

Confusion raced over his eyes and then they widened in nothing short of terror as she brought him before the golden gates – practically smashed him into them – and it was like the gold became the fire she needed, purifying anything unworthy of what lay behind those gates.

He whimpered and tried to close off his mind, but it was far too late. Flames filled him from the inside out and he all but exploded from her grasp, a leaping fireball catapulting across the room.

"What the—" Anton was on his feet in seconds.

Ronan twisted round as soon as he was free of him, pulled the stake out of his left hand and drove it into Anton's heart through his back.

Joseph's fist found Ronan's face, throwing him into Sophia, and they both went hurtling to the ground. Ronan was on his feet before Sophia could blink. He hugged her around the waist from behind, whispered "kick" into her ear as he swung her up and around with force.

On pure instinct, she did as he said *just* on time as her boot went into Joseph's chest. Maybe there was some super strength in her after all – or maybe it was Ronan's strength combined with hers. Whichever it was, her kick was strong enough to send him flying towards the window, his own weight breaking it to pieces as he launched out of it.

Gasps and shrieks sounded from below. She followed Ronan to the window and they both looked down to see Joseph dusting himself down and staring right at them – at *her*.

He let out a roar, pointed a finger at her, and then, in a blur, disappeared.

"He won't be back anytime soon," reassured Ronan. "Not with what everyone's just seen."

Sophia teetered where she stood, the reality of what just happened – *what she just did* – crashing down on her. The bite mark on her hip radiated pain.

And *now* she was hungry. Charged and hungry.

Ronan's bloody hand permeated her sinuses.

Her fangs grew.

He sensed it.

Turning to face her, he took her in properly – her eyes, her teeth, her heaving frame with its beating heart; looked at the charred dust on the ground that had been Manuel, then back at her. "Holy Mary, who the fuck are you and where'd'ye come from?"

She couldn't speak and had no strength for much. Using the last of it, she met his gaze, locked it to hers, and threw up the image of the golden gates, just like she'd done with Jacque on Daniel's couch. Or maybe he'd been the one to do that, she couldn't really remember.

Whichever it was, it worked.

Ronan's stare became one of disbelief. "Aingeal?" he asked, softly; stunned.

Her gaze veered towards the protruding vein on his neck and stayed there. Eliza had been right – she knew exactly where to bite and how. Her fangs felt bigger than they'd ever been and they ached like nothing else; felt almost itchy. "P-please," she managed to stutter.

Understanding came over him. He took her with him to one of the conference chairs, sat himself down, then pulled her onto him, angling his neck. "You saved me from a world of pain, stóirín. Take what you need."

She didn't need a second invitation. It was as if the ends of her fangs had nerves and knew exactly how much pressure to use. She bit far more softly for the fierce need she felt within. The first lave of blood over her tongue was pure heaven. She moaned and sucked.

She felt Ronan's entire body harden beneath her, then relax on a sigh as his arm came up and around her to support her feed.

A hushed string of words left him as he pulled her in closer, his thumb stroking her skin under her top.

She barely heard them. Registered nothing. Not the door opening; not Jacque and Eliza entering the room. There was just the sweetest red nectar of life gliding down her throat, rebuilding her from the inside out, and bringing her home.

Chapter Twenty-Six

"I'm sorry if I got you in trouble with Jacque," said Sophia as they pulled up outside Jacque's house. She was in Eliza's car, and Jacque had accepted a lift back home from Ronan in his. Jacque and Ronan, it turned out, were not unfamiliar to each other, albeit had not seen each other for nearly a thousand years.

Apart from an initial and brief appraisal to make sure she was all right, Jacque had yet to say two words to her.

"But," she continued, "I had to do it, Eliza. They were going to torture him. I'm not sorry for jumping in."

"And the feeding part, Sophia?"

"What do you mean?"

Eliza let out an exasperated groan. "I asked you to go mingle with the *humans*. Feed on *humans*. You drank from a vampire."

"I needed it after—"

"Humans aren't supposed to drink from vampires – not really. And you've drunk from two. Vampires drink from vampires, and vampires drink from humans, not the other way around. *He's* linked to you now, just like Jacque is and actually, I don't even know what happens with that. I don't *know* humans that feed on vampires. I don't know what the consequences are when a human feeds on *two* and links with *two*."

Oh. It wasn't like she was really thinking at the time – just needing. "I *feel* okay. Is Jacque mad at me?"

"I have no idea – he hasn't said a thing to me since we found you."

Great. She sighed.

Further up the drive, Ronan had already parked up. She saw them both get out of his car and head into the house. "Guess I'd better go face the music."

"We're all going in. Jacque pretty much called a meeting as we left – said Ronan has a lot he can tell us about the party on Friday. He's going to be there too."

"He is?" And Abigail had no idea a small collection of vampires had been invited to her parents' do. She wondered why they'd invited their daughter at all. As far as she knew, there were going to be vampires there, churchy people there, probably Resurrectors since there was a hidden history between the stately home and her family name, and Abi had mentioned some kind of ceremony. Why on earth invite a woman who knew nothing about any of that – *even* if she was their daughter? What was the point?

Jacque and Ronan had spoken briefly for a few minutes, alone, after she'd finished her feed. (They'd let her finish – was that a good thing? It seemed a polite thing, anyway.) Ronan, it turned out, owned the feeding house. He and his employees had had to reassure guests after Joseph had gone flying out the window and put a few things in place before they'd left.

"Daniel will be here in a minute. Jacque asked me to call him."

"Full house, then."

"One thing's for sure, Sophia." Eliza threw her a light smile. "Life's a lot less boring with you around."

Eliza and Daniel sat there, stunned, bewildered, and lost for words, as they looked at the scars etched into both Jacque and Ronan's backs through new eyes. They now knew what had caused them. This was how the meeting had started. Sophia hadn't quite expected it – not after Jacque's reasoning as to why he'd never told them about the vampire's angelic origins – but clearly an important discussion had been had in the car riding home, and the two males had obviously come to an agreement that if Daniel and Eliza were to be involved, they had to understand the angelic aspect to everything.

Sophia was chewing at the bit to know what they'd talked about. She was also not wholly comfortable with Daniel and Eliza's now rising anger at having never been told such a pivotal truth by their sire. The words were starting to come out. Jacque had a lot of explaining to do.

"All the times we spoke of the mythologies, the stories – you could have told me *then*!" That was Daniel.

"Does it affect *our* blood in any way?" Eliza asked, her hurt clearly audible.

"No, not in the slightest."

"You didn't trust us to know about this?"

And it went on and on. They hadn't even brought up *her* angelic traits yet, and she kind of wished they wouldn't, but knew it was inevitable.

Quietly, Sophia left her seat in the living room and made her way into the kitchen. She needed a glass of water and some breathing space. Having just heard one ruckus in a meeting room, she wasn't quite ready for another. It reminded her too much of her family arguing about her – *because* of her.

"The pot's certainly brewin' in there." Ronan strolled in and took up a seat by the breakfast table. "There's only so much I can say in Jacque's defence. I've now left him to his own demise."

Sophia smiled and took a sip of her water. "Would you like a drink?"

"I don't need a drink, thanks."

"Um, Ronan, I just wanted to say thank you for letting me feed from you earlier and I'm sorry if it's put you in a strange position with the blood link. I wasn't really in the place to think things through."

"I can think for myself, stóirín," he replied, softly. "I knew you had a heartbeat – the fangs are an interesting twist to *that* story – and you showed me those golden gates loud and clear. I made a choice, and I made it happily. You might have just saved my life tonight. I should be thanking you. I *am* thanking you."

She smiled again, shrugging off his thanks.

"Although..."

She raised her eyebrows. "Although?"

"A little head's up you were Jacque's would've been appreciated."

Her mouth fell open as his words sank in. "I am *not* Jacque's. Is that what he told you in the car? I belong to myself, and I didn't even know you knew each other back—"

Ronan laughed. "All right, all right, no need to be eatin' me head off. And no, he didn't say those actual words – I just wanted to see your reaction. But he explained to me about your childhood and what he had to do."

That caught her off guard for a moment. "He did?" He must surely trust Ronan implicitly to divulge such a thing.

"He did. But I wasn't talkin' about your blood link. I'll have that drink now – glass of water like yours would be lovely."

"Oh ... er, sure." She opened the cupboard for a glass.

There was a moment of almost uncomfortable silence as Ronan watched her pour his drink, then he said, "Did Jacque ever tell you how he lost his wings?"

She stared at him, surprised. "Erm ... no." She'd kind of just imagined them 'falling off' or something. Hadn't really had time to consider there might be more to it.

He smiled a sad smile. "You know, when we fell as angels all that time ago, we landed scattered across the earth. We had no sire, no creator; we had to cope alone until we crossed each other's paths again. It was anguish. The physical form needs food for sustenance, and our food was blood. If we became addicted to blood – craved it beyond reason – we would lose our wings. Many of us lasted a good two thousand years or so before that happened, but even if we overcame the bloodlust, there were other ways to lose our wings. Jacque and I crossed paths early. I was always grateful for that – that we had each other to lean on; to understand what the hell was going on most of the time."

Sophia handed him his glass of water.

"We both kept our wings for quite a while – for five, maybe six thousand years. Time moved differently then; different calendars and also a different feel to everything, so the years are an approximate.

"Jacque lost his wings after Dalila."

"Dalila?"

"Mm-hmm. She ripped his heart open in all ways but actual. And more." He studied her carefully as he had a sip of water, his eyes keeping their cheerful twinkle despite the heaviness of the story. "It was the time of the great pyramids – there were pyramids all over the planet, but Egypt was a hub – and what a time that was, filled with powerful magic – both good and evil – and the strangest technologies. It was a time of angels on earth, too. Not all fallen had lost their wings yet.

"Dalila was a Pharaoh's daughter – a beautiful and wily one who everyone adored except those who knew her best. Jacque pretty much fell in love with her in an instant."

She suddenly felt uncomfortable knowing this intimate thing about Jacque, especially if there was a woman involved. "Ronan, why are you telling me all this?"

He smiled at her in a contemplative way. "Just balancing the scales a little. Jacque has known you – and a lot about you – for twenty-two years and you've only just been given the chance to catch up. You should know *something* equally important about him."

Was that an okay answer? She couldn't deny she wanted to know more about Jacque because she felt woefully inadequate next to his supernatural vastness.

He continued when she didn't protest further. "Jacque didn't always used to be so closed off. That was Dalila's doing. Jacque was – and I say this without trying to sound like a complete langer – the light of my feckin' life. Optimistic to a fault. Saw the good in everyone before the bad. I swear t'ye, he's the reason I kept my wings as long as I did.

"Dalila wanted his wings, Sophia. Dalila wanted his wisdom, his joy, and a seat in Heaven along with the immortals: she wanted his blood in her chalice.

"He told her angels, fallen or otherwise, cannot make humans immortal, but she'd already heard of the angels that had *lost* their wings – the vampires – and how they *could* make humans immortal, so she plotted and planned how to make him lose his.

"Nothing worked at first. She tried hexes and curses, and they failed. She convinced those he trusted to betray him – that didn't work either. And he was none the wiser that *she* was the one creating all the chaos in his life behind his back. Oh, there were, for sure, a couple of souls who tried to tell him, but most never spoke against that woman for fear of retribution from the Pharoah.

"After many failed attempts, Dalila finally understood, the one person who really moved him heart and soul, was her. So, *she* betrayed him. One night, she drugged him with herbs and magic. And while he was sleeping a death-like sleep, she cut off his wings herself."

"No..." Sophia's heart dropped.

"She did. He awoke to bloody, shredded stumps of ragged feathers. His grief was too enormous to contain. It turned to madness, and our madness is usually only quelled by the bloodlust..." He faltered then, his eyes glazing in memory.

She got the distinct impression he was replaying the scene, filtering which parts to tell her.

"And he killed her," he said. "Never giving her the immortality she craved, mind. Thank god – the world can do without the likes of *her* being undead. But when he killed her, the stumps that were left fell off. That is how Jacque lost his wings."

The silence that followed stung. Sophia just shook her head. No one word seemed big enough.

"The truly sad thing is, if she'd have just fuckin' asked him, with all the honesty and valour she never had, he'd probably have shed them for her, fool that he was." Although he'd said that affectionately; softly. "Because that's how he loves.

"He disappeared from my life soon after that. Took off in a raging mess, and by god, I missed him. And I worried for him. The next time I saw him was just under a thousand years ago. He was all dressed up as a Knight of the Templar and he was different. Distant. Mission-led. Armoured. Certainly no talk of women – the Knights abstained from all those urges. But he had found a semblance of sanity again – that was a blessing at least.

"Again, we lost touch. I heard of him through an acquaintance around four hundred years ago – heard he was living life as some solitary farmer or something along those lines. The 'solitary' part told me nothing had changed." He gazed at her steadily. "Until little under two hours ago, when he broke the lock of one of my conference rooms in a bid to save you – a woman – and *what* a woman no less, with your pyrotechnics and your living pulse. The look on his face was one I hadn't seen since before that witch ruined him."

Dumbfounded, she didn't know where to look. She brought her arms up around her. "Ronan, I don't think—"

"And then he told me in the car how he'd met you, what had happened, and so on, and it was suddenly clear as day to me, that no woman between now and six thousand years ago could *ever* have snuck under his defences. But a child could. And a child did." He chuckled. "And then he got himself into a right pickle, didn't he, because the child he formed a blood-link with solely to keep her safe, grew into the very kind of woman he'd refused to let in. So"—he finished the water and slid the empty glass towards her—"well done, stóirín. Thank you for bringing my Jacque home." He stood, stretched his back, and said, "Sounds like it's quietened down a bit in that front room, so I'll risk headin' back in."

"No ... Ronan, you're ... I'm not—"

"His. I know – you said. That's all right, you don't have to be his. You're not ready to be his, and given everythin' I've heard that's happened to you over the past few days, that's hardly surprising. I'm sure he knows you might *never* be his. That's why he'll never ask it of you. But you've brought him back regardless, so you have my gratitude. And you have my protection. And I guarantee you, stóirín, however it is you feel, now or in fifty years, *he* is yours."

Everyone had returned to the front room. Eliza and Daniel sat on the smaller sofa, Eliza glaring at Jacque every now and then as Ronan shared what he knew. Sophia sat on a single seater between Ronan and Jacque; Jacque on his armchair and Ronan on the main, larger sofa.

Ronan was filling them in on everything he knew about tomorrow's party and how he'd gotten mixed up in it. "Joseph Marino has been bullying his way into feeding houses for the last five years looking for a special kind of blood, which I'll get to in a minute. No one wants to get caught up in his web, but he threatens you with violence, loss of money and reputation, and anything else he fancies at any time, including loss of human life which we definitely don't want – some of us have built quite a friendship with some of our donors.

"You do what he asks, he leaves you well alone and even compensates you. You refuse and you may not be able to get by in this country again, or any other he's got sway in. He came into my feeding house about two years ago and try as I might, I couldn't get rid of him without causing a whole heap of trouble." He glanced at Sophia and nodded. "Until tonight, anyway, although the trouble will come, I'm sure.

"The blood he's after is associated with something called Project Veil. It is believed that Project Veil was first drafted in the Middle Ages – that's when it began. The paradoxical thing about the project is that no one is a hundred percent sure it exists, or – even more absurdly – what it actually is, and yet anyone determined to get their hands on it seems willing to die to do so."

"That makes no sense," said Sophia.

"It does if you're fanatical about a promise of salvation, even if it's a delusion. The rumour has always been that the project is all about finding a way to bring vampires to ascension."

"Back to the Resurrectors, then."

"Yes, and the rumours also have the Resurrectors as very much aware and aligned with Project Veil. It was Joseph that got me an invitation to the event at Bannerman House tomorrow night. We know there's an old library on the grounds of the house – we think in the lower ground or cellar, according to the floor plan – and in that library, there's talk of a book which holds the key to everything Project Veil is since its conception to now. It's like a five-hundred-year-old record book that's still being written in."

Sophia sat up in her chair. "I'm going to the party with my colleague tomorrow – it's her parents that own the house. She's distanced herself from both her parents and the house, but she likely knows where the library is. I can ask her if she can take me there – she knows how much of an antiquarian I am, so it won't be suspicious of me to ask."

"The more I'm hearing about all this, the more I think you shouldn't go," said Jacque, unhappily.

"If that book is really causing all this trouble, I'm your best chance to get it."

"I agree," said Ronan. "We can find a way to go in with her."

"Can you walk into the private residence as vampires?" Sophia asked.

"The party invite is enough – it's an official invitation. And with Daniel and Eliza now coming too, we can scout above ground as well as below."

Jacque grunted.

"We need to get hold of that book before Joseph does," pressed Ronan.

"Why does he want it."

"For salvation, like so many others. But he's become increasingly mad over his desire for it. The past six months, he's been unpredictable and downright dangerous with his movements and tactics."

"Why *this* project?" asked Jacque. "There have been a few promising salvation since our existence and most vampires can't stand anything associated with the Resurrectors."

"Word amongst its most loyal devotees is that the project was started by a vampire, *not* the Resurrectors. He just managed to get some of them on his side, that's all. That's why it's managed to survive for hundreds of years and, allegedly, is still an active project."

"Started by a vampire?" asked Jacque.

"And overseen by one. Specifically one like us – a fallen. One who wants to go back home badly enough. No one knows who, though. Most of the original angels-turned-vampires are long gone now – there are, I think, maybe six of us left. That's it."

"Are all who fell men?" asked Sophia.

"Not at all – we had quite a few women, but they're all gone now. Only one left as far as I know: Miriam. Last I saw her was out in the Middle East somewhere, maybe just under three thousand years ago. Then there's Jacque and myself, and Joseph's also a fallen."

Sophia gasped. "*Him*? A fallen angel before becoming a vampire?"

Ronan nodded. "He was the last to lose his wings," he said, quietly, a trace of sadness evident. "Rumour has it he was one of the Bratvashka until whatever happened to make their numbers dwindle. And I'm not sure who the other fallen are."

"So *that's* why he wants salvation? He remembers his origins?"

Ronan looked at her and held her eyes. "The belief amongst we fallen-turned-vampires is that there is *no* salvation for us. If and when we die – however that happens – we go poof. No afterlife. No returning home. Our souls are just no more. Someone at some point in history decided that if we found a way to regain our wings, we could retain our souls and return home to the angelic realm."

"The place with the golden gates?" asked Sophia.

"Yes. On the tail of that new belief, Project Veil was seeded. It's also around that time when the Resurrectors started to believe they could rid the earth of *all* vampires through their own version of what an ascension would be."

"Wait, wait..." Her mind was spinning. "About five hundred years ago, this fallen-turned-vampire created Project Veil – which we know nothing about – as a means to go home, and the Resurrectors got wind of this idea and have since run with it, creating their own ideas about how to rid the earth of *all* vampires... Have I got that right?"

"In a nutshell, yes. And some Resurrectors decided to work with the vampire – might still be working with him – because they see it as a more sure way to get their own outcome."

"This is crazy. It's all just based on belief. That's it."

Ronan threw her a wry smile. "Surely you've noticed, stóirín, belief is pretty much what everyone fights for and always has."

"Okay, fine, if you're playing that card, Daniel told me vampires *do* actually have souls. Surely that means you will return home no matter what."

"Sophia, why is it that humans believe in an afterlife?"

She shrugged. "Um, not all do. But of the ones that do, I guess they've seen something or felt something to substantiate it for themselves."

"Exactly. How many vampire relatives do you think come back to visit us from beyond the grave? How many vampire ghosts to you think have been seen? The answer to both of those is none. Ever. And vampires don't dream, so there's no chance of hellos and goodbyes with dead loved ones in our sleep. No vampire has ever experienced or preached of such things. Since our fall, until now, not one single hint of an afterlife exists for us."

"Oh." She didn't know what else to say to that. It just seemed profoundly sad.

"So perhaps you'll understand better that when something like Project Veil comes along, no matter how vague it is, a fallen like Joseph will hold onto it like it's the chalice of life itself, because there *is* nothing else for us.

"Now ... here's the clincher that changed everything; that

finally made belief into something tangible." He looked around the room to make sure he had everyone's attention. "About two decades ago or so, a vampire allegedly came out of the woodwork, said he was associated with the project and swore he'd drunk the blood of something that made him immune to sunlight."

Sophia froze where she sat.

Eliza leaned forward. "He what? And he was believed?"

"He was believed for a very good reason. He proved it."

Her gut churned. All she could hear was blood rushing to her ears. And words. Words she hadn't understood at all when six years old – hadn't even taken note of, the pain in her wrist far more urgent – but suddenly understood for the first time, this very second, when the memory erupted in her mind like a fist to her stomach.

"Look ... can you see? Sophia, look." He held his hand out under the sun, his brown eyes lit with glee. "I'm not burning."

"This vampire was in good standing with the Nocturnes, and it was the Nocturnes who went on to spread the word – *they* claim he showed it to them himself. He stepped into the sun and did not burn."

She felt sick. That had been a Nocturne near the cemetery on their grounds.

Because they knew Uncle Hugo – he moved in their circles.

"He swore he'd bring them the blood to try themselves—"

"You have something very special and your job is to let me have it, do you understand?"

"—but refused to give them any information about what that blood was – animal, vampire, human, or other. He said it was part of Project Veil and he was sworn to secrecy. I don't know why he was so involved with the Nocturnes, but he was deeply embedded enough to vow they were the only ones he'd told. Maybe he was like a spy for them or somethin'. He told them he was going to experiment with the blood a bit more in secret. The story goes he never told the other members of the project about this blood. He convinced the Nocturnes to give him more time learning what the blood could do."

"Uncle Hugo, no!"
"Your veins are too small. I need an artery."
"NO!"
"You're the only one who can stop us burning."

She crossed her legs and drew them in, wanting the chair to swallow her up.

"Because the project has always had its place on a pedestal amongst certain vampires – the Nocturnes being one of them – they accepted this for now. Unfortunately – or maybe fortunately – they never saw their vampire spy again."

Because I set him on fire. I killed him.

"And that's all I've got. I know all this because of the work Joseph blackmailed me to do for him. He's been raiding feeding houses all over the country to try and find the source of this blood." His voice darkened. "I've taken my share of bullets from him trying to keep my donors safe."

He then sighed and stretched his legs as if finally laying all that on the table was a weight off his shoulders. "I've no fecking idea what this party's about tomorrow, in all honesty – I'm not on any terms with the Resurrectors at all – but my aim is to go anyway and get that book before anyone else gets it for Joseph. Maybe if I destroy it or convince him it's been destroyed, or convince him it doesn't exist after all, he'll finally leave us all be."

"I've only heard of Project Veil in passing," said Jacque, thoughtfully. "I've never paid it much mind – thought it nothing more than a fanciful delusion. The only dealings I've had with the Resurrectors are through the Auclairs, first about eight hundred years ago; then, five hundred years ago, I fell out with them because of their growing obsession with the vampiric ascension, and then I very briefly entered their lives again when I met Sophia, but they never brought up the project with me. I've never had access to that information. They *did* insinuate..." He hesitated, his gaze flicking over Sophia; probably not wanting to upset her. "That they were working on a hybrid birth for the purpose of the ascension. That's why they called me – they wanted an evaluation of"—he was obviously considering his words carefully—"Sophia's wellbeing since she was demonstrating vampiric traits."

"They wanted rid of me," she added, flatly. "Once it became apparent I wasn't whatever pure thing they'd bred for their ascension, they couldn't bear to touch me." Except her mother at the very end. And Hugo. He hadn't been afraid to touch her at all, had he – the only other monster in the house. Repulsion coursed through her.

Ronan clasped his hands behind his head and winked at her. "Don't worry yourself over it, stóirín, there are worse things than being the monster that ruined Dr Frankenstein's illusion."

Sophia recoiled.

Jacque threw Ronan the most scathing look. "Tact was never your gift, was it?"

"What? That's a *good* thing. I'm not saying anything bad about her – she's their victim here."

Vomit surged up her throat. She coughed as she swallowed it back. What the fuck *was* she? No one else knew about the sunlight thing and for the moment, no one in the room was putting two and two together. To think that Hugo was the one to have found that out. *Christ*. She felt his teeth puncture her anew. He was the *only* one to have ever—

"Are you okay?" asked Eliza, gently, a world of sympathy in her tone. "We *don't* think you're like Frankenstein's monster, by the way."

Daniel hissed Eliza's name, sharply in Sophia's defence – the first time he'd said anything.

Maybe Eliza and Ronan could compete for the gold medal in tact. "I'm fine." She nodded and glanced at Jacque. "I'm okay."

He didn't look convinced. "Do we have a name for this vampire who professed to have conquered sunlight?" asked Jacque, probably thinking he was changing the subject for her sake, oblivious to the fact the subject of the miracle blood was still her.

"Do you believe in miracles?"

Oh, god ... her mother's words to her in those final moments. *"...your blood is special; your destiny is great. There are people who will try to steal it all – some with good intentions, and some only for themselves."*

She had known. Hugo must have told her. Threatened her with the information, more like...

And now she was dead. Everyone was dead. Because they'd created *her*.

Sophia's head swam, dizziness and nausea competing for purchase.

"There is no name. The Nocturnes went very quiet after the vampire disappeared, deciding to keep any little information they had to themselves—"

She closed her eyes recalling their visit to the library.

"I do wonder ... what sunlight tastes like."

Because Hugo had fucking told them.

"—and you know what they're like, they'll give you riddles and nothing else."

"Maybe they're lying," threw in Eliza.

"I second that," added Jacque.

"They have no reason to – they're pretty revered among vampires." Ronan looked at Sophia to explain. "They were never fallen angels, but they're the only species of vampire to have regained wings in some form or another. Most vamps tend to hold them in high regard because of that alone, so I can't see why they would *need* to lie about this. What would there be to gain?"

She felt ... wrong. Wrong inside.

A final, chilling thought hit her, engraving that wrongness into her being. Everyone in this room would want her dead if they found out her blood could make vampires immune to sunlight, after all, they wanted the book destroyed for so much less. She was more than a book, she was fucking dangerous. Vampires walking in sunlight? Everyone would want her dead – fallen angels, vampires, humans, Resurrectors – *everyone*. Or forever alive for the taking. If anyone took it upon themselves to protect her, they would be as condemned as she. Her eyes went straight to Jacque. That was *worse* than them wanting her dead.

Jacque was focused on what Ronan had said. She followed his gaze, but couldn't look their new ally in the eye. "Asking the wrong person, I'm afraid." Her voice broke. She coughed again to hide it and stood up. "Sorry, guys, I need the bathroom. Someone take notes for me." She hoped her legs didn't look as shaky as they felt, and she *tried* to walk out at a regular pace, though took the last few strides to the bathroom door as fast as possible.

Once inside, she locked the door, pulled up the toilet lid and puked.

Chapter Twenty-Seven

She'd chickened out. Couldn't go back into the front room to join the others. After vomiting (mostly saliva with a tinge of blood), she'd sat on the floor feeling gross. It wasn't just Uncle Hugo and what he represented – *him* finding this secret inside her no one knew – or the fact every vampire on the planet was going to want her trussed up to needles and vials once they knew what her blood could do, or that she was a danger to all those she cared for, or the fact she was some kind of chimera hybrid *thing* – never a child that was wanted for normal reasons – or the fact she could feel Manuel between her legs right this second because the whiskey she'd thrown over herself and her clothes suddenly reeked in her sensitised state. It was *all* of it. Her skin crawled.

There was a shower cubicle in this downstairs bathroom she was balled up in, so she shed her clothes, got in it, and turned on the hot water. There was no shampoo that she could see, but there was soap, so she used that to scrub herself everywhere including her hair. She frothed up some water with it, then rinsed her mouth out too. Not that any of it worked. Nothing got clean. The smell of whiskey seemed bonded to her. Even with her skin as red as it was under the scorch of the water, she couldn't get clean. She could set everyone else on fire, but couldn't burn herself away.

She had no idea how long she'd been in there by the time she turned the water off. It felt like forever and not long enough. She spied a bath towel and grabbed it, dried herself as best as she could, then wrapped it around herself.

After bunching her clothes up, she piled them in one corner, not wanting to take the smell of whiskey to her bedroom. She'd deal with them later.

Opening the door, she poked her head out first and listened. Silence greeted her. She couldn't hear any chatter coming from the living room and was sure they'd wondered why she'd taken a shower in the middle of a meeting like a crazy person. She had no intention of explaining why. The least number of vampires who knew what her blood could do the better. She was putting everyone in danger by existing. If no one knew, she could remain a rumour; a mystery that need not be real. And after the party tomorrow, she'd disappear. She'd learnt a lot being in witness protection – she might be able to pull it off herself. She'd get them that book from the library at Bannerman House tomorrow – it was the least she could do – then they'd never see her again. And Jacque would just have to understand. She'd *make* him understand, or maybe there was a way she could erase the blood link, after all, her blood wasn't exactly normal. Maybe that blasted Project Veil book could explain how to erase the link.

She stepped out and padded upstairs as quietly as she could. When she reached her bedroom door, she opened it, closed it, then jumped out of her skin to see the silhouette on her bed.

"Everyone's gone," said Jacque. "It's ten o'clock."

She looked towards her window at the night sky.

"You were in the shower for nearly an hour and a half."

Oh. "Sorry," she whispered.

"Your skin looks red enough to blister."

She looked down at herself and couldn't see much in the dark. His night vision was clearly better than hers. She pulled the towel a bit tighter around her. "I couldn't get myself clean."

Her mobile phone sounded from somewhere downstairs.

Jacque grunted. "It's gone off five times since everyone left. I'm placing bets it's Deiniol since I had to bribe him to get the hell out of my house. He wanted to break down the bathroom door to make sure you were all right."

"Sorry," she whispered again.

Jacque stood and made his way to her. His hair caught what little faint light there was first, before his eyes came into view, a captivating shade of blue in the near darkness; and then his face, his shoulders, his chest in the navy blue, matte satin shirt he'd been wearing all evening; until there was only an inch between them.

She met his eyes.

By god ... he was stunning. For the first time, she allowed herself to see it and think it. He was *stunning*. And more so now that she was going to leave him.

She tried to conjure up the Jacque who'd played dressed-up chess with her and couldn't quite do it. She'd known that Jacque three days, and it had changed her life. She'd known this imposing and breathtaking version of him three days, and it had changed her life. The gap between three and three was fast fusing shut and day seven had an air of foreboding about it. The party, the vampires, the Resurrectors, her blood... It would be a glorious new beginning or a cataclysmic end.

He cupped a hand around her arm and she closed her eyes, the feel of his touch raising every hair on it. Then, he trailed it down until he clasped her hand. "Look," he said.

She blinked her eyes open, first to his face – he was watching her intently – then down to the hand he'd raised. She could just about see small blisters forming on its surface.

"We need to get something put on this – on all of you. You've damaged your skin. And it's drying up."

"I heal fast."

"Sometimes. And sometimes not so fast."

There was barely a centimetre between them now. If she stood on her tip toes, her lips would meet his. And she was selfish. Very selfish. Because she yearned to know him that intimately now she'd decided to leave. "I didn't really mean to ... I just couldn't get cl—"

Her stomach growled embarrassingly.

Jacque's lip twitched into a smile. "Was your earlier feed not adequate? I won't tell Ronan – let the man keep his pride."

She attempted a smile, but wasn't quite there. "It was more than adequate, but I ... threw up in the bathroom, so ... that's probably why."

The smile fell away. His eyes darkened as he studied her.

"Are you upset?" she asked suddenly. "That I drank his blood?"

"I learnt to drown that detrimental green-eyed monster, specific to a vampire's blueprint, a long time ago." He placed his forearm on the wall above her head and leaned into it, his nose almost brushing hers as his stare bored into her. His jaw clenched. "Mostly."

She swallowed hard. "I don't know how to drown it. I heard you this morning – in the cabin in the garden."

His brow creased. "I'm sorry."

"You don't have to—"

"She was food."

"I heard you moan." Her face flamed. Her fucking stupid jealousy propelling her fucking stupid mouth. She hadn't wanted to say anything and yet there it was.

He exhaled sharply, leant right in and brought his mouth to her ear. "No you bloody didn't. When you *really* hear me moan, you're going to know the fucking difference."

And then she was off her feet and in his arms as he carried her out the door and across the landing, pushing his bedroom door open with his foot before taking her inside.

"Jacque—"

"I have mint oil. We use it ourselves for burns. You'll be a sight for sore eyes tomorrow if we don't get it on you now."

He placed her on his bed.

Battling with arousal, her still-lingering jealousy, and the vow she'd made to leave, she was about to protest, but all possible arguments left her mind as she took in his bedroom with its intricate dark wood furniture, including the bed frame, all of it against white walls. The light was a bit brighter in here with the waxing gibbous moon shining straight in through the window. His bed sheets were a dark burgundy and rich, smooth cotton. She'd not been in here before. It was a sensual combination of gothic and bohemian.

She barely noticed him back by her side until the scent of mint filled her.

He poured oil into his hand from the bottle, then put the bottle on a flat carved edge of the bed frame.

"It's beautiful in here. I'll bet everyone says so." She glanced at him. It was the most discrete way she could ask how many women he'd brought in here without actually asking, and it turned out, she really wanted to know, although she couldn't quite figure out if it was to placate the tempestuous jealousy, feed her possessiveness, or if it was plain old curiosity.

He threw her a stare as if he knew exactly what she was asking, which he likely did as there was no subtle way to ask that question (especially on the tail of her little episode), then took her arm, starting with her blistering hand and massaged the oil in. "You're the only other person who's ever been in this room, undead or otherwise."

Yep. Her possessiveness was really fucking happy about that.

He worked his way up her arm towards her shoulder, avoiding where the towel met her body, then started on the other arm. After a minute, she sighed, closed her eyes, and let herself relax into his care, not knowing if it was a good idea or bad idea, but needing it nonetheless. It was truly frightening, actually, how much she needed this. *Just another reason to go after tomorrow*, she whispered to herself. *If it's this hard now, you won't be able to leave after a week; after a month.*

When he was done with her second arm, he repositioned her slightly on the bed and raised a leg at the knee – just a bit – and brought her foot onto his lap.

She kept her eyes closed.

After a moment, he was sliding oil into the ball of her left foot, her toes, her heel, then her ankle and up her shin.

The moan left her unbidden; it felt so bloody good. "No one's ever done this before," she found herself whispering. And she wasn't sure she'd have ever *let* anyone either. It was more involved than she usually liked to be. There was a vulnerability in it. She'd shielded too well against vulnerability after the fire; by the time she'd reached adulthood, this kind of sensation had felt impossible to reach.

She shivered as he finished, high up on her inner thigh. She daren't look to see how much her towel was even covering at this stage, but kept her eyes firmly closed.

The bed bounced gently beneath her as he shifted to her other side, and the entire process was repeated with her right leg.

There was no denying she was aroused now, and there was no way he didn't know because his fingers brushed across the sheen of dampness slicked between her thighs as he finished with her other leg. It wouldn't take much at all to bring her to orgasm.

"Sophia."

Her name came from far away, but the way he said it still managed to ignite a powerful swell of feeling within her. She opened her eyes and her breath almost stopped at the way he was looking at her. She wasn't even sure there was a word for it –

they all seemed woefully inadequate – but if this was the way he'd looked at that Dalila woman, she'd been nothing short of evil to do what she'd done. A faint anger rose at the thought of it, in spite of the fact it had happened six thousand years ago and there wasn't a damn thing she could do about it.

"Stand up." It was a low and husky instruction.

She followed it and stood in front of him.

"Turn around."

She did, her back now facing him.

She felt him stand up behind her, his hands grazing the top of her towel.

"Let it go." His breath played with her hair.

It didn't fall as she'd half expected it to. He caught the towel and brought it down to below her waist, then brought his arms up around her to pass her the corners of the towel.

She took them and wrapped it around her front, leaving her back exposed.

He pulled her hair to one side and started at her neck, working the oil down, kneading in all the right places, and not until this second had she realised every single knot of tension she'd been holding onto, now releasing on every moan and whimper that left her as he worked her shoulders and back, and when his hands glided down her sides, grazing the sides of her breasts, she gasped softly and arched, letting her head fall back on his chest.

That drew the first uninhibited sound from him she'd heard, an almost vulnerable groan that shot desire through her faster than any touch. She squeezed her thighs together to relieve the fast growing pressure – the harsh tease of that orgasm building.

With a patience she just didn't have, he took his time reaching the small of her back, let his hands slide to her hips, then turned her around, and she just about lost it; couldn't quite take his closeness anymore when every inch of her body felt cool and hot at once. She leaned up to kiss him, but he pulled back just enough, shook his head, and smoothed the remnant of oil on his hands across her face – forehead, cheeks, trailing it down the front of her neck... "I haven't finished," he whispered hoarsely. Then, "Drop the towel."

It took a ridiculous amount of effort to unclasp the towel from her hands, she was clenching it so tightly to keep herself from coming too soon.

In the end, it was he who tugged it loose with his right hand while his left held a fresh pool of oil. The towel fell free and for a second everything stopped. Cold air wrapped around her where her towel had been, pimpling her flesh and tightening her breasts, and Jacque took her in, his gaze dark, heated, with a need that matched hers. That gaze finally trailed back to her eyes, staring into her so deeply she felt far more exposed than her nudity made her. "You're beautiful beyond words."

Tears rushed to her eyes, his sentiment profound in ways she couldn't quite grasp, but felt to her core.

His hands stroked oil across her stomach and sides. When he reached the undersides of her breasts, she had to grab his shoulders to steady herself, her breathing beyond her control now as it came out in ragged gasps.

She tried to step closer to him, needing that kiss, the fulfilment of that connection, but he held her where she was.

His hands slid down to cup her backside, pressing oil into every inch of her curves before sliding back up to engulf her breasts.

Jesus Christ. She threw her head back, rocked; cried out when he circled her nipples more than once, every part of her tightening as her climax loomed.

Jacque suddenly stopped, pulling her completely into his frame. He was fully erect behind his trousers; breathing as hard as her; but he held her still as he moved his hand down to her navel – below it – and pressed it into her scar. His voice was low in her ear. "Sophia ... I want you. So badly it hurts. But you're in my bedroom – mine – and this *bite* isn't mine. I won't hurt you, and I won't drink from you, but his mark has no fucking right to be on you and I want it gone. Do you understand what I'm saying?"

She did. Completely.

She was his.

Or would be once he'd healed that scar. She could feel that telltale possessiveness simmering somewhere deep inside him. She was starting to recognise it – small waves from Daniel, larger waves from within herself, and god only knew how possessiveness moved within a fallen-turned-vampire. Jacque, Ronan, and that Joseph guy all had statures beyond most vampires – a certain look, gait, and air to them that made them stand out; made them formidable.

And would it be so bad, teased her mind, *to let yourself, just once, be possessed by a man who knows you inside and out.*

The thought almost undid her. Pierce hadn't been hers at all and neither had Daniel in the end. Ronan had unequivocally told her Jacque was.

Just once. Before it's gone forever.

She knew it was dangerous – dangerous to play this game with her heart. Wasn't this every single thing young girls were warned about? But she was already seeking out his hand; placed hers over his and over her scar. She nodded against the crook of his neck. "Make me yours."

He groaned in her ear.

She *sensed* his fangs grow.

His hand slid down between her wet thighs; parted them. "There's more than one way I'm going to be doing that." He pressed his fingers against her clit and stroked.

"Oh, god!" It really wasn't fair she reacted so swiftly to his touch, but she'd been on the edge for too long already.

He rubbed, pressed, circled, and she came right there meshed up against him, one leg wrapped around the back of his as she gripped his shoulders and pushed herself against his fingers over and over and over.

He cursed the sweetest of sounds, then she was on the bed with his weight across the lower half of her body, almost in agony because it wasn't enough; everything inside her still clenched with need.

"Jacque ... please..."

"This first." His tone was steel and his fangs were bare as they hovered above the scar below her navel, and even though she trusted him and knew he'd be careful, ice cold washed over her, the memory of Hugo's actions too fresh after the conversation earlier. She went rigid under his touch, the part of her that had frozen with that scar twenty-two years ago, fighting for control over what was about to happen.

It wasn't his fangs she felt, but his lips. He kissed her marred flesh; kissed around it. With his thumb, he began to stroke it just as he had last night, and it wasn't too long before warmth tingled and ice melted.

With his left hand, he reached for hers and laced their fingers together. "Trust me, *seraphia.*"

She blinked, starting to lose herself as warmth turned to heat. What had he called her?

"Touch me." His voice held a plea.

She looked down at him, his head across her abdomen as his free hand worked her skin. He stared at her, his pupils so dilated it looked like he had two blue rings around each midnight orb. His expression was one of devotion.

The only place she could reach him from this angle was his head, so she touched him there, running her fingers through his dark blond hair.

A delightful noise, like a purr, emanated from him. Satisfied, he lowered his head, still gripping her hand in one of his and rubbing her scar with the other.

All she felt was heat now. She didn't even feel it, at first, when the very tips of his fangs sank into the two old puncture wounds that blemished her. When she did, it was like being pricked with two needles – sudden and sharp – but only for a second. And in those two very precise spots, heat turned molten and rushed to the core of the injury. The sensation was as paradoxical as the vampire who gave it: a poisonous sting that aroused a grating pleasure.

She groaned and tried to thrust upwards, unclear as to whether she wanted to go towards the agitation or away from it.

Whichever it was, she went nowhere. Jacque held her down with unmovable strength and sounded a predatory growl that filled the room. A warning.

Her primal self responded before any other part of her, heeding it and obeying.

But the hand he'd twined with hers, squeezed hers with affection. *Keep still*, said the movement. *Nearly done.*

She felt one more injection of his venom (*medicine*) inflame her skin from the top down. That molten heat which had settled deep inside her abdomen began to spread – fast – lava hurtling through the deeper tissue beyond her scarring; rushing through every capillary and vein it could find, filling her hips; filling her chest.

Unable to help it and on a moan of almost anguish, she thrust upwards again, to find this time, she could. Jacque was no longer pinning her still, but moving his lips down towards the crease of her thigh, his nose brushing past her pubic mound until his tongue laved her entrance – *just* as a surge of his healing venom found the stem of her brain and blasted through it. It was a brutal bliss, and her cry was feral.

She felt a sudden movement, the bed depress, and managed

to focus her hazy vision – barely – on the male stripping off his clothes. She risked a glance down at her scar and noted there was no blood at all. He'd kept his promise and hadn't drunk from her. He'd injected her, not bitten her.

Her body was trembling with needed release; his fluid in her creating pandemonium in every cell.

Her eyes went back to Jacque, naked and … her gaze fell to his cock. It was as impressive as the rest of him, and she appeared to have little control over her functions anymore because the oddest noise left her throat and before she realised it, she'd arched her back and pulled her legs up and open for him, her body responding to the sight of him without any provocation.

The tiniest part of her human self, still conscious, asked what the heck she was doing; the vampire in her, very much dominating all her senses right now, wanted *him* in his entirety and it was non-negotiable.

His eyes were impossibly dark, never leaving her form. When he climbed back on the bed, it was with the precision of a predator and far, far, too slowly.

She waited as she was, her muscles humming with the ache of holding herself ready for him.

A low constant rumble sounded from somewhere around his chest, and the intensity suddenly became too much – she needed him and his dominance *now* or she'd fall into some bottomless chasm, lost.

A tear slipped past the corner of her eye, falling down her temple and onto her bedding below. She whimpered and opened herself as wide as her shaking thighs would allow, physically begging him to take her, aware her entire body was responding to his every movement no matter how small.

The same growl erupted from him as before, in warning for her to keep still as he climbed her body until he was right above her, positioned at her entrance and angled to perfection, and *not touching her.*

Another tear slipped. She was prey – completely his for the taking and she *wanted* to be taken, and it was singularly the most intense, consuming, carnal demand she'd ever felt from herself.

The ruthlessness in his gaze shifted, and he brought his cheek to hers; kissed her there, kissed her again. Every inclination of every word he spoke held his restrained need for her. "What did you ask me to do? Say it again."

His words squeezed a whimper out of her. "Make me yours."

He pushed his hard length into her in one unforgiving stroke.

She didn't hold back her cry, his sound of procurement almost matching it as she bucked and writhed under the size and force of him.

He held still, breathing hard, and let her struggle against him as she sought her adjustment until the struggles turned to rocking, submitting to his intrusion; small, rhythmic undulations from her hips, pleading for his thrusts.

He obliged, each thrust stronger than the next.

She was softening around him; melting around him. A lustful groan left her as her coaxed wetness gushed around him and between them.

Then he stopped.

She protested, but he hissed gently, and she waited, feeling him shift his position ever so slightly, then shove forwards, once, hard. There was a sharp nudge where he met her, the briefest of pain and the tinge of fresh blood; his length pulsed, something hot filled her and before she could sound her surprise at what the hell that was, her body went mad with a surge of arousal, her hips jerking against his, uncontrollably, as she cried out in bliss.

His moan was a sensual resonance of victory, vulnerability, pure need, and almost desperation, and he'd been completely right – it sounded *nothing* like his earlier feed. He moved inside her with urgency – an urgency she matched as her climax rushed to greet her, the immensity of it astounding and filling her eyes with tears at both the pain and pleasure of it.

Her gums thrummed as her fangs grew larger.

Jacque leaned down, turned his neck for her, and she bit with the same force of his thrusts, sucking hungrily, captivated at the way every jerk of his hips pumped his blood into her mouth that little bit harder.

When her orgasm swallowed her, she sank her teeth into him further, up to her gums.

He bucked and groaned and came, his entire frame heaving in desire and release, and something else – relief. Relief she heard in his breaking voice as she slathered her tongue over the wound she'd made, sealing it as best as she could. "Now you're mine, Sophia." He shuddered inside her, still climaxing, and she all at once realised he'd been warring with the fact she might walk away, or despise him for what he'd done, or never want him at all.

He sighed and sank onto her, hugging her to him. "Now you're mine."

Chapter Twenty-Eight

The peace and contentment was astounding. She was floating and weightless, and although she knew Jacque was also without form, Sophia sensed him all around her and in her, as if in a constant embrace with him.

"Are you awake?" she asked. Although being a dream, she'd said it in her mind. There was no reply, but a pulsing of his essence as they filled this space within the golden gates. "I want to stay here forever."

Another pulse – an agreement – a tightening and loosening of the embrace, all of eternity in that action.

A whistle sounded from somewhere beneath them, down below, outside the gates. "Come with me," she said, feeling the pull to respond to this new call, but the embrace slipped and she was suddenly without Jacque, floating towards the gates to find the source of the whistle.

She protested, not willing to be without him now she'd found him, but could not resist the tug and pull of whatever had her bound.

She reached the gates, grasped their glowing, golden bars, and looked down. Far, far below her stood Ronan, his shock of red hair giving him away.

It was night down there. He looked up at her, his arms crossed over that broad chest. "You have work to do, stóirín – no time for rest. There's a long way to go."

She looked back at where she knew Jacque was, but was

suddenly yanked through the gates and falling ... falling...

After what felt like forever, she landed on soft grass, her heart heavy – everything heavy.

Brushing herself down, she stood, her form now solid in a dress the same colour as the gates she longed to return to. "Ronan?"

He'd disappeared, but to her right lay a rectangular table and chairs, a child pouring drinks from a teapot into toy cups.

She walked over to her, until she was standing right in front of her six-year-old self who looked up and smiled, and continued pouring drinks. Red fluid – blood – ran from the teapot's spout into a cup that was placed before a male doll with dark blond hair and blue eyes. Another filled cup of blood was placed in front of another doll, also male, this one with red hair and very light blue eyes. "Jacque and Ronan?" she asked as she looked around the whole table.

Six chairs surrounded it. The dolls took up two of them, leaving the rest empty, but her young, past self poured blood into every single cup – all six. When she was done, she handed her Jacque's cup and said, "Drink."

She obliged and placed the cup back down, and watched in fascination as a white wing sprang open from the girl's back, high up near her left shoulder.

Young Sophia giggled with delight, then picked up Ronan's cup and handed it to her. "Drink," she said again with more excitement in her voice.

She took the cup, drank the blood, and couldn't help but smile when her young self laughed in glee as her second wing fluttered out.

"What about all the empty seats?" she asked her, looking at the four cups of blood remaining.

Little Sophia smiled and small fangs peeked out from under her lips. She was the cutest vampire ever – with wings. "They're not here yet, but they're coming." She skipped around the table, bent down and pulled out something from under it – another doll. This one had black hair, almost black eyes, and two scars across its face above a beard.

Growing cold, Sophia took a step back and shook her head, but young Sophia wasn't fazed by her reaction. "They all need to come – no exceptions." She'd said that to her in a stern expression and the tone of a school teacher.

Something landed on the table with a thud, seemingly from the sky, making them both jump. It was her mother's crucifix, the wings out. The heavy pendant had landed in front of the blond doll just as a ray of sun beamed across the grass near their feet. Its ray was so bright and unexpected, they both looked towards it.

"Uh-oh," said young Sophia, shaking her head. "This is bad. It's not supposed to happen."

The beam spread as the sun emerged.

The girl looked up at her, her large amber eyes panicked. "Run, Sophia," she said.

"But what about—"

Jacque's doll caught fire as the sun hit it.

The girl screamed, and then screamed the word again. "RUN!"

Sophia woke with a start, her heart thumping, although she couldn't immediately recall why. Some bizarre dream with a tea party and dolls. Was she young in the dream or old? Had Jacque been there?

The night's fervidness came back to her and seized by a strange panic, she turned on the bed, relief washing over her when she saw Jacque's frame on it, his back to her, his two grievous scars just about visible in the dark. The pull to take him in her arms was enormous, but she hesitated, not sure if she wanted to wake him.

She couldn't see a clock in here, but it felt like it might be around three in the morning.

A beam of moonlight cut a path across the bed. Frowning, it triggered a flash of something from her dream, but she couldn't remember what.

Looking back at Jacque and his scars, she was suddenly reminded of her own. Scooting herself down into the moonlight, she glanced towards her navel and took in a sharp breath. It had gone. Hugo's bite was completely gone. Not a trace of it remained.

Her gaze was drawn to the staining between her legs – dried seed, her own desire, and a hint of blood. God, he really had taken her – with forceful, powerful dominance. Her cheeks flushed hot. And she'd enjoyed every second of it and craved more.

The mattress under her shifted and Jacque's hand spanned her belly as his lips found her shoulder.

She sighed at the feel of him.

"Are you all right?" he muttered, sleep coating his voice.

She turned her head and met his eyes, and *just* about managed to stop herself falling headlong into them and losing her train of thought. "Hugo's bite is gone. There's no trace of it."

He made a sleepy harrumph sound of victory. "And good fucking riddance. Are you all right in here?" He stroked her across her belly button. "I'd never have been so rough without the healing venom in you – it should have fixed you pretty much straight after."

She smirked. "Rough? Jacque, you were brutal."

He blinked, suddenly uncertain, concern taking over lingering sleepiness.

Sophia turned fully towards him and rubbed her nose down the length of his. "And I loved it. I want you to do it again."

Relief – and a flicker of lust – coloured his shadowed face.

"And you're right, I don't hurt inside at all." In fact, she hurt *nowhere.* There wasn't even a smidgen of the aches she sometimes had – a slightly pulled muscle, a twinge to her neck when she slept funny – nothing at all. It was bliss. "I'm afraid we made a bit of a mess of your bedsheets, though."

He smiled slowly and surely, reminding her of a few days back when he'd worn a similar smug expression on Daniel's couch. "Your come and blood on my sheets fills me with a rather sinful pride."

She laughed. "Is that so?"

He lowered his eyes, staring at her through his eyelashes, both boyish and devilish, and nodded. And any last doubt she was truly his just evaporated into the night because her heart fell in on itself at that fierce and vulnerable expression, proving last night had not just been physical desire. He was there in her heart – as a lover, a friend, a reluctant saviour, and something else, too, that was too ethereal to name but felt a lot like eternity. If she lost him, she'd lose a part of herself.

Damn, what was that dream … something *wrong* had woken her up.

He scooped her up – was good at that – and drew her onto his lap straddling him. "I will never be brutal with you without care, I promise. Now, why is there a frown on your face?" He planted a kiss on her cheek.

"It's nothing, really. I think I had a bad dream, but I don't remember it. Listen, do we *have* to go to the party tomorrow night? I mean, if all the others are now going, maybe we could … you know," she smiled, "stay in bed all night?"

"Mmmm." He kissed her neck, trailing more kisses down to her shoulder. "Don't tempt me. But we have to go. Vampires are surfacing everywhere and with all the attacks, it's getting too public. Vampires aren't usually like this. We need to find out why and how to stop it and if it's you they're targeting. That thirty-mile radius of attacks around you suggests it might be an energy you bring rather than you specifically. I don't really like the idea of you being there, but I'd like it less leaving you here alone given the attacks. It seems like we might find a lot of answers at the party. And I thought you didn't want to let your friend down."

That was true – she didn't want to let Abi down.

"We made a plan last night while you were having your Guinness World Record shower."

She threw him a look and his lip twitched. "Very funny. What's the plan?"

"You head into the library room with your friend in search of that Project Veil book. Only take it if you feel it's safe. If not, leave it, but at least we'll know where we can find it before the end of the night. The public guest list shows around two hundred people in attendance, so Daniel and Eliza are going to scout the guests and see if anyone knows about this vampire who claimed to be immune to sunlight."

She tried not to stiffen in his arms or show any reaction to his words. She should probably tell him about her blood, but she all at once was certain – especially after last night and his dominance – there was no way he'd let her go to the party amongst other vampires if he knew. He'd deem it too dangerous for her. She'd be left alone, here, without him, and there wasn't a chance in hell she was going to let that happen – not after waking up feeling so unsettled. She *needed* to be by his side.

"Ronan's going in search of Joseph's next moves and will be speaking to the owners of any of the other feeding houses who might be there. If he can get them on board to form some kind of alliance against Joseph's violent tactics, they may be better able to keep him away."

"And what about you?"

"I'm going to hunt out information about the owners of Bannerman House and any association they have with the

Resurrectors. After your family perished, a lot of that went very quiet – the Auclairs had been the crux of the Resurrectors for a while. Of the vampires we know going tomorrow, all of them received an invitation signed 'The Estate'. No names. But the invitations all had the Resurrectors' logo on it – the same image as your mum's crucifix."

That had been in her dream – the pendant. At least, she thought so. "Did you get the envelope I left you detailing what Les found out about Aunty Rita?"

"That she might still be alive? Yes. It's an interesting notion and if true, possible she might be involved with Bannerman House given the owner's names and details are not so easy to find. Her supposed death would mean she'd need to stay low."

"I'll ask Abi if she knows anyone called Rita."

He nodded. "She might not have kept the same name, though. And Sophia..." He held her gaze, his expression grave. "Please consider that Abigail might not be what you think she is."

She sighed. "I understand your concern and the logic behind it, but honestly, I would be shocked if she knew anything. I don't even think she knows about vampires, although it's concerning that her parents likely do. I'm more suspicious as to why they've never told her. I've worked with her for a whole year and the first time she ever mentioned her family to me was a week ago when inviting me to the party because it's her birthday. I doubt she's *that* good an actress."

Jacque studied her. "Is her birthday actually today? On the summer solstice?"

"Yes, I think so. Why?"

"The whole event's just a bit odd. We know there's going to be a ceremony, but Catholics don't usually celebrate the solstices."

"Maybe the Resurrectors do, though."

"Perhaps. I've been out of their business for a long time now."

"What was that vow you made to them? The one my grandmother blackmailed you with to take my memories?"

"It wasn't anything overly extraordinary. The Auclairs took me in and helped me half a millennium ago when I had lost my way after having no direction. The Templars were gone, it was a relative time of peace in terms of wars, and without anything to keep my mind off ... I lost myself a bit. They helped me find my way back. Soon after that I found Deiniol and life got a lot better. I made a promise to return the favour to the Auclairs."

"Daniel became your new mission," she stated, softly.

He looked at her a bit surprised, and then thoughtfully. "I suppose he did. I had not sired anyone before him as I was too dedicated to any cause that came my way. It gave me a new perspective on the possibilities that lay before me."

Gave him people to care for and a reason to live without missions and wars ... a reason to continue living without wings. "He will forgive you, Jacque," she said, softly. She reached for him and cupped his face, and this time it was her turn to gaze at him through her lashes. His entire body relaxed beneath her and her gaze, and she relished the power she had to make him react. *To her.*

"Seraphia, are you trying to seduce me with that look?"

"That depends," she teased. "What does seraphia mean?"

"Did you read the book I left you?"

Oh, the 'Seraph' book. She had tried to read it in the car when parked by the river after calling her dad, but had been far too distracted and emotionally drained. It was currently in her handbag with most of her stolen literary collection. "I only managed a page; I couldn't concentrate on it properly at the time."

"Seraph means angel that burns. There are as many types of

angels as there are vampires, and if there's any angel in you, you seem like a seraph to me."

"And the 'ia' part?"

He shrugged, looking sheepish. "It's just the end of Sophia. So you're 'seraphia'."

She laughed. "You turned me into a lexical blend?"

"It's a beautiful sounding lexical blend – rolls off my tongue like your clitoris."

Her mouth opened in genuine shock, not expecting that kind of audacity mid-conversation, and three seconds later a gasp escaped it when he repositioned her against his semi-hard erection and rubbed said clit.

"Rolls around quite nicely here, too," he added, huskily. "I do believe you're already wet."

She narrowed her eyes at him. "I've been sitting on you, naked, for five minutes."

She lost her snark to an almost embarrassing whimper the moment he enveloped her left breast in his mouth, sucking, nibbling, flicking... Her whole body arched towards him, needing him inside her. That beautiful, deep purring noise he made vibrated through her skin.

"And what exactly should we do about that, seraphia?" he asked as he released her. He brought her forward and positioned her above his ready cock, now fully erect.

She took his face in both her hands, held herself steady, and stilled, taking a moment to take *him* in – not his body, but his face and eyes and soul... "Kiss me," she said.

His irises met hers, alight with a fiery adoration. And much, much more than that.

"You've made me yours, but you haven't kissed me yet."

Reaching up, he cupped her cheek and brought her mouth down. And stopped. Her lips hovered a centimetre from his. His gaze roamed every curve and swell of her face from her forehead to the dip of her nose, the groove below it, the smooth lines of her jaw, and back to her eyes again.

How the hell did he do it? Her body warmed and tingled, the beginnings of an orgasm already kindling. Tears filled her eyes at the overwhelm and solid certainty of every feeling she'd ever had for him.

"I can't cry," he whispered. "But I promise you, I share those tears." Reaching forward one aching millimetre, he stroked her top lip with his tongue, and then her bottom lip.

Those unruly tears fell. Her whole being flamed for him.

"Sophia." Their eyes locked once more. "Everything I have is yours. I'm yours." His words fluttered across her lips as if sealing an oath and everything inside her clenched around those words, branding them to her. A searing wave of euphoria shuddered through her.

She tightened her hold on his face, but he was stronger than she and held her where she was.

His top lip touched hers.

His bottom lip touched hers.

"*Jacque,*" she breathed into him, unable to hold back the next wave; unable to hold herself on whatever precipice he'd pulled her to.

His tongue darted out and barely – *just barely* – caressed the inside of her upper lip and she came on the deepest orgasm of her life, her cry filling his mouth as her whole body clamped downwards.

He plunged his tongue into her and sealed her lips with his, letting her have every aching inch of him as he pulled her down onto his cock, groaning as her body, still quaking, took his to completion.

And still they kissed, each meeting of lips and tongue a vow unto itself.

She wasn't leaving after the party – fool to think she even

could.

She'd find another way – *with* him.

She was committed.

She was complete.

And for the first time in her life, she was in love.

PART IV
The Party

Chapter Twenty-Nine

Daniel unlocked the door to the apartment above his, hoping six o'clock was too early for Les to be up. He needed breathing space. He needed solitude for a damn second. But he also found he needed the familiarity of family – human family. Humanness.

Les was up, sitting on the sofa, biting through a slice of toast as he read a paperback. He glanced up as Daniel walked into the room.

"Sorry. I thought you might be asleep."

"At my age? I sleep a bit here and there; wake up at the crack of dawn though. What can I do you for?"

"I just..." Words failed him. "Um..."

Les stared at him for a second, and then closed his book and put it down. "You gonna stand there all morning? Take a seat." He gestured to the space beside him.

Daniel did as he suggested.

"Have you heard from Sophia since last night?"

Daniel and Eliza had filled him in on everything when they'd arrived back home at around nine thirty last night. "No." And that was a sore point. She hadn't replied to his texts – on the phone *he'd* given her – which meant she hadn't seen them or she wasn't okay.

"Eliza sleeping?"

He nodded. "She's turned in."

"And you're here and not sleeping because...?"

He sighed and slumped back on the sofa. "I just need a moment of quiet," he mumbled. "The last week has been a whirlwind. I've just found out *angels* actually exist and created the first vampires. My mind feels fucked."

"Mmmn," agreed Les. "A hundred and eighty on your belief system will do that."

"It's not just that. It's ... hard to explain."

"You were with Sophia and then you weren't."

He looked at Les and raised his eyebrows. "Maybe not that hard, then." He rested his head on the back of the couch and stared at the ceiling. "It's not like I'm in agony or anything – it only hurts a bit. And I don't even know exactly why it does. I suppose ... I really connected with her, you know? In a human way. She's so *human* – or was – and I'd forgotten what that was like. It's been a while since Amelia. To be in the company of that kind of softness – a heart that beats that way... And then I dreamt for the first time because of her. Being so close to her; explaining about vampires to her, and my own history, it was like it all came back to me – not just my own past, but my own humanity – my past *before* I was turned. I hadn't thought about it in so long. I thought in Sophia I'd found..." He glanced at Les to see if he was making any sense of the gibberish coming out of his mouth.

"Yeah, I'm listening." He stuffed the last portion of toast in his mouth.

"Me. I thought I'd found me. It made me want to be human again. I wasn't expecting it. And I pushed it to one side, but hearing everyone talk last night about the vampires who were angels wanting to return home..."

"You wanted that too – for you. You wanted your human heartbeat back."

"I did. And I thought Sophia was – I don't know really. It felt like she was going to be a part of that, and then suddenly there was Eliza at my door. And I love that she's come back. I still love her – we never got a chance to finish – but it's not what it was, and we're having to get to know each other all over again. She's changed a lot. I guess I have, too. But I can't shake this feeling like I've lost a chance with Sophia."

"With Sophia specifically? Or a chance to touch humanity again?"

Daniel smiled. "Maybe the latter. I'm not sure. I just know she was the reason for it."

"Is Sophia with Jacque now?"

"If she isn't yet, she will be pretty damn soon. Whatever's between them was palpable from the moment I saw them in the same room together, even before her memories returned – it's why I lost it with him a few nights back. It took me by surprise and opened the old wound with Eliza. Sorry, Les. I'm sure this isn't the peaceful morning you wanted. I'm just feeling kind of thrown by everything."

"Hardly surprising, is it? But you'll pull yourself back together again – you always do."

"Yeah, thanks."

A few seconds of silence ensued, and then Daniel turned back to Les. "Do you think – if there is some kind of heaven or god, or whatever the existence of angels means – that I'm ... worthy of ..."

Les reached forward and squeezed his hand, his eyes glistening. "There's no one I know, human or otherwise, more worthy."

Moments like these were his heartbeat. "Thank you."

Les rose from the couch, but Daniel took his arm instead. "Wait ... son..."

He sat back down.

"Tonight ... stay in the car park. Stay hidden. Stay safe. Read your book, or do a million crosswords, whatever it takes. Just stay out of harm's way. I have a sense of foreboding about this party. It's a bloody cult gathering is what it is – with wayward vampires, corrupted humans, and the lot. And I'm not ready to lose you yet. Not yet, Les."

The old man blinked hard. "I wasn't planning on giving up my retirement and my last decade, god willing, soaking up the sun along the various beaches of the Caribbean."

Daniel chuckled.

"So, do me a favour, follow your own advice and keep your undead self alive. Don't give me a bloody heart attack now – I want my cocktails with those paper umbrellas stuck in 'em."

He pulled him in for a tight hug which was returned. "Do you mind if I crash here for a few hours? I'll make my way back down to Eliza after midday."

"Be my guest. I'm about to check the car over for tonight, then I might get some shut-eye myself. It's gonna be a long night."

No sooner had Abi walked out of her bathroom and into her bedroom, did her mobile phone start to ring. It was seven-thirty in the morning. She looked at the screen to see her mother's number flash across it. *Damn it!*

She considered letting it ring out, but knew her mother would just keep pestering, calling every half hour until she answered so she could get whatever point she wanted made across.

With a resigned sigh, she took the call. "Mum?"

"Sweetheart!"

Already annoyed, Abi rolled her eyes, put her phone on loudspeaker and dropped it onto the bed so she could get changed.

"Happy birthday, darling!"

She towelled her hair as she replied. "You called me at this time of the morning to wish me a happy birthday?" Not once had she ever called her to wish her a happy birthday.

"It's your twenty-fifth – this is going to be such special day."

"You mean like my thirteenth and sixteenth and eighteenth and twenty-first..." There'd been no celebration on those traditionally special anniversaries. She wasn't sure what made twenty-five so special.

"Darling, make sure you wear something special – something that makes you look beautiful and slim, not fat like usual."

Her gut turned in on itself at her mother's words and she bit back an angry exhale, not wanting her mother to hear it. Not wanting her mother to know she could still affect her in any way.

Although she didn't want to look, her eyes automatically wandered to her reflection in the wardrobe mirror. Naked now she'd lost her towel, she forced herself not to see herself as ugly, having fought her mother's verbal abuse ever since she could remember. She was curvy, sure – maybe even a little 'round' at her breasts and hips; her abdomen had a small bump, but it covered a womb – she was a *woman* for god's sake. She wasn't made for Hollywood, but she was in proportion. *You're gorgeous as you are,* she told herself, even as she blinked back tears.

"Is that what you called to tell me?" she snapped, her voice hard to hide the wobble in it.

"One of the things, yes. I would have thought you'd love the chance to dress up for a change, Abigail. Don't you tire of being so normal. It must be dull, surely, working in that library and being the way you are, and looking the way you do with those glasses. I hope you're wearing contact lenses tonight."

Give me strength. She'd make it a point to make sure her glasses stood out particularly well against what she was wearing tonight.

"Also, your father's very much looking forward to seeing you."

Her father was the only reason she'd initially agreed to go.

She never saw him. He barely ever left the house. Since she was old enough to form understanding of how cruel her mother could be, she'd held a small amount of anger at her father for being utterly under her thumb. He had never stood up to her and had barely ever stood up *for* his daughter against her. But Abigail loved him and sometimes missed him, and on the rare moments they managed to catch some time alone, just the two of them, she found she could actually feel like someone's loved daughter for once.

"Tell him I'm looking forward to that, too."

"Is your library friend still coming?"

"You asked me that two days ago."

"I know, but now Friday's upon us, I just wanted to be sure."

She decided she wasn't going to enable her mother's overbearingness by answering her. "Mum, what exactly are you expecting from me tonight? I won't know anyone there, and I don't think I'm going to get anything out of the church ceremony thing you're putting on. What's the point in me coming?"

"I so hate to ruin surprises. But I will say we do have one for you, darling. A big one. A quarter of a century is a big deal." Trust her mum to make twenty-five sound like she was about to keel over and die of old age.

"Did *you* organise the surprise for me?"

"Absolutely!"

A nest of vipers? A poisoned birthday cake? She ran through her mind all the things it could possibly be.

"It'll be pure magic, darling. Six o'clock pick-up, remember. You'll arrive just after seven. I'll see you then." Her mother made some superficial kissing sound on the phone and hung up, not even bothering to hear her say goodbye too.

"Good riddance," she said instead, as she got herself dressed for work.

A text message came through. It was from Sophia: **I'm so sorry I didn't get back to you last night. Yes, I'm definitely coming in to work – just leaving now. Looking forward to seeing you later and to the party. Xx**

She felt a bit bad at the amount of relief that swam through her at Sophia's message. She didn't want to introduce anyone to her mother's shit, and maybe she'd find a way to keep Sophia away from her mother all night, but she was hoping having Sophia by her side might cool her mother's tongue and make the night a bit easier. On herself.

Definitely selfish on my part, she chided. But never mind. If it all turned out to be terrible, she'd find a way to make it up to Sophia.

Her phone sounded again.

Doing up the final button of her blouse, she glanced at the screen then picked it up. It was from Anthony: **Happy birthday, Abi! I'm so sorry I've been silent. So much to do here. I won't be able to speak to you tonight, but I'll be thinking about you. Anthony x**

A fresh bout of tears prickled the corners of her eyes, but she blinked them back in a hurry. *He's not worth it.* Sophia had been right – she deserved more. One kiss at the end of that text, no 'I love you', and not even a hint of affection, really. What was she even doing?

Shaking her head, she gathered both her holdall bag with her evening wear, and her handbag, double-checking she had everything she needed. Her mum had told her the party wasn't ending until dawn, but like hell was she staying there that long. Her aim was to leave soon after midnight.

A bizarre feeling stole over her; a crazy sensation that she might never come back to her little flat again.

That's how much mother dearest unnerves you, Abi. She shook her head to rid herself of the notion and left for work.

♦

Peace. It had been a fucking long time since Jacque had felt honest, true peace that grooved a channel so deep inside you, you'd never forget how perfectly you fit in the world, even if that world was falling apart. Experience told him it wouldn't last long, so he sank into its perfection and stayed where he was in the corner of the hallway, watching Sophia scurry this way and that, getting showered, getting dressed, getting packed, absent-mindedly eating her breakfast while she hurried so she wouldn't be late for work. And every now and then her movements wafted a soft gust of air his way and his heart would fill at, not just her scent, but his. The scent he'd marked her with, deep inside, where life begins in all humans.

He should probably have told her he'd done that – in all honestly, he hadn't quite meant to go that far, but it turned out thousands upon thousands of years of controlling that vampiric possessive urge hadn't quite prepared him for what would unleash when she'd openly and readily asked him to make her his. The moment he'd entered her, it had become imperative – *vital* – that every vampire in every continent damn well knew she was *taken* and unavailable, and stayed the hell away from her. And he wasn't even the main reason they needed to stay away.

He'd tell her later and face the consequences – maybe after she'd had a glass or two of wine. Right now, he didn't want to spoil the beauty of the peace.

She threw him a look of amusement as she breezed past him for the twentieth time on her way to the kitchen. "You know, you could *help* me get ready for work."

"And have you leave sooner? I'm good. I'll watch." He couldn't hide the husky desire in his voice. "But if you keep *swaying* like that as you walk, you will be leaving late." She looked particularly beautiful this morning with her white jeans and dark emerald green top setting off the colour of her hair.

She threw him a knowing smile – one that implied she was completely ready to be taken again – and glanced at him through her eyelashes. *That look.* He inwardly groaned, suddenly unsure he could let her leave in five minutes without another taste of her.

He hadn't seen her coming – not a week ago and not twenty-two years ago. Back then, of course, his only inclination was to keep a remarkable child safe, not least from her insane and horrid family. Her innocence and fighting spirit, despite the foulness of those around her, had warmed his heart and kindled a sense of guardianship within him – one he could do nothing about because a child, human or otherwise, had no place in a vampire's world. He would look after her how, exactly? He'd chosen the only way he could think of to look after her, even though it had broken him to do it.

He'd watched her constantly from a distance until he'd known she was safe with her new adopted parents, and then he'd left, his role as guardian done. For the most part, anyway. He'd come back every now and then just to check in; swore a few curses at the idiot *married* human male toying with her heart while she was at university, and then had walked away properly because he'd sensed it then for the first time: a trace of possessiveness – *his own* possessiveness – over her.

He hadn't come back again. Not until the sudden sharp tug he'd felt when she'd been attacked in that alleyway a week ago. Deiniol had also felt that tug because she'd latched onto him *through* Jacque's mind and he had gotten there first. By the time Jacque had arrived the only things left were their scents.

His possessiveness had stirred again, and a feeling of hurt that Deiniol had her. But he was glad she was at least in good hands. Burying the hurt, he'd considered leaving her with Deiniol and taking off again.

But she'd found herself in danger again two days later, and he was the only one with the blood link to feel it – not Deiniol. Reaching her at that man's accommodation (seriously, *why* had that useless cheater still been around?) during the Hupogeios vampire attack, had changed more than he'd been prepared for. He'd seen her up close and properly for the first time in two decades. She'd grown from a fierce child into a fierce woman with eyes that shone the colour of those golden gates when she was angry or aroused, and – despite his progeny's scent all over her (*that* had taken some willpower to put aside) – he'd *seen* her attraction to him and *felt* their connection the minute he'd taken her hand.

Walking away had no longer been an option.

"Sophia." He caught her arm next time she strutted past, her almost comically large handbag now over her shoulder. The vampire in her was very much awakened because a soft purr emanated from her chest the minute he pulled her body into his. *Christ,* she was gorgeous. "Deiniol brought this over last night in case you wanted it." He pulled the crucifix pendant from his trouser pocket, its wings extended, otherwise he wouldn't even have been able to touch the damn thing. "I think you should wear it tonight."

A mixture of sadness and anger took over her features. "I can't wear that now. After knowing it hurts you? After knowing what it was created for – what *I* was birthed for by these people? No."

"Wear it wings out so it doesn't hurt any of us." She went to protest further, but he cut in. "It will help you fit in and not look so suspicious to others there, especially if you're asking questions about the library at the house and family affairs. They'll think you're a Resurrector."

She huffed and pursed her lips, but he knew she could see his point. Reluctantly, she took it and put it in her handbag.

"Thank you."

"I feel like I'm betraying you by wearing it."

"You're not."

She suddenly stilled in his arms and looked up at him like she wanted to say something. The look in her eyes was one of grief, and maybe a little guilt, but it went quickly, replaced by that fierceness he loved.

Fuck – I do. I love her. Completely.

She cupped his face, and her tone was serious when she said, "Jacque, I will *never* betray you. I swear it."

"Sophia, I know—"

She shook her head. "Wait ... I need to talk to you about something, but not now – there's no time – after the party."

"We can make time if it's—"

"I want to feel you bite me and take my blood into you."

Good god... His teeth almost ripped his gums the way they'd just erupted and if she was in any doubt what his sudden show of fangs meant, his full erection pressing into her should make things quite clear.

She smiled a little at the feel of him, but was all seriousness again. "I want to be yours completely, and you mine, completely. With nothing in the way. But we need to talk first about it. About my ... blood."

"Christ, seraphia, I would never drink your blood and seal our link without us talking about it first. The implications are too—"

She smashed her lips to his, shutting him up, then she pulled back and stared at him, deeply, her arousal clear in both her eyes and her aroma. "I love you."

She'd knocked all words out of him. He just stood there, soaking in everything she was.

She nodded, as if confirming it to herself now that she'd said it, and said it again. "I love you."

Fuck the time. He returned her kiss and picked her up, speeding them both into the living room and onto the sofa. Her bag was dropped on the floor, her hands now racing over the buttons of his shirt to undo them; his were already yanking her jeans down, her underwear with them.

She gave up on his buttons and scrambled to pull his trousers off.

He hurriedly helped her with them, and then he was inside her and it was bliss. Pure bliss. Better than bliss.

The sounds she made for him were everything he needed. Her hands roamed his chest under the damned shirt that hadn't quite come off, and he almost came right then, every touch of hers was heaven.

"Jacque ... oh, god, please..."

He took her over the edge with long, hard strokes, making sure he'd driven every sweet cry out of her before he let himself go. "I love you, too, Sophia. So much."

More than he'd ever thought possible.

"How do I look?" asked Abi. And she felt stupid asking it because Sophia looked stunning to a degree she'd only seen on super models and celebrities. She'd looked stunning all day, even in her jeans and green top, as if yesterday's rest had *literally* healed her on some fundamental level.

Her colleague stood there in her long, dark green silk dress, which showed off every single contour of her slim body and somehow still managed to be curvy in the right places. Her dress was to die for. It was some kind of silk, lace was etched into the bodice and sides in such a sophisticated way and every stitch was so tight and discrete, Abi wondered if it had been hand sewn. High slits travelled up each thigh so she could take long strides, and every stride was perfection in itself. She could have stepped straight out of the early 1900s, except her dark brown, chestnut hair was worn loose in soft waves.

Sophia turned to look at Abigail as Abi tried not to throw her arms in front of her massive waist, far too snugly encased in her dark red satin dress. She'd gone for one that accentuated her breasts and hips – if you've got them, flaunt them, as the saying goes. But now, she just felt woefully self-conscious and despised herself for it.

Do not start to sound like your mother. Burn in hell before you go there, Abi. Don't ever *treat yourself the way she treats you.*

With some effort, she straightened her back and held her head up.

Sophia's smile was wide and genuine. Her eyes sparkled. She didn't know what make-up the woman was wearing today, but somehow they made her irises look more golden than usual. "Abi, my god ... you look *so* beautiful."

She suddenly felt daft for keeping her glasses on. She must look like a nerdy dumpling next to Sophia. Her eyes fell to the necklace she wore around her neck and felt a sudden chill. It passed quickly, but it had pressed on something in her mind. She'd seen a necklace like that before – and angel on a cross – but a long time ago. She couldn't remember where. It felt like a childhood memory – one of those ones you can't recall because you were too young to hold onto it. Her first memory was from age three or four, so it must have been before that.

"Wait, wait, I have something for you." Sophia rummaged in her bag.

They'd locked up at five o'clock. Their ride was arriving in ten minutes and Sophia had said her friends were also meeting them with their chauffeur and would follow them all the way there. She didn't mind at all – the more the merrier – but it was a bit weird how Sophia's acting buddies were suddenly all *there* even though she hadn't mentioned them – or acting, for that matter – before the nightmare in the basement.

But Sophia had explained she'd left the acting group last year before she'd even started working at the library – they'd only contacted her as an emergency because of her mother's sudden demands. And apparently, the play might not even go ahead now as the religious ceremony – or whatever it was her mother had cooked up – was taking precedence.

Whatever. She was so done with her mother's antics, she was starting to regret going tonight.

"Here." Her colleague handed her a small present and card.

"You didn't have to do this!" She took the small bundle and tore into the envelope.

"It's your birthday and I wanted to. The minute I saw this, I thought of you. Open it now, okay, before everyone gets here."

The card was so thoughtful and she said so. Feeling a tingle of excitement, because this wasn't a present from her mother which always ended with Abi feeling hurt or disappointed, she dug her finger into the wrapping paper and opened it.

A small jewellery box was inside it. When she opened the box, the little thing inside took her breath away. A gorgeous, small and delicate glass swan pendant sat on a sterling silver chain against the black velvet box. It refracted rainbow colours as the light caught it. "I don't know what to say – this is one of the most beautiful gifts I've ever received. Thank you *so* much."

"Put it on," encouraged her friend, her face flushed with Abi's obvious gratitude. "As soon I saw this, I thought of how you are with people and with your customers – so graceful and caring, even with the difficult ones – and the way you just breeze through each day without letting anything ruffle you, even when on your own the past few days when I couldn't be here. Strong and untouchable, just like a swan. You are such an inspiration."

Abi blinked. Then blinked again. She closed the clasp of the chain around her neck and stared at herself at the inadequate, small mirror in the staff room.

Sophia let out an exclamation to match her grin. "I knew it would look gorgeous on you!" She gave her a hug and Abi felt a bit bad for standing there like a lemon. She was about to hug her back, but Sophia was off her and looking at the clock. "Five minutes. I have something quick I need to do then I'll meet you by the front door, okay?"

Abigail nodded, and the woman was out of there in a flash.

Feeling somewhat numb, Abi brought her eyes back to the little swan in the mirror, and let her tears surface.

Strong ... untouchable...

Graceful.

An embarrassing sob broke through, but she breathed through it until she had it under control. She used to pretend she was. Years ago. No one had ever said she was like ... like a *swan* before.

Her heart swelled with ... she didn't even know what the feeling was. She felt vulnerable. But she felt ... *seen*.

And she felt grateful. Grateful there were wonderful people in her life.

Straightening her shoulders, she grabbed her clutch bag. Tonight was going to be fine – she was done with Anthony. She'd tell him it was over before she left the party. And whatever her mother threw at her, she would deal with it. Because she *was* strong.

Sophia let herself into the basement. She'd wanted to come down here earlier, but the library had been very busy today, teeming with customers. The part-timers were back from tomorrow and she was glad – she couldn't take any more time off work, but she needed space to think. She felt like a different person to who she'd been a week ago.

She made her way to the middle of the room and called out to Jane. "It's the big party tonight, but I just wanted to say thank you so much for your help with those Nocturnes two days ago."

Silence.

"You saved my life. I can't stay – our rides are probably here by now – but is there anything I can do for you, Jane? To return the favour? Please just let me know if there is."

She was about to turn and leave when the scraping noise of a book sounded. And then another, and then another.

She hurried towards the sounds, now quite used to whereabouts they all came from and the kinds of books they might belong to. She found three sticking out of place down three separate aisles, and she *really* had to hurry now, or they'd be late.

Grabbing them, she hurriedly looked at the titles of each: *Born Free, Cry Freedom,* and *Trap Door.*

Trap door?

Her heart thudded as sadness gripped it.

A final book was flung from a shelf and landed on the floor in front of her. The pages flipped. When they'd stopped, Sophia glanced down at the chapter heading: *Free Me.*

Jane didn't roam the basement willingly. She was trapped in here.

Steely determination settled in her as she closed the book.

Sophia nodded. "Give me time. I'll see what I can do."

Chapter Thirty

Jacque was out of Les' car as soon as it had parked up in the designated field of the stately home, thanking the heavens for an overcast evening. While the sun didn't officially set until past nine o'clock in the summer, that was only under two hours away and it looked like they wouldn't be seeing any sunset at all.

He didn't love long car journeys on a good day, but what was getting his goat right now was that somewhere along the 'A' road, after a roundabout and in busy commuter traffic, they'd lost the other car.

He could *sense* Sophia was okay, but until he clapped eyes on her again, he couldn't relax.

"She's fine," came Ronan's Irish drawl behind him. "I turned Location on for all our phones. They got stuck on the A27 – should be here in ten minutes or so."

Jacque nodded his thanks.

Daniel, Eliza, and Les were stretching their legs a good few metres away on the other side of the car.

Ronan rested his hand on his shoulder. "Walk with me. I want to run something by you."

He glanced at his friend as they wandered a little bit further away from prying ears. 'Friend' was quite an understatement for what they were to each other, and it mattered little that he hadn't spoken to Ronan for a thousand years or so – warrior, brother, best friend, and loyal, there was no one else he trusted to the same degree, whether in a battlefield or in his house.

When Ronan was far enough away from anyone else around, he stopped and said, "I had a vision last night."

Jacque stilled at his words as he processed them. "How long has it been?"

"There have been none since I lost my wings."

All fallen angels had possessed something uniquely 'them' – something they lost right along with their wings through their vampiric transition. Ronan's was prophetic vision. "Why now?"

"I have a few ideas – one of them is the aingeal you've fallen in love with."

He raised a brow. "Is it that obvious?"

Ronan chuckled. "I can feel it, which is the other thing we need to talk about, but first, the vision. I'm sad to say, it wasn't pretty. I saw the sun – giant thing rising up from the horizon right in front of me, taking up the whole landscape like I was just a few metres away from it. It burned us all, Jacque – it took all of us with it. I woke up thinking I was ash. The second thing I thought is we need to be the feck out of here before dawn. Way before dawn."

The male shivered, which told Jacque everything he needed to know because Ronan was never easily spooked. "Ronan," he began in a bid to calm him, "the last time you had your visions, we lived in a different world. Millennia have passed. Demon tribes no longer walk the earth, the days of Merlin and the Fay are gone, magic holds nowhere near the power it used to, and vampires have been relegated to the pages of fiction for god's sake – we live very much in the human's world now, so perhaps your vision does not mean something as daunting as you might think."

He shook his head, his lips pressed together. "I don't want to be here anywhere near dawn."

Jacque sighed. "All right, Sophia told me Abigail wants to leave soon after midnight. We could aim to have all our scouting done by then and leave together. We'll have at least four hours – it should be plenty of time."

"Let's do that. That vision can *not* become reality." He glanced at Jacque and held his gaze just a fraction too long.

"What aren't you telling me?"

The right corner of his mouth rose. "You know me too well."

"Likewise. What is it?"

He paused and seemed to contemplate his words. "When was the last time"—those light blue eyes met his again—"you felt our mergence?"

Oh, hell. *Fuck*. Jacque looked around him, then ran a hand through his hair with a sigh. One big, fucking, complicated sigh. "Not since my wings went."

"Same. Except ... I felt that, too – last night."

Jesus Christ.

Ronan had been one of the few determined to get through to Jacque about Dalila – over six thousand years ago now. He'd had vision after vision of her malice and Jacque's downfall.

Jacque hadn't just woken up to his wings destroyed, he'd suffered severe blood loss with no way to quench it. Wings were not skin – they did not heal the same. Hundreds of thick arteries ran from the heart through each wing. And while angels were immortal, damage to those arteries and such blood loss could send one mad; and combined with the loss of the wings themselves? It had driven Jacque over the edge of sanity.

His blood had flowed in rivers. It was Ronan who had found him in a mess. And such is the thirst when near to death – such was his surging madness from the reality of what Dalila had done to him – that he'd sunk his teeth into Ronan's neck and drunk, and Ronan hadn't been able to stop him, Jacque's hysteria-fuelled strength outweighing his. Maybe that had been the first awakening of the vampire in him.

A vampire (or an angel) driven by blood loss cannot see reason; cannot see the person in front of them; cannot control their needs. Only mania exists. And they will drink anything in their path without hesitation or mercy.

Growing weaker by the second and in desperation and fury,

Ronan had lunged, bitten him back and swallowed in a fraught attempt to reclaim his blood.

And the link had been sealed.

But they had both been angels at that point – not vampires. And angels could not share blood in the way vampires could – an anomaly occurred when they tried: a total mergence of the two souls. Or as total as corporeal bodies allowed. Ronan had found himself in Jacque's mind and vice versa. Emotions were fused. Physical pain was shared.

Confused, raging, and in agony, Jacque had not taken his turn from angel to vampire well.

And due to the enforced mergence, Ronan had felt it all.

Had felt Jacque's descent into madness. Had felt the completion of his fall when he'd taken Dalila's head off.

After that, what was left of Jacque's wings had fallen. Ironically, with the wings gone, Jacque was no longer angel, but vampire, and the mergence between them was thus proven short-lived – it had severed after less than two days actualised.

However, he'd fled. Jacque had fled into his own darkness and left Ronan to pick up the pieces of the wreckage he'd left him with. When they'd reconvened by accident, five thousand years later, Jacque had fallen on his knees before him and asked for his forgiveness.

Ronan had already forgiven.

"When I had the vision, I didn't know if it was me in the vision, or you in the vision – I couldn't tell the difference. It was *just* like the short while we were merged. So, I reached out to see if I could feel the mergence, and I could. I did. I'm not sure how, but it's reinstated itself. Right along with my visions."

"How do you know for sure? What did you feel?"

"Do you *really* want me to give you the details of the beautiful place you were in last night? The smell of mint? The feel of *her*?"

He growled.

"We're good." He raised his hands. "I'm just making my point. And I didn't hang around in you long."

Jacque reeled himself in. He was too frazzled at Ronan's admittance to feel possessive. And it was Ronan. If it had been *anyone* else... "Shit. So what do we do?"

"Can you try and reach out to me now? I want to see if it's both ways."

"Okay." Although he needed to calm the fuck down first. Taking a couple of deep breaths, he centred himself.

"Try and speak to me – mind to mind. Say something random. Nonsensical."

Jacque nodded, and then reached out when ready: *Potatoes, salad, spaghetti, corn on the cob, anchovies—*

What the— Is this what you feckin' had for dinner last night?

Jacque cursed. "I can hear you loud and clear."

Ronan delved into the inside pocket of his jacket and drew out a flick knife. "Hold your palm out."

He did, knowing exactly what was coming.

Ronan sliced into his own left palm first and they waited, staring at Jacque's in exactly the same spot.

Nothing happened. He then sliced Jacque's right palm, and they waited.

Nothing.

"That's good at least," nodded Ronan, putting his knife away. "We can rule out a physical resonance. At least for now."

Across the field, the car carrying Sophia and Abigail pulled into a space not far from theirs. Daniel and Eliza spotted them and headed over.

"We have to tell her," said Ronan, grimly. "She has both our blood in her – she might be affected too."

He was right and there was no way out of it. "Not tonight, though. Let's get this godforsaken party over and done with first."

"I agree. The mergence isn't as bad as the vision I had."

Jacque nodded. "We'll plan to reconvene here at midnight. We'll be home well before dawn."

"Good. Let's organise it with the others."

They made their way towards them, and then Jacque stopped, catching Ronan by the arm.

The redhead halted, turning to him, but a bunch of people walked past, and they were too close to the others now, anyway.

So Jacque shot his words into his mind. *If something happens to me, she's yours. I know you'll take care of her.*

Ronan's eyebrows went up in amusement, although his expression remained grave. *Are you intending to give her any choice in the matter? And I've seen her in action – she can take care of herself just fine.*

I mean it, Ronan. There's no one else in this world I'd trust with her. And I saw you both when she was feeding from you. She trusted you then, without even knowing you. Promise me you'll take her if I die.

For Christ's sake, the purpose of telling you about the vision was not for your eulogy – you're not dyin', you eejit. Ronan was pissed off. *I'll die before I let you die, how's that for a promise?*

And then Sophia was there, looking like the best damn thing that had ever happened to him. Because she was. "Hi!" Her eyes sparkled as she greeted them both.

"Hi, yourself." Jacque brought her into his arms, and it was close to a miracle that even after that conversation, his entire body relaxed as her frame moulded into his. God, she was like some kind of drug. And he needed it.

He glanced at Ronan over the top of her dark hair.

Ronan pursed his lips and shook his head, and Jacque knew – knew he was feeling her against his own frame in that second.

Still shaking his head, Ronan walked away, but not before he heard him curse his name. *Fuck you, Jacque. You know I'd do anythin' for you. Fine. I promise.*

♦

"I don't want to leave Abi talking to Les for too long, but I wanted to let you know I had a chance to chat with her quite a lot in the car."

Jacque's arms around her waist were almost distracting her from her mission, they felt so damn good.

"Her family surname is Carey – that's from her dad's side and he sounds like your average guy. I think he married into the Resurrectors even though the estate is in his name, although I'm betting his wife gets everything when he dies. His wife is her mother and she assumed the surname Carey, too, but guess what – her first name is Rita."

Jacque let out a long exhale. "There we have it, then."

"I know. If it's the *same* Rita, then Abi's my cousin."

"We need to find out more."

"I agree. I want to go with Abi and see Rita for myself."

His hold on her tightened. "I'm really not sure about that."

"I could handle Rita as a child – she's tame. She was always so scared of me."

"What if she recognises you? What if she already knows who you are and she's the *reason* you're here?"

"Maybe it means she's been wanting to make contact with me and the only way she felt she could do it was through Abigail, and maybe she felt it was safer in a party setting in front of other people, too, in case the reunion went horribly wrong – it gives us both an easy excuse to walk away."

"Having spoken to your family, I don't think their intentions for you are good ones."

"I would agree if it were anyone else, but I'll bet Rita on her own is harmless. Come with me and Abi if you want to – I don't mind. I want to ask Aunty Rita about my birth. Without my other family members breathing down her throat, she might just tell me what the hell I am and why. As my only living relative, she could be my last chance to know."

"What about Abi? Does she know any of this?"

Sophia pulled a face. "I haven't told her on the off-chance it's a different Rita. I don't know *how* to tell Abi, but if it *is* my Aunt Rita, that'll then be the perfect time for the truth to come out. And Abi and I get on really well – I'd love to be her cousin. I'm sort of hoping the truth will just play itself out in the best way it can once I know for sure it's really Aunty Rita."

"All right." He nodded. "I remember Rita – I don't want to scare her. It might be easier if it's just you and Abi. But use this." He prodded her crucifix. "Push the wings back in when you're away from us. I don't want vampires hovering around you."

She narrowed her eyes. "Oh, and there I was thinking you'd taken care of that little problem when you marked me with your scent."

"Aaah."

"Yes, aaah." She poked him in the chest. "Eliza told me outside the library because, of course, *every* vampire can smell I'm 'taken' now, you absolute *male*. Is that what that hot liquid feeling was before ... you know. Don't you think you should have asked my permission first?"

He dropped his voice to a whisper. "I recall you were quite turned on by your total submission to me."

She flushed hot.

He damn well *felt* her flush hot. "You came fucking hard, too."

"Don't think we're not going to finish this conversation later."

"I'll look forward to it, but I'm not sorry – no vampire is

coming near you. Sophia"—he pulled her in, right against the erection he'd grown in the past fifteen seconds, but his gaze turned urgent as he went back to the other, more pressing issue —"I want to know where you're heading to meet Rita. Find me, or text me where you're planning to see her before you do. I want to be close by."

"I will. It might not be for a bit yet – I think Abi wants to put off seeing her for as long as possible." She rose up and kissed him. "I love you, you cocky arse."

He deepened that kiss without any hesitation. "God, I so wish I could spend more time with you tonight. You look bloody amazing in this dress, by the way."

"If we're leaving at midnight, we'll be home before two in the morning." She dropped her voice. "You can have me from then until I need to go to work, and you can peel this dress off me with your teeth."

"Mmmn ... you have me very hard, seraphia," he whispered. "Tell me, when between now and 7 a.m. do you intend to sleep?"

"Sleep is overrated when you're lying next to me."

His next kiss was one of those delightfully hypnotic ones, or at least it was heading that way until Abi's cough sounded to her left.

Sophia pulled away from Jacque, then laughed at Abi's amused expression.

"You know," Abi said, "I knew there was something going on between you two when I saw you in the library basement together." She held out her hand to Jacque. "I'm Abi, and your name probably isn't Romeo, is it?"

He smiled and took it, repositioning himself subtly so the bulge in his pants didn't show. "Jacque."

"Wow." She glanced at Sophia. "Nicer than Romeo."

"I've been told it's your birthday," he added. "Many happy

returns."

"Thank you."

Sophia gave Jacque's hand a squeeze. "I'll see you a bit later."

"See you later." His eyes begged her to stay safe.

She gave him a last peck on the lips and whispered, "I'll be careful."

"I love you," she heard from behind her as Abi led her out of the parking field and onto the main grounds.

It was just gone nine o'clock and Daniel was leaning on a tree trunk, his jacket on the ground by his feet, bored out of his mind, and completely out of his comfort zone. Social gatherings had never been his thing – definitely Eliza's thing, even when she'd been human – but never his. Throw in the eerie religious aspect to this entire event and he had the creeps. He'd seen first-hand the consequences of religious dogma and fanaticism growing up in the late 1500s and was more than happy to be out of that era.

In a far field, he saw a huddle of priests and Catholic folk (probably Catholic, anyway) preparing for whatever ceremony was going to take place. No one was allowed near enough to see the preparations, but what looked like large planks of wood lay on the ground next to tarpaulin. Were these people Resurrectors? Probably. He found the whole thing confusing. His religion was nature and always had been: nurture the land and the land gives back. What the hell else was there, really? Everything you could ever want was in the water that rushed down the mountains, the soil that fed you, the sky that fed the soil, and the sun's light that brought it all to life.

Okay, so he wasn't on best terms with the sun nowadays, but he hadn't forgotten it – the feel of it on his back as he'd worked his crops; how it lit up dark days and had brought his children out of the house with smiles on their faces.

Turning his head from the little thicket of trees he was currently taking a breather amongst, he spied Eliza about fifty metres away in deep conversation with another vampire. He'd had no luck at all getting information from anyone about the mystery vamp who could walk in the sun. Few had even heard of the rumour; the one or two that had, mumbled something about Nocturnes and kept their mouths shut. Maybe Eliza would have more luck; she looked far more at ease chatting to everyone about everything, and her enthusiastic, openly curious demeanour was magnetic, even for vampires.

There was a kerfuffle in the tree above him. Daniel looked up at the irritated chirrups coming from a bird's nest some ten feet above him. Baby birds. He couldn't see or sense their mother around, and suddenly there was a flutter of a shadow and a tiny form was falling.

In the blink of an eye, he caught the baby bird that had tumbled out of its nest. "Whoa ... gotchya little daredevil." With a lithe flex that all vampires had, he scurried up the tree to pop the baby back in its nest. There was no need to worry about his scent putting off the mother – he was undead and vampires only exuded scent for mating or for marking.

That brought his thoughts to Jacque and Sophia and he had to tamp down his annoyance. Jacque had only gone and fucking marked her – *heavily* – and even though he'd resolved to let Sophia go, he was still irate about it.

But the talk with Les earlier had allowed him to see it was the *human* connection he'd had with her that he was possessive about, and not necessarily Sophia herself. He could work with that, but it still felt like a bruise to his gut, not least because his connection with Eliza was ... not all there. She was harder than she used to be; steelier around the edges. She was now undead.

With a sadness, he'd asked himself this morning if when he'd loved her as a human, he'd loved her *because* she was human.

Amelia, Les' mother, had also been human.

With a sudden clarity, he'd understood it was the humanity of a person he always fell in love with, and he had no idea what to do with that information because he wasn't bloody human – he was a vampire.

He took his last step off the tree back onto solid ground and froze. His forte as a vampire tended to be his 'feeling' of a thing, not his sense of smell, yet, the most enticing musk surrounded him; filled his nasal passages, all the way up the cortex of his brain; set his mind and body alight.

A tremor ran through him and ... he was hard. Instantly and intensely, his cock was erect and the sensation was so urgent it almost hurt. It was more than alarming, and it was not a response he was used to – his vampire was a considerate, cautious one; not one led by some primordial ego to mount and mate.

Startled into new awareness, he turned and scanned the cluster of trees he stood in until his gaze landed on a woman. A female. A vampire. But not like one he'd ever seen before.

She was almost as tall as he, her body athletic, firm, and made for climbing fortresses despite the delicate looking lilac dress she was wearing. Her skin was a stunning shade of tan; her mid-length hair a sandy brown with a luminosity to it. Her eyes were an exotic and lethal pale green, but soft in shape. They exuded a compassion not at all common among his fanged kin. And those eyes glowed. *For him*. And he knew this because the musk in the air that licked his senses was her arousal. No doubt she was very aware of his own. *For her*.

She took one step towards him and he took one step back right into the damned tree. Her lips turned up in a smile that made him ache, but her eyes remained kind.

He wanted to bury himself inside her.

"Daniel!"

Fuck.

Eliza waved from barely fifteen metres away and he sped out of the thicket to greet her, not wanting her to catch the scent of—

"Hey, are you oka— Whoa."

He whisked her away by the arm back towards the crowd he loathed. "I was watching you mingle. Did you find anything out?" Guilt had him by the tongue, desperate to find any subject she could cling to so she wouldn't ask what he'd been doing.

"Er ... not really. Are you all right?"

"Mmm-hmmn, just needed a moment of quiet away from the chattering."

She suddenly halted all movement. Her nostrils flared.

He held his breath; felt like he was about to be mowed over by a freight train.

Then, Eliza smiled, slowly, her blue-grey eyes gleaming, and pressed herself into him; melted into him. "So," she teased, "you were watching me mingle?" Between them, her hand found his hard shaft.

Caught somewhere between arousal, guilt, and the craziest feeling he was betraying the *other* female, he gulped, caught her wrist and pulled himself back. "It's too busy here."

Her gaze wandered behind him to the thicket. "We could go—"

"No. Um ... I just want to get this party over with so we can make our way home."

"Oh."

"To bed," he added, because the disappointment in her face was evident.

That helped a little, and another small smile took over her disappointment. "I guess I can wait. But give me something to go on." Before he could stop her, she was back on his cock, giving it a rub and a squeeze, and he was going straight to hell – no angels or golden gates for him – because he hissed and grew at the contact when green eyes flashed through his mind.

He brushed her away more harshly than he'd intended.

She just rolled her eyes – always at him for his more reserved nature – then said, "Hey, where's your jacket."

Damn it. He'd left it by the tree. "I forgot it. I'll be one second."

"I'll come with yo—"

"Jesus, just give me *one second.*"

Hurt flickered over her and he felt like the shittiest creature alive.

"I'm sorry. I'm just skittish because of all the people and this event really isn't my kind of thing. I'm sorry," he repeated. "I won't be long. I was feeling too warm so left it by a tree."

Before she could protest and before he could ramble further, he turned and sped into the thicket.

She didn't follow him, thank god.

Finding the tree he'd been standing by, he picked up his jacket, gave it a shake, and couldn't resist glancing around for the female who'd been there with him. Of course, she was gone, but her scent wasn't. And he was in deep trouble because that scent was *in* him now, affecting him in ways he couldn't easily control.

Closing his eyes, he breathed it in deep, committing it to memory – committing it to his every goddamned cell – then turned and left, discarding the primitive and virile need within him to track whoever she was down and make her his.

Joseph Marino was here, or so said the vampire Ronan had just been speaking to – an owner of another feeding house in the Midlands, he was willing to take his word for it. Ronan had convinced him to help him build a network – reach out to other houses so they could confront Joseph's makeshift mafia together. He'd seemed keen. Numbers were exchanged. He'd follow up next week.

But he could do without seeing Joseph, and he could do with keeping Sophia away from him, too, given his first impression of her may well have kindled a deep-seated wish to kill her.

Fuck. He shouldn't have been here. No doubt he'd decided to join the party because Ronan – who he'd sent – could no longer be trusted to get his damned Project Veil book. He was probably looking for the bloody thing himself now.

Ronan muttered a curse under his breath as he scanned the grounds he was on and whatever he could see of the next field over. He was about to phone Jacque when a light and husky female laugh sounded from behind him.

He turned to find green eyes on exquisitely refined, golden-brown skin, and everything felt better. "Good Christ, Miriam!" He grinned as he took her in an embrace. "Three thousand feckin' years?"

He felt her nod and her kiss landed on his cheek "And then some. Good to see you, you Gael."

It was hard to put her down, but it had always been hard to put Miri down, especially in the early days. When she'd lost her wings, the whole world had mourned without knowing why. "Of all the vamps here tonight, you're the last I would have expected." He finally let her go and took her in. She was just as he'd remembered – maybe a tad more world weary, but weren't they all.

"I had no intention of coming, believe me. I was surprised when I got the invite a couple of months back. How the devil are you?"

"Hopefully not too close to the devil just yet." He found himself looking at the congregation in the far field, in their cassocks and robes.

She followed his gaze. "This entire place is freaky, Ronan."

He snorted. "Don't see anything you like, then?"

"I've seen *one* thing I like." Her voice lowered almost seductively and wrapped itself around that statement possessively. Her pupils dilated slightly.

Interesting. God help whomever she'd set her eyes on because Miriam left no one the same way she found them.

"One bright star among a horde of dark souls, especially in there." She nodded to the main house. "I don't want to know what's in there."

Which probably meant that's where he was headed. "So what brings you into the crowds? I know how much you love the whole social butterfly gig."

She let out another laugh. "I may actually have to move back to the mountains if I can't get a handle on what happened last night." She looked at him, grimaced, then said. "It's back. The empathy. Hit me like a ton of bricks at around three in the morning – chest-crushing, soul-crushing ... I can feel everything and everyone and I need to learn to switch it all off again."

As an angel, Miriam had brought empathy to earth when she'd fallen. Just about every fallen angel had been in love with her, or rather, the unconditional compassion she exuded. She'd been *needed* and she'd fed them all in many ways. In the early, less populated days of earth, that had been possible. But once the numbers of humans grew, and most fallen had lost their wings, giving way to the expansion of vampires, she had had to retreat. Emotions became denser, darker; humans and vampires alike yearned her whenever she was present to balm their souls and share their anguish, and it had been too much. There'd been no one able to feed Miri the way she fed all others. She'd left civilisation behind and sought out the quiet spaces of mountains, valleys; anywhere unpopulated. She had still had her wings then, and Ronan had no idea how she lost them – she'd never divulged it to anyone – but he did know *when*, because every single living creature had wept that day, even if they'd been ignorant to why.

"There's something else, too." She met his eyes. "I cried."

Well, that left him dumbstruck. "You ... cried?"

"Tears. Real ones. I have no idea why. Do you? That's why I came – hoping to find answers because there was nowhere else I could think of to go. I thought if I'd been invited, maybe others, like you, were too."

"Good thinking. And you're not alone. My visions are back – also from around three in the morning."

"What the hell happened at three in the morning?"

He pursed his lips. He suspected it had something to do with a blond Gaul, his healed heart, and the returned memories of the aingeal hybrid he was in love with, but he had no idea where any of it was going or why. "I'm still trying to figure that one out. Jacque's here, by the way. So's Joseph, but he's an insane fucker now, so I'm staying out of his way."

"What about Elijah?"

"I've never met Elijah? He a fallen?"

"He is – lost his wings earlyish, about eight thousand years ago or so."

"Listen, come back with us to Jacque's tonight. We have a ride. We're meeting in the parking field at midnight and heading off straight after. What happened to you last night is exactly what we're discussing."

"Okay, I'm in. I have to be – the thought of doing this all over again"—she placed a hand between her breasts, over her heart—"with eight billion on the planet *before* you include the vampires, is terrifying. And I don't want to have to retreat again. The isolation is just as bad." She turned to Ronan for another hug and he gave it. "I'm so glad I found you here tonight." She pulled back just as quickly. "Midnight in the parking field, then."

He nodded. "You leaving me already?"

"I'm rattled to my bones." She stared, again, at the robes in the field, then at the main house. "I can't place exactly what it is – it's like so much here is shrouded; there's blindness and twisted feelings. I'm on edge. And have you seen the gargoyles on the roof?"

He grimaced. "Let's hope they stay asleep – last thing we feckin' need."

"I won't be going anywhere near them. I'm going to find that star again."

"Be gentle with the poor thing."

She laughed.

"Male or female?"

"Male. I dunno ... I saw him and everything inside me stilled. It was even more quiet than after the empathy had gone. It was soothing."

And not once had he heard her say that before about anyone or anything. "Then, I definitely wouldn't pass up on your star. Off wit'ya. I'll see you in a couple of hours or so."

She squeezed his arm and left.

Ronan looked at his watch. It told him it was 9:45 p.m. He then looked at the large stately home where Miriam had sensed a horde of dark souls. And headed towards it.

Chapter Thirty-One

"Ronan!" Sophia approached him up the side of the house just as he was arriving, her strides long and confident, her dark chestnut hair caught by the lamp light to her left. She looked nothing short of stunning in that dark green dress, and her eyes shone with a keen awareness and determination that was always there, giving away the consequences of some of the hardships she'd been through. She hadn't hesitated a second taking on that Manuel bastard. It was no wonder Jacque had fallen hook, line, and sinker.

Ronan steeled himself against the scent of Jacque on her – *in her* – throwing up a host of complications inside him there was no time to deal with tonight. "Stóirín," he greeted her.

She paused mid-thought, staring at him with her head slightly tilted, then asked – finally – "What does that mean?"

"It's a term of endearment."

After a couple of seconds, she smiled and shook her head. "You and Jacque are so alike in some ways. Do you know where he is? I texted him over fifteen minutes ago and got no reply, and he's not picking up either."

Ronan reached for him with his mind, just enough to connect and know he was alive and not in panic or pain. "He's around and doing fine. Anything I can help you with?"

"I'm going in the house with Abi to meet her mum – did Jacque fill you in?"

"On the massively coincidental familial connection – yes, he did."

"He wanted me to let him know where and when."

"I'll watch your back. You goin' in now?"

"Yep. We caught up with Abi's dad earlier – a very lovely and very normal guy, if you get what I mean. He seems totally out of place here. Rita phoned him while we were with him and said she'd like to see me and Abi. Abi will be here in a sec, then we're going in."

"I'll stay out here near to the house – I can sense you better when we're close, but be careful in there – I got word it's ... not very nice."

"Which reminds me – the cellar that was supposed to contain the library? It's gone. Abi's dad told us all the books down there were moved twenty years ago for safer keeping, but guess where everything was moved to?" She lowered her voice. "The bloody library I work in – in the basement. It all makes sense now: why the books are so old; why they're not in a museum... For fuck's sake, I could have just searched it earlier today for the damned book we're looking for!"

"Hmmn, do you think it's luck you got a job in the very same library? Perhaps you were led there."

She shrugged. "I found the job in a library leaflet that came through my door over a year ago."

"I'm not liking this whole thing with you and your family. It stinks to high heaven."

"I agree it's weird. Abi was furious. She had no idea that's where all the books came from. I think she trusted the library was a safe haven from her family – something that was just hers – only to find out they'd infiltrated their way into her work."

"I don't know how mixed up your friend is in all of this. I'm not feelin' better about you going in that house."

"I'll be cautious. At least I no longer need to find that book tonight. We've only got two hours – I'm going to focus on speaking to Rita about my own birth and what I am. We're going home with answers one way or the other, and honestly, I can't wait to get away from here. Abi's chewing at the bit to leave, too. Oh, here she is now."

Abigail appeared around the corner and walked up the path towards them some twenty metres away.

Ronan took Sophia's arm and waited until he had her full attention. "If anything happens in there, you *scream* for me, you got that? I mean in your head. I'll feel you."

Holding his gaze, she nodded. "But what about Jac—"

"I'll fill him in on everything you just told me as soon as I see him."

Something like worry flickered across her irises, then she said, quietly, "I had a dream last night – about three in the morning. I don't remember it, but I think ... I think something happened to Jacque. I woke up needing to..." She couldn't finish that sentence, but her eyes watered.

He stroked her arm where he held her. "Never, in a million years, stóirín, will I let anything happen to Jacque." And he couldn't help it, damn it. The way his voice nearly broke over the male's name.

She stared at him – at the impression his own words left on him – and understanding seeped across her face.

Abigail's heels on the tarmac clattered.

He dropped her arm.

She nodded. "Thank you." Then, she turned to her friend. "All ready?"

"Yep," smiled Abi, grimly. "Let's meet the dragon and get this over and done with."

They linked arms, and with a last look over her shoulder at Ronan, Sophia headed into the house.

Abigail hadn't set foot in this house since she left at eighteen years old and the minute she entered it again, she knew exactly why she'd hurried out. The atmosphere was oppressive to say the least. Something odd had always clung to the air here and it reeked of her mother.

She had heard there used to be a library in the cellar – in fact, she thought she had very vague memories of it – but to learn that library was the very same one now in the basement of her place of work was horrifying, fury-inducing, and made a hell of a lot of sense. No wonder the basement had always given her the creeps.

"Miss Carey!" A house maid called Marjorie hurried over to greet them. "It's been such a long time."

Her eyes twinkled and Abigail wondered how on earth this lovely woman had coped in these walls all these years. Marjorie – and her dad, the times he hadn't seemed bewitched by her mother – had been the only nice thing in her life growing up. "It's wonderful to see you, Marjorie. I've missed you, although I can't say I miss this house."

"I do remember how you wanted to leave. Happy birthday, by the way."

"Thank you. This is Sophia, my friend."

Marjorie bowed slightly with a smile and Abi bit her tongue, hoping Sophia didn't find the gesture strange.

To her credit, Sophia smiled warmly and took it all in her stride.

Abi turned back to Marjorie. "My mother's expecting us?" And it was so weird – almost like she had to ask permission to see her mother on her own birthday. But truthfully, she'd rather not see her at all.

"Yes, she asked me to bring you down to the cellar."

"The cellar?"

"Yes, ma'am. She moved her office down there a few years back for more privacy."

Irritation stirred. Again. "She wants to see me in her office?" she asked, flatly. So cold. So typical. But then, she couldn't actually remember having ever received a hug from her mother. It had been her dad who had provided those when she was little, and he was always ready to drop her the minute her mother showed up. She turned to Sophia. "I guess we're going down. Are you all right with that?"

"I suppose so," Sophia shrugged, although she did look a little nervous. She looked back towards the front door.

"Are you *sure* you'd like to meet her? Please don't feel you have to. I have no idea why my mother's taken such an interest in my work colleague, but she does like to interfere in my life whenever she can. I'm even starting to wonder if she had anything to do with my getting the job at the library now, learning all the books in this house have ended up there." God, that had knocked her for six.

"No, I'd love to know *you* better, and I'm happy to meet your mother."

"We don't have to stay long. I don't *want* to stay long. She said she had a birthday surprise for me and I've never been a fan of her surprises."

Marjorie looked expectantly at them, back and forth, while they chatted.

"All right, Marjorie," said Abi. "Lead the way." She knew her own way around the house just fine – she even knew her way around all its underground tunnels having spent many a year as a teenager fantasising about escaping her mother's clutches – but didn't want to take the job of hospitality away from the dedicated woman.

Nothing had changed too much in seven years. The large hallways looked the same, the front rooms all looked the same from what she could glimpse as they were ushered past them, and the kitchen looked the same. Even the door from the kitchen that led to the stairs going down to the cellar looked the same.

"I have instructions to leave you here," said Marjorie at the top of those stairs, almost apologetically. "Do you remember your way down."

"Of course. Thank you. And it really is good to see you again. Has she been treating you well, Marjorie?"

"Oh, same as always, Miss Carey."

No, then.

"We'll see you on our return," smiled Abi. And then she was leading the way down the stone steps – not too dissimilar to the ones at the library. Sophia followed. Abi looked over her shoulder at her. "So, what are your thoughts, history buff? Is the house to your liking?"

Sophia's smile looked grim. "It certainly has a vibe to it. It reminds me of where I grew up, actually – the house that got burned down, I mean."

"Feel free to burn this one down," Abi mumbled. And then they were at the bottom of the steps. An iron gate stood in front of them, open, which led into the cellar. A very large cellar.

Sophia's eyes widened at the torches – actual torches, with flames shooting out of the oil-soaked rags wrapped around their tops – that decorated the walls and gave light to the gloomy interior.

"This is just like my mum," whispered Abi, "to go whole hog with the aesthetics." Aesthetics was right. Shelf upon shelf of jars of herbs, and oils, and gemstones, and *things* lay against one wall. In front of the shelves stood two tables cluttered with books, mortars and pestles, oil burners, candles, and god knew what else. This was a witch's cellar and no mistake. Her mother fitted the description of 'black witch' perfectly as far as Abi was concerned.

Glancing around the span of the cellar, Abi spotted the other iron gate to the underground tunnel that she knew branched out to many more and ran the length of the grounds all the way to the outer fields.

Sophia looked more anxious now, and she felt bad for bringing her down here. She shouldn't have. She'd thought her mother would greet them upstairs in one of the front rooms.

Sophia was flaring her nostrils, frowning at whatever assaulted them.

Abigail turned her attention to the hag sitting at a desk on the far side of the cellar, her back to them. *Rude*. But she always had been.

Let's get this over and done with. "Mother."

Behind them, iron scraped and clanked. It sounded like the gate to the cellar shutting.

"Darling!" came her mother's reply, and she felt Sophia stiffen beside her.

But then a familiar voice called her name. "Abi, over here! Happy birthday!"

"Anthony?" Surprised, she found him opening the other gate and beckoning her over.

"I'm sorry I said nothing," he replied, excitedly, "but we wanted it to be a surprise." His grin was wide and because it was *his* grin, completely contrasting her mother's coldness, and because she was slightly numb from the bewilderment of seeing him, she went straight over.

"No," hissed Sophia. "Abi, wait."

She heard her mother rise from her chair, but didn't have time to take in much else because Anthony grabbed her hand, yanked her through the gate, and kissed her. At any other time, she would have welcomed this display of affection – *finally* – but now she shoved him off her, everything feeling more than strange. "What the hell do you—"

"We need to go now. Time is everything." He pulled her into the tunnel away from the cellar.

"Wait, no." He was stronger than she remembered, but he'd

never treated her so roughly before. She looked over her shoulder, stumbling, and the last thing she saw before the tunnel got too dark was Sophia's horrified expression as her mother turned to face her.

♦

The tone of Ronan's phone made him jump. He was already on edge. Miriam hadn't been wrong about this house – the longer he stood here, the longer he felt tainted by its presence. He was itching to go in and haul Sophia out of there.

Jacque.

He answered it. "Hi." And then walked away from the house towards the grounds so he could see if he could spot him.

Jacque's voice was harsh and urgent. "Where's Sophia?"

"In the house with Abigail." Using his senses, he homed in on who he *thought* was Jacque, just a small blurry silhouette from this distance, bounding across the far field.

He cursed. "Get her out now! We all need to leave – we're surrounded by the blackest fucking magic. They're moving the goddamn sky, and her aunt's not who she thinks she is."

Moving the— "What?"

"*Now*, Ronan."

And then the screaming came. Many screams.

"Jacque?"

The line went static.

"Jacque!"

Across the horizon, a dark haze cloaked the land, rising from the ground into the sky.

"*Jesus Christ*," he heard his friend whisper, the screaming grew louder, and then the phone went dead the same time that bounding, blurry, silhouette got swallowed by the darkness, along with everything in its path.

♦

"I'll just be five minutes. I don't see the problem – there are so many more people to talk to. We came here to get information and that's what I'm doing." Eliza had finally lost her patience with his restlessness. She wasn't exactly wrong – they *had* come here for information and she was doing a far better job than he at getting it.

And Daniel *was* restless. Not just because of his illicitly beautiful encounter earlier, but because the *wrongness* he could feel in the air around him was very real and nothing he could put into words. This was how animals felt before an earthquake.

He exhaled and ran a hand through his hair, trying to gather himself. He wanted to get to the car and to Les. It was 10:15. They had under two hours before midnight and he'd given up. He figured he'd just sit in the car and chat to his son until everyone made it back. But Eliza wasn't making that easy. He could leave her to it and head back himself, but the unease he felt made him reluctant to leave her alone.

A whinny cut through the still air. He looked towards it and saw a stable about a hundred metres away on top of the slope they were on. "Okay. I'll be in the stable – find me there when you're done."

"The stable? Seriously? Why don't you just hang around and have fun?"

Because it isn't fun. "I *like* horses." And he didn't feel like fighting or justifying himself, so he leant down, gave her a quick kiss on the cheek and headed off. "I'll see you soon."

He could feel her stare bore into his back as he walked away. But then he heard her footsteps swivel on the grass and pad off towards the groups of people she had yet to meet.

He sighed, half in regret of their difficulties and half in relief he could get away to somewhere quiet.

He was greeted by four beautiful stallions in four stalls when he walked through the stable door. The one nearest to him came right up to greet him and he gave him a smile in return. "And how's your evening going?" he asked the brown brute, running a hand down his nose.

His reply was a neigh and a quick stamp of his hoof.

Daniel tutted when he spied a near empty water bucket in the horse's stall. His hay was dwindling, too. "We need to sack your keeper, my friend. I'll fill you up." And he did. He took off his jacket, rolled up his shirt sleeves, and after finding the barrels of water, he filled the bucket and then brought a fresh bale of hay from the corner of the stable, loosening it a little with a rake to make feeding a bit easier. Feeling too warm already, his tie came off next along with the top two buttons of his shirt.

Hell, that was better. He could breathe now.

The stallion butted him in the shoulder in thanks.

"You're welcome."

He was about to check on the other three stalls when he felt a strange ... *vibration*. He thought he'd imagined it at first, but all four horses started stomping and shaking their manes.

"Okay, okay..." He soothed the one he'd just fed. "You feel it, too?"

He made for the stable door, and the horse protested, neighing louder than before. He looked back at him. "I just want to see what's going on. I won't be long."

He made his way towards where the slope began to dip, spotted Eliza almost straight away near where he'd left her, chatting to three other vampires, and then froze. It was mostly dark now, and yet ... a darkness darker than night began to seep up from the grass across the whole grounds.

He blinked, thinking he must be seeing things ... and then the screams started.

Those standing began to collapse to the ground in fives, in

tens...

"Eliza!" He ran to her, or tried, but the darkness got there first, consuming her in it, and then something barrelled into him and he was flying through the air, back towards the stables, landing on his back a good few metres from where he'd been, a heavy weight upon him.

Familiar green eyes met his. "*Run!*"

Winded and stunned, and pushed and pulled by determined hands, he scrambled to a stand and ran, both of them racing back to the stable, the black haze that rose from the grass at their heels.

"Help me shut the doors!" she cried – that female from the thicket – as they sprinted into the outbuilding.

The horses were toing and froing where they stood, upset.

He took one door and she took the other, both sets of lower doors and upper doors bolting into place, and not a moment too soon as the deadly haze reached them.

The small structure rattled as the darkness swathed it.

A poof of black seeped through the wood of the stable doors and the female tumbled into his arms, alarmed.

He held her tight – as much for his sake as hers.

And then it all stopped.

Two minutes passed as they breathed heavily into each other before either dared move.

"What the hell was that?" he whispered, his throat dry.

"Magic," she said. "Powerful, dark magic. I've seen it used in pockets of the Middle East. Africa, too. Not for a long time in this country – not since the 1200s."

Still holding her, he reached into his trouser pocket, his hand trembling, pulled out his phone, and dialled Les, trying to ease the panic building in his chest at the old man's safety.

"Hello," Les answered, and Daniel breathed heavily in relief.

"Are you in the car?"

"Yeah – where else would I be?"

"Stay inside it – don't get out for anything. Did you see anything strange a minute ago, on the grass or in the air?"

"From inside the car? No. But it's dark. Do you want me to—"

"No! Les, stay *inside* the car. Promise me. Until you hear otherwise."

"Er, yeah, sure. Are you all right?"

"So far. There's some nasty shit going on here though. I'll call you as soon as I know more, but stay *in* the car."

"Roger that." Les' tone softened. "You take care."

"I will."

No sooner had Daniel hung up than his phone rang. *Ronan*. "You okay?" he answered, not bothering with formalities. His unexpected companion was still nestled into him, but watching and listening intently, her vampiric hearing no doubt picking up on everything that was said.

Ronan's voice was just above a whisper. "Just about standing. Did you see the same fecking black haze thing I did?"

Before he could answer, the female leaned towards the phone. "Ronan?"

After a second: "Miriam?"

Okay, then ... so they knew each other. Daniel dropped the phone lower so they could both speak and hear.

"Yes, it's me. This is like Djinn magic, Ronan. I don't know who's commanding it, but they're evil to the core."

"I'm feelin' the evil."

"I'm *not* exaggerating. Haven't felt this level of it since way back – it just doesn't exist nowadays."

Another pause. "How are you inside, Miri?"

Her arms tightened around Daniel's waist. "Good for now."

"Stay that way. I'm not losing you to this, too."

"Too?"

"Jacque got swamped by the stuff."

Fuck it. Daniel reined in his panic and anger. His sire's life hanging in the balance had only happened once in their history together and it was like a scorch across the blood link. "So did Eliza."

"They're not dead," added Ronan. "At least Jacque isn't – I can feel him. Maybe you can, too, if you focus. It's like he's in a deep sleep or something."

Daniel resolved to try and link to Jacque after the phone call – he deliberately hadn't for over two centuries.

"It's an enchantment," said Miriam. "Over the grounds of the estate."

"I'll take your word for it. Okay, listen, I have to be quick: I took cover in the main house and I'm hiding. Sophia's in here somewhere, I'm going to find her and get her out. Those put to sleep by the black haze are all outside in it, but *only* vampires are affected, I think. I saw a maid come out the house and walk over the grass – she was human and she didn't falter. I'm not sure animals are affected either. I've seen two birds fly through it, still alive, and one of the house cats just went wandering out – also fine. Spooked, but fine. We've got to avoid the ground it covers – don't step on any of the grass it cloaks. And don't let the stuff seep into wherever you are, or you'll also end up walking on it."

Daniel interrupted. "We're shut in the stable north of the house. Ronan, Les is fine. I'm not sure the black stuff reached the parking field, but I've told him to stay in the car no matter what."

"Good, we all need to get back to the car as soon as we can, somehow or another. We'll find a way to get Jacque and Eliza." There was a shuffling noise, Ronan cursed, and the line went dead.

Exhaling sharply, Daniel pocketed his phone, aware of the woman – Miriam – watching him very intently, and then finally met her eyes. He should have steeled himself a little more before he did – the attraction was still there. In spades. And despite the hazardous situation they were in, he knew if he carried on looking into that soulful gaze, his sexual arousal would stir.

Maybe she was on the same wavelength, because she loosened her hold on him and tentatively started to draw her body back from where she'd moulded it against his. Tentatively was an understatement, though. Her movements were cautious to an unnerving degree, as if every inch she distanced herself might lead to some kind of destruction.

He held himself still and let her untangle herself, sensing something more was at stake than just the comfort of his nearness.

Only her hand remained on him now – a palm on his chest. She held it there a few seconds longer, then that went, too.

Relief fluttered across her features. It didn't hide the hint of desire in her eyes. "Did I drain you?" she asked, quietly, clearly worried at the prospect.

It was bizarrely difficult to find his voice. "I don't know what you mean."

"Are you feeling strong?"

Strong? He did a quick check of his body with his mind. It felt just fine. Apart from the sheer terror of whatever hellish magic was out there, he felt the same as he always had. Plus sexually aroused, damn it – that hadn't taken long. "I feel no different to usual."

Satisfied with that answer, her shoulders sagged and she looked around the stable, taking in their surroundings for the first time.

"Miriam," he said. And he had no idea why he'd said it. It was as if his brain wanted to try her name out on his tongue. "You're one of the fallen, aren't you?"

She studied him, then after a moment, she nodded. "And

you are?"

"Daniel."

There was a silence that was almost awkward, with them both consciously ignoring their want for the other because it was massively mistimed and misplaced.

She broke it first. "Any ideas on what we're going to do?"

"I vote for taking a moment to catch my breath. Then ... I don't know. Is there any way to tell if that black stuff's still around us?"

Before she could answer, he'd already made his way to the door and—

"What are you doing?" she asked, alarmed, and literally planted herself between the door and him.

"Relax. I'm not opening the door. I just wondered if I can see anything through any of the cracks in the wood."

"That's risky, too. Did you see the way it started to seep in?"

He wanted to protest – they needed to do *something* – but her anxiety seemed greater than just a fear they might collide into the dark haze. And out of place. With her stance, and athletic build, the force behind her eyes, and just knowing she was cut from the same cloth as the likes of Jacque and Ronan, he was certain she could hold her own in almost any situation. She was either terrified of the magic, or something she hadn't disclosed, and he suspected it was the latter. Since they had no choice but to stay put for now, he decided to let it go.

Finding a bench to perch on, he tried to calm himself down, closed his eyes, and focused on the link he had with Jacque instead, opening himself up to it for the first time in ... too long, actually, because when it hit him, it was like coming home. It was guardianship and surety and the protectiveness that had nurtured him into becoming what he now was. He felt a little calmer on the connection.

And Jacque was alive. Which meant Eliza probably was, too.

When he opened his eyes, he almost jumped out of his skin at Miriam perched next to him on the bench, looking *into* him with open curiosity. "Jacque means a lot to you, doesn't he?"

Daniel frowned, not feeling as surprised as he should at her intuition. "He's my sire."

Slowly, she nodded, then looked towards the doors again, then back at him. "I'm empathic. Or, I *am* an empath. At least, I am now ... again. I haven't had to shield myself from it for thousands of years. I can feel everything outside: the darkness, the fear before everyone hit the ground, and they don't know it – they can't help it – but when I'm around, they reach for me. Both vampires and humans. Whenever they need soothing or calming. I'm out of practice coping with it, I'm afraid – it will take a few days on my part to remember how – but you..." She hesitated, looked a bit embarrassed, but her inquisitiveness was bolder. She stared straight at him. "You don't do that. You don't take from me and when I'm near you, I ... there's just stillness inside. I just feel peace. And I've never felt that before."

Her words were like an intimate confession. It was like something deeply personal and private. It was like he'd been inside her, and he wanted to stay. And perhaps most peculiar of all, he understood with breaking clarity exactly what she needed. "I take from the earth," he said, quietly.

Her green gaze widened.

"When I need soothing, I mean. The trees, the animals, the mountains, the rain, and the sun when I was human – that's where I go."

"Then, you're extraordinary," she said, and she was completely serious – no teasing, no mockery, no sarcasm. "I don't know any other vampire that does what you do."

"That's why you asked me if you had drained me?"

She nodded.

"Because you felt ... healed? From our contact?"

A flush passed over her cheeks as she nodded again, and a soft protectiveness passed over *him*. It felt like water on a hot day, refreshing and rebalancing. He *wanted* to be the quiet she craved.

But the 'hot' was still there, under the surface. He could also feel her more carnal desire for him, and his own yearning wasn't going anywhere any time soon. That was probably something to be discussed at some point. But not now.

Now, Daniel let himself sink, just for a minute, into the leaf green of her eyes which held an enticing dichotomy of hardness and compassion. It would be a travesty if that compassion was ever shattered. "Then, let's make sure you stay that way."

Chapter Thirty-Two

It felt like stepping into a black hole; being sucked down a void – through time – when her aunt's face came into view under the flames of the torches surrounding them. Not Aunt Rita's, but Aunty Fiona's.

"You," Sophia said, weakly.

She looked almost just the same – hadn't aged a day – except ... there was an oddness in her aura, like the room shimmered slightly around her. A foul energy seeped from her that made Sophia cringe.

Fiona smiled, but it was taut and grim, the hatred she'd always had for her niece shining clearly through her gaze. "Haven't you turned out to be a pretty monster."

"How..." She didn't know which question to ask first; wanted to run out of there as fast as possible, but her shock, and perhaps a morbid curiosity, kept her rooted to the spot.

"How am I here? I never died. I *almost* did, but you didn't quite manage to best me, my love."

Sophia's gut churned on the mocking contempt behind her last two words. "But Rita..."

She blew air between her teeth in irritation. "That crybaby was always stealing my things. She wanted to be me. Ironic how that worked out in the end – *she* died in the fire wearing my things, so everyone thought it *was* me. It very much played to my advantage in keeping the mission going. Covertly, of course. She was so dotard in everything she did, the one good thing being that everyone felt very *safe* around her. Me being *her* meant no one batted an eye as the Resurrectors regrouped. Very slowly, mind. It's taken two decades. And here we are, on the precipice of an unforgettable resurgence, marked by the summer solstice and a ceremony to die for." Now, she grinned. "And there will be death. In under two hours, every vampire here will be giving up their life tonight in the greatest sacrifice of our history – an offering to our new deity to help us finally rid the world of the unclean undead."

"New deity?" Sophia's mind spun. It was an unsettling realisation that her aunt was certain Sophia wasn't getting out of here alive, or she wouldn't be divulging so much.

"'God' hasn't done much for us in hundreds of years – *my* Resurrectors will be better taken care of under new instruction. This ceremony will cut our ties with 'God' once and for all and welcome in our new king. And he's already been so good to me, Sophia. I never thought much of ancient deities and the magic they facilitate until *he* found me and saved me from that house fire, cured my burns, even allowed me to keep my poor pet. He led me to you even when you were hidden from us, but disciplined me to bide my time – this solstice only comes around once every two-and-a-half-thousand years. He will bestow power upon me like no one has had for an age after tonight. That kind of power is the only way to cleanse the earth of the undead."

"Jesus," she whispered on a breath out. "Have you always been this unhinged?" *Yes*, came the answer in her mind. Fiona had always talked this way, like she was above anyone, and with utter disgust for those she deemed inferior. In the past though, Fiona's mother had provided firm rules and held her on a tight leash. A leash that was now gone. Her best bet was to keep her talking and get as much information as possible, and *hope* she'd find an escape route to warn the others. "What about Abigail? Does she know?"

"Know?" Fiona laughed, *genuinely*, like she'd been told the funniest joke in the world. The sound was jarring. "Know ... ha ... no ... that child was such a mistake. My parents thought *you* were such a success, I wasn't given much choice but to carry my own experiment – she was a 'plan B' in case you went wrong; inseminated on the summer solstice, twenty-five years ago. She spent the first three years of her life with her father to keep you both separate – we couldn't have one experiment affecting the other. After the house fire, we moved in here." The woman sighed with a grimace. "Abigail's displayed nothing worthy in all these years – no super senses, no strength, ugh – no anything. She's utterly normal, ignorant to the core, and as ugly as her father. It was a relief when she moved out, but we couldn't just *leave* her – she's still an experiment. We tracked her; arranged her job at the library. Of course, it was imperative she never knew this. But she can't ever escape us or what she is."

"I can't believe the way you're talking about your own daughter."

The woman scoffed. "The only useful thing she's ever done

is bring you here – that's why she had to come – that and the Resurrectors have a use for her in their ceremony."

"Brought *me* here? Why do you even want me here if you hate me so much?"

"I *don't* want you here," she snapped. "You're no use to the Resurrectors now. With our new deity in place, we don't need failed experiments such as you to 'save' us. I tried persuading my mother to end your life." She paused and gathered herself. "But there *is* someone who wanted you here and he's dying to see you. For closure. And what better time than this solstice when everything changes. I've given him permission to kill you, and it really should be him that does. My pet deserves that much after what you did to him."

A cold dread settled deep within her. She could *not* be meaning who she thought.

Speaking became hard. "You've ... tracked me like Abigail, haven't you? You arranged my job at the library."

"And your move to Emerson. We waited years, watched your development from afar in case you *actually* showed some kind of divine intervention, and finally saw our opening, and just in time, wouldn't you say? The way the monster in you has started to emerge once more."

She felt sick. "You needed Abi to bring me here for..." For Hugo. It didn't bear thinking about. Hugo *couldn't* still be alive... But she'd run. She hadn't watched him turn to ash.

"Oh, I'm sorry, Sophia," she pouted. "Did you think you were destined for something more? Always did think highly of yourself, didn't you? I suppose my family's reverence of you didn't help."

He'd never told her. Hugo had *never* told her about what her blood could do or she certainly wouldn't want her dead.

"It was the *vampires* I wanted here, especially the old ones. It is only with our new deity's help that we can purge them from our world, and what a sacrifice they'll all be for our new god. *Him*, especially – the French one."

Protectiveness burned through her. On impulse she hissed and leapt at the woman before she could stop herself, not quite expecting, or prepared for, that surge from her vampire.

She didn't get far. The air crackled around Fiona and she found herself bouncing off a dome of energy around her, landing on the stone floor with a groan.

The woman laughed again, more quietly this time. "There she is – there's your true form." Fiona's eyes narrowed as she looked down at her, her gaze darting across her throat, then she extended her hand, and pain lanced across Sophia's neck.

She yelped at the sudden sting, then saw her necklace in Fiona's grasp.

"Thief," she snarled. "This was your mother's, wasn't it? I think I'll have it back." She fastened it around her own neck then stared at her with a victorious smirk. "And what cute teeth you've grown, darling. But they're not going to save Aubert. We're already preparing him for the ceremony." Her tone took on a note of reverence. "Have you read our journals about him?" she asked, breathlessly, as she stroked the pendant now resting against her chest. She pressed its notch and the wings emerged. "They're magnificent. Everywhere he's been; everything he's done. He'll make a wonderful sacrifice."

"Don't," said Sophia. Her voice broke over the single syllable. She pushed back her tears as she stood, knowing this woman would only take pleasure in them. "Please don't hurt him."

Fiona's eyes flickered white and Sophia recoiled. She waved her hand in front of her and an electrical charge fizzed, as if she were recharging her forcefield. This was when Sophia noticed the ring she wore – a coiled serpent of some kind. The metal of it seemed to shimmer with her eyes and in time with her forcefield. Then, she wore her own eyes once more. "He's already hurt, my darling, but if it's any consolation, he's in the deepest of slumbers and won't feel a thing. I have to go and prepare for the ceremony now. If my pet lets you live, maybe you'll come and watch. You're more than welcome – you have no power to affect anything. The wheel's already set in motion and it can't be stopped. There's nothing anyone can do now but watch."

"No! Wait ... what's going to happen?"

She smiled as she gathered the things from her desk she needed. "Once every two and half thousand years, on the summer solstice, the earth's rotation combined with the gravitational pull of all the planets in the solar system, means that the Arctic Circle expands to include Great Britain within its radius. At least, it does with a little help from a certain deity. This means the high summer sun can be seen in perpetuity throughout the day and night, for one night only." Her smile widened as she strode past Sophia, crackling her energy field, and headed towards the gate Abi had been taken through. "The sky outside is currently covered with a black haze." She pulled the gate shut and locked it once she was on the other side. "When it clears, at exactly midnight and at the peak of our ceremony, all the vampires on the ground will be treated to a polar day – a midnight sun. It's going to be wondrous. And Jacque Aubert is going to be the star of the show."

She left.

"*No!*" Sophia sprinted after her, cursing her heels, then cursing her mostly human strength when the gate didn't budge. *Ronan ... Ronan, Ronan, Ronan, if you can hear me, or feel me, get here now!*

"She's always had a flair for the dramatics, hasn't she?"

Everything sank inside her as she held onto the bars of that gate. His voice was more hoarse than she remembered, but even without looking it was still *his* voice – sickly sweet and revolting. "I killed you."

"You didn't. You burnt me. If Fiona hadn't found me when she did and thrown me into the downstairs shower room before the pipes popped and burst, I'd be nothing but wisps of acrid air."

She turned around, pressing into the bars as if she could somehow squeeze through them.

With half a head of hair, a heavily scarred face and neck, and a deformed right shoulder, Hugo's mouth widened into a misshapen grin, his fangs gleaming. "Hello, sweet Sophia."

♦

"Anthony, stop!"

For two minutes, he'd been pulling her and dragging her, holding one of those torches that had lit up the cellar, and Abi had, at first, been too shocked to do anything. His grip was hard and he wasn't gentle. He was also talking gibberish. Utter nonsense about the ceremony, some kind of ascension, and she thought she'd misheard him when he'd mentioned vampires, but then he'd said that word again and it turned out that vampires appeared to be the main focus of whatever baloney came out of his mouth.

With the dark of the tunnel, the brightness of the torch, the insanity of Anthony's actions, and the mortification she'd left Sophia alone with her mother, her senses had gone into overdrive and she hadn't been able to function.

Realisation, however, was starting to set in and so was the clarity of her situation. But it wasn't the fact she was being roughly handled through a dark tunnel that cut her the most. It was the fact that Anthony was as delusional as her mother had always been – *that's* the clarity that she saw – and she had been blind to it. Completely blind.

"*Enough*!" she yelled, and she yanked her arm out of his

grasp with a brewing anger that felt a shade darker than she was used to, but years of suppressing everything about her mother and her verbally abusive childhood had created a pressure cooker simmering for far too long.

The torch swivelled towards her and she caught Anthony's look of surprise as he stared at her.

"You are going to tell me *right now* what the hell is going on and why I'm in this tunnel with you."

"Abi," he said, surprised, as if this were not a thing she should find strange at all. "Have you not been listening?"

"If I'm to believe the drivel you've been speaking, it seems you fancy yourself as some kind of vampire hunter. Okay, Van Helsing, let's play along." She felt the edges of her own sanity fraying. "Why exactly does that mean I need to be dragged through a tunnel with you?" She also wanted to ask him why the hell he was talking to her when he'd specifically said he would be ignoring her all night, but that seemed far too a normal question for the events of the last few minutes.

Anthony paused, still with that bewildered look on his face; then he gathered himself and gave his clergy collar a tug as if to straighten it. "I am so sorry you've been kept in the dark about all of this, Abigail, and I wanted to tell you, but I had to keep it from you for your innocence. It's important you're as pure as possible for the ceremony and vampires have a way of seduction about them – even *knowing* they exist can make you ... *want* them. I needed to keep you away from that kind of lustful debauchery. It's why I felt you should keep lots of holy water with you at all times. Your mother was not keen for you to take part in the ceremony at all, but the bishop and I thought you a fitting addition; a symbol of the cleansing of the land, and we finally convinced her, although," he frowned, "she did sort of start to take over everything once she'd agreed."

A strange flutter deep inside her stirred. It felt like a tickle and sounded a lot like hysterical laughter, but it remained a ghost of a sensation as she took in his words.

"Take ... part? In the ... ceremony?"

He smiled, gently, and looked at her adoringly.

That fluttering tickle inside her got a little bit stronger.

"It's why we couldn't make love until now. It all had to be saved for this moment on the solstice: you and I finally consummating our relationship, and I know how you've wanted to for a while now – that's your birthday surprise. But time is of the essence and we need to get to the site of the ceremony."

"Consummating?" She felt like a robot, repeating words back at him, but this entire thing felt like an odd film she was watching. It was happening to someone else and she was watching.

He blushed.

He *actually* blushed under the torch light and took a step closer to Abi, the most love for her on his face than she'd ever seen before. "I am so looking forward to making love to you at midnight. It would have been special anyway, but to have your pure virgin blood be part of the ascension ceremony and for me to be the one who draws it is such an honour."

There it was again. The tickle. Crazy hoots of laughter bounced around her skull, but that's where it stayed as she stared at Anthony. And stared.

He ... thinks I'm a virgin?

He seemed unsure all of a sudden. Probably because she had lost all ability to move or speak. "Um ... like I said, I had to be quite firm with your mother about this, but she decided to grant the consummation to keep the peace with the Resurrectors, after all, we've acquiesced an awful lot to her own demands over the past few years. Um ... I'm sorry about prying into your virginity and all that, but that aspect was quite important and your mother guaranteed no one had ever taken an interest in you."

Ooooh... Oh, my mother *said I was a virgin ... right. Because I'm a fat, ugly, boring librarian. Of course.*

Well, at least that part made sense. She could absolutely see her mother utterly shocked at the sheer possibility that Stuart, one of the summer stable boys, popped her cherry right here in these tunnels when she was fifteen. And that she'd very happily initiated it; that he'd very happily complied. Had been *dying* to comply because he'd *liked* her.

"And, er..." He seemed to be fast losing his confidence. "Well, I know it might seem a bit weird to be making love for the first time on the altar in front of everyone, but it's like work – it's just business – you can ignore them. They'll be chanting, not looking."

Oh ... my ... god.

Abigail finally moved. She took one slow step after another until she was standing right in front of Anthony and stared very deeply into his eyes, searching for the joke, mockery, the last laugh he wanted to have, the fucking plot twist, *anything* but what she actually saw there: total sincerity. He believed every word he was saying.

Just like her mother.

A strange sound left her. It was the beginnings of that bubbly laughter that had been rising inside her, but it got stuck. What rose instead was her fist, aimed directly at Anthony's nose, and it made him yell and knocked him flat, the torch bouncing out of his hand.

"Abigail!" he cried, shocked. And hurt. He had the *audacity* to look *hurt*.

She'd drawn blood. His nose was gushing. Part of her knew her hand was probably smarting quite a bit, but she couldn't feel it. She was in that bizarre place where make believe met reality.

Anthony pulled himself to his feet, whimpering, and then looked at her like he wanted to tell her off. "How could you! Do you have anything to say for yourself?"

From behind him, a large, dark shape loomed. But it was fine. It was fine because she was watching a film. A tall, broad man appeared with murder in his eyes. Maybe he *was* death. Menace and rage rolled off him in waves. His eyes and hair were dark, he was half in shadow, and two scars ran across the top if his skull, right across his face, ending somewhere beneath his beard.

Even though he made no sound, when his large fangs emerged, Abi swore she could hear the roar in his head as his gaze focused on Anthony's neck: his prey.

She should probably have screamed. She should probably have felt something like terror, or horror. But her mind was functioning on some other level. What Abigail did, instead, was answer Anthony's question in a very calm and matter-of-fact way. "I'm not a virgin."

The man with fangs lunged and sank them into Anthony.

Anthony shrieked and sort of gurgled as his shriek ended, and Abi heard the man swallow ... heard swallow after swallow as he ... drank Anthony. To death.

Because he was a vampire.

And that's what vampire's did.

The ... *vampire* ... stared at Abi with his dangerous eyes while he drank, as if he was proving his victory; as if he were demanding she see his conquest; as if he were daring her to run, or trying to warn her she was next; as if he could actually hurt her after every single damned bruise her mother had pounded into her heart and soul for the last twenty-five years.

He's a vampire.

The tickle finally erupted, a displaced mania rose, and Abigail's laugh bounced around the stone walls of the tunnel.

♦

"You do realise," said Sophia, her eyes darting around the cellar for anything she could use as a weapon, "that Fiona is completely insane now."

"I'm afraid so," agreed Hugo. "Not much I could do once she'd gotten a real taste of power."

"That magic on her is not what power is."

He grunted. "It's not my *preference* of power. But it kept her busy and out of my business and I conceded to *waiting* two fucking decades for this blasted solstice to finally get what's mine. But I needed to know how strong you were first. So wrapped up is she in her new god, she didn't even notice when I sent that vampire your way last week."

She inhaled as realisation dawned. "The female in the bridleway."

"With my Nocturnes keeping a very close eye, at least until the Bratvashka scared them away. And then there was your very sweet little neighbour."

"*You* killed him?"

"I was hoping he'd find me a way into your house or draw you out, but you had a bloody vampire watching you all night – how *did* you manage that, I wondered? Then, after I sent the Nocturnes into the library, I learnt that French nuisance was back in your life. No matter – Fiona already had plans for him which works to my benefit. And here you are – *now* you're finally mine."

"I have never and will never be yours."

"Your blood is *in* me. Tell me, did you never once *feel* me thinking of you in all these years?"

Oh, god... Every throb and stab of that scar erupted in her mind. *That* was why? She almost retched. "Why did you never tell Fiona what my blood can do?"

"She's reckless and selfish. She'd have squandered your wonderful gift. *Your* blood is true power, Sophia. But before we continue the friendly banter," his voice dripped honeyed sarcasm, "I hope you don't mind me taking precautions."

He disappeared in a blur.

Sophia swore under her breath, not able to see him, then before she could register the blur was back, a bucket of cold liquid hit her from head to toe.

She screamed, ducking her head and squeezing her eyes shut, but her eyes still stung. While the liquid was cold, it also seemed to scour her, and she all at once recognised its pungent smell: petrol.

"You even *try* to set me on fire, you're going up with me."

She coughed through the stench, her nasal passages now stinging as much as her eyes. The stuff felt heavy on her skin and also seemed to tighten it. "You're a bastard."

Her hands were yanked above her head where they were held as she was pulled to the ground and dragged along it, her fangs breaking through at the pain of the stone floor ripping the bottom of her dress and grazing her skin. And she couldn't open her fucking eyes; tried to by blinking rapidly, but the petrol on her eyelashes stung too much.

He suddenly flung her onto her front and sat on her back, winding her as her ribs bashed the ground. Her hands were pulled sharply behind her back and tied with something that felt like thin rope; so tightly, the binds bit.

Forcing her mind from panic into logistics, she rubbed her feet together and managed to pull off her high heeled sandals – if she needed to run, they'd only hamper her. She attempted to flail out, not so much to get away but to test her strength and discern which parts of her body she could actually move. Her shoulders strained from how tightly he'd secured her, and it was now apparent the rope had also been trained up her arms to bind her elbow to elbow. Any hope she might have had of trying to slip her wrists loose were gone. Her breasts were starting to hurt pressed against the floor.

Hugo didn't appreciate her struggling and settled the length of his body directly on hers to keep her still.

She yelled as his weight landed too heavily on her hands and arms, stretched as they were. She stilled herself so nothing snapped or dislocated.

"Good girl," he breathed into her ear, pressing her face into the ground with his. "That's better. I don't *want* to hurt you, Sophia. Drinking from you doesn't have to be painful."

"Why do you want my blood so badly? Do you really crave daylight with the way you look? Do you think you'll fit into the human world?"

He growled quietly, his breath hot just under her earlobe. "Before you *deformed* me with however you managed to start that fire, yes, I wanted to move in daylight. I was never ugly to the eye. For months afterwards, my skin tried to heal, but no amount of blood helped, and I finally had to accept the hideous way you left me. But now? I'll be handing you over to the Nocturnes after midnight – they're nearby, waiting, and they're compensating me very handsomely so I never have to worry about my food or needs looking the way I do. They're secretive, but have always treated me better than Fiona ever did. I don't worry myself about what they want your blood for long term – but they've promised me free access to you. I'll be tasting you first, though, Sophia. Before they take you."

No! "What's Project Veil?" she blurted out. Anything to delay him biting her.

He paused, and then he laughed. "Someone's been feeding you information – the French irritant, no doubt. I seem to remember he thought he knew everything. I've never been allowed to see the project, but *you,* Sophia are its latest success."

"How was I made?"

"The only person who had that information was your grandmother. If she didn't inform the project with the details, she took it to her grave. Now..." She felt him trace the vein in her neck with his finger. "The flavour of petrol on you is a shame, but needs must."

"Don't!" she gritted out between bouts of pain as she tried to shift away from him.

He moved her hair out of the way, crawled a bit higher up her body, brought his nose into the crook of her neck and sniffed.

And froze.

A strange stillness suddenly surrounded him; enveloped them.

She felt his demeanour change, but couldn't quite place why, or what that meant until—

"You've been marked." His voice lowered and strained over those three words with ... possessiveness.

And then arousal.

Alarm bells rang in her mind and she instinctively tried to squirm out of his grasp, even though she knew she couldn't.

He clamped himself harder down on her with a hiss this time. *That* hiss.

And with a nauseous sinking of her stomach, she felt him grow hard against her backside.

He made no other move, though. He was rigidly still above her. His next words were laced with a strange confusion. "I've ... never considered you ... like this before."

He was warring with himself and Sophia daren't speak or move, as unsure of his thought process as he was.

"I ... wasn't expecting that. I..." He hissed again, although it seemed to be directed more at himself than her. "No, your *blood* is more important."

But he didn't seem to be paying much attention to her neck

anymore. He let out a growl, and like the hiss, it seemed self-directed, until it suddenly dropped an octave and slowed right down. He brought his mouth back to her ear. She could feel his whole frame trembling on her; strained; *re*strained. He whispered, "It's not easy the way I look. It's been a long time since I've pleasured myself on a woman."

Tears rose to her eyes at the way this was heading. It managed to clear the sting of the petrol a bit, and she had a better vision of where he held her – pretty much in the centre of the cellar with not much around them. Nothing she could see to help her escape, although with crushing reality, she realised there would be nothing she could do anyway. Even if surrounded by weapons, she wouldn't be able to get them. If she tried to set Hugo on fire, she'd seal her own fate the same way. Not just because she was doused in petrol, but because both gates were locked and she was tied – any fire that successfully took in this cold, stone cellar, she would not be able to run from to save herself.

"Tell me, Sophia, has any other vampire ever drunk from you?" He *kissed* her. First below her ear, then on the back of her neck, dropping to between her shoulder blades, his tongue tasting her there. It was devastatingly intimate.

She clenched her jaw, refusing to give him an answer.

"No," he answered for himself. "Of course they haven't or they'd know, wouldn't they? About the sun. I would have heard about a vampire walking in the sun." Another kiss on her shoulder. And then his body hardened around her, his growl returned, deep and coated with possessiveness, and he shoved his erection between her legs as if trying to find entry through their clothes. "I'm your first and only. Which means you're *mine*."

Everything that happened next seemed to happen at once. He ripped her dress at its waist, cold air hit her backside, and she screamed and bucked and kicked and flung herself, no matter how futile it was because there was no way in hell she could just *let* him do this.

She barely heard the shriek of iron on stone over her own screaming and his grunts – a tremendous grating sound accompanied by crumbling stone – and then a final clash when the wrought iron gate from the entrance to the cellar landed in front of them, the iron bent. She didn't really take any of it in, her vision still somewhat blurred; her sole focus on squeezing her thighs shut against fingers that shouldn't have been where they were.

Hugo saw Ronan first.

In that blur of vampiric speed she wasn't really used to yet, she was hauled off the floor and against Hugo's chest. There was a momentary shift in direction when he sped her away from Ronan's massive form entering the room. She registered a shelf with metal rods on them, chains hanging from above it; her blood ran cold when her head almost collided with a six-inch nail jutting out of the wall, then she was spun around again, held in Hugo's arms, his left hand gripping her right breast, his right clamped between her legs, fingers digging into both and lifting her off the floor in a feral display of ownership. His fangs bared and he growled.

Ronan's face came into view, lit fully by the flame torch in his hand; the rest of him followed, and gone was any of the usual cheer to his features. 'Berserker' was a more accurate description of the fury before them. His growl shook stone as he swung the torch towards Hugo.

"She's soaked in petrol!" he shouted, panicked. "You can smell it. You burn me, she goes up in flames."

Ronan's menace didn't falter, but he did pull in his torch.

Hugo took them both a step back.

The image of the six-inch nail bloomed in Sophia's mind. If she had it right, it was pretty much directly behind them. If she had it wrong, it could still be enough of a distraction to buy

Ronan some time. All she needed was the ground to push back from, but she was held aloft.

As if someone, somewhere, heard her plea, Hugo suddenly moved the hand between her legs to reach for something to his right – one of those rods, which he held up and out in defence. His grip on her breast tightened to keep his balance of her, but her feet and weight were back on the ground and that was all Sophia needed. The moment she felt she had a decent grip on the stone below her, she dug her heels in and heaved herself and Hugo backwards with a cry, not stopping until he hit the wall.

Something squelched. Hugo made a coughing, gasping noise, and then Sophia was on the floor, fallen from his grip. She landed on her side with a grunt and stayed there as Ronan swung into action. Not as quick as those around her, and compromised by her restraints, Sophia only caught the end result through hazy eyes, which was an iron bar wrenched from the gate, driven through the vampire's torso and into the mortar between the stones behind him, pegging him into the wall.

Hugo screeched, hanging there.

She heard Ronan breaking something – furniture? – and then she was pulled up to her knees. He cut through her binds with a flick knife.

She groaned once her hands and arms were free, blood rushing back into them as she was helped to her feet. She wasn't given any more time than that.

Ronan pushed a splintered desk leg into her left hand, brought her right hand up to its other side, then enclosed them with his own, turned her around and brought the makeshift stake in line with Hugo's heart. His voice was more vicious and heated than she'd ever heard it. "Your kill." He removed his hands from hers, but stayed right behind her.

It should have been easy. She'd done it once before, remembered what it felt like, but this was the first time she *knew* the person she was about to kill and the first time it was personal; the first time it *meant* something, vampire or not; monster or not.

She knew if she didn't do it, Ronan would.

A moment of judgement caught her – did her life mean more than Hugo's? Did she have the *right* to decide it did? What did she *want* this moment to mean?

The impaled vampire caught her train of thought far too easily and laughed – from his throat, anyway; his lung was ruptured by the nail. "Kill me as many times as you want, Sophia; I'll always be the first inside you and the one you think of."

Ronan's temper flared. He hurled a verbal stream of savagery at the male in a language she assumed was his native Gaelic.

She blocked it all out, and it was Jacque who filled her mind instead: his threat to Hugo outside her Dad's office, his anger and pain at having learnt he'd bitten her, his loving healing of the legacy that bite had left...

Even after everything, she couldn't kill him for herself, but she could for Jacque.

With a roar, she rammed the jagged wood into his heart as far as it would go, until all that was left was dust.

Chapter Thirty-Three

At approximately three in the morning, the 'gift' that Joseph Marino thought lost forever, returned to him. And it had scared him beyond reason. He didn't want it back, not now; not after everything he'd done. To *feel* it run through him, igniting that ... connection to *life* he'd turned his back on...

That was the reason he'd come to this ridiculous and lavish party – the very kind he detested. He needed answers of a personal nature.

His reasons had been all business before: he'd given his invite away, blackmailed that Irish boor to come instead to hunt for Project Veil, not wanting to do the dirty work himself; not that he could trust him anymore... But the traitor was now the least of his worries because everything had changed in those early hours of the morning. He had been looking for salvation ever since he lost his wings. Now, he wasn't sure he wanted it – not if feeling *this* was the consequence. There was no relationship with life without also bedding guilt, remorse, shame, and the *humanness* that lurked on the other side of those feelings.

Coming here tonight, though, had been one of the worst decisions of his long life. He'd lain low; had stayed out of everyone's way, preferring to observe for his answers rather than ask. He had spied Ronan, but he wasn't alone or with his usual crowd. He was with that fallen called ... Jake? Jack? He couldn't remember and didn't know him well – had heard of him by reputation only. And he'd been with that woman who had killed Manuel. His rage had simmered at seeing her, but he'd held it in check, far more concerned about the unexpected changes to his biology to get drawn into revenge for now.

Later on, he had spied Miriam, and he had almost approached her. Apart from Ronan, he had not spoken to any of the fallen for a very long time – they reminded him too much of everything he no longer was – but she had always been ... accepting. He remembered that. She had never looked upon him or anyone in judgement, and she could also take him in a fight. He had a lot of respect for her. But it seemed she was just as elusive as he, staying hidden and away from the throng of people sprawled along the grounds.

So hours had passed, and he'd decided to loiter where the Resurrectors were setting up their ceremony or whatever the hell it was. It looked unnecessarily biblical. *Blind idiots*. He had stayed on the fringe of the Resurrectors for hundreds of years, wanting his salvation, but never really agreeing their methods were in any way helpful or progressive.

And then, suddenly, a hundred screams had filled the air. A strange, black, dense mist rose from the ground and Joseph, without thinking about it at all, had unfurled his 'gift' in an act of self-preservation against the haze that smelled wrong and shrieked all kinds of badness. That was the only reason he'd not collapsed onto the earth like every other vampire he could see.

Shrinking into the shadows of a few nearby trees, no one spotted him. All the humans – all of them Resurrectors as far as he could tell – got straight to work once all the vampires were down, and with sharp understanding, Joseph knew this was *part* of their event and every single vampire needed to get *out* of there ASAP. They had been tricked into coming.

There was no way he was going to risk using his gift along the whole of the grounds, competing with this eerie black magic, especially not with his gift feeling so rusty after so long out of commission, so he'd resolved to head into the underground tunnels and escape near the main road beyond the outer field. He'd memorised the plan of the tunnels to his best ability.

As he was making his way to where he thought the nearest tunnel was, he'd come across that fallen's unconscious body. Ronan's friend. Where had he settled in the early days? France? Sweden? Croatia? He couldn't recall.

Jack – he was going to call him Jack until he remembered what his name was. Halting in his tracks, he had considered trying to get him underground, too, when he'd had to scurry into hiding again as four people approached. And what they did to

Jack – to his body – horrified him more than the return of his gift.

With a scream in his throat, he'd wasted no more time speeding himself into the first tunnel he found. As he'd scrambled through it, his fear had grown, but so had his rage. *Fools* were they to ever trust humans. Vampires had been persecuted since the very beginning, some humans fearing their darkness, some craving their darkness, and even as fallen angels, humans had greedily lusted after the light they exuded. You couldn't be *different* in their world – you had to hide if you were.

Before too long, he realised he'd been so caught up with in his anger, he hadn't paid attention to the route. He couldn't remember if he'd taken a turn and he wasn't sure where along the tunnels he was.

So, now, he was lost. His frustration at his stupidity added to his rage, taking over any terror, and that's when he heard voices ahead. Training his night vision and his hearing, he slowed down and skulked silently towards the voices, the near black of the tunnel, his ally.

He saw the back of a priest – one of those bloody Resurrectors betraying his kind under their noses – at least that what he thought he was given the garb he was wearing. And standing in front of the priest, he caught a glimpse of a woman. He noticed her glasses first, the lenses reflecting the flames from the torch the priest held, and then, rather curiously, his gaze was drawn to the other thing on her reflecting the light of the fire: a pendant on her necklace – a swan, he thought, although it was hard to tell with the way it lit up, throwing rainbows everywhere, making this woman look oddly innocent and enchanting in the black of the tunnel under the corruption that was taking place on the grounds above. She looked out of place. Didn't belong in the dark at all. She wasn't tall, but she was voluptuous, and the torch light on the red dress moulded to her curves, gave her a seductive appearance that was a direct juxtaposition to the innocence also evident. She was ... *different*. Not quite like anyone he'd seen before.

She was staring at the priest with the widest, most bewildered eyes he'd ever seen under those glasses. And something else: rage. He recognised it. It simmered low – very low – and he wished it wasn't there. He wished he could take it away from her because he knew where it led and all the consequences of that one-way journey.

And then he caught himself.

What the fuck?

Was he *really* standing here waxing lyrical over the emotional choices of a human woman he didn't know?

The return of that goddamned gift – this is what it's going to do now.

He gave his head a shake, knocked that thought right out of his head, and let his own rage take up the space it left. He had to bury it all – bury his abilities and make sure he never, ever used them again. Up there, it had been an accident – he'd needed to save himself, so he let it pass – but no more. He'd turned his back on all that for a very good reason, and now he tortured people – and sometimes vampires. He maimed. He hurt. He needed to kill something. *Now.*

The priest suddenly said something that prickled his skin and he had to fight through the rage pounding in his ears to hear him properly.

"...making love to you at midnight."

Rage ... pounding ... ears...

"...your pure virgin blood be part of the..."

Pounding ... pounding...

"...and for me to be the one who draws it is such an honour."

Something was wrong with Joseph inside his body. A disturbing, burning heat filled his chest and it felt a lot like his ribs were being ripped out. Or that he wanted to rip the ribs out of the priest. He wasn't actually sure which it was, but the latter was more his MO.

For the first time in centuries, he didn't quite know what to do. He didn't understand the signals he was receiving. His mind was telling him one thing, his body telling him something else.

And there was the rage. It needed an outlet or he was going to blow.

"...making love for the first time on the altar in front of everyone, but it's like work – it's just business – you can ignore them. They'll be chanting, not looking."

Joseph's face twitched.

The sudden image of this complete moron pounding his dick into this very unusual woman like she was an exhibition, while everyone *watched*, was just...

He saw red. He was going to kill him.

But before he could get there, the woman punched him in the face, and it was one hell of a punch because he went down and bled.

The heat in his chest warmed into a pride-like feeling.

He had to catch himself again. *No, no, no...* Sadistic bastards like himself couldn't become *attached* to anything.

The idiot priest rose to his feet.

Joseph dipped into the scent of fresh blood and let it fill him. His old self returned and it felt fucking good. He stalked his prey and felt a traitorous sense of *something* he couldn't name when the woman saw him. It made him shiver. He silently homed in on the man's neck, the man oblivious to his presence.

He had the insolence to speak to this woman like he wanted to discipline her.

Cunt. If anyone's going to discipline her, it's going to be me.

Before Joseph could question where that odd notion had come from and what exactly it meant, he bit into flesh, locked his eyes on *hers* as the warm blood gushed into his mouth, and swallowed.

Her final words to the soon-to-be-dead priest made him growl into his neck. Utter imbecile to not see her for everything she was – no damn way was she a virgin with *that* dress on.

Those conflicting feelings were back. Her gaze was like a magnet to his, neither looking away. Several dichotomous thoughts and demands went through Joseph's mind – which to be fair, had been fraying for quite a few centuries:

See? I'm protecting you.

Run, bitch, you're next.

Fucking blockhead doesn't deserve you.

Scream – I want to hear you scream for me.

No one's ever going to hurt you again.

Get on your knees and say thank you.

The priest's heart stopped beating, his blood stopped flowing, and Joseph let him fall to the ground. His entire body thrummed with power at the life he'd just drunk (mostly because the woman was now free of this halfwit thanks to his kill) and at the anticipation of her scream and the chase that would follow.

That didn't happen.

Instead, she laughed. And laughed. *And laughed.*

A scowl started to form across his brow, but stopped when he realised there was no mockery in her laugh – it was ... just a laugh. Either something was hilarious, or she'd lost the plot. He knew what the latter was like. And now he didn't know what to do. He'd been gearing up for a chase.

After a gradual slowing, her laughter came to a stop, and she all at once seemed just as confused as he. She met his gaze again, but he saw no fear there. Just a resignation that both aggrieved him and delighted him.

With a sniff, she pushed her glasses up her nose and was

about to reach for the still-flaming torch on the ground when Joseph caught a scent. And then faint footsteps.

Fuck! It was that witch! He'd seen her earlier near the main house – knew vaguely her history with the Resurrectors – but had smelled and sensed some evil shit coming off her. He'd kept his distance. It was the same fucking evil that had swarmed around Jack when the humans had gotten him.

He grabbed the woman, clamped a hand over her mouth, and ran until he found a dip in the tunnel walls he felt made a good enough cover.

She appeared too startled to struggle and he was glad because he did *not* want to confront the witch.

When the sound of footsteps fell into the range of human hearing, he felt the woman stiffen in his arms, and there was an intake of breath through her nose and behind his hand when the witch walked past, as if she recognised her too.

The witch stopped at the priest's fallen body, mumbled something about his incompetence, and carried on down the tunnel, barely a break in her stride.

There was a twitch, and then *fury* from the female in his arms. He felt it in every cell of her body against his – she wanted to tear after the witch and destroy her.

Well, that wasn't going to happen because Joseph was not going to end up like Jack. He held her still and pressed her more firmly into his frame. For a fleeting moment, and it was very fleeting, he thought he caught a scent of her sex as he held her – *awakened*.

But he was clearly overstimulated by fear, anger, his recent kill, and every contradictory thought and feeling cascading through him, so he shoved the bizarre notion she was turned on to one side so it wouldn't distract him from getting the fuck out of here.

She did smell bloody good, though.

Finally, when the witch's footsteps had faded from his vampire hearing, he let the woman go.

With a growl that reminded him of a puppy, she threw herself away from him, then turned around and chewed his fucking ear off. "Maybe *you* can see in the pitch black, but how the fuck am I supposed to see where I'm going now? I needed that torch! Go back and get it!"

He blinked, not quite knowing what— Had she just *ordered* him to—

"I mean it! Do you want to get out of here or not? I know these tunnels like the back of my hand. I can get us out to the main road in twenty minutes *if* you get your vampire-arse back there and pick up the torch Anthony dropped."

The priest's name was Anthony? She shouldn't be saying his name.

"Don't you hiss at me. You know what? Forget it. I'll get myself out of here in the dark – I'll *feel* my damn way. *You* can wander around in circles. Nice knowing you. Goodbye."

No!

He grabbed her with a growl, brought his face right into hers in a threat, and then swallowed his growl when she glared back in unshakable defiance. *Fuck*... Her blue eyes were *steel*. "You want to come with me, *get* the torch."

She was his best bet getting out alive. At least that's what Joseph told himself when for the first time in his undead life, he voluntarily acquiesced to a woman's demand. He blurred away, then blurred back with the torch.

She startled at his return, clearly not expecting him back so soon, and a flare of *appreciation* flitted across her eyes as she took him in.

That heat spread across his chest again.

She ... *smiled* at him. "Thank you." She took the torch, turned around and led the way. "Let's go."

♦

Ronan had been on the phone to Daniel for five minutes, pacing up and down the galley of the kitchen bare-chested, his trousers still wet. Sophia was sitting at the breakfast table in his long, white shirt. There were no signs of any other person – human or vampire – in the house.

After staking Hugo, her first and last thought had been of Jacque, and as Ronan had carried her out of the cellar and into the house, she had told him everything Fiona and Hugo had told her – or at least she thought she had. She'd been babbling, hopefully not too incoherently, her fear for Jacque at its peak, the skin on her face burning – all of her bruised – and her brain doing its best to put everything that had just happened into a little box for now, because she just didn't have time to deal with it.

When Ronan had bulldozed them into the bathroom, she'd protested – they needed to go save Jacque *now*. At that point, he hadn't yet told her they couldn't go outside for fear of falling into unconsciousness.

He had ignored her, stood her in the shower – the water acceptably warm – put a bar of soap in her hands, with a "Petrol can blind you," comment which she figured was supposed to encourage her to wash herself.

She'd stood there, mostly numb, understanding she needed to soap herself down, unable to, and not quite knowing what to do about it. It had occurred to her, at that moment, she'd had a ridiculous number of showers for upsetting reasons over the past seven days in various people's houses, and almost laughed.

Then Ronan had walked into the cubicle, perhaps realising she wasn't getting very far. Socks, shoes, and shirt off, trousers still on, he'd stripped off what was left of her dress, taken the soap from her and washed her under the spray. She'd been relieved.

He'd worked methodically, patiently, and quickly, lathering soap everywhere, then rinsing, from the top of her head and hair to her toes.

She'd refused to look at herself, because when she caught a glimpse from the corner of her eye, she saw horrible bruises and welts along her arms, wrists, and on her ribs; purple and yellow marks around her right breast where she'd been held, and she didn't need to see it all anyway, because it was clear enough in Ronan's methodical clench of his jaw as he cleaned all traces of petrol – and everything – off her.

He'd turned the water off, pulled her out of the shower, wrapped her in the nearest bath towel he could find, then had brought her into his arms and held her tenderly, but firmly, where she'd finally cracked and sobbed.

But only for a minute. Her fear for Jacque's life allowed her no more than one minute.

With no words spoken other than her earlier babble, they'd dried off, Ronan had given her his shirt to wear which reached the middle of her thighs, and he'd briefly brought her up to date on the 'black haze coming out of the ground' thing, what had happened to Daniel and Miriam – who she had yet to meet – then as if on cue, Daniel had phoned.

Finally hanging up, he turned to her, a small amount of hope shining in his eyes. While he hadn't quite returned to his more chilled, happy self, the 'berserker' had retreated for now. "Can you ride a horse?"

She shook her head. "Not properly."

"It's fine. I'll take you on mine. Daniel's bringing four horses. He and Miriam tried their luck and it turns out the horses aren't affected by the magic. As long as we stay on them, we're not affected either. You might not be anyway because of your human nature, but with the vampire in you too, I'm not sure we should take the risk. Anyway, Daniel managed to ride out and hoist Eliza up on the horse. She's still unconscious, so he took her to Les. The magic doesn't reach as far as the parking field. Les is on standby in case we need him. We're going to ride out and get Jacque – given what your aunt told you, we all agree he's likely in that field where they were setting up for the ceremony."

"And Abi?"

"If she went with the priest, she's likely there, too."

That made sense. And Fiona had said she was needed for the ceremony. She hoped to god she was all right whatever had happened to her. To think she had no idea of her mother's real name or origins. She wondered if the priest knew. "What about Fiona? She's running the whole show. She needs to be disarmed somehow."

"Miri might be able to help there – speak to her when she's here and tell her everything you know about Fiona and how she displayed her power. Miri's lived in and experienced multiple cultures throughout the world, over millennia – more so than other vampires. She's likely seen something like it before."

"Ronan ... the midnight sun..."

He rested his forearms across the breakfast bar. "That's where I come up with a blank. Everything we do, we need to do before midnight, and before that haze clears, and we need to be in the shade when it does."

"I have the solution." She bit her lip, wishing she didn't have to say it, but seeing no alternative. "It's my blood that's immune to the sun. It was Hugo that drank from me – that's how he found out. I know it made him immune for at least two hours because that was about the length of time from him biting me to finding out. Beyond that, I don't know. I have no idea if it's temporary or permanent. I'm so sorry I didn't say anything. I—"

"We knew, stóirín," he said, quietly. "Or at least, Jacque strongly suspected and filled me in."

She let out a long, shaky breath. "He did?"

"He didn't want to bring it up with you – make you relive what that bastard put you through – so he played it right down when I brought it up at his house. He figured you'd bring it up yourself when ready and having now seen that son-of-a-bitch uncle of yours for myself, I fully concur." Berserker flashed into the room for half a second then exited just as quickly.

And it dawned on Sophia like an epiphany: Jacque's behaviour last night, his tenderness with her after everyone had left, his refusal to bite her, his *need* to mark her...

"...I'm not sorry – no vampire is coming near you."

He'd marked her to *protect* her and keep anyone from wanting to bite her. Because he'd known about her blood. He hadn't wanted to hurt her by bringing it up with her, so he'd done the only other thing he could think to do.

Tears welled, her love for him swelling. "We have to get him back."

Ronan reached over and clasped her hand in his. "We will."

She shook her head. "Fiona said it was too late."

"I'd rather believe in my own gut than that hag."

She shook her head again and pulled her hand back. This *had* to work. They *had* to win. "You all have to drink my blood – you, Daniel, and Miriam – before we all go out there."

His gaze grew hard. "Save your blood."

"No! Ronan, this is what it's for. This is how we win. We *need* time and the only way to gain that is to go beyond midnight."

"Sophia—"

"One swallow. I don't think Hugo even took that much the first time."

"*Damn it*, all you've known of what's supposed to be a bonding moment is someone taking your blood by force and this is no different. You deserve—"

"It's completely different."

"—to be giving it in a moment of love and tenderness or—"

"That's *exactly* what this is, Ronan, I love Jacque. That's why you have to drink. Please. I *need* him back."

He stared at her for a few seconds, then exhaled. "Daniel and Miri can decide for themselves. You may have to sweet talk them as I don't think either will be keen to break into your bruised wrists."

"They can drink from any other vein, and the bruising on me is nothing compared to how I'll feel if Jacque dies."

Ronan mumbled something she didn't quite catch, but she got the gist.

"Ronan, please ... if Jacque's weak or unconscious, we need *you* to help us – you may be the only one able to take his full weight if we need to carry him – and we need you not going up in flames."

He stood up sharply from the table and paced, tugging at his hair as he stretched himself in his internal anguish. "Sophia ... Jacque and I ... we have a..." He was obviously struggling for the right words.

She stood and went up to him. "I promise you, nothing you say will be enough to change my mind on this."

He looked down at her and his shoulders sagged a little. "My blood is in you. Jacque's blood is in you. Both of those things are permanent because of the human in you. Throw in the part of you that's angel and I ... I don't know what happens if you and I seal the link."

She met his gaze and held it. "If you can't do it for me, do it for Jacque. Please." At any other time, guilt would have eaten at her for putting him in such a position.

His voice cracked when he said, "You know I will."

A whinny sounded from the front of the house along with clops along the tarmac.

Ronan gave her a small smile and clasped her chin in his hand, that jovial twinkle back in his eye, and Sophia realised that twinkle she adored was, at least in part, an act of self-preservation. "They're here."

Chapter Thirty-Four

Daniel was staring at Sophia with a mix of anger and mortification. Anger at the state Hugo had left her (she'd already had to calm him down after Ronan had filled him in), and mortification at the thought of biting into her in spite of that state. On the *tail* of her having just endured what she had less than an hour ago.

Miriam regarded her with open curiosity and some warmth. Her presence had a way about it and put her at ease straight away, like a sedative to her anxiety.

"It's forty minutes 'til midnight. You know my blood is the best chance we have the second that black haze clears under the midnight sun." Sophia was starting to sound like a parrot trying to convince everyone.

Daniel brushed a hand over his eyes and pinched the centre of his brow. "Christ, Sophia..."

"It's the *one* thing about me Fiona doesn't know. It's our greatest advantage against her, especially with all that magic she's got working for her. She won't be expecting it."

Miriam hadn't said a word yet beyond a heartfelt greeting. She spoke now. "She's not wrong, Daniel. Sophia's very sure about doing this, and she's strong – that's clear as anything to me. The blood flows how the heart beats, which means we're drinking from a human, so her blood should not affect us beyond two or three days as usual after feeding – the sun immunity part notwithstanding, but I'm prepared to take whatever risk that comes with for Jacque. If we do nothing, we're likely as good as dead. And there's going to be far too much death tonight – we can't save all those vampires out there on the grounds." They all fell silent at that reality. "So, I'm grateful we've at least got a chance. I'm in." She nodded at Sophia and smiled. "Thank you."

Sophia smiled back with relief, then looked at Daniel, expectantly.

He stared at her, somewhat sorrowfully, and on impulse she reached over and took his hand. Daniel had known her intimately and she knew he was protective. He'd been the first to so carefully school her on the sacredness and implications of sharing blood, and had sworn not to drink from her without the utmost thought and care. She knew he was loathe to take from her like this. "I know this is hard for you. I'm so sorry, Daniel. But this is something I'm more than willing to do."

"I know," he whispered, and then he swallowed hard before squeezing her hand back. "I know. We're also out of time and Jacque needs us. I'm in."

Her breath left her in a rush. "Thank you."

He nodded.

"Good," said Miriam, gently. She turned to Sophia. "About Fiona – from everything you've described and the ring you said she was wearing, it sounds like her deity is Apopis. He's an Egyptian god of chaos and disorder. We don't have to worry about Apopis – deities cannot directly hurt humans and won't; they very much play their own games between themselves and work to their own rules. They instigate situations where *humans* meddle with humans – largely for their entertainment. Stripping Fiona of her magic should also strip her of her link to Apopis and his power, and I think I can do it. I know how. I just ... haven't done anything of this nature in a long time."

Daniel frowned, gazing at her, his objection already slipped past his lips. "Miriam..."

She took Daniel's other hand, and it was starkly different to how Sophia had done so. Some undercurrent of energy rippled between them, and Miriam *stroked* her thumb across his, making it seem so much more than that. He laced his fingers through hers, almost absent-mindedly, still churning through his thoughts.

Oh, lord ... and Eliza? Sophia chanced a glance at Ronan to see if he'd noticed.

He had. He raised his eyebrows at her and shrugged.

"I may need you with me when I confront her," Miriam said to Daniel, quietly.

"That's good because I won't be anywhere else. We'll need to stay on our horses, though."

She nodded. "I can start that way. Once I've got a hold of Fiona's feelings, I may be able to risk the ground."

"Why on earth has she entered a contract with an Egyptian deity?" asked Ronan.

"Your guess is as good as mine."

"I don't remember there ever being a mention of anything like that in my early years," threw in Sophia. "Not from any of my family members."

"All right," Ronan stood. "The whys of it are less important than stopping it. We're a five-minute ride to that field. We need to make headway. Sophia, are you ready?"

"I am. I, er ... I don't mind where you choose to drink from, and one swallow should be all you need." She felt a blush rise to her face at how inadequate she felt concerning all things vampires did. She didn't even know if she was saying it all right.

No one seemed to notice. Daniel turned to her where he sat, letting her hand go, but keeping hold of Miriam's from behind him. "May I do this right here, Sophia?"

"Of course."

"I'll take from the middle of your forearm – from your veins just here, near the surface."

The middle of both her forearms were free from welts or bruises. Her sleeves were already rolled up, but she rolled them even higher, wanting him to have full access and no doubts.

Miri placed a hand on her shoulder, briefly. It felt nice – *she* felt nice, and Sophia wondered if she had some kind of magic of her own. Ronan had sort of explained the empathy she wielded, but not in enough detail for Sophia to really understand it. "I'll take from the same spot straight after," she said. "Don't seal the wound, Daniel."

He nodded. "Let me know when, Sophia."

"I'm ready now."

He held her gaze intently, and she let his beautiful dark gold eyes fill her senses, just as she had the night she'd met him. He dipped his head to her vein.

She tensed for one second, not meaning to, but it was her legacy reaction to being bitten. Hugo's final words came back to her, or at least they tried to invade her mind, but she pushed them away, along with the sorrow they invoked over the brutality of their truth. She focused instead on the beautiful male in front of her, letting her affection for him swell her heart.

It was quick and fairly painless. When he broke her skin, she gasped, then bit back a small moan at the sensation of his sucking – one swallow, and then it was done.

He and Miriam swapped places without breaking their hand contact, and Miriam didn't waste any time sinking her teeth into the exact same puncture holes.

The sensation was more intense this time, and Sophia felt a euphoric wave run through her despite the very practical and hasty nature of the moment. Heat pooled between her legs, and for the first time since her shower, she was aware she had no underwear on.

Bloody hell. No wonder feeding could get all blissful, although she could now also clearly feel how different it was from the kind of joy love's intimacy brought. She knew her body well enough to know if the circumstances were different and they'd all had time to fully lean into the moment, that wave of euphoria would likely have taken her to a very lascivious place. Yet, it would be nothing compared to last night with Jacque.

Her mind took her to the feeding house and the lust of all the donors and vampires in it; it then shot back to hearing Jacque in his cabin with whomever that had been.

Miriam looked at Ronan from her position on Sophia's arm.

He shook his head, and Miriam sealed the wound.

Sophia frowned. "Ronan—"

"Just give me a minute, stóirín." He addressed the other two. "If all's good, can you both get the horses ready and give us a moment?"

They nodded. The four horses had been brought *into* the house, tied to the banister of the stairs and left with two large bowls of water. Their arrival had had them all holding their breath and trying to come up with ways to block the haze from entering the house once they'd opened the door. Fortunately, they didn't have to worry about it. There seemed to be a block from it entering the house in the first place, and Sophia suspected it was deliberate, so Hugo didn't succumb to it.

"We'll have to leave one of the horses here, but I'll come back for it if I can," Daniel said.

When they'd left the kitchen, Sophia's eyes widened in surprise.

"You all right there?" asked Ronan as he sidled up to her.

She stared at him in wonder. "I can feel them. Daniel and Miriam – I can feel where they are from *inside me*."

"Hmmn. That's the part of you that's *not* human. Like Miri said, it should only last a couple of days where they're concerned. Come join me over here."

A little dumbstruck at this new awareness, she followed him to the sofa situated at the open end of the kitchen. Once they were seated, he turned to face her. "It'll be permanent with us."

She nodded. "I know." Although only now, with the experience of her blood in Daniel and Miriam, did she understand the enormity of what he was saying. And the enormity of what Jacque had done for her all that time ago.

"And what you felt when they bit into you – and when they took from you – that's going to feel ten times stronger."

Blood rushed to her face. Did it matter? He'd just showered her. She'd deal with it. "It's fine."

He stared at her for a couple of seconds, then pulled her onto his lap by her waist, and not in the practical methodical way he'd showered her at all. She was *on* his crotch, her legs either side of his hips, with her hands on his bare chest for balance.

He grasped her chin. "Look at me, stóirín. And listen to me."

She met his eyes, questioningly, and started at the trace of lust there. She'd never seen it before, but then she'd never seen 'berserker' either until an hour ago.

He ran his nose down the length of hers, then kissed her cheek before returning his gaze to hers. "There's no time to do this properly, but I can't just take from you like I'm not already in you. This isn't romance. This isn't love. This is blood and *sensation*; it's nature and need." His lips closed around the skin under her ear in another kiss, his tongue flickering out to taste her there, and by god ... if they weren't doing this to save

Jacque... She wasn't going to come back from this on any level.

Heat rose faster than she was prepared for.

"Let yourself sink into it," he said into her ear. "Let it happen, stóirín, because I'm not a bastard who's going to leave you needin' just before I take you into that darkness outside."

Holy fuck.

She was hot and tight everywhere just from his words and kisses.

His tongue trailed down her neck along her vein and she stiffened.

"Easy, easy," he whispered. "I'm not biting you yet. Let yourself go." He shifted his position until he was propped up against the arm of the couch, taking her down with him as she straddled him. His left hand grasped her neck and stilled her as he lavished it with his mouth, preparing her vein for his bite.

She wasn't aware she was moving against him until his erection was suddenly there, massive and hard under the fabric of his trousers. Embarrassment piqued. She was using him to get herself off.

She stilled, uttering an apology, but he wasn't having any of that. He grabbed her hip, pressed her back down, and thrust himself into her. "Don't you dare stop," he groaned, his voice hoarse, the rawness in him sending an uncontrollable fiery thrill through her, so incandescent, she moaned.

His right hand slipped between the juncture of her thighs, travelling the length of her slit before settling at the base of her clit and stroking her there.

"Oh, god!" The cry escaped her before she could stop it. Everything went from hot to scorching.

His mouth was back on her neck, by her ear. "Do you want more?"

All she could do was whimper some nonsensical non-word, but he just kept going, his words guttural, "You're soaking for it."

She heard the unique sound of bones shifting against soft tissue and knew his fangs had emerged.

He slipped his fingers inside her and pumped her hard, his thumb rolling over her swollen nub.

Another moan escaped her, loudly, along with a curse; all her senses frazzled as she fast approached the brink. *Way* too fast.

"That low-life in the cellar was wrong. He lied to you, Sophia, because I'm going to sink inside you so fast and deep you'll be feeling me the rest of your life and you're going to beg me to fucking do it. *I'm* the only damn thing you'll think about whenever teeth break your flesh."

She cried out at his words, her orgasm cresting, and then Ronan stopped all movement, his fingers pushed in deep. "What are you—"

And then he pulled out of her completely.

"No!" The desperation in her voice was *appalling*, but she was crazed with desire. Rabid with it; all fire inside with nowhere for it to go, and she knew how that ended. Maybe it was his blood in her; maybe her body was making up for the numbness earlier; maybe it needed to reach some kind of peak after Daniel and Miriam's feed; or maybe Ronan had some kind of secret vampire touch – like the aphrodisiac in the bite fluid, only it was on his fingers. She ached where he'd left her. "Ronan..."

She felt the tip of his fangs scrape her skin over her carotid vein, and before she could stop herself she leaned *into* his teeth, needing him inside her – fingers, fangs, anywhere as long as they filled her.

He held himself back, just out of her reach.

She growled in frustration. "Fucking vampires!"

He chuckled despite himself, finding that highly amusing, before pressing her clit again and circling it.

She bucked and almost screamed.

He entered her deep, then pulled completely out.

"Please don't."

"Look at me," he rumbled.

She did – realised she hadn't actually met his eyes since they'd started. She almost came right then. His light blue irises shone like jewels, his face was flushed, his chest was flushed, his fangs were *gorgeous*—

"Tell me what you want."

"Inside me," she panted.

"Who inside you?"

"You."

"Say my name. *Tell* me what you want." He leant forward, scratched her vein with his teeth; teased the wet heat between her thighs...

"*Fuck*. Ronan ... Ronan, please, I want you inside me, I want you deep inside me."

His groan ran right through her. It was one of acquiescence and approval. It happened without warning. He slammed his fingers inside her and *thrust* just as his long canines punctured her neck, and she came. Hard and instantaneously. She clamped down on his fingers and *felt* her blood spill into his mouth the same time she felt her gush onto his hand.

He sucked and swallowed twice, not just once, filling his mouth both times, and it was like nothing she'd ever imagined. Somewhere inside her, she sensed their blood join – the link sealed – but it was a faint feeling for now; a blossoming of something vast and non-corporeal. But the coalescence was intense despite its – perhaps because of its – wispy, teasing faintness.

A second orgasm overwhelmed her.

Even as he extracted his teeth from her neck and sealed her wound, he didn't stop fucking her with his hand, making sure she took everything she needed.

The third orgasm was harsh and final, blade-like and unforgiving. She finally collapsed on top of him, unable to speak.

And he was right.

Her eyes brimmed with tears. *That* was her first time bitten. Everyone else would have to compare. Ronan would always be her first.

Gratitude swelled, dropping her tears onto his chest. She turned her head and kissed them away. Kissed around them.

He let out a gentle moan, his voice barely above a whisper. "Your lips fluttering on me feel divine, but we've got to go."

"Wait." She pressed into his erection with her hip and lifted her head up to meet his eyes. "You haven't come. Let me help."

He smiled and shook his head. "I'll save it. A bit of sexual frustration channelled into focused anger on the battlefield's never a bad thing. I'll have this, though, if you don't mind." He withdrew his fingers from inside her. They were completely coated in her juices. And then he put them in his mouth, closed his eyes on a small groan, and sucked.

She'd thought she was all worn out, but no – a small flurry of ecstasy at the sight of him enjoying her made itself known in her core.

When he'd licked all of her off, he opened his eyes, his pupils fully dilated.

The first thread of confusion slipped its way into her. She wasn't ever going to see him the same way again. She went to speak, but he got there first, reading her with startling accuracy.

"Jacque and I have quite a history, some of it complicated, and some which we need to tell you about." He stroked her hair and then her lips. "This wasn't a betrayal, I promise you. Jacque will understand."

"I don't feel like I've betrayed him." She'd have to ponder on that later because it confused her as much as anything else – after everything she'd been through with Pierce...

She'd asked Jacque last night if he was angry she'd drunk

from Ronan. His answer had been vague and not really an answer at all. The truth was, she felt close to Jacque being with Ronan – very close – almost as if he'd actually been here with them. "But I have no idea how we progress from here."

"One step at a time, stóirín. First, let's go get our Jacque back."

♦

Stepping out of the tunnel and into the night air was more than a relief, especially when it was clear that freaky black stuff coming out of the ground didn't reach this far. The night was strange, though – lighter than it should be – but Joseph wasn't hanging around to figure out why.

His accidental companion turned to face him, her jaw set, her features stony. The flame on their torch had died out five minutes ago, but they'd been so close to the opening, that between her knowledge of the tunnels and his night vision, they hadn't needed it. "Well," she said, "this is where I hitch a ride home." She frowned, looked toward the stately home, seemingly upset about something, then sighed and shook her head. "I'd say it was nice knowing you, but..." She shrugged. "I guess it's been interesting, at least. Learnt something new and all that."

His brain urged him to say something. The instruction ended somewhere before it reached his mouth.

"I'm pretty certain I'll wake up tomorrow and think it was just a bad dream." She turned then, and left, walking towards the main road twenty metres away.

The urge to run after her and make her stay by his side was nonsensical and foreign, so he ignored it and glanced around him. He had a dwelling in the south of London. If he ran full speed, he'd make it there in an hour. A car would be far more preferable, though, but no fucker was going to give him a lift in the dead of night with the way he looked.

"Hey!"

Joseph whipped his head towards the voice that sounded over a rumble of an engine. A car pulled up by the side of the road next to the woman.

That didn't bloody take long, did it? Woman looking like her... Of course it was a bloke who'd pulled over, and while, on a normal night, the chances he was a genuinely helpful person was higher than him being some kind of perv or murderer, Joseph was well aware that those with darker intent gravitated toward the kind of magic in the air around the estate.

He clenched his jaw around a growl and crouched amid the long grass, staying silent. He focused his night vision on the car and its owner.

Joseph had never asked the woman her name. (Although if he recalled correctly the vermin-priest had called her Abigail.) In fact, he was pretty sure he hadn't said two words to her as she'd led them out of the tunnel. A part of him scolded himself for that, but she took him to a different place he wasn't used to – *emotionally*. He didn't want to encourage anything of that sort. She needed to be gone and he needed to insist she went.

"Are you okay?" The car was a blue Ford. Its owner was a thirty-something brown-haired simp who needed to learn to shave better.

"Long story; bad night. Are you heading anywhere towards Emerson? Or Winchester would be great – I can get a cab from Winchester."

"Sure, I can do Winchester. Hop in."

"Thanks."

"If you're okay waiting a second, I was going to stop anyway to take a leak."

"No problem."

She got in and the guy switched off the engine, then hopped

out of the car. Halfway into the hedges, he turned back to look at her, then fidgeted with the hem of his shirt, which got Joseph's back right up, his senses unequivocally telling him this guy couldn't be trusted.

He continued walking further into the darkness beyond the hedges. There was no way the woman could see him now, but Joseph still could. And hear him.

He pulled his phone from his pocket, dialled someone, and held the device up to his ears.

Joseph turned his head to a better auditory position.

The guy lowered his voice. "Hey, Tony."

But the person at the other end didn't bother. "Phil?"

"Yeah. Picked up this chick hitching a lift. You game if I bring her back to yours?"

"Fuck, man, I thought we weren't doing that shit tonight."

"Yeah, but she was just standing there, man, and she's kinda hot, you know? In this sexy red dress and all curvy the way I like."

"Why she hitching? She a skank?"

"Nah, she looks all classy, like, rich or something."

"Why my place?"

"Dave's at mine – I told him I'd be out."

"What the fuck, man, can't you just do her in your car or something?"

"Nah, man, come on."

"Whatevs – you drug her before you get here, got it? I ain't having no police looking for some classy rich bitch at my place."

"Cool, I'll take care of it. Thanks, man."

He hung up and Joseph smiled. It looked like he'd just found himself the car he was looking for.

◆

Abigail was in a state – one she didn't have a name for. She'd been spitting mad at Anthony and then he'd died – just like that. Because a vampire had killed him. Anger had turned to shock, and then her body had done something really bloody weird when she was pressed up against that vampire's body, which she wasn't going to think about at all, other than to put it down to shock.

Shock had quickly turned to fury at seeing her mother stride past them in the tunnel and that had been what she'd held on to to get her through the next twenty minutes or so. She'd morphed into some superhero version of herself and clung onto it for dear life, because she *had* to get home. She *had* to get home and into bed and only then would this horrible dream end.

She felt guilty as hell for leaving Sophia behind, but figured if her mother wasn't with her, Sophia would be okay – she was a survivor. And Abi knew she could get a lift back in that other car with her friends – she had loads of friends looking out for her. She'd phone Sophia once she was home and grovel her an apology.

This birthday really sucked.

As she got into this stranger's car, part of her brain told her she was being a fool doing so, but vampires existed, so her brain could go do one. Compared to vampires existing and watching Anthony fall dead in front of her after being drained of his blood, getting into a car with a stranger seemed pretty fucking normal, thank you very much.

She still had her clutch bag – in it, her phone and wallet – so things could be worse. Sophia got attacked a week ago and lost her bag, and her ex died, so Abi was doing just fine.

She wondered if vampires spoke or if she'd just found herself a mute one.

She wondered where he'd gotten those scars on his face.

They made him look mean as fuck, but she'd found herself bizarrely horny over them and the darkest grey eyes ever, unless the flame of the torch had been deceiving her.

She frowned. She wasn't going to think about that – the horny feelings. Jesus, she was such a weirdo. First a priest, now a vampire?

See? You are *dreaming. It's all just a dream.*

"All done!" Her driver was back.

He got in behind the wheel and said, "Winchester, right? Want me to pull up by the taxi rank at the station for you?"

"That would be great, thanks." She heard herself speak, but only from quite far away.

"I'm Mark, by the way. Oh, wait, I almost forgot." He got out of the car again and headed for the boot. "I have a bottle of juice somewhere in here." He fumbled for a while, mumbling as he tried to find it, then finally shut the boot lid and returned to the front. He handed her the bottle – some kind of red berry concoction from one of the superstores. "In case you wanted any, it being a hot night and all. And sorry it's open – I started on it earlier. Otherwise, you'll have to wait 'til we get to Winchester – it's all I got."

She took the bottle of juice and he shut the door. "Thanks."

"Figured it might help, it's an hour's drive at least."

As he tapped instructions into his Sat Nav, Abi popped the lid and drank.

Wow – she was actually thirsty.

"Whoa, whoa..." The guy – was it Mark? – grabbed the bottle from her. Not all in one go – shit." He looked a bit scared.

"Sorry – did you want some?"

"Er ... yeah," he laughed, nervously.

"Oh, sorry."

"It's cool."

His Sat Nav told them it would take one hour and four

minutes to get to Winchester. He started the engine, but eyed her warily.

And suddenly Abi felt wrong. She'd done everything wrong. She should never have gone to the party and she shouldn't be in this car with Mark who she all at once suspected was not called Mark.

Should have stayed with the vampire.

"Wait..." She reached for the door handle and found she couldn't quite grasp it. Her forehead pricked with sweat and a hot flush engulfed her. Her heart seemed to speed up, her breaths growing ragged.

"It's cool, sweetheart. You're fine." Not-really-Mark stroked the back of her neck, then his hand dipped, stroking the top of her chest. "You're really pretty, you know that?"

Her head lolled back and turned so she was looking out her window. God, she wanted him to stop touching her, but she also wanted to sleep. Sleep forever.

She saw a shadow loom as it came nearer the car. She recognised it straight away; could still feel the way he'd held her – it should have frightened her to death, his hand over her mouth like that and pinning her to him. It hadn't. She'd just felt safe. He'd been mute and angry, but he hadn't hurt her. "Gonna bite you," she sang out. At least, she thought she had – she couldn't really feel her throat and mouth anymore.

"What was that, baby? You wanna bite me?"

She somehow managed to swing her head around to face pervy not-Mark.

He smiled at her, goofily, his hand on her boob.

The world swam in and out for a second, then in again, and before it swam back out, she saw her beautiful scarred shadow yank the driver's door open and grab not-Mark by the throat in a choke-hold.

She smiled back.

Chapter Thirty-Five

Riding up to the ceremonial field, Sophia couldn't help feeling they formed a rather dishevelled version of the four horsemen of the vampire apocalypse – or it would have been four if she could actually ride a horse. As it was, she was nestled in front of Ronan on his, trying to ignore the fact she was barefoot with no underwear and only a long shirt for clothing. Ronan was still bare-chested, his trousers slightly damp from the shower; Daniel was in his formalwear, and Miriam had her lovely lilac dress hiked right up to her waist so she could ride. Yeah, the four horsemen were a haphazard, unplanned quartet.

The sight of vampires scattered across the grounds was unnerving to say the least. This was a graveyard in the making. They'd all be dead soon because there was no way they could clear them all before the sun broke through. That Daniel had managed to take Eliza to Les was a small blessing amid this mess. And Jacque? They had followed the Location emitted from his phone to his clothes on the ground and his mobile lying on top of them. None of them had been surprised, but their frustration and fear had been, and still were, palpable.

"I can't see him anywhere," she whispered to Ronan.

His tone was as grim as hers. "Neither can I. Can't feel him either. Can't link with him. Daniel?"

Daniel turned on his horse to face Ronan.

"Jacque?"

Daniel shook his head. "Nothing." His sire link was just as blocked.

Sophia couldn't see Abi either. Wherever she was, she didn't appear to be with her mother.

Fiona stood at the foot of all the robed priests and clergy. She assumed the bishop was the one with the tallest hat. The hundred or so humans wearing regular clothing, she assumed were Resurrectors. The congregation stood about a hundred metres from them. Behind them, tarpaulin laid stretched across the ground covering whatever they had been preparing earlier for the ceremony. Daniel had said he'd seen planks of wood or wooden structures from a distance, but not much else.

She glanced down at Ronan's watch. Quarter to midnight. They needed to put an end to this now, but without knowing where Jacque was, it was impossible to know if he'd get caught in the line of fire or under the sun when it burst through at midnight.

The four of them sidled closer to each other on their horses so they could converse. Miriam stared at Fiona. That strange, shimmering orb encircling her was more visible under the night sky. "Sophia, that's her, isn't it? I'm certain if I draw her power from her, the enchantment breaks, but it means the haze and clouds all clear at that moment. The sun will shine through then. I doubt the course of the planets will change their alignment, so the night sun is happening one way or another. I don't know how long I can hold her in a stalemate until you find Jacque."

Ronan cursed under his breath. "This is next to impossible without a link to him."

A sudden hush fell over the congregation.

The bishop turned to address the crowd, and then Fiona stepped up beside him. "My faithful Resurrectors," she began, her voice loud and shrill across the field. "We gather here today as a reward to ourselves, and as a token of our devotion to the god who has kept us safe from the unliving disease which continues to sweep across our sacred land, even after millennia. Tonight, the gods join forces to eradicate the disease once and for all."

"I take it we're the disease," scoffed Daniel, unamused.

"Persecution at its finest," replied Ronan.

"How vampires ever sided with Resurrectors, I'll never understand."

"Fear can make a blind servant out of anyone."

"Jacque told me no one really knows about the angel origin of vampires anymore," said Sophia. "For the Resurrectors it's a belief. I wonder if they'd revere vampires instead if they knew for sure."

"Reverence is not a blessing, stóirín. And no, I don't think they would – I think they'd become even more desperate for their perceived salvation."

Fiona raised her arms and gave her next words some force. "Tonight, at the two-and-a-half-thousand-year mark of the midnight sun, we will show through sacrifice and dedication, our commitment to our cause and mission to see blood flow pure through our sacred earth once more!" She gestured to the unconscious vampires on the ground. "We offer the sleeping undead for the sun to take. And we offer to the sun, as a special sacrifice, one who is over a thousand years old – a king amongst the unliving and the undead."

Cold fear ran through Sophia as she gasped.

Ronan's left hand tightened on the reins; his right came up around her waist. She could feel his tension.

To her right, Daniel hissed quietly.

Don't let her be talking about Jacque. But Sophia already knew she was because of what she'd told her in the cellar. They had no idea how old he really was – to those who had heard of him, he was simply an 'old one' – over a thousand – because of the written records about him.

"Behold!"

People scurried behind the congregation. The bishop said something in Latin Sophia couldn't immediately translate because she was frozen in dread, and then everyone started chanting as a massive object rose behind them all, pulled up by about twenty people using too many ropes to count. It was protected by a giant tarpaulin, which slipped further and further as the structure rose to vertical and slotted into the ground, and then the tarpaulin was pulled off completely.

There were audible gasps, some shouts, some cheers, Daniel groaned in pain, Ronan's grip around her tightened and trembled, and the scream that tore the night in half – her own scream – shattered any illusion that lingered about the horrific sight before them.

Sophia wasn't sure if later she would be able to recall what happened next. It all happened fast, yet it all happened slow under the weight of sorrow and desperate terror. Daniel was on the phone to Les shouting instructions – she couldn't hear what for the ringing in her ears.

Ronan was also shouting instructions. Miriam was nodding at his instructions, a haunted look in her eyes.

And then he was saying other things; shaking her by the arms.

Her face was grasped and turned. "Don't look! Don't look at him. Look at me. I'm going to bring him down, but I need you here – I need you with me. Sophia..."

Bring him down...

From up there. From the cross.

Jacque had been crucified. They'd crucified him.

The vision of his pale, drained body hanging on that wood was as scarred into her mind as every word and symbol on his flesh.

His flesh...

They'd branded him with their beliefs on his grey-pallored skin after slicing through every major artery as severely and methodically as a butcher did to meat. How long? They'd lost him ... two hours ago? He'd been seeping blood for two hours... Fiona's words scoured her – *the wheel's already set in motion and it can't be stopped. There's nothing anyone can do now but watch.*

He'd been bleeding for *two hours*.

"Sophia!"

Lips landed hard on hers and two fingers entered her harshly from below and pressed into her. And it fucking worked.

She blinked and gasped, pulling away from Ronan as she landed back in her body, one primal sensation of shock and survival overtaking the other.

He let her go and grasped her chin. "Are you here?"

"I am," she croaked, and nodded. "I am."

"I'm going to get him down. Daniel and Miri are making their way there now. Miri's going straight for Fiona. Les is coming with the car. We can make out a small platform by the cross. I'm going to put you down there, then Daniel's going to take you on his horse – I need mine to carry Jacque. Are you with me?"

She nodded.

"And don't fucking look at him," he said, his voice strained. "That's not him." He kicked his horse and they were off.

Ronan was wrong. That was Jacque. That was her Jacque. *Hers*. The memory of their first meeting near the cemetery filled her mind – as did their last one all that time ago when he'd given her his blood. And last night when they'd moved against each other, so *alive*. And so at peace.

Another memory surfaced, this time of the dream she'd had last night, or at least a part if it – they had flown in peace together behind those golden gates. She hadn't wanted to leave him, but had had no choice, Ronan calling her back down to wherever she needed to be.

Those golden gates...

"I usually keep it a secret because it's in my head, but if that's where you're from, we can share the secret, can't we?"

"Yes, we can."

Somewhere inside, under the shock and horror, determination forged. Jacque had *always* been hers. She wasn't leaving him. And she did look at him as they came nearer to that cross, even though it didn't bear looking at – what they'd done to him.

He hung unconscious, only large nails holding him up by the wrists and ankles, embedded into feeding points. They hadn't bothered with binds for him. The gashes across his arteries had not closed. His muscles had already lost their weight suggesting the letters and symbols on his skin had been carved before they'd drained him. He sagged as he hung, lifeless, but not dead.

"Here." They'd arrived at the platform by the cross. Clearly, those who had hauled the cross up had used the platform for leverage.

Angry shouts sounded, all aimed at them. She and Ronan had been spotted and a mob was forming, running towards them. All they were missing were the pitchforks.

"Fuck it." Ronan looked around as if hunting for solutions.

Miriam was circling Fiona on her horse. Daniel was fending off anyone trying to get to the two women, using his horse as his weapon. Everyone had their hands full.

But it wasn't the human mob that caught them out in the end. High-pitched shrieks filled the air and a colony of furred bodies swarmed them.

Their horse flailed and reared.

Ronan was catapulted off first, his weight taking him backwards as bats attacked him from all angles.

Sophia managed to gain some footing on the side of the saddle and pushed herself off the horse, clumsily, but with some control, landing on the platform with a thud before rolling on her side. The Nocturnes, unaffected by the enchantment in their animal form, did not seem to see her as a threat at the moment, concentrating their full attack on Ronan.

She stood, shakily.

Daniel was getting more and more swamped by the priests, but suddenly there was a shift in something – a few shouts and screams rippled through the crowd along with the noise of a revved engine.

Les sped his Range Rover Autobiography through anything in his way including people – the sensible ones ran – and Miriam leapt into action. Literally. She *leapt* from her horse and landed on top of Fiona and that's all Sophia saw because the black haze that coated the sky above her crackled and rippled on the attack, drawing her attention upwards.

If Fiona was disabled, the haze would be disabled and the midnight sun would come out.

She stared at Ronan unable to tell if he was winning his battle with the Nocturnes – only that he was trying to squash and maim every winged mammal he could get his hands on – but regardless, the Nocturnes would be dead as soon as the sun hit them.

But Ronan would survive because of her blood.

And it was like the sun suddenly rose in *her* making everything bright and clear.

She looked up at Jacque, saw the metal rods that had been nailed into the wooden structure, all the way to the top, so it could be climbed for maintenance, and knew exactly what she needed to do.

Not thinking on it further, she took a run at the cross, jumped onto the first metal rung, and then climbed up its back as fast as she could.

She ignored the scent of stale blood. From this close, she could see his flesh had also burnt where it had lain on the cross, and she ignored that scent, too, and all the childhood memories it conjured. She ignored the violation of Jacque's skin, the anger that boiled within her over the carvings on it, and most of all, she ignored Fiona's voice telling her it was too late to save him. She filled her mind with golden gates and that's the only thing she let in.

When she reached the top, she swung her legs and torso around to the front while keeping hold of the highest rungs with her hands, until she was straddling Jacque's form the best she could, her face level with his and her arms stretched either side of it. He'd lost so much weight, she could get her feet around his width. She used whatever rungs she planted her feet on to support her.

"Jacque... You're not dead. So I know that somewhere in there, you can hear me. I'm not leaving you. I'm not." She brought her right hand to her mouth, extended her fangs, pleased that she'd finally learnt to do that on command this morning (her squeals of delight had amused Jacque very much), and bit two fingers, then brought her bloody digits to his lips and forced them into his mouth. "Wake up. You need to feed."

He didn't move. At all.

"Don't you fucking ignore me." Her voice broke. She leaned in and placed her lips on his, darting her tongue in where they were now parted, and stroked his tongue with hers. "You swore you wouldn't leave me again, so you get back here right now, do you hear me?" Giving up wasn't an option, so she bit her wrist this time for greater flow and greater scent, aligned the wound with his open mouth and pressed it in. "Drink. Drink from me, damn it."

She couldn't turn to see what was going on below her or she'd lose her balance. She didn't want to know anyway – her focus was all here. But above her, the black haze started to roll – a little at first, and then in a clear dispersal of darkness.

"Now – *now*! Jacque, please..." And she was pleading. Crying unashamedly. "You *have* to drink." She kept her wrist where it was and pressed her whole self into him as much as she could. "Come on – hear my heartbeat. Feel it. It's yours. Take it."

He didn't move.

Below them a cacophony of yells and shouts continued on.

Beyond them, a beam of sunlight streamed onto the grass from a break in the haze and clouds above. It would have looked so fucking beautiful if it hadn't meant his death.

She sobbed. Racked her sobs into his body as she held him; sobbed so hard, she almost didn't feel the faint – very faint – flick of his tongue against her wrist.

Unsure she'd felt it at all, she stilled and waited, and there it was again.

"Jacque? Jacque, drink. Drink it all."

Another flick. And then *suction.*

Her heart leapt with hope. "More. Drink more." And she watched his throat for a swallow. One swallow might be all it took, although in his condition, she really wasn't sure.

There was definitely a ripple of his neck muscles, but then he rolled his head to the right and groaned.

"Don't stop. Jacque, drink more."

His eyelids fluttered, then opened, and his eyes...

A chill swept through her. His blue eyes had lost most of their colour, but his *pupils* ... they were completely dilated and not in passion as they had been last night. It was in hunger. Feral hunger. She knew it, sensed it, understood it all from an animalistic perspective.

A barely-there hiss sounded from his throat and his canines grew. And grew. And as they grew, his eyes found their focus, and every single thing about him awake and conscious, homed in on that focus. Every muscle still working, trained on it.

His open mouth drooled as his fangs took over, about four inches in length and formed solely for survival.

His head turned, his gaze landing on her face, but seeing nothing. It dropped to her neck, her shoulder, and then his pupils became pin-pricks amid starving, cloudy irises.

That was the moment she knew she'd die. He'd drain her completely.

She undid the top two buttons of Ronan's shirt and pulled it off her left shoulder; pulled her hair away from the left side of her neck. Bracing herself with her feet and hands – because she *mustn't let go* – she turned her head to give him access.

His nostrils flared, some vague recognition flickered through his eyes, and she suddenly understood two things: one – he could smell Ronan as well as herself because of the shirt, and two – for some reason unknown to her, this was the trigger he needed to yield to his thirst.

"*Sophia*! *No*!" That was Ronan shouting from below, oddly confirming what she innately knew.

Ronan had survived the Nocturnes. She felt comfort in that. But the sun was out. It covered the whole field next to this one and its ray was speeding towards Jacque.

She moulded herself into Jacque's body, and brought her neck up as close as she could to his mouth while holding onto the rungs for dear life – his life. "I love you, Jacque. Take it. Take my blood."

She felt his body tremble against hers, and then it rumbled, a roar ripped from it, and it was not her neck he sank his teeth into, but her shoulder – *sliced* into it like butter.

There was no pain at first, and then agony.

Her scream never sounded, as if he'd cut into whatever made her voice box work. This was not just feeding, this was possession complete and total. This was absolute ownership of her blood and carcass.

She felt the moment he pierced her subclavian artery with the tip of his fangs, *deep* in her anatomy. And she felt her heartbeat change. It skipped, stuttered, trying to find a rhythm, finding it only when he sucked ... drank ... sucked ... drank ... sucked ... drank...

Her heart beat to his taking of her.

Her hands slipped from the rungs and landed on his back where she attempted to hold on so she wouldn't fall.

The sun touched his hair.

With a growl that vibrated *inside* her heart chambers, he tightened the fist of his left hand and forced his arm off the cross. It came away, nail and all. He brought it around her waist – around his quarry – and held her up as he sucked ... drank ... sucked ... drank...

The sun spread across his shoulders and back, and he *did not burn*.

Internally, Sophia sighed in relief, although no sigh sounded. Her breath was his. Her voice was his. Her pulse was his.

I did it. He'll live now. He'll live.

Her feet lost their hold on the rungs, and fell, as feeling left her body,

It was all right – he had her. He had her. She could let go. She was his now, her entire body pulsing to his every need; her life flowing into his.

Unexpectedly, a wave of pleasure coursed through her; a moment of unconditional bliss at knowing she could provide for another in such an intimate and vital way.

The sun shone in her eyes. Gold. And when her eyes lost

their focus and fluttered shut, golden lines, like the bars of grand gates, impressed on the vision behind her lids. In a minute, she'd fly home.

Consciousness faded. She could feel nothing that was hers anymore – just him. He surrounded her; he penetrated her; everything was him.

Maybe it always had been.

Epilogue

Coming back from the brink of death was a lot like waking up from the deepest of slumbers, to the point where Sophia wondered, while teetering on the edge of returning consciousness, if we all actually died most nights when we fell asleep. Because she thought she merely *had* been sleeping, all the events of ... before ... nowhere near her waking memory when the taste of blood finally pulled her into the current reality.

Her eyes felt heavy, swollen, and achy. Opening them was a chore, but she finally managed it. Getting everything to stop being one massive blur, though, wasn't quite as easy.

She swallowed, reflexively, as she tried to wake and realised the taste of blood was on her tongue, but not fresh – it was as if she'd fed maybe half an hour ago.

With a soft groan, she tried to turn her head, the hues and blurs in front of her slowly taking more shape and definition.

There was a gasp from somewhere, and then a hurried voice said, "She's waking up! I'll get Ronan." Eliza's voice.

Footsteps sounded – two sets going in different directions – and then she sensed a warm presence hover above her. Her blurry vision, her nose, and her blood in him, told her it was Daniel. The warm hand that fell on hers certainly *felt* like Daniel's. "Welcome back, darling." His voice held nothing but affection.

She opened her mouth to speak and didn't quite manage it.

"Hush. Don't say anything. There's no rush. Ronan's on his way."

"Daniel." She mouthed his name rather than said it.

She felt his hand cup her face. "I'm right here."

She sighed into it ... almost fell back asleep.

More shuffling and footsteps, a shift in positions, and then the side of her bed going down, just like when she'd sat on Jacque's bed with her eyes closed while he'd—

Jacque!

She fought to sit up, gasping his name, every single thing that had happened hitting her right, left, and centre.

"Easy, easy..." Familiar words from a familiar mouth.

"Ronan," she croaked.

"Jacque's alive."

He's—

Ronan's arm encircled her and pulled her back down onto the bed. "He's alive," he repeated. "But you'll do yourself injury. You're not healed yet and neither's he."

She was dizzy as hell.

Something thudded on the floor and then Ronan was lying next to her, drawing her to him.

"He's alive," she said, not knowing what else to say, and doubting she had the strength to say much.

"He is. You saved his life. That it damn well nearly killed you is something we'll talk about another day. But you did save him, stóirín, I wouldn't have got to him before the sun."

Relief rushed through her. She relaxed in Ronan's arms and let his presence soothe her. She was vaguely aware Daniel had left the room. She wanted to talk to him, though. She'd do it later.

"You're in Jacque's house in your bedroom. He's in his own room. He's alive, but just like you, he's needed to sleep and he hasn't come back to consciousness yet. Until he's properly awake and aware of who he is, we can't put you in the same room as him – his thirst is still there for now. He lost almost all his blood. Give it a couple more days."

She blinked, then blinked again, and was finally able to see the things around her. She turned her head towards Ronan, wincing at the pain in her left shoulder, until she met his light blue eyes.

"Hi." He smiled down at her.

"Hey," she replied.

"Daniel and Miri are both well. Fiona's dead. Daniel cut her head off with a ceremonial sword the bishop was wielding – he was left with no choice. The woman was mad and Miri couldn't hold on. Miriam took on quite a lot of her darkness; Daniel eased her and they're both fine. Eliza's awake and knew nothing of all of it until we told her. She basically slept through the whole thing and is more refreshed than any of us."

"Les?"

"Is grumbling about retirement."

Sophia smiled despite herself. "I hurt all over."

"I'm not surprised. By my guess, you'd nearly lost forty percent of your blood volume by the time I could prise Jacque out of you. He wasn't properly conscious even then – it was a primal feeding."

"It was a Blood Surge," corrected Sophia.

Ronan looked at her sombrely. "You know about that, then?"

"Daniel told me about it last week."

"Hmmn." He stroked her arm. "We'll talk all about that later. There's not much we can say about it now."

"I didn't know he'd feed that way, but I don't regret it, Ronan. When he opened his eyes, I knew he'd drain me – that I wouldn't come back from it. I could have run then. I could have left him."

"Nah, you couldn't – no more than I could. You're a fierce lady, stóirín." He bent down and kissed her forehead, tenderly. "Everyone on the grounds had run by the time I carried you down; the vampires on the grass had all gone up in flames. I fed you while Daniel brought Jacque down. None of us burnt under the sun thanks to you, so we could do all of this quickly right where we were. We then got in Les' car and sped home. And by the way, that old man is quite the race car driver, let me tell you – missed a calling there."

She smiled again, but her need for sleep was already trying to take over. "Abi?"

"There was no sign of her. You've been asleep for over twenty-four hours – call her when you're able."

Twenty-four hours? Shit. "Work."

He tightened his hold on her and spooned himself further into her side. "There's nothin' for it now, and you'd be as useful as a sack of potatoes. Let it go – we'll sort all of that out when you're better."

No, of course she couldn't go to work, but she hated the idea of leaving it all, not that she could argue with him.

An uncomfortable sensation pressed against her abdomen as she tried to turn. She realised it was her bladder. "Ronan." She wrinkled her nose. "I need to pee, but I don't think I can stand without falling over."

"If you were in hospital, you'd have a catheter. Come on." In three seconds, she was in his arms, then in the en suite bathroom.

She bit her tongue against every ache that shot through her at the movement. "Should I be in a hospital?"

"I've been keepin' an eye. Was worried my blood wouldn't be enough – that you might need a human transfusion – but you fed without any problems and it's good that you're awake now. I made a call – we have one of our doctors coming to see you tomorrow to make sure." He lowered her onto the toilet seat.

She was still in Ronan's shirt with no damn underwear on, but that at least made it easier to do her business. She'd shower and change as soon as she was able. "Like a vampire doctor?"

"Yes. And if he approves it, I'll bring a human donor in to feed you."

She was so light-headed, she almost fell over on the seat, then had to catch her breath when it felt like all oxygen had left the room.

He grabbed her and steadied her for balance, and she tried not to let the stark sound of her urine hitting the water get to her. "Need me to clean you?" he asked.

Heat went to her face, whether over feelings of embarrassment or frustration at her uselessness, she couldn't tell. "I've got it."

When done, he brought her to standing and flushed while he held her, then took her to the sink where she washed her hands before he could do it for her. For a minute, it was Daniel's kitchen sink that flashed through her mind; Daniel washing blood and glass off her.

Ronan stayed standing behind her, arms either side of her in case she fell, and she was grateful, because the world wouldn't stop spinning and her legs felt like floss. She frowned though, when she saw unhealed bite marks on both his wrists. She stared at him in the mirror and he was staring right back, not missing a thing. "I've been feeding you every four hours. I've been feeding Jacque too when I can, but he's also got Daniel and Eliza."

And she only had Ronan and Jacque. She couldn't feed on another vampire without a permanent link being formed. So Ronan was it. Or a human, and she really hated the idea of snacking on a human. She dried her hands. "I hate that I've put you in that position."

"There are many terrible things I've had to do in my life. Feeding you is not one of them, I promise you."

She turned to face him, swayed at the movement, and she was in his arms again, heading back to bed. "I'm still human then, if no one else can feed me."

"As far as I can tell, you are, indeed, still human. 'Though how your heart's still beating is something of a mystery to me." He placed her where she'd been on the bed and got in beside her, assuming his previous position.

"My heart beat differently during the Surging."

He fell silent for a good few seconds, then kissed the side of her head. "We'll know more about that in the coming weeks."

A yawn crept up on her, exhaustion coming in fast after that small amount of activity. "I want to see Jacque."

"Tomorrow. He'll likely heal better with you beside him, but someone's got to stay with you both – you can't be alone with him yet."

She nodded, understanding, although her heart weighed heavy.

"Sleep, stóirín. I'll hold you 'til you do. And someone's always watchin' over you."

She wished she didn't have to sleep, but no sooner had she thought it, than she was out like a light.

♦

The beautiful, rounded, sweet-bitter taste of hashish was not something Ronan had indulged in in a fair while. As a vampire, he was largely immune to its physiological effects, but the *taste* of it he'd always liked – it was calming in and of itself. He was shattered and he needed something to get his mind off the state that was Jacque. It wasn't yet clear to him if he'd pull through unscathed – physically, anyway. He certainly wouldn't be all right emotionally once he realised he'd Surged with Sophia.

But he couldn't fucking smoke the stuff right now in case it affected Sophia's recovery through his blood. So, he paced the edge of Jacque's garden at two in the morning, focusing on the small things he was grateful for: no more visions just yet, thank fuck – he wouldn't be able to cope with those right now – and Jacque was alive. And he couldn't deny the times he, Miriam, and Daniel had spent *under* the sun today had been ... spectacular. It had been a fucking miracle. Daniel, especially, had been greatly affected, his memory of what the sun felt like, more fresh for him than for anyone else.

"You're going to wear the grass out," Miriam said as she approached him. She looked well considering the storm she'd been through. He hadn't been there to see her battle with Fiona, but he'd seen some of the aftermath. This female had had her body racked with whatever evil shite had come off the human hag and if it hadn't been for Daniel...

"How's your star, aingeal?"

"I'm a vampire, Ronan."

"You'll always be the most aingeal of us all."

"Except perhaps the heroine you're feeding."

"Hmmn ... except perhaps," he agreed.

"And Daniel is well. He's just fed Jacque, and has now gone to his home to speak to Les and rest. Eliza wants to stay here with Jacque – she'll be feeding him next – so she's bedding in the living room."

Ronan nodded. "And you?"

"I haven't decided anything beyond the next five minutes."

"What's happening in the next five minutes?"

"I'm feeding you, Ronan. I came to offer you my vein."

"Ah, Miriam, is anlann maith é an t-ocras."

"I'm going to guess that's you saying no, but I'm going to ignore you."

"You're gonna force yourself on me, Miri?"

She came right up to him, shaking her head at his stubbornness. "I'm going to tell you you look like shit. You're a bit sallow, your eyes have lost their shine, you're skinnier than you should be, and it's hard to breathe when you're trying to keep two people you care about alive, let alone do anything else."

He sighed. "You're not gonna let up, are you."

"Nope. If you want to help Jacque and Sophia, take my vein. I know you have your human donors, but human blood's not enough for the amount you've been giving. Come on."

He side-eyed her.

She threw him a lop-sided smile. "Sulk later. Feed now."

"You know I don't like the feelin' of feeding on vamps."

"Because it actually *makes* you feel? Yeah, I know. Wondered how the hell you'd cope taking blood from Sophia last night, but you managed that."

"She's human."

"Only in part, and *not* the part where her blood makes us all immune to sunlight, so let's not kid ourselves."

"Fine," he grumbled. "Where – here?"

"Here's good."

"Wait – there, against that tree. Lean on it and hold yourself up – I won't be touching you."

"Be as clinical as you like, Ronan, but take from the carotid so you get your full dose, all right?"

He said nothing as she positioned herself against the tree, still in her lilac dress. None of them had had time to change and they all agreed it felt wrong to wear Jacque's clothes. He'd been horribly violated. None of them wanted to go hunting through his private drawers and closet.

"It didn't *sound* very clinical when you drank from Sophia last night."

"Miri," he said, in warning.

"You may have your visions, but I *see* a hell of a lot through *this*." She rammed a finger against his chest, over his heart. "And your life has changed, my friend – one hundred and eighty – and you need to start opening up to it because it's all going to move faster than you can ever imagine."

"I'm not—"

"Does she know?"

"Jesus, woman, know what?"

"How in love with Jacque you are."

"I'm *not* talking about this."

"How in love with Cara you were?"

Fuck. Anger flashed through him – not at Miri, in spite of her pushing him, but at that point of his life he never took himself to because it was done, over, impossible to change, and *far* too long ago now. Only Miriam had met Cara. Even Jacque never had – Cara was after he'd left in his fit of madness, and he'd never told him about her. "I didn't realise agreeing to feed from you meant putting up with unnecessary chatter."

She raised a brow at him. "Have it your way." She pulled her hair to one side and bared her neck. "Bite, and feel nothing."

He growled. "If I wasn't exhausted and hungry—

"Jacque's hungrier than you," her voice softened, "and Sophia's more exhausted than you. But if you don't feed, you'll become so. Come on. I'll be silent now."

She kept her promise.

Planting his arms above her head, he leaned in and bit into her vein; couldn't help his moan as her blood filled his mouth. *Shit*. He *needed* this. His stomach growled even as blood filled it.

He didn't touch her, just as he'd vowed. He'd never go there again with any female. Sophia was an exception that had been necessary – they'd *had* to drink from her. It had been life or death, and he couldn't take from her so coldly after everything she'd been through; after everything he'd seen in that cellar. But the urgency was over now and he wouldn't drink from her again.

And she was Jacque's. Clearly and obviously head-over-heels in love with Jacque and he with her. He'd always look after anything that was Jacque's.

So, we're just going to forget about the permanent blood link you sealed together?

Fuck. Pushing away the sudden and alarming notion Sophia was *his*, Ronan leant into Miri's vein and drank deeper – just a few seconds longer. A few seconds and he'd be strong enough to once more hold everything and everyone up.

"Sir?"

Elijah's focus didn't wane as his employee entered the room. He stared out of the window of his home. Here on the fifth floor, he had an astounding view across Vologda.

"Have you just flown in, Damien?"

"Yes, sir. Came here first."

Elijah caught his own reflection in the pane of the window. Despite his naturally indomitable size, he looked more worn than he should, his blond hair and beard on the dry side, his brown eyes clutching at dullness rather than their usual softness. Feeding didn't usually enliven him the way it did most vampires, but he might need to up his weekly dose. "What news of Elle Auclair's daughter?"

"Reports claim she was killed. Her body, though, we could not find."

He sighed. "Killed how, Damien?"

"Beheaded with a sword."

Gosh ... a rather chivalrous death for the twenty-first century.

"And you found no head?"

"And no body, sir. Sorry."

The only creature that survived a beheading was an angel. Fiona had certainly been no angel. Something else was afoot, and the peace he hoped he might find after the summer solstice eluded him. It looked like he was going to have to pay the Albion Island a visit after all. "How many deaths?"

"Nearly a hundred vampires, sir."

"And the fallen?"

"None, sir, although ... one was a 'sacrifice' by the Resurrectors. Jacque Aubert."

His face twisted in disgust. Resurrectors and their bloody sacrifices.

"They crucified him, sir. But he was rescued. I am ... unsure as to his current condition."

Fucking dinosaurs. A crucifixion in the modern western world? In the twenty-first century? He could damn well imagine the male's current condition – he'd seen a Resurrectors' crucifixion before. To have it happen to someone like Jacque Aubert... Elijah knew him only by reputation, but it was one hell of a reputation. He stroked his beard and finally turned to face his messenger. "How was he rescued?"

"We believe four of the fallen were there in total. Two of them rescued him with help. They ... appear to have had some protection."

Four out of the six left were there. "Miriam?" he asked, hoping his voice didn't betray him. Her name on his lips had always been a weakness. A fucking beautiful weakness he missed.

"She was there, yes. Ronan McLaughlin was the other. They both were seen with Jacque by a handful of humans ... under the sun, sir."

Ronan ... the red-haired brawn if he remembered, correctly. "Can these humans be trusted? Were they frightened into delusional states?"

"They were unrelated humans speaking to various contacts of mine, all reporting the same thing."

"Under the sun..." he pondered. He turned back to his view, delighting in the vastness of this country he'd settled in; the country he and Ivan had birthed the Bratvashka after seeing how the fallen suffered so, right after their turning, inciting chaos too easily. Russia had remarkable gifts for any being able to befriend its mountains and valleys. Its landscape taught endurance and discipline. In the olden days he used to bring the newly turned here so their bereftness and rage could be honed and polished into something orderly. There was no place for chaos amongst vampires in a human world.

Vologda was the only city he really liked, much preferring the rugged and isolated terrains, but there was a reason *here* was the place he'd found a second home. His gaze wandered over the beautiful domes of St Sophia Cathedral. Five hundred years ago the planning for Project Veil had begun – a project he both cherished and loathed.

"We are not yet clear on why or how they managed to withstand the sun, sir."

He had an idea. Not that he was willing to share it. "And Joseph Marino?" Joseph had been a valued member of the Bratvashka three thousand years ago, and the only one to have retained his wings, but became something of a loose cannon after they'd lost so many of the fallen vampires after the last accentuated midnight sun, two-and-a-half-thousand years ago. His wings were gone now and it was a damn shame. He'd been one of the most disciplined of all. Rumours said he bordered on insanity now.

"Joseph was there, but disappeared early. No one saw him leave. There were two human killings, sir. One was in the tunnels underground – bitten and drained, but impossible to know if it was Joseph's work. He could have left through the tunnels, though. The other death was off the grounds, south of the property near the main road – choked to death, not bitten or drained."

Elijah inwardly groaned. Human deaths were a pain to deal with. And he didn't consider the Auclair woman human – not if her body disappeared after a goddamn beheading. But these others ... at least it was just two. "The clean-up?"

"It's underway. Miriam and Ronan – they tidied up after themselves, but they had to flee with Aubert and couldn't cope with the rest. There were ... erm..."

Elijah turned back around and stared at Damien. "Yes?"

The man cleared his throat. "The stately home ... there are gargoyles..." His voice faltered and he went silent.

Jesus fucking Christ. Elijah winced and lowered his voice. "Do they need appeasing?"

"We don't believe they were woken."

He hissed through his teeth, perturbed. Gargoyles were the most chaotic of all creatures. Worse than bloody dragons. Thankfully, they were barely ever woken which was good because they *hated* being woken. The last gargoyle awakening had been – he didn't know when. But given this particular solstice and its midnight sun...

The only way to appease them was with the blood of a fallen – angel or vampire, it didn't matter. Fuck it – he'd go there himself. "I'll sort it all out, Damien. All right. Good. Thank you. Please ensure the clean-up is pristine. If memories need to be wiped, do it intelligently." He now knew he was needed in England, not that he wanted to go. (Not if he had to deal with *gargoyles*, fuck it.) He much preferred to remain in the background while others showed their faces and reported back to him. But something had begun last night – no before that. At five in the morning, local time, over forty-eight hours ago, he had been struck by the return of his beast, absent for over eight thousand years. Gift or curse, he couldn't say he was delighted. Hmmn, maybe that was why he felt he needed to feed more.

It all appeared to have been kicked into motion by the solstice and he wasn't sure what that was all about, but... His gaze reverted to St Sophia Cathedral. He'd find out more in England rather than here. "Book me a ticket to London for tomorrow, please. And ask Ivan to call me at his convenience." *Always at his fucking convenience*, he thought, bitterly. "Tell him it's urgent."

"Yes, sir."

He doubted Ivan would join him, but the lazy fool had to hold the fort here and he had to fucking *do* the boring work for once. "And Damien."

"Yes, sir?"

"Arrange a car to take me to the main feeding house, and ask them to have three donors ready. I'm hungry. Oh – wait." Miriam's face entered his mind. He closed his eyes and let himself go there; could remember every single part of what it was like to sink into her, even if it had been centuries ago. "One of them should have light brown hair and green eyes – the lighter the green the better."

"Yes, sir."

His body needed calming and he had a damn fine imagination. He'd do more than feed tonight.

"*Apopis*," had been the last word tumbling from her lips just before her head had left her body. She'd been *furious*. He'd promised her immortality. She was clearly not going to get it from anyone else.

Later, amid the veils of the in between, Apopis had laughed at her. *"To be undead, you have to first die. What were you expecting? You asked, I gave. And as for immortality, if you wish to live forever, you can wait to have your request fulfilled. Time matters no more."*

"Wait for what? I am ready now."

"But the world is not. Who should perish so you can live? Forever, no less. No – you will arise from dying flesh. You will await your portal."

She had waited, and waited, and waited, and waited. And then, one day or night, in the span of a second or minute, she had tumbled through the veils, Apopis laughing at her scream as she fell out of the in between.

Her father would have been furious. *"Making deals with deities, you foolish child!"*

But deities were her domain – their *land* was built by deities, or so every person would have her believe, so why not play the game of deities?

With a groan, she stood – or tried. She fell twice, got up both times, until finally, her feet remembered what it was to take her weight. She could not tell if it was night or day. It looked like night, but the sun was ... *there*. The grass felt different under her feet than what she remembered – softer. Much softer. And the earth smelled sweeter. Where were the aromatic spices that usually tinged the air?

Looking gingerly around her, she half walked and half tumbled in any direction that felt right until an abode loomed ahead. A structure far different to any she had seen. A house? Or place of prayer?

Whichever the answer, that was the way she went.

She was walking more upright by the time she reached it, now also able to understand she was unclothed and alone. No one else appeared to exist here, although *someone* did, for she saw things only human hands could fashion.

The door to the building was open. She walked in to be greeted by a horse bound to a staircase. Relief flooded her on seeing a beast she recognised. Stroking it for comfort, she finally pulled away and decided on ascending the stairs. Things of a godly nature were so often kept near the top.

Is this your doing, Apopis? Is this my rebirth? Am I immortal now?

She had no answers and knew he would not give them to her. He only gave clues, enjoying the way humans struggled to find the answers they craved. But gods always gave well, even as they took away, so she would look for the hidden gifts. *What have you left me, Apopis? What have you left for me to find?*

She did not have to wait long for the first gift to appear. In fact, it was right there on her person, only now noticed by her new eyes as her hand rested on the banister: his symbol on a ring adorning her finger. She stroked the coiled snake. She had her first answer: yes, her rebirth was Apopis' doing and she had returned by his grace.

At the top of the stairs were many doors along a vast strip of floor. She went into the one nearest to her. Wherever she was, she knew she did not have long. She had to find all the clues quickly then leave without being seen. She would have to listen and learn. It might take a long time before she could finally emerge amongst people and survive.

A bed lay in the middle of the room. A chest of drawers stood to the right. This was a chamber of some kind – a sleeping place. Opening drawers, she found... *Oh, these might be for wearing.*

The clothing was strange, but she had two arms and two legs and so did the items she found. She put on what she could and bundled together others she liked. Hunting for a carrier of some kind, she found something suitable in a closet. She would carry what she could until she understood what to do.

In another drawer of the same chest, she found small sheets that looked like papyrus, although they did not feel quite the same. There were different images on some of them – heads of important looking people and she had the sudden understanding that they were representative of different regions. *Rulers* of different regions, none of whom she recognised. The symbols on them, she did not understand, save one, and she gasped in delight when she saw it.

Home.

A pyramid with a glowing top decorated the left side of this papyrus. She traced a finger around the symbols in the middle with a frown, wishing she could understand what they said, for she was sure they explained what she was holding: ONE DOLLAR.

No matter – this was both a clue and her second gift. She picked up all the papyrus she could find in the drawer and put them into her carrier. Under the papyrus, at the bottom of the drawer, she saw coins. *These* she recognised as currency for trading and she suddenly wondered if the papyrus was simply a different kind of currency since they were grouped together in the same drawer. She took the coins, too, thinking whomever they belonged to must be a frequent traveller to different lands. Even in her time, different lands had held different currencies.

Making quick work now, because she knew she could not stay, she hurried through every drawer. She saw a tool for combing her hair – that's what she would use it for, anyway – and took it.

There was another room adjoining this chamber. She wandered into it and saw... After a bit of consideration, she guessed it must be a water system. Maybe this was where bathing took place and in such a small area, this could not be a public house – she was in a private residence.

The reflective shine of a large rectangular panel on the wall caught her eye, and her breath caught. She had had her own mirrors of copper, although her favourite had been gold, but neither had been so *clear* as this.

Making her way to it, she deliberately stayed out of its view, suddenly terrified of what she would see. She was no fool. This was not her land and not her time, and it would stand to reason, this could not be her body she was wearing.

Yet, Apopis had once told her he was quite enamoured with her body, and his voice had been wistful, as if he had not been toying with her for once. Dare she hope he would let her keep her form?

She pushed aside the hope – it was too much to ask for, despite the words he'd teased her with... *"If immortality means so much to you, perhaps I should make you a seat by my side and a space in my bed. Your form under mine could create beautiful havoc."*

She shivered at the memory. He had not lain one finger on her, but she had heard tales of gods that had bedded mortals. Not that she was mortal anymore. She grinned.

Breathing in deep, she gathered her courage and stepped in front of the mirror.

An exclamation left her throat and tears brimmed, then fell. "Apopis..." All her gratitude in his name, she laughed at her reflection – *her* reflection. *Her.*

He had allowed her her real form.

Through watering eyes, she smiled back at herself, her long, dark hair tumbling in waves as it always had, her almond-shaped eyes framed by majestic brows, her full lips unchapped and unscathed by time; her smooth skin still the same brown as the rich soil of the earth.

Gold glistened around her neck, and she frowned. She had

not been aware of this when clothing herself in her haste – indeed, she had not properly *felt* her body at all as she had ascended the stairs. She was much more acclimatised now.

Reaching for the chain, she pulled the necklace out from under the fabric now covering her chest. An angel greeted her. An angel who looked rather aggrieved at whatever his predicament was, and of course the angel that rose sharply in her memory was *him*. The one who had ended her life in a fit of rage and pain.

All at once, she knew he was here. *Still here*. Surely this was Apopis' final clue for her. Or was it a gift? Would the angel ... love her again? He had certainly been a remarkable lover.

Or was it revenge she sought? Truthfully, she had not thought on revenge in all this time, her sole focus on the rebirth Apopis had promised her, no matter how vague the promise had been.

She had not blamed her lover his rage, after all, fair was fair in games of love and war. She knew he had seen differently – loved her *too much*. She had played too hard with him, so had accepted her fate even as it had frustrated her to have her life end so early – which was the very reason her deity's name had been the last word she'd uttered. Even at the bitter end, she had sought her immortality.

Oh, but the last word *he'd* uttered ... her poor, lovesick angel. The last thing he'd screamed as he'd brought his sword down across her neck had been *her* name.

She met her own eyes in the mirror, the memory of her ending now sharp and clear in her mind, her angel's voice echoing in her ears as if he'd screamed it yesterday. She brought her hand up to the mirror and stroked her lips, remembering his touch in other ways; remembering the sound of her name when it toppled from his tongue in throes of passion and ecstasy...

"Dalila."

To be continued...

Coming Soon

Book two of the *Blood Surge* series is in the works with a tentative release planned for December 2026. All updates can be found at diannahardy.com

If you loved this story, please share your thoughts and consider leaving a review somewhere, or telling everyone you know – word of mouth is the most valuable source of marketing an author could ask for and we really do appreciate it more than you could know! Thank you so much.

Also by Dianna Hardy

The Witching Pen series
And the companion novel, *Saving Eve*.

Witches, angels, demons, Heaven and Hell all come together in a dizzying story of friendship, love and forgiveness. A titillating mix of paranormal romance and urban fantasy brings you a sensational series you won't forget.

Eye of the Storm series
This international bestselling fantasy series is now complete. Werewolves living in the Surrey Hills come face to face with family secrets, ancient mythology, and monsters – both human and created – that want them extinct. Humorous and highly erotic in places, this is dark paranormal fantasy, not for the faint of heart.

Blood Never Lies (Duet)
Two companion novels to the *Eye of the Storm* series that also stand on their own and act as prequels to a brand new series each. Dark Urban Fantasy.

Once Times Thrice series
Practical Magic meets Serendipity in a beautiful, fun, and magical series about love, family, and second chances, set in Cornwall, England. Follow Merri, Jamie, Pippa, Jimmy and Candy as summer turns to autumn. Contemporary romance with a touch of magic.

Broken Lights
One gunshot, one scramble for life, one unlikely couple, one very long night ... can one damaged woman and one ordinary man, find the extraordinary in the very last second they're given? This is a gritty, romantic suspense story set in Whitechapel, London.

'Til Death Do Us Part
(an Adult Retelling of The Little Mermaid)
An adult fairy tale novelette. In this dark and passionate retelling of The Little Mermaid, can a love founded on humanity stand the passing of time, an angry sea-God, and even death itself?

A Silver Kiss (Vampire Poetry)
A dark and daring addition to the literary world of vampirism, this is a collection of rhyming and freestyle poetry that explores the often taboo themes of power, possession and seduction.

Emotionally charging, each poem is written from a different perspective, be it the hunter or the hunted and inspires a deeper look into the psychology of the human mind and the darker aspects of human relationships and society.

All books can be viewed at
diannahardy.com

About the Author

Dianna Hardy is the international bestselling author of *The Witching Pen series* and the *Eye Of The Storm series*.

She writes (often cross-genre) fantasy fiction, combining anything from paranormal romance to horror, to creation myths and god-punk, as well as a healthy dose of the erotic into her writing. Her stories are action-packed, and fast-paced, with a focus on both character development and the plot.

She currently lives in South Hampshire, UK with her partner and their daughter, where she writes full-time.

Website: diannahardy.com
Email: dianna@diannahardy.com

Facebook: facebook.com/authordiannahardy
Twitter: twitter.com/thewitchingpen
Instagram: instagram/diannahardy.author

www.ingramcontent.com/pod-product-compliance
Lightning Source LLC
LaVergne TN
LVHW041053080826
845145LV00007B/1553

* 9 7 8 1 9 1 6 8 4 0 1 1 9 *